Dangerous
Illusions

Dangerous Illusions

AMANDA SCOTT

OPEN ROAD
INTEGRATED MEDIA
NEW YORK

This is a work of fiction. Names, characters, places, and incidents either are the product of the author's imagination or are used fictitiously. Any resemblance to actual persons, living or dead, businesses, companies, events, or locales is entirely coincidental.

Copyright © 1994 by Lynne Scott-Drennan

Cover design by Mimi Bark

978-1-5040-5285-6

This edition published in 2018 by Open Road Integrated Media, Inc.
180 Maiden Lane
New York, NY 10038
www.openroadmedia.com

To Catherine Coulter,
Whose talent is exceeded only
By her generosity of spirit and friendship,
Thank you, for every pearl of wisdom.

Dangerous
Illusions

One

June 18, 1815, Waterloo

They say Lady Daintry's got a mind of her own, Gideon," Viscount Penthorpe said, leaning his lanky, rain-drenched body against his horse's sodden flank, "but even though I ain't such a dab-hand with the fair sex as you are, I'll wager that if Boney don't get me first, once I wed the chit, I'll soon bring her round my thumb, all right and tight."

Major Lord Gideon Deverill, a head taller than Penthorpe and blessed with a far more imposing figure, was scanning the mist-dimmed scene before them through his telescope, listening with only half an ear to his friend's account of his recent betrothal. He was damp and cold, and well aware that his usually immaculate uniform was heavy with mud, but he knew, too, that his men were equally bedraggled and uncomfortable, and he was conscious of an increasing tension among them as he strained his eyes to pierce the mist, to try to make out details of the enemy troop movements across the valley. Though he was certain their tension stemmed not from fear but from expectation—for they were all brave men who had proved themselves in battle—it nonetheless reminded him yet again of his deep responsibilities as their leader.

Throughout the seemingly endless, rainy night and dismal morning they had occupied a long, low ridge bordering the plateau called Mont-Saint-Jean a mile south of the Belgian village of Waterloo, their squadron flanked on the right by the rest of Major General Sir William Ponsonby's brigade and on the left by Major General Somerset's. The other nine brigades of Lord Uxbridge's gallant corps of cavalry waited in the valley behind them, while the hillside below writhed with restless infantry units. English artillery lined the entire crest of the ridge.

Not one of Gideon's men was sitting down, for the entire ridge appeared to be composed solely of sharp rocks and muddy puddles. Moreover, in anticipation of the fierce battle that lay ahead, they had been ordered to spare their mounts any extra weight for as long as possible.

Gideon's attention returned to Penthorpe when that gentleman sighed, glanced up at the gray sky, and said, "At least the rain has stopped, but by Jove, I'd give my soul for a dry bed and a willing wench in place of all this damned waiting. Can you make out what's happening, Gideon? 'Tis a bad business, this, and dash it all, for once I don't believe the Duke knows what he's about. They say Boney's so confident of victory that he's ordered his men to carry their red and blue parade uniforms right along with them so as to have them at hand to wear when they march into Brussels. That little upstart just might be the death of us yet!"

"Nonsense," Gideon said crisply, but surveying the scene around them and feeling a surge of pity for the cold bodies, shaggy wet beards, and filthy clothes of his men, he repressed the impulse to say more, to reprimand the man whom for years he had counted more as friend than subordinate. Penthorpe's face was so mud-streaked that scarcely a freckle could be seen. Even his hair, a flaming red that usually could be seen for miles, could be discerned now below his helmet only as more blobs of mud. Realizing that the others, sharing Penthorpe's physical discomfort, most likely shared at least some of his doubts as well, Gideon wished he could somehow relieve them.

The rain that had fallen so heavily all night did seem to have stopped, but the mists were still heavy in places and the ground saturated, with muddy pools filling every hollow. Ahead, between their forces and Bonaparte's, soggy wheat fields crisscrossed by two highroads sloped gently down for a quarter of a mile, then rose the same distance to a second ridge. Peering again through his telescope, Gideon saw, less than six hundred yards away, dark enemy cannons mounted against the gray horizon.

Despite the drab day, the scene itself was not dull, for the French fighting uniforms were even more colorful than their parade dress. Not only did each regiment wear colors different from the others, but many wore colors similar to the British, Dutch, and Prussians. In the heat of battle, Gideon remembered glumly, one could scarcely ever tell Allied soldiers from French. Glancing again at his men, he realized with a grim, sinking feeling that once the fighting began, mud would coat everyone equally, making it nearly impossible to tell friend from foe.

Below to his left he could see outbuildings, a garden wall, hedges, and a small grove of trees that clustered about Chateau Hougoumont, presently occupied by the Allied forces. Directly before him, in the midst of the wheat fields, lay the farm known as La Haye Sainte, where the Duke of Wellington, commander of the Allied army, had spent the past night—hopefully a less disturbed one than Gideon's own. Unable to sit or to lie down in the sea of rocks and mud, he and his men had dozed standing or in their saddles, and several times during the night, when horses had broken tether and galloped down the hill, Gideon had snapped awake, tense and alert, believing the cavalry charge had begun.

The two armies now facing each other were almost equal in size, and he could see that Bonaparte had drawn his men up in three lines. Clearly, his infantry would launch the attack, followed by the cavalry, while behind them, utterly formidable and terrifying, the famous French Guard, in their familiar tall bearskin hats, were poised to charge in for the kill.

"Gideon, what do you see?" Penthorpe repeated more urgently, moving nearer. "Dash it all, even from here it looks as if Boney's about ready to make his move. We'll soon be done for."

"No, we won't," Gideon said, ignoring a small voice at the back of his mind that traitorously urged him to share Penthorpe's fears.

Still peering through the telescope, knowing full well that his men would quickly sense any lack of confidence in him, he added firmly, "The Duke knows precisely what he's about."

"Dash it all, how can you say so?" Penthorpe demanded. "We've already had to retreat once!"

Looking straight at him, Gideon said, "That withdrawal, my lad, was a vastly different affair from any retreat. Come now, think about it," he added when Penthorpe looked skeptical. "The move from Quatre Bras was accomplished at no more than a smart parade march. The Duke wanted to be nearer Blücher, that's all, for he had determined that Boney was attempting to drive a wedge between the two forces, so as to defeat Blücher before he had to deal with us. Nearly did it, too," he added grimly, but in that same moment the memory that Wellington had outsmarted Bonaparte brought his usual confidence surging back. What the Duke had done once, he could certainly be depended upon to do again.

"They say Blücher was dashed near done for," Penthorpe said.

"His horse fell with him," Gideon said applying an eye to the telescope again. He had heard Wellington tell Lord Uxbridge that the splendid white charger given the Prussian commander by England's Prince Regent had been killed in that battle, but seeing nothing to be gained by imparting that information just now, added only, "Blücher was merely bruised, nothing more."

"Merely bruised," Penthorpe muttered. "Look here, Gideon, I've got a devilish queer notion we ain't going to see England again. Daresay that impudent young woman of mine won't ever know what she's missed. Nor will I," he added in a more despondent tone. "Ain't even laid eyes on the wench yet, but my uncle's as good as promised me she's worth twenty thousand a year, and truth is, I could do with more income. Still and all, I ain't a man to rush headlong into things. By Jove," he added, clapping a hand to his head, "what am I thinking? She's from Cornwall, ain't she? Dashed if it ever even crossed my mind before, but she must be better known to you than she is to me. Lived there for years, didn't you, before your father came into his title?"

Lowering the telescope, grateful for the change of topic, Gideon smiled and said, "Deverill Court is in Cornwall, right enough, and my father still seems to spend a good portion of the year there; however, I cannot really say I've lived there, Andy. What with school and the military, I've not done so for years."

"Still, you must know the family," Penthorpe insisted.

Gideon's smile widened. "It is possible that I do, of course; however, not only have you scarcely mentioned your betrothal before now, but you've never once told me the chit's surname. I'll grant you that Daintry is a name I'd remember, especially since there is only one family I know of that might run to heiresses of such magnitude, but as I recall, the Earl of St. Merryn's daughter is called Susan, so it cannot be she."

"He's got two daughters," Penthorpe said. "Fact is, it was Daintry's being Lady Susan Tarrant's sister that let me swallow such a dashed odd betrothal at all, and the reason I haven't talked much about it till now is that I was in no great rush to try explaining how it came about that I've never so much as clapped eyes on the wench I'm intended to marry."

"Fact is," Gideon retorted with a teasing grin, "that you put off talking about it because you *always* put off things you don't much want to do. You are the worst procrastinator I know. But tell me what Lady Susan had to do with all this. I don't know her, but I've been told she's something of a beauty."

Penthorpe sighed. "I don't mind telling you, if I'd been eligible ten years ago when she made her come-out, I'd have tried my best to cut Seacourt out, though I haven't got an ounce of his cleverness with females, and I was only nineteen at the time. You remember him, don't you? Several years ahead of us, of course, but an Eton man, all the same."

Gideon nodded. Certain memories of Sir Geoffrey Seacourt made him frown, but Penthorpe did not wait for comment.

"Don't signify," he said, "because I hadn't a notion then that I'd come into the title. Didn't do so until four years ago, you know, and didn't have a penny to bless myself before. If I had shown my face to St. Merryn then, he'd have sent me packing, but now, for reasons best known to himself and my uncle—school chums like us, they were—he's hot to match his younger daughter with my humble self, and he wants the whole business handled by proxy, which makes me think Lady Daintry must be past praying for. Wench is twenty, after all, so she's nearly on the shelf. When my uncle pressed me to do so, I agreed to a proxy betrothal, but I dashed well want to see her in the flesh before I marry her. Dash it, any man would. You do know the family, you say?"

"Oh, yes. Their land adjoins ours on the moor for several miles. The fact is that my father—"

"Good God, don't say Jervaulx harbors ambitions for you in that direction! Of course, it's only natural if St. Merryn's daughters will come into twenty thousand a year, but look here, Gideon, if I had known—"

"No, no," Gideon said, laughing. "Quite the reverse. I just told you I wasn't even aware of a second daughter. I've never laid eyes on the first, and I don't expect to do so unless by some unforeseen circumstance our paths should cross. My father and theirs don't speak—never have, as far as I know. Our respective grandfathers had a falling-out long before I was born, when my branch of the Deverill tree was still the junior one, and there has not been an amiable word spoken between the families since. I don't even know enough about the Tarrants to tell you if Lady Daintry is as pretty as her sister."

"Well, she ain't, because I do know what she looks like," Penthorpe said, reaching into his inner coat and withdrawing an oval miniature in a gold frame. Handing it to Gideon, he said, "There you are. My uncle sent it. Too dark for my taste, but she's pretty enough, I suppose. Not that one can go by miniatures. Only look what happened to the Regent, thinking Caroline of Brunswick was a fine-looking woman, then getting stuck with such an untidy, vulgar sort of wench in the end."

Gideon murmured, "But then, Caroline was shown a picture of Prince Florizel, as he liked to call himself, painted a good ten years or more before she saw it. And you cannot say Prinny was any great prize on the Marriage Mart, Andy, aside from his rank, that is." Gazing at the miniature Penthorpe had handed him, he didn't think his friend would be as gravely disappointed as the Prince of Wales had been twenty years before.

What Gideon saw was a pair of laughing blue eyes, a tip-tilted nose, and pouting cherry-colored lips in a piquant little face surrounded by a cloud of sable ringlets. Her cheeks were the color of dusty roses, and except for the merry twinkle the artist had managed to capture in her eyes, she appeared to be both fragile and sultry. Her lips looked as if they longed to be kissed, and her lashes were so thick that they seemed to weigh her eyelids down, giving her a most beguiling look. An instant, intriguing sense of gentle warmth spread through Gideon's body, stirring curiosity and much more primitive sensations, and he found himself wishing he might see her smile like that at him.

"Looks a bit spoilt, I thought," Penthorpe said. "Her sister was much the same till she married Seacourt. But maybe you didn't know she'd married him. You ain't been back in a while, now that I think about it. I went home last year, after the Peace, of course, then joined up again to be in on Boney's capture, but you stayed over here the whole time, raking and larking about with Lord Hill's people, didn't you?"

Gideon nodded, still looking at the miniature. Reluctantly and with an odd sense of loss, he returned it, thinking back to a day in his youth, not many months after his mother's death, when he had told his brother, Jack, that he meant to learn all about the feud between the Deverills and the Earl of St. Merryn even if he had to go to Tuscombe Park and demand that the earl tell him what their father would not. Jack had informed on him, of course, and he had taken a thrashing for what his father had called his damned insolence. He had not thought of that feud in years, but now, gazing at Lady Daintry's fascinating likeness, he began to think he ought never to have allowed a mere thrashing to deter him from learning more about the Tarrant family.

Not that opportunity had often come his way. He had been sent to Eton soon after that unfortunate episode, and except for school holidays—spent as often with his maternal grandparents as with his father—he had enjoyed little time in Cornwall during the intervening years. First there had been Cambridge, and then, because he was the second son, a career in the army. That his father had become sixth Marquess of Jervaulx the previous year (following the unexpected demise of the last male twig on the senior branch of the Deverill family tree) had changed little in

Gideon's life, although the one letter he had received from Jack in the meantime indicated that his graceless brother greatly enjoyed his position as the new heir to that great title.

"Gideon, look there," Penthorpe said suddenly, his words accompanied by an ominous thunder of cannonfire from the opposite ridge. "Boney's moving on the chateau!"

Startled, Gideon saw at once that Penthorpe was right and ruthlessly dismissed all thought of Cornwall from his mind, riveting his attention instead on the formidable duties at hand.

That opening salvo, accompanied by a rhythmic beat of drums and a strident blaring of horns, could have been heard for miles and filled the misty air with a heavy cloud of smoke. Eight thousand men stormed Chateau Hougoumont, but Gideon could see at once that the huge fortress would be nearly impossible to take. That realization strengthened his confidence, and he said calmly, "They may take the orchard, Andy, but our lads will hold firm inside." Handing him the telescope, he added, "Keep watch now, for I must see to the others. And guard your fears, man. Our position is strong. This line extends for three miles along the ridge, and Boney can't even see the reserves in the valley behind us. He's in for a shock. You may take my word for that."

Gideon maintained his air of confidence as he moved from man to man of his squadron, checking to see that each was awake and that men and horses alike were ready either to defend their present position or to charge if the order came. But his earlier concern had not been banished entirely, for that annoying little voice at the back of his mind soon reminded him that Wellington's advantage of position was counterbalanced by Napoleon's superior artillery and cavalry. And while British morale was certainly equal to that of the French, the same could not be said of the Dutch, Belgian, and North German troops who also fought under the Duke's command. Wellington had tried to offset that shortcoming by mixing his troops so that halfhearted and inexperienced men—of whom he had far too many—would be supported and influenced by those who were better disciplined and more accustomed to battle. Gideon could only hope the plan would work.

When he returned to his place beside Penthorpe, he saw with satisfaction, even before he took back the telescope, that the British still held Chateau Hougoumont. A ring of dead French soldiers encircled the place, their once gaudy uniforms scarcely recognizable now for the mud in which they lay, and most of the remaining activity appeared to be shifting to a new target.

"Damned reckless of them to have expended so much effort on an invincible target," Gideon muttered, "but how like Bonaparte to indulge in such a waste of lives and resources, as though men were unlimited. Surely, it will lead to his undoing in the end."

"I hope you ain't counting on it," Penthorpe said testily, "for there is Ney now, moving his men on the farmhouse. I know it's him, because I saw that red hair of his even without the telescope, when he took off his helmet for an instant just before they began to move."

Gideon chuckled. "I hope you, of all people, don't condemn the Frenchman for the color of his hair."

"Well, you ain't one to talk either," Penthorpe said with a grimace. "Yours may be dark enough now to pass for auburn, but as I recall the matter, you began life at Eton as Carrots Minor."

"So I did," Gideon said cheerfully. "Recollect that Jack's hair was reddish then, too. He had long since convinced everyone to call him Deverill, however, so he was even more displeased than I was when Carrots Minor stuck, because some of the cheekier lads promptly dubbed him Carrots Major."

With a thoughtful air, Penthorpe murmured, "I wonder how this lot behind us would enjoy addressing you as Major Carrots."

"Just you try that on, my lad, and see what you get for your trouble," Gideon warned, straightening to his full height.

"Oh, I'm mum," Penthorpe said, grinning, but the grin faded at the sound of a fresh salvo from below, and he added more grimly, "I say, Gideon, try as I might, I can't get shut of the notion that today's my last one on this earth. If Boney gets me, will you go to Tuscombe Park and tell them I'm frightfully sorry and all that, but . . . well, you know the drill."

"I do, indeed, but don't be nonsensical, Andy. You'll make it through this day and whatever follows, if only to go to Tuscombe

Park yourself and see if this aged and decrepit lass still looks anything like her miniature."

A sudden silence fell, broken almost at once by another roll of drums and a trumpet call. Staring into the valley, Penthorpe said quietly, "I hope you're right, but even though you've pulled me out of some awful scrapes in the past, Gideon, I don't believe you can do it today. I'm no coward, truly, but please—"

"Don't trouble your head," Gideon replied gruffly. "I'll do it if I must." Wanting to divert Penthorpe's thoughts and still keep an eye on the activity below and an ear cocked for orders, he said, "How is it that this Lady Daintry's such an heiress if she's got an older sister? For that matter, St. Merryn's fortune ought to go with the property. Isn't there a son?"

"Oh, aye, to be sure, her brother, Charles Tarrant. Poor fellow went to Harrow is why you don't know him. He gets the Tarrant estates, of course, but it seems that besides the settlement her father will make, my wench will inherit the fortune of a great-aunt, a truly redoubtable old lady, according to my Uncle Tattersall. In her seventies, she is, though, so she can't last long. From some cause or other she has money all her own. I don't understand it myself, because she ain't a widow, so it don't stand to reason that she ought to have much—lives with St. Merryn, too—but my uncle assured me the wench is due to come into at least twenty thousand a year from her, just like I said."

A French horn sounding the charge below diverted Gideon's attention again, and he saw instantly that the French, under cover of the heavy cannon smoke, meant to break through Wellington's center to open the road to Brussels. French bombardments were centered on the Dutch-Belgian divisions below, and even as he snatched the reins of his horse from the soldier who held them and snapped at Penthorpe to get to his unit, he saw the foreign troops break ranks and throw down their weapons. In wild confusion, pushing and sliding on the slippery ground, they turned and surged back up the slope toward the safety of the Allied main line with the French appallingly close behind them.

Leaping to his saddle, Gideon shouted to his officers to prepare to support the infantry. The order to charge came a split second later.

Riding powerful horses and waving their long sabers, the British cavalry attacked with murderous fury, cutting through the densely massed French columns to wreak terrifying mutilation and death. The trampled wheat grew red with blood, and even in the thick of battle, above the din of horns, drums, clashing swords, pounding hooves, and gunfire, Gideon could hear the shocking screams and appalling groans of wounded and dying horses and men.

Despite his best efforts to keep his units together, they soon became scattered, though the Allied forces held strong. When they regrouped sometime later at the base of the ridge, he did not see Penthorpe, but Wellington was waiting for them, astride his magnificent chestnut war-horse, Copenhagen. Ordinarily reserved in his manner toward his men, the Duke was so pleased that he received them now with a slight lift of his low cocked hat and the words, "Life Guards, I thank you!" Gideon grinned at his nearest officer and saw his own pride reflected in the man's widened eyes and parted lips.

But the battle was far from over. The British infantry quickly formed squares, turning the ground into a chessboard and entangling the French cavalry, whereupon the British cavalry charged again, driving the French back; but Bonaparte called in his reserves, and his army rallied, threatening Wellington's center and forcing the Duke to call in his reserves. By half past seven that evening, with the sun nearing the western horizon, the British main line had become badly weakened.

Gideon caught sight of Penthorpe near an inn called *La Belle Alliance,* but soon afterward Bonaparte hurled a huge wave against Wellington's line, nearly breaking through, and by the time the French had been repulsed, Gideon had lost sight of Penthorpe again. The center was crumbling, the Duke's men exhausted, and his reserves were used up. But with bulldog tenacity Wellington had already begun to reorganize his forces.

Bonaparte had the edge, Gideon thought, watching grimly as he signaled his men to regroup. The little upstart's men still thought they would get to wear the parade uniforms they carried to march into Brussels, but the Duke could yet prove them wrong.

French cannons were fired, the British replied in kind, and the smoke grew so heavy that for a time the enemy troops were lost from sight. Hearing the cry *"Vive l'Empereur!"* Gideon knew a new charge had begun, but still he could not see. Then, as he raised his saber in warning to his men to expect a command, the smoke cleared briefly, revealing line upon line of flashing bayonets appallingly nearer than he had expected.

"Fire!" he cried, and the command echoed down the line till it was lost in a thunderous explosion of cannon fire. When the smoke cleared again, three hundred of Napoleon's Old Guard lay dead or dying on the ground. Moments later Wellington galloped along the entire front line on the magnificent Copenhagen, waving his hat aloft and shouting, "The whole line! Advance!"

The battle was won. The French infantry, cavalry, and artillery had merged pell-mell into a great seething mass of panic. Some units tried to hold formation and fight, while others were trying to effect an orderly retreat, but the panicked masses were bent upon fleeing the blood-soaked wheat fields as fast as horses or their own legs could carry them.

The sun had set, and in the gray dusk, clouds of low-lying smoke enveloped whole sections of the field as Wellington's army pushed its way through the wreckage. Mangled bodies of dead and wounded men and horses lay jumbled together, surrounded by the debris of battle—plumed helmets, shakos, bearskin hats, gaiters, odd shoes, boots, knapsacks, metal breastplates, mess bowls, knives and forks, cannonballs, lances, sabers, torn bits of gold braid and lace, epaulets, flags, bagpipes, bugles, trumpets, and drums—each item telling its own sad story.

Grimly fighting his stomach's reaction to the gory sight, Gideon forced himself to keep his mind on his duty. Realizing he was near the inn, he looked anxiously around for Penthorpe but did not see him. His men waited quietly for orders, and when Wellington raised his hand, Gideon spurred his horse nearer to hear what he would say. As he did so, he saw an infantryman stoop suddenly to pick up something from the ground, and there was still enough light left for him to see the dull flash of gold. Swerving his mount toward the man, Gideon snapped, "What's that you've found there, soldier?"

The man looked up, saw his epaulets, and quickly saluted. "Damned if it ain't a lady's picture, sir," he said. "These Frenchies've dropped some o' the damnedest things."

"Let's have it," Gideon said, his stomach clenching in apprehension. The soldier handed up the miniature, muddy but perfectly recognizable. Not bothering to conceal the tide of fear that swept over him, Gideon scanned the nearby ground, his gaze passing swiftly over bodies that could not be Penthorpe's but lingering wherever a shape seemed at all familiar. Bodies lay all around him, and the dreadful groaning and screams of pain were such that he knew he would hear them in his dreams for years to come. Suddenly, in a hollow not far from where the miniature had been found, a lanky mud-covered figure caught his eye. The man lay facedown in the mud, but his helmet had slipped to one side, revealing a few locks of relatively clean reddish hair.

Flinging himself from the saddle, Gideon rushed to the fallen man, grabbed his shoulders, and pulled. The thick, oozing mud clung to its captive, reluctant to release him, and although Gideon's strength prevailed, his effort was futile. Bile surged into his throat. The man's face had been blown away.

Just then Wellington cried, "Bonaparte's taken horse to *Quatre Bras!* After him, lads!"

Fighting down his nausea, Gideon turned back to the waiting foot soldier and indicated the body. "He was a friend," he said. "The picture belonged to him, so I shall keep it, but I must go. You stay here to protect the body from looters and see it gets a proper burial. Here are a few yellow boys for your trouble," he added, digging for guineas. Tossing them to the man, he tucked the miniature safely away inside his jacket, flung himself into the saddle, and forced himself to concentrate on his badly depleted brigade and the mission that lay before them.

The battle of Waterloo was over, but pursuit of the French would not be abandoned, for the Duke was determined this time to drive Napoleon all the way back to Paris if necessary, and then to occupy the city. Only the dead on the blood-soaked field would rest tonight, Gideon thought.

Sending up a silent prayer for Penthorpe's soul, and ruthlessly repressing a vision of tears replacing the laughter in those blue eyes in Cornwall, he looked back one last time and saw, scattered here and there in the mud where they had fallen from torn French knapsacks, a vast number of still colorful red and blue parade uniforms.

Two

September 26, 1815

Lady Daintry Tarrant, having finished the final episode of the romantic tale she had been reading in the *Ladies' Monthly Museum*, sighed, cast the issue aside, and said to the only other occupant of the morning room, a stout, gray-haired lady, "I simply do not understand, Aunt Ophelia, why every silly female ends her tale expecting to live happily ever after only because she is getting married. It puzzles me how so many women—in stories, at least— find just the right man and, at no more than a nod or a wink from him, fall quite desperately in love."

Looking up from the journal in which she was writing, Lady Ophelia Balterley said, "One does not *fall* in love, dear child. One steps in it, rather like one steps into something in a stable yard. 'Tis a fact you should recognize yourself by now, having sent three no doubt eligible suitors to the right-about before getting yourself stuck with a fourth young man."

Daintry sighed again, pushed back a stray dark curl that was tickling her nose, and turned to glance out the nearby window at a dreary prospect that looked more like February than late September. Gray clouds drifted low over the trees of Tuscombe Park, and a light drizzle dampened the landscape. One could not call it rain, for the water in the quiet courtyard fountain showed not a single ripple and the lake beyond the vast sweep of the front lawn looked like a slate-colored mirror. But it was not yet a day for riding, so here she was, sitting on a sofa with nothing more interesting than a magazine to occupy her time.

Glancing at her great-aunt, seated too near the hearth but seemingly unaffected by the heat from the roaring fire, she saw that Lady Ophelia was still watching her, having abandoned the journal resting on the wide right arm of her writing chair in hope of conversation. Short of stature and square in shape, Lady Ophelia was solidly built and enjoyed long walks each day as much as she enjoyed her studies. Having entered her seventy-seventh year, she was remarkably well-preserved, still able to read and write perfectly well without the assistance of spectacles, and possessed of a mind that was sharper than most minds of any age whatever. Lady Ophelia was an acknowledged Bluestocking, an admirer of such radical females as Mary Wollstonecraft and Mary Anstell, and not the least bit likely to apologize for the fact.

Smiling, Daintry said, "Do you suppose there really is such a thing as true love, ma'am—between a man and a woman, I mean? I do seem to be attracted to certain gentlemen, to be sure, which is just as well, since Papa is determined above all things to see me married to one, and I try to believe each time that perhaps this man will do; however, in the final event, I find he won't do at all, so now here I am, betrothed to a man I have never even clapped eyes upon, merely because Papa has decided I am incapable of choosing a husband for myself."

"Your father is scarcely a better judge of men than you are, for goodness' sake," Lady Ophelia replied. "Only look at the specimen he picked for your sister, Susan, for no better reason than that Seacourt Head lies opposite Tuscombe Point."

"But Seacourt is a most charming gentleman," Daintry protested. "He is very handsome, and Papa still says—even after ten years—that it was an excellent match, since it brought all the land around St. Merryn's Bay into the family."

"Well, it did not do any such thing, since the Seacourt portion will no doubt go to Sir Geoffrey's son, if he ever has one, but property and money are all that matter to the English male. It was precisely the same when I was a gel. Fortunately for me, my papa was a man of foresight and vision who saw no good reason for me to live, after his death, in another man's pocket—or under his thumb, which was most likely to have been the case, of course. I've got a perfectly good man of affairs in Sir Lionel Werring, but I call the tune, and really, my dear, there is no urgent need for St. Merryn to cast you into marriage at all, for you will inherit half of my fortune, after all, which will make you quite independent of any male."

"Yes, ma'am, but I have not inherited it yet, nor do I desire to do so in the near future," Daintry said, twinkling at her. "And until I do, it is my duty to obey Papa."

"A duty made up by males to suit themselves," Lady Ophelia retorted. "Men created the entire world to suit themselves."

Daintry chuckled. "You know Mama has a spasm whenever you say such things, and Reverend Sykes does not approve either."

"Oh, quite, but that does not alter the fact that men have it all their own way. Do not tell me that any woman had a hand in deciphering the word of God, for I know she did not, nor did any female write the Bible or dream up the nonsense written about the Creation. Moreover, women used to have a great deal more power than they have today, for recollect that amongst the Greek and Roman gods females were quite as powerful as the males, and in even more ancient societies, females frequently ruled the roast. It was thought, and not unnaturally," she added dryly, "that man was born of woman, rather than the other way round, making Eve, not Adam, the first inhabitant of this earth. But men, once they began to sort out religion to suit themselves, promptly decided to make Eve a villainess, blaming her for that whole stupid apple affair just as if Adam had had nothing to do with it. I am quite thankful to know that had it all happened in England, the courts would have held *him* responsible, though they would have done so out of the foolish notion that only men are wise enough to make the important decisions in life."

"Yes, ma'am, so you have frequently told me," Daintry said, making no attempt to conceal her amusement, "but I am not certain that an English magistrate would go so far as to admit to anyone, ever, that he would have supported Eve in that particular case."

"Yes, well, I am glad to see you still think for yourself," Lady Ophelia said briskly. "For that you must thank me. Your father would never have taught you to do so, nor would he have been stirred to provide any governess who could teach you more than the basic accomplishments thought suitable for a female to learn. You would have learned no Greek or Latin, though you might have got a bit of Italian, and I daresay he would have let you learn French. Despite that rascal Napoleon, the language still enjoys favor with the *beau monde,* though not as much as it once did, to be sure. Perhaps it will come back into fashion now that the Continent has been made safe for travel again."

Daintry laughed. "Only if that dastardly Bonaparte does not break free again as he did last year. And as for my learning Greek and Latin, ma'am, you know perfectly well that I have not got the least turn for either language."

"You know as much as most men who fritter away their time at Oxford or Cambridge," Lady Ophelia said acidly, "and much more than most women. If we are ever to regain our proper place in this world, women must be better educated. 'Tis absurd to teach them only to be entertaining and decorative. Why, in ancient Celtic tribes, women fought right alongside their men in battle, and I can tell you that if a woman had locked up that dratted Napoleon, he would not have got loose again for a hundred days or more to work his dreadful mischief. Only men are stupid enough to believe that others will play by rules that they themselves have ordained, just as only a man can be stupid enough to believe that a gel who has unbetrothed herself three times in as many years is likely to remain betrothed to a fourth man only because he commands her to do so."

Daintry was accustomed to her great-aunt's penchant for changing a subject mid-sentence, so she didn't blink, saying only, "Papa threatened dire consequences if I fail to obey him, ma'am, and you know he is perfectly capable of keeping his word. I doubt I have the courage to jilt Penthorpe, in any case, since I do not even know him. What possible reason could I give?"

"I should think not knowing him would be reason enough, myself. Good gracious, child, he could be a rake or a scoundrel. Even your father don't know him, and only arranged the thing because he was exasperated with you. Also, the lad is a viscount, and it suited St. Merryn to be connected with his old friend's nephew. I daresay he knew Penthorpe's father, too."

"Yes, because they were all at Harrow together. It is the one fault he can find in Penthorpe that from some cause or other the poor man had the misfortune to go to Eton."

"Well, your father would have gone to Eton, too, in the old days and not have thought it any misfortune," Lady Ophelia said tartly. "Had it not been for the falling-out between his papa and Lord Thomas Deverill, he would never have gone to Harrow, nor would he have sent your brother Charles there. All foolishness, that feud. I never had any patience with it. When Jervaulx lost his elder son in that tragic riding accident just days before Waterloo, your father would say only that he's got another son somewhere and that he ought to get on back to Jervaulx Abbey instead of lingering in Cornwall, pretending a concern for all the miners out of work, when he is neither needed nor wanted and really desires only to keep up the price of Gloucestershire corn. However, that is all by the way. I meant only to explain that Eton was always the Tarrant men's school before that idiotish feud, and your father certainly did not let Seacourt's having gone to Eton dissuade him from giving your sister to the man."

"I do not pretend to care which school any man attended, ma'am. They all seem much of a muchness to me. I know Charles hated Harrow while he was there quite as much as any man I know who went to Eton hated it there. All of them are harsh places, are they not? I have observed that it is only after men leave their schools that they seem to acquire a love for them."

The morning-room door banged back against the wall just then, and a damsel who looked a good deal like Daintry, with the same rosy complexion, dark curls, and twinkling eyes, burst into the room, her white muslin dress rucked up under its blue satin sash, and her right stocking crumpled around her ankle. A second child, ethereally fair and slender, followed gracefully and silently in her wake, her light gray eyes wide and watchful.

"Charlotte," Lady Ophelia exclaimed, "what have you been about? Pull up your stocking at once, and try to remember that a lady enters a room with dignity, not like some whirling dervish."

Seeing Charley bend swiftly to do as she was told, Daintry smiled at the second child, patted the place beside her on the sofa, and said, "Come, sit by me, Melissa, and tell us what you two have been doing to occupy yourselves this dreary morning."

Melissa looked guiltily at Charley but moved obediently to sit beside Daintry, giving no response to her question.

Nor was it necessary for her to do so. Tugging at her second stocking, Charley looked up with a laughing face, her eyes twinkling mischievously as her gaze darted from her aunt to Lady Ophelia and back again. She said, "We've done away with Cousin Ethelinda. We decided to amuse ourselves without her today."

Stifling laughter, Daintry looked at Lady Ophelia, but although the old lady disliked untidiness, she was as immune to being shocked by Charley's declarations as Daintry was. "And just how have you accomplished that feat," she inquired placidly. "Did you murder the poor woman?"

Charley chuckled appreciatively and straightened up to deal with her sash, saying, "No, though it is frequently a temptation, ma'am. She is such a wet-goose, you know, and says such dreary things to us. She doesn't *know* anything at all."

Lady Ophelia said, "I cannot argue against that fact, but it is scarcely a proper sentiment to hear from the lips of a gel no more than ten years of age."

"Really, Aunt Ophelia, it is the latter end of September, as you must know since we celebrated your birthday more than six weeks ago, so my eleventh birthday is less than half a year off, and Melissa will be ten, two whole months before that. We are growing quite old. Soon we shall be turning down our hems and putting up our hair, and we do *not* like stitching samplers, which is all that Cousin Ethelinda can think of for us to do."

Daintry glanced at Melissa, sitting quietly with her hands folded in her lap. "Surely, our cousin also teaches you to play the pianoforte, and to work with globes and read improving works. I know she possesses many worthwhile accomplishments, and my governesses taught all those things, as well as trying to teach me the sort of things Aunt Ophelia was determined I should know."

"Well, at least the things Aunt Ophelia teaches one are interesting," Charley said, giving a final twitch to her skirt before turning and flinging herself down upon a cushion near Lady Ophelia's feet. "I do not intend to become a weeping willow like Cousin Ethelinda. She is not a proper governess, in any case, but is merely attempting to oblige so as not to seem so much of a barnacle upon Grandmama as she otherwise must appear to be."

"Charley, you simply must not speak in such an ill-bred manner," Daintry said, exchanging another look with her great-aunt. "It does not become a little girl to speak disparagingly of her elders."

"But it is true," Charley protested. "Even Melissa knows the only reason we have got stuck with Cousin Ethelinda is that Grandpapa said it is not his business but Papa's to choose a proper governess for me now that Miss Pettibone has gone. Melissa has her own at home, of course, and has only been sharing Miss Pettibone, but since both our papas are still in Brighton, of course Cousin Ethelinda insisted upon looking after us, because she feels obliged to make her way here, and if she is not hovering over Grandmama, she is making us do stupid samplers. We want to ride, Aunt Daintry, if you please." The last statement was made with a melting look cast at her aunt.

Daintry, trying to maintain a stern demeanor, could not do so in the face of that look, but she shook her head and said, "You cannot ride until the roads dry, darling. This drizzle is enough to soak you through in minutes. It is no use begging me, either. Indeed, it would be as well for you if your grandpapa does not discover that you have escaped from Cousin Ethelinda."

Melissa got up at once, but Charley waved her back to her seat. "Grandpapa never comes back to this room once he has gone down to his library, and it's warmer here than in the schoolroom. Tell us a story about when you were young, Aunt Ophelia."

"Oh, yes, please," Melissa said softly, breaking her customary silence at last.

Lady Ophelia was no more resistant than Daintry was to such pleading, and if the story she told was not quite one about her own youth, it was nonetheless interesting, for she told them about Bonnie Prince Charlie and the Jacobite rebellion, and if the tale was not precisely the version that would find greatest favor with the little girls' parents, it was no doubt closer to the truth of the matter than was the generally accepted English version, or the accepted Scottish version for that matter, since she did not glorify the prince but described his many faults.

Daintry had heard the tale many times and sat back to watch the little girls, seeing in their eyes the same fascination she remembered feeling the first time she had heard it. Lady Ophelia had a knack for making history sound like a fairy tale, and it was only years afterward that one realized how much one had learned from her. Daintry found herself listening again and was as annoyed as the two children were when they were interrupted.

"Oh, here you are, you naughty girls," Lady Susan Seacourt exclaimed, hurrying into the room, her pale-blue muslin skirts swirling around her slim ankles. She was taller than Daintry, fair and slender like her daughter, and her general demeanor was gentle, but at the moment she was clearly displeased. "Cousin Ethelinda has been searching the entire house for you," she said, "and we were just about to send a footman to the stables to look for you there. Here they are, Mama," she called over her shoulder, "safe and sound with Daintry and Aunt Ophelia."

"Oh, thank heaven," Lady St. Merryn said weakly, entering in Susan's wake, clasping her many shawls closer about her thin body as though she felt a chill. Leaning on the arm of a harried-looking plump woman with faded blond hair, she tottered toward the sofa nearest the hearth.

Charley got to her feet at once, saying, "Goodness, Grandmama and Aunt Susan, did you think we'd got lost? I always take very good care of Melissa, you know. I'd never lose her."

"No, darling," Lady Susan said, "I know you would not lose her, but you must know that proper young ladies do not run off and do as they please, especially since Cousin Ethelinda has so kindly undertaken to look after you both until we return to Seacourt Head. Of course, if your papa and mama were at home, Charley, they would see at once to hiring a new governess for you, but until they can do so, you must obey Cousin Ethelinda." She turned to her daughter, adding gently, "I am surprised that you would allow your cousin to lead you to be naughty, dear."

Melissa, who had also stood up politely when the others entered, said nothing, but her eyes filled with tears at the mild reproof, and Susan fell silent, looking helplessly at Daintry.

Miss Ethelinda Davies, who was helping Lady St. Merryn arrange herself on the sofa, glanced up and said quickly, "Oh, pray do not scold her, Cousin, for I am certain it was no doing of hers, and indeed, one cannot wonder at it if the children do not heed me." She laughed behind her hand, adding, "I fear I am not the sort of tyrant who knows how to enforce obedience. 'Tis a grave fault in me, as I know you would say, were you not too kind to do so. Now, Cousin Letitia, let me find you a cushion, for I know that the stairs must have tired you. Oh, thank you," she said when Charley offered the cushion she had been sitting on. Stuffing it behind Lady St. Merryn, Miss Davies added kindly, "There now. Your salts bottle is ready to hand, and I shall ring for a footman to fetch your very own fire screen from the drawing room, for I know you do not like the one in here. We do not like to see your cheeks grow too red, do we?"

Lady St. Merryn fluttered a limp hand in response, and Lady Ophelia, who had been watching the whole procedure with patent displeasure, said tartly, "Cease your prattling, Ethelinda, for goodness' sake. Letty cannot have been worn out by climbing one flight of stairs, nor will she or her precious rouge melt from this paltry fire. Moreover, a good brisk walk in the fresh air would do her a great deal more good than those nasty salts, but if you are going to ring for a footman, pray tell him to bring more logs. I cannot think why no one has filled the basket. In another quarter hour there will be only ashes on that hearth."

Lady Susan said, "You girls, go with Cousin Ethelinda now, and do your lessons. Perhaps if you are very good, Aunt Daintry will take you riding when the weather clears."

"Yes, I will," Daintry said. "It will be clear soon, just as it has been every afternoon this week, and we can ride toward the sea if you like."

"May we go down onto the shingle?" Charley asked. "Melissa says she will not be frightened to do so if we are with her, and she wants to ride right into the biggest smugglers' cave."

Daintry looked at the smaller girl. "Is that right, darling? You were quite frightened when we rode down before."

"The waves were too loud then," Melissa murmured. "My mare didn't like them, and her fidgets made me nervous, but Charley has promised she will not let her bolt with me."

"Tender Lady?" Charley's eyes lit with affectionate laughter. "I could stop any horse in Grandpapa's stable from bolting with you, as you must know by now, but that old cow wouldn't bolt if we put nettles under her saddle."

Susan said, "What a dreadful thing to suggest!"

"Well, it is not as if I would do it," Charley replied indignantly. "I meant only that Tender Lady is a complete slug."

Lady St. Merryn said feebly, "Oh, do go away, child. Take her away, Ethelinda. I do not know why you allow her to speak so loudly. I tell you, she makes my head ache quite dreadfully."

Daintry shot a quelling look at Charley, who looked mutinous but shut her mouth obediently and motioned to Melissa. The two little girls followed Miss Davies from the room.

"I do wish," Lady St. Merryn said plaintively, "that Charles and Davina would come home and take that child in hand."

Susan said lightly, "There are two children, Mama."

Lady Ophelia said, "And do you pretend not to know which one your mother wants taken in hand? It is fortunate that neither Charles nor Davina is so foolish as to believe Charlotte's spirit ought to be stifled or her curiosity bridled, for in all candor, I find her much easier to deal with than Melissa. Too quiet by half, that child of yours is, Susan."

"Melissa is admirably well-behaved," Lady St. Merryn said, reaching for her salts again, "but because she acts as she should, you find fault with her, Aunt. You are very hard."

"If you ask me," Susan said stiffly, "neither Charles nor Davina takes enough interest in Charley. They are far too busy being members of the *beau monde*, flitting off to London for the Season and to Brighton for the Regent's birthday. Next there will be shooting parties and house parties, then hunting in the shires after Christmas. Then London again. If they pause long enough to hire a new governess, I shall own myself amazed."

"Pooh," Lady Ophelia said, "you enjoy London yourself, my dear, certainly more than I do and more than you would if you had the trouble I have trying to sleep there! Moreover, you'd have gone on to Brighton in a twinkling if you hadn't been laid low by a feverish cold. I will say, though, that I do not suppose anyone could ever accuse you of neglecting your child. Your deep feelings for Melissa are clear to anyone who knows you."

Susan blushed, and Lady St. Merryn said, "Most unfashionable is she not, to take such an interest in Melissa? Folks would have thought it most odd in me always to be fretting after my children. Not that I did, of course. St. Merryn would not have permitted it, even had my health allowed it. It simply was not the done thing. Of course, it would be better if Susan had two or three more. I cannot think why she has had only the one."

Daintry had been watching her sister and thinking she looked much healthier than when she and Melissa had arrived at Tuscombe Park more than six weeks before. Both had had colds then, and Susan's had been particularly severe. Now she looked her old self, if a trifle self-conscious as a result of Lady St. Merryn's tactless remark. Knowing Susan would dwell upon Sir Geoffrey's disappointment that she had not yet given him a son if she were not diverted, Daintry patted her hand and said, "It is just like the old days, Susan. You do everything right the first time and thus need not try again. Melissa is an angel."

Susan smiled. "She is, isn't she? Geoffrey says that Charlotte—for I must remember not to call her Charley; he detests such boyish nicknames—that she is a bad influence on Melissa, but I told him that dearest Melissa is much more likely to be a good influence on Charlotte. Don't you think so?"

Daintry nearly laughed aloud, but a certain look of anxiety in Susan's eyes gave her pause and made her respond more diplomatically, "I suppose that if anyone can influence Charley, Melissa will. But Charley is a handful for anyone."

Lady Ophelia said, "A limb of Satan, that's what the child is, and much the better for it, if you ask me. A female needs a great deal of spunk to get on in this world."

Susan said gently, "Manners will take her farther than spunk, ma'am. Geoffrey says she ought to have a sterner governess, and he said that even before Miss Pettibone left. He did not know she meant to go, of course, but he said—"

"Oh, for goodness' sake," Lady Ophelia snapped, "spare us from hearing every word Seacourt has said these past ten years. Do you say nothing for yourself anymore, gel? I declare, for six weeks all we have heard is what Geoffrey says, and from all I can tell he never does say anything worth listening to!"

Flushing deeply, Susan bit her lip, looking suddenly very much like her daughter. "I-I'm sorry, Aunt Ophelia, I did not mean to offend you."

Daintry said gently, "You have not offended her, Susan. You know you have not. It is only that she prefers to hear what people really think, not what they think they ought to think, or what other people think they ought—Oh, dear," she said with a comical look, "what a tangle my tongue makes of my thoughts! I shall never learn to explain them clearly, but you do understand what I mean, do you not?"

"Oh, yes," Susan said, sighing. "Your meaning is perfectly clear. It generally is, you know, even when you think you have got it garbled. I am the one who can never seem to make people understand what I mean. Perhaps that is why I so frequently quote others instead. I think, if you will all forgive me now, that I will go upstairs. Geoffrey and the others will be home soon, I believe, and I must begin to sort out Melissa's and my things so that Rosemary can begin our packing." She got to her feet as she spoke and was gone from the room almost before anyone else understood that she was going.

When the door had shut behind her, Lady Ophelia said grimly, "Sorting clothes as though Rosemary were not a perfectly good maid! She will be darning stockings or fussing in the kitchen next. Susan is growing to be like you, Letty, all megrims and grievances. Thank heaven your daughters are different in their natures, or I should have become so dreadfully bored here that I must have set up my own household out of self-defense."

Daintry laughed. "You would never have done such a thing, ma'am. Fancy how frustrating it would have been for you always to be wondering what sort of a fix we had got into without you here to put things right! And life here would have been very dull indeed," she added with a teasing look.

The old lady smiled back at her, and Lady St. Merryn said testily, "Just you wait, Aunt Ophelia, until Daintry is finally married, and see if she don't change like Susan did, and like I did myself, for that matter. I am persuaded I was quite a lively girl before my come-out, but marriage is a sobering business, as you might not realize yourself, never having been asked."

Daintry looked swiftly back at her great-aunt, thinking the old lady would take offense; but, seeing that she was struggling to keep from smiling, Daintry relaxed.

Lady Ophelia said, "It was certainly not from lack of being asked, Letty, but if you are trying to tell me that I ought to have married, I simply cannot agree with you."

Lady St. Merryn tossed her head like the pettish beauty she clearly once had been. "I am sure I should not be so impertinent as to tell you what you ought to have done, ma'am, but to be telling married ladies how things ought to be when you have no experience of the married state is rather the outside of enough."

"One needn't always experience something to understand that it would be bad for one," Lady Ophelia said, "and having discovered quite early on in life that I had practically no respect whatsoever for men, it would have been unconscionable of me to pretend to submit both my mind and body to the direction of one of the creatures, do you not agree?"

"It would be most unbecoming in me to agree to any such thing," Lady St. Merryn said, leaning back against her cushion. She looked at Daintry. "You will find, my dear, that once you are Viscountess Penthorpe your ways will have to change, for no gentleman will tolerate for long having his opinions challenged by a female, and you are far too likely to do that very thing. Your father has told you, and I tell you now, that to go on as you have become accustomed will soon lead to your undoing."

Daintry grimaced, thinking again as she had so frequently thought since the day her father had commanded her to cease her foolishness and agree to marry a man she had never met, that the road ahead was fraught with peril. Certain that she was bound to say something she would regret if she remained in the room much longer, she said that she ought to send word to the stables to have horses saddled for herself and the little girls just as soon as the weather cleared. Neither Lady Ophelia nor Lady St. Merryn made any objection, and when Daintry closed the door of the morning room behind her, she breathed a sigh of relief.

Deciding she might as well walk down to the stables herself rather than send a footman, she went to her bedchamber to collect her red-wool hooded cloak. Flinging it around her shoulders and drawing on a pair of York tan gloves, she returned to the gallery and was approaching the right wing of the graceful, divided stairway that swooped down into the massive front hall, when her father came out of his library and the hall porter swung open the heavy front door to reveal a visitor, a tall, broad-shouldered gentleman in an elegant, many-caped gray driving cloak.

His gleaming Hessian boots seemed to belie the dampness outside as he stepped across the threshold onto the black-and-white marble floor and doffed his beaver hat, revealing a ruggedly handsome face and a head of thick auburn hair.

"Upon my word," St. Merryn exclaimed, hurrying to greet him, "it's Penthorpe, is it not? By heaven, lad, I'd recognize you anywhere with that head of hair, though damme, it's darkened a good bit since last I saw you. "You can't have been more than ten at the time, so that is not to be wondered at. Come in, come in. You are Penthorpe, are you not? Confess it, man. You've come at last to claim my daughter, and not before time, I can tell you!"

The gentleman reached for the clasp at the top of his cloak, lifting his chin as he did so, and his gaze met Daintry's. She saw that his eyes were sunk deep beneath dark brows, his nose was straight, and his cheekbones and square jaw were rather pronounced. So that was Penthorpe. She thought him handsome but very large. His lips had parted, revealing even white teeth, and he had seemed about to speak, but after gazing at her for a long moment, he closed his mouth. Then, visibly collecting himself, he said in a pleasant, deep voice, "Aye, sir, I'm Penthorpe."

Three

Gideon had not so much as paused to think before speaking, but for the moment at least, he did not regret the impulse that had overcome his good sense. Lady Daintry Tarrant was even lovelier than her portrait.

She had not moved but still stood poised with one tan-gloved hand resting lightly on the polished banister. Her scarlet cloak accented the glow in her cheeks, and her eyes were so brilliant a blue that he could see their color from where he stood. Her elfin chin had lifted when St. Merryn called him Penthorpe, and her full, red lips had parted, but he could see that she was not particularly happy to think her betrothed had arrived at last. The thought cheered him, but he was wrenched from his pleasant reverie when the footman took his hat and St. Merryn seized his hand to shake it. Feeling sudden warmth in his cheeks, Gideon hoped to God he wasn't blushing like a damned schoolboy.

"Delighted to see you, my boy," St. Merryn exclaimed, clapping him on the shoulder as he pumped his hand up and down. "Not but what I haven't been on the watch for you this past month. Knew you'd sell out the moment that rascal Boney was clapped up again, but I daresay there were any number of details to see to before you could get back to England, and I can't doubt you went to Tattersall Greens before you came here to us."

"Yes, sir," Gideon said, thankful that that much at least was the truth. He had certainly sold out, but he had not done so as quickly as Penthorpe would have; not until he had received word of Jack's death, and that disconcerting—not to mention tragic—news had been more than six weeks in reaching him. But he had indeed gone to Tattersall, believing Penthorpe's uncle would desire to learn how his nephew had died. It had not occurred to him that Lord Tattersall might be wholly unaware of Penthorpe's death, but he had not been surprised to discover that was the case, for the losses at Waterloo had been so staggering—between forty and fifty thousand men—that he knew some families would never receive official notice. They would be told only that their relatives were missing and presumed to have died, and even that much information would take months to reach them.

The thought gave him pause, but a glance at the haughty, silent beauty standing at the top of the stairs, and another at her beaming parent, steadied his resolve. He was an honorable man, but he was also a crack cavalry officer, trained to take the line of least resistance, to accept whatever challenges came his way, and to seize even the slimmest opportunity that the Fates provided. Thus, though his initial reaction had been to set the earl straight at once, one look at Lady Daintry, added to the certainty that St. Merryn would send him packing the minute he discovered he was a Deverill, made up his mind for him. It would do no harm to masquerade as Penthorpe for the short time it would take him to get to know the lady better.

Realizing that St. Merryn was demanding news of Penthorpe's uncle, he collected his wits and gave his full attention to the earl. "He is as well as can be expected, I suppose, sir."

"Still in the gout, is he?" St. Merryn nodded wisely. "I had a letter from him in the spring, and he complained about it then. Quacks himself, of course. Do him a world of good to get out of the house now and again and onto a good horse. Used to be a damned fine hunter, old Ollie was, but now he just sits in a chair and mutters to himself about his gout. Puts him right out of temper, too, but I daresay he was pleased to see you. Only thing I've ever heard him complain of in you is a tendency to procrastinate, but he can't have complained this time, can he?"

"No, sir. Lady Tatt . . . that is, my aunt is well, too," he added, wanting to change the subject and unable to resist discovering what his lordship thought of that formidable dame.

St. Merryn grimaced. "Can't stand the woman. She's the one that's turned poor Ollie into a petty tyrant, what with all her nagging, and what good is she? Only the one child did she give him and too old now he's gone to mend the matter. If I've told him once, I've told him a million times to take a firmer hand on the reins, for it don't do to let a female get the upper hand. You remember that, lad," he added, turning to glare up at his daughter. "Give 'em an inch, and they'll take an ell."

Stifling laughter, Gideon looked up to discover that her ladyship did not share his mirth. Her lovely mouth had hardened into a straight line, and the little chin had taken on a firmness that clearly bespoke a defiant nature. Finding himself more intrigued than ever, he smiled at her and turned back to St. Merryn, saying, "I am not so easily cowed, sir."

"Have to say you don't look the sort to be ruled by a petticoat," St. Merryn said. "Come now and meet the family, lad. Daintry, don't stand like a stock, and take off that damned cloak. Can't imagine where you thought you were going."

"I am going to the stables, Papa."

"Don't be absurd. Make your curtsy to the man you are going to marry, and let me hear no more of stables."

"I promised Charley and Melissa I would take them riding when the rain stopped," she said, "and I believe it has."

"Then send a footman with your message," he snapped, moving toward the stairway as he spoke. "You've not the least need to go down there yourself. Whoever heard of such a thing?"

He was working himself into a temper, but Gideon did not think Daintry seemed much disturbed. He watched her as he followed in the earl's wake, feeling rather pleased when she stood her ground and made no effort to remove the offending cloak. Neither did she evade his own gaze, giving him back look for look until the earl reached the top step. Then, just at the moment when Gideon thought St. Merryn was about to explode, she swept a deep curtsy, still without looking away from Gideon.

"Saucy chit," St. Merryn growled, glancing over his shoulder as though to gauge Gideon's reaction. "Might as well warn you from the outset, Penthorpe. She's got her head stuffed with a lot of damn-fool notions. Daresay you'll knock them out soon enough, but you might as well know what you're up against."

"It certainly helps to know the opposition, sir," Gideon murmured, watching her eyes. "It is a pleasure to make your acquaintance, Lady Daintry."

"Is it, sir?" She rose. "You are taller than I'd expected. I have met Lord Tattersall, and as I recall, he is rather short of stature, so I'd expected you to be much the same."

"I hope you are not disappointed."

Her eyes widened, giving him that sudden urge to laugh again, but before she could reply, St. Merryn snapped, "Much good it would do her if she were. Where's your mother, girl? Must make Penthorpe known to her, you know, if she ain't laid down on her bed or some such thing." He grimaced at Gideon. "It's no secret that my Letty's worse at quacking herself than old Ollie is, and she's got a damned cousin of hers lurking about, whose sole use seems to be to encourage her to imagine her ills. I tell you, lad, if I had to look at Ethelinda's ugly face every day, I'd let the undertakers have me and be glad of the change."

"Mama's with Aunt Ophelia in the drawing room, Papa," Daintry said evenly, but she turned so sharply to lead the way that her cloak swirled out, and then, glancing back over her shoulder, she said matter-of-factly, "You might as well be warned from the outset, Lord Penthorpe, that I have been betrothed three times before now, only to cry off each time before the wedding."

St. Merryn caught her by the arm and swung her around, giving her a rough shake. "You'll not cry off this time, by God, and don't you forget it. Upon my word, girl, I've had enough!"

Gideon, knowing he had not the least right to interfere between man and daughter, still had to fight an instinctive urge to do so. He watched, feeling no surprise when she stiffened and the light of defiance leapt to her eyes again. What did surprise him, however, was that when she glared at her father, St. Merryn released her. Not until then did she say grimly, "I promised you I would not cry off,

Papa, but as you have frequently said yourself, he has every right to know the worst of me."

"Yes, to be sure, he has every right," St. Merryn blustered, "but if you are hoping he'll cry off himself, now he's learned of your nonsense, you wrong him, girl. Penthorpe is a gentleman."

Conscious of the fact that he was behaving in anything but a gentlemanly way, Gideon resisted an impulse to compound the matter by pretending outrage and demanding to hear the details of every broken betrothal. There was something about the girl that made him want to provoke her, to stir her passions. That there were passions to be stirred, and not far beneath the surface, was obvious to the meanest intelligence. He could see that her father had quite failed to tame her, and he had a strong itch to attempt the feat himself. That it would be a challenge was clear, but he had never been a man to run from a challenge.

They had come to a pair of double doors at the end of the gallery, and Daintry pushed them open, saying lightly as she did so, "Here is a surprise for all of you. Lord Penthorpe has arrived. You may all wish me happy, I suppose."

St. Merryn said testily, "That is no way to introduce a gentleman to your mama. If you cannot do the thing properly, say nothing at all and I will do the honors. Come in, Penthorpe."

Finding himself facing what seemed at first like a roomful of women, but all unknown, Gideon breathed a sigh of relief, for it had occurred to him only as he crossed the threshold that he might easily encounter someone he knew. His home was near enough Tuscombe Park that they must have several local acquaintances in common, and the utter lunacy of what he was doing struck him with incredible force. *A fine soldier you are,* he thought sourly. *Just pure dumb luck you didn't walk straight into an ambush.*

His gaze lighted on the most formidable of what proved to be only four females, a square-shaped elderly lady with gray hair pulled ruthlessly into a bun at the nape of her neck. Not only did she not smile at hearing Penthorpe's name, but her pale blue eyes narrowed speculatively and the look she gave him was much the same one she might have employed to search out rats in her pantry. He had difficulty returning that look, and he had the odd notion that, in the brief moment before he shifted his gaze to the next lady, the first had seen straight into his soul.

The plump one hovering over the sofa clasped her hands at her bosom and exclaimed, "Oh, goodness me, a true English hero!"

St. Merryn snapped, "Don't be a fool, Ethelinda! Pay her no heed, Penthorpe. My wife," he added, indicating the thin, mouse-haired lady reclining on the sofa. "Letty, dear, I present your future son-in-law. Have the goodness not to have a fit of the vapors till he knows you better. I've no tolerance for it now."

"Or ever," the old lady said, adding abruptly when Gideon glanced back at her, "You say you are Penthorpe, young man?"

Totally unable to lie in the teeth of that look, he had all he could do to conceal his relief when St. Merryn snapped, "Didn't I just say so, Ophelia? Knew the instant I clapped eyes on that red hair of his. Damned if I don't think you're growing deaf in your old age. That . . . that female is my wife's aunt, Lady Ophelia Balterley," he added for Gideon's benefit.

"It is a pleasure to make your acquaintance, my lady," Gideon said politely before turning to the lady who had declared him a true English hero, "and yours, ma'am, as well."

For the first time since his arrival he saw Daintry smile at him. Though it was only a little smile, he thought it worth waiting for. She said, "That is Cousin Ethelinda, sir . . . Miss Ethelinda Davies, that is, who is Mama's most devoted companion and quite the kindest person in our household. But I thought you had gone upstairs with the children, Cousin."

Blushing deeply, Miss Davies murmured something about having set them to writing letters and then having just popped back downstairs to make certain of dearest Letty's comfort; whereupon, Gideon, recognizing his cue, made her a profound leg. When he straightened, he saw to his deep satisfaction that Daintry was regarding him with near approval.

Grinning, he held her gaze, and was rewarded with another hesitant smile in return. Then, visibly gathering herself, she indicated the fourth lady and said, "And that is my sister, sir, Lady Susan Seacourt."

Recalling in dismay that Penthorpe had described Lady Susan, Gideon saw an apparent abyss about to open before him. Having counted heavily on the viscount's assurance that no one in the household knew him, he recollected now that Penthorpe had agreed to his odd betrothal only because he had admired Lady Susan enough to consent to marry her sister, but Lady Susan's polite look encouraged him. She clearly did not think him an impostor.

"I believe I was at school with your husband, Lady Susan," he said calmly. "He was years ahead of me, however, and probably remembers me only as a repulsive scrub." He nearly added that Sir Geoffrey had been much better acquainted with his brother but remembered in the nick of time that Penthorpe had no brother.

Susan said quietly, "He will be sorry to have missed meeting you, sir. He and my brother are presently in Brighton—along with everyone else of any importance," she added with a smile.

"So the *beau monde* still flocks to the seaside from Prinny's birthday onward," Gideon said, returning her smile.

St. Merryn grunted. "You make it sound as if you've been away for a decade, lad, but Ollie wrote you'd sold out before Boney got loose and went back just to help hunt the rascal down."

Gideon said smoothly, "Perfectly true, sir, but though he abdicated in April, I did not get back to England till September, and went straight to Tattersall Greens. I didn't go to Brighton at all, and since Bonaparte escaped the first of March, before I had got round to stirring a foot from home, I was in London only long enough to sign on to return to the Continent."

"Ah, well, that's all behind you now," St. Merryn said comfortably. "It is all very well for a young man to serve when his country has need of him, but when it don't, he's better off putting his house in order and setting up his nursery. I daresay my Charles would have liked nothing better than to purchase a pair of colors and follow the Duke, but what with his being my only son, and heir to the earldom, it wasn't to be thought of."

Without thinking, Gideon said, "Lucky for us, Lord Uxbridge didn't let that stop him, sir. Even after he inherited the earldom three years ago, he remained in the thick of things, and if it hadn't been for losing his leg at Waterloo, I daresay he'd be in service yet. To be sure, he was not the only son, but both of his brothers also serve in the Army."

"A gallant hero, Uxbridge," St. Merryn said, taking no umbrage, "though we must call him Anglesey now that he's been made a marquess for all his heroic deeds."

Lady Ophelia said dryly, "He might be a gallant hero, but that won't get him inside most London drawing-rooms, St. Merryn, not after the shameful way he treated his first wife—an earl's daughter, I remind you—and not when he seduced his second while she was still married to Wellington's poor brother. Any man responsible for two divorces has much to answer for in this life. And as for his brothers," she added, looking straight at Gideon, "Sir Arthur Paget, at least, is just such another, stealing Lord Boringdon's wife and creating yet one more scandalous divorce."

Lady St. Merryn said sharply, "Do not mention that word. My nerves simply won't stand it, for I cannot imagine how anyone can bear to be part of such a scandal. Moreover, you cannot blame Uxbridge, or whatever we must call him now, when it was his own wife who brought suit against him, which I am persuaded was a most unnatural thing for any female to have done and could only have been accomplished in such a backward place as Scotland."

Gideon, to whom Uxbridge's faults were as well known as his virtues, waited expectantly to see how Lady Ophelia would reply, but Lady Daintry forestalled her. She had been staring at her sputtering father and said now with the same air of surprise as if neither her aunt nor her mother had spoken, "Surely Charles will be as surprised as I am to learn he has any desire to go to war, Papa. I have always thought him the most devout coward."

"Hold your tongue, girl. How dare you say so! Charles is a bruising rider to the hounds and a first-rate shot to boot. He'd have made an excellent cavalry officer."

Gideon did not know Charles Tarrant, but he rather thought he had more faith in Lady Daintry's description of him than the earl's. Realizing that she had purposely drawn St. Merryn's fire, he waited with interest to hear what she would say next; but Lady St. Merryn, diverted from the scandal of divorce, sighed loudly and said, "I am persuaded you must want to send me to an early grave, sir, for you know perfectly well my nerves would never have stood for my darling Charles to have been wrenched from my side. Why, I grow quite faint at the thought."

"Well, you needn't do any such thing," the earl retorted, scowling at her. "He didn't go, did he? I only said he might have done well as a soldier. Who's to say but what he might not have ended up on Lord Hill's staff, or Stuart's?"

"Now that," Daintry said, cocking her head a little to one side, "is entirely within the realm of possibility, for I have heard it said repeatedly that those gentlemen are best known for their noble connections, their gallantry with the fair sex, and for a certain amount of skill at the gaming tables."

"They are skilled on the hunting field as well," Gideon said with a chuckle before he could stop himself. Then, seeing the look of outrage that leapt to St. Merryn's face, he added quickly, "But there are any number of good men on Hill's staff, certainly. The Duke mentioned several in his dispatches."

His first observation had earned him a look of amused appreciation from Lady Daintry. Ignoring the rider, she said with the same thoughtful air as before, "Charles does like to hunt, but he would not have liked being anywhere near the field at Waterloo. As to the rest, Davina complains frequently about his expertise with the opposite sex—she is his wife, you see," she added for Gideon's benefit, "and a fair hand at flirting, herself, so she ought to know—and she certainly complains about the time he spends at the gaming tables, but I should think Hill and Stuart would prefer their staff members to display at least some small sense of responsibility to their duties, and that Charles would fail utterly to do."

"Damn it, Daintry," St. Merryn growled, "I told you to hold your tongue. See what I mean, Penthorpe? I wish you well with the chit, that I do. If you take my advice, you'll begin with a sound beating—on your wedding night—to teach her who's master."

Lady St. Merryn raised her vinaigrette swiftly to her nose, at which ominous sign Miss Davies knelt hastily at her side, patting her hand and murmuring anxiously, all the while casting beseeching looks over her shoulder at the earl.

Daintry had stiffened angrily, her cheeks crimson, her eyes flashing sparks, and Gideon thought her more beautiful than ever. Without thought for consequence, wanting only to prevent an explosion, he stepped forward, unfastened the clasp at her throat with a flick of his fingers, and said as he placed his other hand at her shoulder to turn her, "It is much too warm in this room for that cloak, my lady. I cannot think why you have not rung for a footman to take it away. Pray, allow me to do so for you."

He heard the breath catch in her throat, but before she could react he swept the cloak from her shoulders. She whirled back, and the speed with which her hand flashed up to strike proved, just as he had suspected all along, that her temper was as quick as his own. Other than to challenge her with a warning look, he made no move to defend himself, but she caught herself and, still glaring, let her hand fall to her side again.

Her high-waisted, pale green morning frock had been worked down the front in pink with a Grecian scroll pattern, but Gideon scarcely noted such details. Nor did he heed St. Merryn's hearty congratulations on the way he had put the fear of God into her, for he doubted he had done any such thing. Moreover, he was too busy admiring the effect of rapid breathing on a softly rounded bosom much plumper than he had expected to discover in a girl at least a foot shorter than he was. The pink satin bow tied neatly beneath it underscored the comeliness of that particular asset. Penthorpe had been much luckier than he had ever known.

"The bell rope," Lady Ophelia said dryly, "is yonder by the chimney-piece, my lord."

Recalled to his senses, Gideon flashed her a glance as he moved to ring the bell, and was inexplicably relieved to note a glint of humor in her pale eyes. There was no reflection of that humor in Daintry's eyes, however, when he turned back to face her after giving the bell rope a sharp tug.

"You have just rung for the butler," she said curtly.

"And a very good thing, too," St. Merryn interjected. "He can bring us some wine. I daresay you'll be glad of a drop after your journey, Penthorpe."

"Too early in the day for me, sir, but don't deny yourself on my account. Shall I ring for a footman as well, Lady Daintry?" he added, seeing her turn away toward the window as though she had washed her hands of him. "You did express a desire earlier to send a message to the stables, did you not?"

"Medrose can attend to that," she said, "but since you are determined to be of use, perhaps you will be so kind as to adjust the fire screen for my mother. Is it not too hot for you, Mama?"

"Upon my word, girl," St. Merryn said testily, "stop treating the man like a lackey and sit down. You can forget about sending any damned messages to the stables, too, for I tell you here and now that you are not going to go dashing off on a horse when we've a guest staying in the house. You are staying, of course," he added, looking confidently at Gideon.

"As to that, sir," Gideon began, thinking swiftly, "I was not by any means certain of my welcome here, since I had not had the good manners to send ahead to warn you of my arrival."

"Don't be daft, man," St. Merryn said, breaking off when the door behind him opened and the butler entered, followed by a tall young footman. "There you are, Medrose. Take Lady Daintry's cloak from Lord Penthorpe, and bring us some mountain sherry. Oh, and tell Mrs. Medrose to prepare rooms for his lordship."

Gideon said hastily, "Really, sir—"

"Medrose, send word to the stables that I want horses saddled for myself and the two young ladies the minute the rain has stopped," Daintry said, interrupting him without ceremony.

Gideon did not object since the intervention gave him time to think, but he shot her a curious look as he handed her cloak to the butler. Surely she had said she was taking *Charlie* and Melissa. Or had he misunderstood? Medrose did not question her order, though he did turn back to her once he held her cloak.

"I shall attend to it at once, Miss Daintry. Shall I take your gloves away as well, miss?"

She looked down at her hands in some surprise. "Oh, yes, of course. How foolish of me." Stripping them off, she handed them over to him. At the threshold, he handed cloak and gloves to the footman and, turning back, closed the doors behind them himself.

A silence fell but was broken when Miss Davies got suddenly to her feet, saying with breathless eagerness, "Do sit down, Lord Penthorpe. I cannot think why you have been kept standing this age when we are all perfectly agog to hear about your noble exploits against the dreadful Bonaparte. Do tell us everything, for I am sure we shall hang in awe upon your every word."

Lady Ophelia said tartly, "Don't be a zany, Ethelinda. His most memorable exploit must be Waterloo, and even you cannot be so insensitive as to wish to hear the details of that frightful conflict. His lordship must have lost many friends that day, so we must not ask him to relive it for our entertainment. Sit down at once, and you sit, too, Daintry, for regardless of what you want this young man to think of you, you have no reason to act as if you'd had no breeding whatsoever. Now then, sir," she said when Daintry had obeyed without a murmur, "you may take a seat, too, and tell us if you will, without further roundaboutation, if you do or do not mean to remain with us for a sensible visit."

"Of course he will stay," St. Merryn declared, beaming at him. "We've plans to make, upon my word."

Fully aware that he was treading on thin ice, Gideon remembered belatedly that the reason he generally took care never to lie, aside from the utter reprehensibility of such behavior, was that he had never, even as a child, done so successfully. He still had enough sense left to stick to the truth where possible and was determined to avoid the obvious pitfalls of an extended visit, so repressing a sigh, he said cautiously, "Since I could scarcely count on such a generous welcome when I had not written first, sir—that unfortunate habit of procrastination you spoke of earlier, I fear—I decided I'd do better to put up elsewhere in the neighborhood until I had paid my respects."

"And where," Lady Ophelia said, "might that be, my lord?"

Realizing that she had not once called him Penthorpe, he wondered if she suspected his imposture. In any case, he must end it soon, and to avoid further untruths, and hoping too that the dratted feud would keep them from paying a formal call, he said, "At Deverill Court, ma'am. I daresay you know—"

"Oh, we know of Deverill Court," she said, nodding. "Do we not, St. Merryn?"

"Upon my word, lad," the earl exclaimed, "what are you about to stay with Jervaulx? Bad enough that he's back in Cornwall at all when we thought ourselves rid of him—and I daresay you know nothing of the relationship betwixt our two families—but damme, I can't have you staying there! You're to remove to us at once."

Gideon stiffened but said with forced calm, "I believe I must make that decision, sir. It would be the height of bad manners to leave before I am expected to do so, but the Court is less than an hour's ride from here, so I daresay you will see more than enough of me in days to come. I have every wish to know Lady Daintry well before we set a date for our wedding."

"Damme, man, but Ollie was right. You're a damned procrastinator!"

For the second time that day, Gideon blessed his friend's well-known dilatory nature. "Be that as it may, sir," he said, "I can see nothing to be lost and a great deal to be gained by going gently to work here." He glanced pointedly at Lady Daintry, who had chosen that moment to look out the window again as though she took no interest whatsoever in the conversation.

Following his glance, St. Merryn grimaced and said, "Oh, very well, but you disappoint me, lad. I had not thought you would so easily discount my excellent advice on that head."

The drawing-room doors banged back on their hinges, and Gideon turned to stare in astonishment at the small whirlwind that blew into the room. "Aunt Daintry, the rain has stopped, and we've got our habits on and everything! Oh, please, may we go at once?" The child was almost an exact miniature of her aunt, and faced with such exuberance, Gideon nearly didn't notice the slender blond wraith who slipped in behind her.

"Upon my soul, Charley!" St. Merryn snarled in outrage.

Lady Ophelia said calmly, "Go out and come in again, Charlotte, this time like a lady of quality, if you please."

Without missing a beat, the child turned on her heel and ran past her silent shadow, out of the room, pulling the doors shut behind her. There was a lengthy pause before they opened again, revealing the stately Medrose with tray, decanter, and glasses. Stepping into the room, he paused for effect before announcing majestically, "The Honorable Miss Charlotte Tarrant, madam."

Gideon ruthlessly stifled laughter at the vision next revealed upon the threshold. Carrying herself with the dignity of a queen, and a far more dignified queen than the present one, Miss Charlotte swept into the room and made a profound, even a graceful, curtsy. Her eyes sparkled with mischief, and he saw that they were not the same color as Daintry's but were so dark as to appear black; however, the roses in her cheeks were the same, and it was as clear as could be that in a few years she would be every bit as beautiful as her aunt.

The second child had not moved from the spot she had taken after their first entrance. She stood so still that it seemed almost as if she were not breathing, and she, too, reminded him of someone. For a moment he could not think who it was. Then, with a start, he realized that Lady Susan must be the child's mother. The fact that Susan had been present in the room the entire time he had been there and had scarcely uttered a word was reason enough to have missed the resemblance. He glanced at her now, seated quietly near the window, and saw that she was watching, warily, not her irrepressible niece but St. Merryn.

Daintry, too, shot a look at her father before stepping forward with a laugh to hug Charlotte. "Charley, you dreadful girl, will you never learn to behave?"

"But I did do it properly the second time, Aunt Daintry, so do say you will take us. Who is that gentleman?" she demanded abruptly when her gaze came to rest at last upon Gideon.

St. Merryn snapped, "Children should be seen and not heard."

"Nonsense," Lady Ophelia retorted. "How is the child to learn anything if she does not ask questions? Introduce him."

When the earl's face darkened in anger, Daintry said quickly, "He is Viscount Penthorpe, darling."

"The man you are going to marry?"

Daintry paused, but Gideon, surprising himself, said firmly, "The very man."

The child looked him over from head to toe, then smiled happily at her aunt. "He is much better looking than you thought he would be, isn't he?"

Gasping, Daintry shot him a look of laughing embarrassment before she said, "If I am to take you riding, girls, I must change out of this gown, so now if everyone will excuse me—"

Seeing that St. Merryn was about to object again, Gideon quickly interrupted, saying, "An excellent idea. I will be very happy to accompany you."

But if she was grateful for his intervention, she did not show it, replying curtly, "We ride toward the shore, sir, not toward Bodmin Moor."

Still determined to frustrate St. Merryn's opposition, Gideon said evenly, "Then we can ride together as long as our routes coincide, my lady. Surely you do not wish to stand here debating the point when you could more efficiently employ the time in changing to your riding dress."

For a moment she looked as if she would stand her ground, but then, with a swift look at the two girls, she nodded, said abruptly, "Wait for me in the hall, Charley," and swept from the room with the same air of dignity that the child had assumed to enter it. Only, in Daintry's case, the attitude was clearly a natural one and inspired not the least urge in Gideon to laugh.

"That's the dandy," St. Merryn said, his humor rapidly improving. "A firm hand, that's what you'll need with the chit. You just show her who's master, lad, and you'll have no regrets."

Lady Ophelia, chuckling, said, "All things are possible, I suppose."

Four

Daintry's air of dignity deserted her the moment the drawing-room doors closed behind her, and she hurried upstairs to her bedchamber, where walls papered above white linen-fold wainscoting in a mock-India pattern of colorful flowers and birds on a sky blue background provided an elegant background for dark wood furniture. The hangings at bed and window were of matching blue silk, and a cheerful fire crackled on the white marble hearth.

Ringing for her maid, she crossed the pastel-colored floral carpet and flung open the doors of her wardrobe. Then, kicking off the pink satin slippers she had worn with her morning dress, she untied her sash with one hand while with the other she riffled through the clothes hanging in the wardrobe.

"Merciful heavens, Daintry, whatever are you doing?" Susan demanded from the doorway. There was amusement in her voice, and when Daintry, startled, whirled to face her, she said, "Wait for Nance to help you, for goodness' sake. You know how much it annoys her when you disarrange the things in your wardrobe."

"Good gracious, Susan, do you try to please even your maid? Nance is very good in her way, and I prefer her services to those of that awful dresser Aunt Ophelia insisted I hire my first Season in London, but I do not exert myself to please her. Where the devil is she, anyway? And what are you doing here?"

"I came to help you choose what to wear, of course, and to discover what you think of your betrothed."

"He is a typical man, overbearing and arrogant," Daintry said, laughing at her, "but you can't fool me, my dear. You just wanted to escape from the drawing room. Not that I blame you in the least, but won't Papa be displeased by such base desertion?"

"I daresay he did not even notice that I followed you," Susan said evenly. "Nobody ever pays heed to me."

Daintry arched one eyebrow and said mockingly, "No one? Not even Sir Geoffrey? Come now, that is carrying things too far, I think. Or have you changed your mind about that handsome husband of yours? Why, I can recall when you thought him the most magnificent, the most charming, the most perfect of men."

"Well, Aunt Ophelia never thought him so," Susan said, moving across the room toward the tall, blue-silk-draped window.

"Aunt Ophelia does not appreciate masculine charm," Daintry said, abandoning her search and drifting restlessly toward her dressing table. "Nor am I generally drawn to aesthetic-looking blond gentlemen, myself, but you did not answer my question. Have you altered your opinion of him?"

"Do not be nonsensical," Susan retorted without turning. She added in a worried tone, "Do you think it is safe to take the girls out so soon after that rain? The cobbles in the courtyard are still wet."

"We won't be riding on cobblestones, silly," Daintry said, watching her and wishing the light had not been behind her when she had asked about Sir Geoffrey. Susan never seemed to want to talk about her husband, and Daintry had little wish to press her now. "We mean to ride toward the sea," she said, "but you need not fret, you know, for I will take excellent care of them both just as I always do. Come unfasten my buttons, will you? There must be fifty of them down the back of this frock, and I cannot reach most of them. Where the devil is Nance? I rang ages ago."

"You are so impatient," Susan said with a look of fond exasperation. She dealt swiftly with the buttons, however, and by the time she had finished, Nance had arrived.

"About time," Daintry said, glaring at her. "I want my red habit, black boots, and black gloves. And please don't be all day about it, Nance. My nieces are waiting."

"Oh, aye, and so they are," Nance said, grinning at Susan. A plump Cornishwoman with warm brown eyes and a rosy complexion, she had served at St. Merryn nearly all her life—as had her sister, mother, and grandmother before her—and if she had ever possessed a formal attitude, she had long since abandoned it. Laughing, she said, "As if I and everyone else in the house did not know who's come to call. And as if it were your custom to wear your best habit on a drearsome day like this one. The old blue one were good enough for Miss Charley and Miss Melissa afore today." Abandoning her teasing attitude the moment Daintry's expression hardened, she said, "What's he like, Miss Daintry? I asked Medrose if he were a handsome lad, 'n all, but you know what a stick *he* is. Mr. Stiffrump, that's him to the life, and not one word would he say to me about my Lord Penthorpe."

"Very proper of him," Daintry said. "I hope you do not gossip with the other servants about my affairs, Nance."

"As if I would," Nance said, whisking the red habit out of the wardrobe and laying it upon the high bed, where with its black cord trim, black-fringed epaulets, and jet buttons, it stood out splendidly against the sky blue silk spread. Returning to the wardrobe, she stretched to reach a box on the shelf above the rack, saying as she did so, "But I still want to hear about that young man, Miss Daintry. I'll not breathe a word—"

"I will not wear a hat today," Daintry said.

"Nonsense," Nance said. "You'll never wear that lovely habit without the hat what goes with it."

"You must not go bareheaded, my dear," Susan said quietly. "'Twould be a most unworthy example to set for the girls."

Daintry ground her teeth but said no more about the hat. Susan was right. It would not do to teach the little girls to scorn the dictates of fashion. Not yet, at all events.

She was out of her frock and into the habit in a trice, and Nance stood back to look her over. "Does your complexion proud, that red does. Suits you to a treat. I'm right glad you and my Lady

Ophelia was able to talk your mama out of having it done up in the light blue muslin she fancied so strong for you."

"Susan is to have that," Daintry said, smiling at her sister. "It will be most becoming to her, and will make up into just what she will want for riding in Hyde Park when we go to London in February. Moreover, muslin, fashionable though it may be, is not my notion of suitable material for a riding dress."

"His lordship will like that red sarcenet better on you," Nance said. "Sit down and let me tidy your hair before we put on your hat. Is he handsome, then? Tell me all about him."

"He is well enough, I suppose," Daintry said repressively. In the mirror she saw Nance glance at Susan again and was not surprised to hear her sister chuckle. Shifting her gaze to Susan's reflection, she said, "I suppose you think he is a marvel of masculine pulchritude." Privately she thought Penthorpe a good deal better looking than Sir Geoffrey Seacourt, but she doubted that her sister would agree.

Susan laughed. "Lord Penthorpe is very large and handsome in a rugged sort of way, Nance, and I think Daintry likes him more than she would have us believe. I cannot think why I never noticed him in London, you know, for although Lord Tattersal's son was still alive at the time of my come-out, and Penthorpe was thus quite ineligible, one would think we'd have noted him before he joined Wellington's army, for he has a vast air of command. He even stood up to Papa when Papa wanted him to stay here."

"Don't he mean to stay? Why not?"

While Nance tidied Daintry's unruly curls into a semblance of order, Susan explained. "He is staying with friends in the neighborhood, and I can tell you, Papa is none too happy about that, for his friends are at Deverill Court, of all places."

"Susan." Daintry said no more than her name, but Susan flushed to the roots of her hair and looked down at her hands.

Nance said, "Now don't be scolding her, Miss Daintry. I'd have learned it all soon enough, if not from one of the maids, then from Annie, since our cousin Sarah works days at the Court." Setting the hairbrush on the dressing table, she picked up the hat, a confection of scarlet silk fashionably decked with an assortment of plumes, ribbons, and black Naples lace, and set it carefully atop her mistress's dusky curls, anchoring it with a jeweled brass hatpin. Surveying the result, she said, "Best you tell me the facts yourself, so as when some fool begins telling fairy tales in the servants' hall, I can set him straight."

"You will do no such thing, Nance," Daintry said, meeting her gaze in the mirror and holding it.

Flushing even more brightly than Susan had, Nance muttered, "No, o' course I won't. I know better than to discuss my betters, and so you should know, miss."

"I do hope so, Nance, and that you will refrain from discussing them even with Annie, since she no longer works here herself. You may go now. I will ring for you when I return."

Without another word, pausing only long enough to collect the clothes Daintry had discarded, Nance left the room.

Susan said, "You've upset her."

"Nonsense," Daintry said, peering into the mirror and trying to decide if the tilt of her hat was as becoming as it might be. Then, realizing that she could not possibly be doing such a thing on Charley's or Melissa's account, she turned to face her sister. "I cannot imagine why you would think I had upset Nance. She is not so easily daunted. When next I see her, she will be scolding me for something or other. You know she will."

Susan smiled. "You are right, I suppose."

"I am. Just because you turn tail whenever anyone looks slantwise at you does not mean that everyone else does."

"Do I do that?"

"You do."

Susan bit her lower lip. "I don't mean to, but I do not like loud voices, and I cannot bear to make people angry. And you—Well, you do become so very . . ."

Daintry chuckled and, getting to her feet, moved to hug Susan. "I do, don't I? Threw my first temper tantrum before I was three, got my own way, and never looked back."

Susan shuddered. "Which just goes to show how different things were for you than for me. The one time I told Mama that I *would* do something she had told me I could not do, she snatched me up across her lap and beat me with her hairbrush till I screamed. That was not the only time, either, I can tell you."

Daintry grimaced. "She never did such a thing after Aunt Ophelia came to live with us, did she?"

"Not like that." Susan sighed. "But I never stopped being afraid she might. With you, it was so different. Even Papa—"

"Oh, come now," Daintry said, chuckling, "you are not going to say Papa never punished me, for you know perfectly well—"

"Oh, I know he did, but he never seemed to become so angry with you as he did with me—or with Charles, for that matter."

Daintry shrugged. "I suppose it was because you both were older. He expected more from you than from me. And, too, when I was small, I was nearly always with Aunt Ophelia if I was not with my governess. Aunt would not permit Mama to strike me, and even Papa respects her wishes. And as for Charles, I can understand anyone's wanting to smack him. I do myself, quite frequently, and I utterly *feel* for Davina, though I do not think she ought to flirt with other men the way she does."

"No," Susan said, "and speaking of other men—"

"Yes, I know," Daintry said, picking up her whip from among the clutter on her dressing table. "Not that it wouldn't do that man a world of good to have to wait a few moments. He has become entirely too accustomed to telling others what to do. If I am going to marry him, that must certainly change."

"You do like him then," Susan said, getting up to follow her when she moved to the door.

Daintry looked back over her shoulder. "Like him? Pooh, he is just a man like any other, though not so bad as I'd feared he might be," she added, remembering a singularly attractive smile, warm golden hazel eyes, and the bemused way he had looked up at her that first moment after entering the hall.

"He is very large," Susan said as they walked along the corridor together toward the stair hall.

Daintry remembered his asking if she was disappointed to find him taller than his uncle. She had nearly given her most private thoughts away then. How could one be disappointed when a man's figure was precisely the same as that possessed by the hero of every romantic novel one had ever read? For regardless of the general disapproval of such reading material at Tuscombe Park, no one had ever forbidden her to read what she liked, and she did enjoy reading a pleasant Gothic romance from time to time.

Realizing that Susan was waiting for a response, she said, "I suppose he is rather large, and he is much too arrogant and overbearing in his manner to suit me. I can tell you, I did not care for the way he took it upon himself to remove my cloak, or the way he invited himself along on our ride, either."

"I should not care to see him angry," Susan said quietly.

"Oh, pooh. Much I should care for that." They had reached the gallery, and peering over the railing, she saw that the two little girls were waiting—one patiently, the other pacing. "Oh, good, the girls are there." Glancing toward the drawing-room door, she added, "If Penthorpe thinks I shall fetch him, or wait while he procrastinates, he has another think coming."

She had started down the stairs before she realized that Susan was no longer with her but had in fact vanished in the disconcerting way she had perfected as a child. Then the sound of the drawing-room door caught her attention, and she turned, sighing at the sight of the large man coming out of the room.

"I hope you were not trying to sneak away," he said.

"At least you did not bring Papa along to insist that I let you accompany us on a nice, sedate ride toward the moor, sir. I promised the children I'd take them to ride on the shingle to see the smugglers' caves, and I do not break my promises."

"None of them?" He was beside her now on the stair, his hand firmly at her elbow. She could feel its warmth through the material of her sleeve, and though she did not require assistance to get down the stairs, she decided it would be unseemly to pull away. Few of her friends in the neighborhood treated her at all protectively, although, in London, gentlemen frequently offered such assistance—generally with a great deal of pomp and flourish that she found most disagreeable. To Penthorpe's credit, he managed the gesture so neatly and naturally that she found, to her own surprise, that she rather liked it

"There you are, Aunt Daintry," Charley exclaimed. "We thought you were never coming. It does not take me nearly so long as that to change a frock. Hello, Lord Penthorpe. Are you really going to ride with us, sir?"

"I am—part of the way, at least—and I promise I shall not try to talk you into riding toward the moor."

"Oh, good," she said, laughing. "Not that I was afraid you would, of course, for Aunt Daintry promised, but I did fear that Grandpapa might insist, and then, of course, we should have had to obey. Not that Melissa would mind. She likes riding on the moor. But today," she added, turning and giving Melissa a nudge toward the front door, "we are going to ride on the shingle and see the caves. Will you come that far with us, sir?"

Daintry stiffened but, determined to avoid outright rudeness in front of the children, managed to hold her tongue.

His smile was extremely attractive. "Not today, I think," he said, then added to Daintry in a lower voice, "I did not speak merely to foist my company upon you, you know, but to keep your estimable parent from forbidding your outing altogether."

She said in the same tone, as the children vanished through the doorway, "I am not ungrateful, sir, and will certainly acquit you of any other motive. My father would not have forbidden the ride, but he might well have insisted that we ride to the moor, and the girls would have been disappointed."

"Where will you ride, exactly?"

"St. Merryn Bay. There are several caves there reputed to be used by smugglers, though I daresay the men are as likely to have been wreckers as free traders, when all is said and done."

"I know those caves from my childhood," he said, frowning. "The path down from the cliff is extremely steep, is it not?"

Feeling her temper rise at the implied criticism, she kept her tone even with difficulty. "Both girls are excellent riders, sir. Charley could ride down that trail blindfolded and sitting backwards, and although Melissa is a more nervous horsewoman, she will not have any trouble, I assure you."

"Nevertheless, I think now that perhaps I'd better accompany you," he said. "That path will be slippery from the drizzle, and even though you will certainly take your groom, you will be glad of more help than his, I think."

"That is hardly your decision to make," she said, annoyed.

He was silent until she looked up at him, and there was an enigmatic look in his eyes when she did, but it vanished, and he said sternly, "Our betrothal gives me the right to make it."

She bit her lip, then said, "You go too fast, sir, if you think to give me orders upon such short acquaintance."

"Do you deny my right? I heard you say you had given your word to honor this betrothal, or is your word worth no more than that of most females?"

Indignation threatened to overcome her. "I do not break my word once I have given it, but if you think to run roughshod over me, my lord, you had better think again. I will make you wish you had never been born if you try it."

He smiled. "Shall we catch up with our charges before they ride off without us?"

She gritted her teeth but made no objection. The girls were already mounted, Charley on Victor, her favorite bay gelding, and Melissa on a pretty little gray mare. Daintry's wiry groom held the reins of the silver-dun gelding she favored, and of a large black-roan stallion with a white blaze between his eyes.

"Oh, what a beauty," she said, moving to stroke the black's silky muzzle. "So tall and powerful, yet so dashing and alert."

"My horses have to be large to carry my weight," he said. "That is Shadow. But come, my dear, your charges grow restless."

She felt his hands at her waist before she realized his intent, and there was a brief, exhilarating sense of weightlessness before she was deposited on her saddle.

Handing her the reins, he said, "Do your leathers require some adjustment?"

"No, thank you. Clemons knows just how I like them." She watched as he swung effortlessly into his own saddle, and she was amused to see that, despite the presence of the groom following at a discreet distance, he kept an alert eye not only on the two little girls as they rode down the drive but on herself as well.

She was proud of the children. Both had light hands on the reins and excellent, firm seats in the saddle. She saw at once that Charley was impatient to gallop, so she said gently, "We will walk the horses for fifteen minutes, my dears, but then you may have a gallop if the road is not too mushy from the rain."

Her escort looked at her with raised eyebrows but made no comment. Sighing, she said, "I suppose you think they ought to be riding with leading reins, Penthorpe."

"Not at all," he replied, smiling back at her in a way that made her look swiftly ahead at the gravel drive. "I might, however, have waited a bit before tendering hope of a gallop. The roads are bound to be in too dismal a state for one."

"Perhaps," she agreed, "but if I had told them as much, Charley would be so anxious to prove me wrong that she would communicate her anxiety to her horse. This way she will be content to ride quietly and will soon recognize, for Melissa's sake if not her own, the foolhardiness of riding too fast on a slippery road."

Though he looked doubtful, he said nothing more for several minutes, and indeed, appeared to be listening with some amusement to the one-sided conversation going on ahead of them. As usual, Charley was doing all the talking, while Melissa listened and nodded. After a time, he turned to her again and said, "Though I would not dare to suggest leading reins, I own I did think they would still be riding ponies at their ages."

Daintry, not surprised that he would hold such an opinion, said, "You and Sir Geoffrey agree on that head, sir. Melissa has a pony at home, but she rarely rides him, and I think that a very good thing, myself, but it is plain to see that you have never taught a child to ride. Ponies are dreadfully unreliable, you see. Their gaits are uneven, and they are much more liable than horses are to bolt across a road without reason, or to stand and kick, or to rear up just for their own amusement. And since they are so quick on their feet, their antics can confuse a child so that even if she does not fall off she loses her self-possession, and becomes quite terrified."

He was silent again, and for a moment she thought he meant to argue the point, but then he nodded and said, "I had not thought about that, but I believe you may be quite right."

"Well, I am, of course, though you needn't sound so insufferably condescending about it. However, at least you admit it. My father still thinks girls ought not to ride at all until they are sixteen.

He says they are not strong enough to control a mount of any sort before that time, and I daresay he doubts their ability even then. Boys, of course, he thinks able to ride as soon as they can walk. I am persuaded that he must have put Charles on his first pony even before that auspicious occasion."

"If your papa disapproves so strongly, how is it that he allowed you all to learn before you turned sixteen?"

"Oh, that is because of Aunt Ophelia. She believes girls are every bit as capable as boys are. Indeed, she believes that females are the superior sex, that it is only because men are more muscular that they have become dominant." She watched to see how he would respond to that provocative suggestion.

He laughed. "Lady Ophelia is one very redoubtable woman."

"She has been called worse things than that," Daintry said.

"I don't doubt it. She terrifies me."

"A perfectly common reaction," she said, smiling sweetly at him. "I mean to be exactly like her."

"Do you, indeed?" The warm smile was still visible in his eyes, and while she could not accuse him of mocking her, she had the notion that he was humoring her. As they continued to talk, she was conscious of a strong wish to know what he really thought of her, or of anything at all, but he was careful to advance no exact opinions of his own, and she could not quite decide whether she admired his verbal dexterity or despised his evasive nature. Before she could make up her mind, they had come to the path leading down to the shingle from the cliff side.

The Channel was not looking its best. Sky and water were much the same shade of gray, and the waves were edged with lacy white foam. They had been able to hear the roar of the rollers long before they could see them, and the breeze had quickened to a light wind, blowing Daintry's curls about and making her glad that the brass pin held her hat tightly in place. Melissa's hat was still in place, too, but Charley had long since removed hers, and her long black curls blew wildly about her face. Her cheeks were rosy, and her dark eyes sparkled.

"Look," she cried, "we can see Melissa's house way yonder on the headland, and here's the path down! I'll go first."

"Oh, no, you won't," Daintry said. "I will."

Her companion shook his head. "The best plan would be for the heaviest horse to lead the way," he said quietly. "Shadow is very sure-footed, and if Charley follows me, Melissa can follow her, and you can bring up the rear with your groom. That way, the pair of you will be in the best position to judge the safety of our course," he added when she opened her mouth to protest.

Daintry's protests died on her tongue. Much as she hated to admit it, he was right. Charley would heed him better than she would either herself or Clemons, and if Penthorpe and Charley proceeded without mishap, Melissa would be safe following them. If it looked as if either of the leaders was having difficulty, Daintry would be able to stop her, while Clemons went to help.

Penthorpe was watching her narrowly, and when she nodded, he said, "Good girl. I knew you were not a fool."

Once again, his attitude stirred mixed emotions. She was grateful for the compliment but wondered at the same time if he thought most women were fools.

The cliff path was easily negotiated, for although there were damp patches, the stiff breeze had dried most of it, and only a bit more than usual care was required. Even Melissa did not seem nervous, and at the bottom, when Daintry drew her silver dun up next to the big black roan, and his rider said, "I will leave you now," she was surprised and a little disappointed.

"You do not mean to accompany us, then?"

Charley, overhearing, said quickly, "Don't you want to see the caves, sir? One of them is big enough to house an army!"

"No, thank you," he said smiling at her. "I have seen them before, and I came this far only because I thought you might require my help, but I see now that you will do very well on your own. Going up that path will be easier than riding down was."

Daintry could not deny it, but she was sorry to see him go.

Gideon looked back from the cliff top and saw that the three of them were still watching him. He waved and they waved back. Then, Charley, who, true to her aunt's prediction, had said nothing more about galloping, suddenly wheeled the bay gelding and took off at top speed along the shingle. With scarcely a pause, the other two followed her.

Resolutely, Gideon turned his face homeward, wondering what on earth he had got himself into. In the next hour he repeated that question a good number of times, and though he told himself he did not regret the impulse that had stirred him to deceit, he did regret the deceit itself, for the simple reason that he would have to confess it and take the consequences of his action. That there would be unpleasant consequences he did not doubt for one moment. He had seen enough of Daintry Tarrant now to know that she would not look kindly on even the briefest deception.

She was even lovelier than he had imagined, and there was something about her that stirred feelings he had not known he possessed. He had enjoyed his share of indiscretions, to be sure, particularly as a carefree bachelor on Lord Hill's staff, but not one of the many beauties who had crossed his path over the years had instantly stirred such feelings in him.

He paid little heed to his direction, for once he reached the bleak heights of Bodmin Moor and saw Rough Tor and Brown Willy rising like sentinels in the northeast, he knew Shadow would carry him home with little need for guidance. He was in no hurry to get there. Having obeyed a command to present himself at Jervaulx Abbey in Gloucestershire as soon as he had rid himself of his commission, he had not expected to find his father in residence in Cornwall a mere fortnight later, and he wondered what his reception would be. The marquess had seemed to have so little use for him at the Abbey that the unpleasant duty that beckoned him to Tattersall had proved something of a relief, in that it had given him an unexceptionable excuse to leave. So lost in thought was he that Deverill Court loomed on the horizon above the west bank of the River Fowey in a what seemed an amazingly short time. Not long afterward he passed through the tall iron gates and onto the gravel drive leading to the house.

The drive was bordered with thick shrubbery, camellias, azaleas, and rhododendrons that, in the early spring, created a magnificent display. Now, though the blooms were gone, the shrubs were lushly green, framing the gray granite house at the end of the drive, backed by its own woods, and looking just as it had since the days of the Tudors. The Tudor house enfolded part of a fortified manor house that had been there when Gideon's ancestor Richard Deverill acquired the property through marriage in 1353, and little had been changed over the years. The Deverills who lived there were satisfied with what they had and had never felt the need expressed by many of their friends and acquaintances to add on extra wings with each succeeding generation, or to tear down the old to replace it with newer, more modern substitutes. The last major addition to the house had been the northwest tower with its muniments room, in 1627.

Gideon loved the old house, but since the day he had first left it to go to Eton, he had never expected to be more than a visitor there, even after his father had succeeded unexpectedly to the marquessate; and although his brother's death had altered many things in his life, he still found it difficult to accept the fact that Deverill Court would one day be his. Only the marquess seemed to find that fact more difficult to face than he did. Jervaulx seemed almost resentful of the fact that his primary seat was now a vast estate in Gloucestershire.

Giving his horse into a groom's keeping, he went inside, greeted the porter cheerfully, then passed through the soaring hall with its elaborate roof supports and vast Tudor open fireplaces to the stair hall, without so much as a glance at the vast collection of arms and armor, pausing only to allow a waiting footman to take his hat and gloves, and to inquire as to his father's whereabouts.

"Lord Jervaulx is in his book room, my lord."

Halfway up the stairs, Gideon slowed his pace, and just outside the door of that apartment, catching a glimpse of himself in a pier glass, he paused to straighten his neckcloth and smooth his hair. Then, drawing a deep breath, he nodded at the footman, who had hurried in his wake, to open the doors, and he went in.

"Good afternoon, Father." The footman closed the door.

Jervaulx, a hawk-faced gentleman with some fifty-five years in his dish, was seated at the large, leather-topped desk, writing. He did not look up at once but continued to write.

Gideon remained silent, watching him.

At last, with a final flourish of his pen, the marquess put it down, leaned back in his chair, and gave his attention to his son. "So, you have come home."

"As you see," Gideon said, wishing, and not for the first time in his life, that he could read his father's thoughts in his expression. But Jervaulx rarely made things so easy. He was never angry, emotional, hurried, or upset. As a boy, Gideon had been terrified of him, certain that beneath the cool surface lurked potential disaster, but over the years, that fear had eased to a certain, sometimes frustrated, wariness.

"One assumes that Tattersall was grateful for your visit," Jervaulx said. "The news of Penthorpe's unfortunate demise had no doubt distressed him."

"He had not yet learned of it and was beside himself with grief," Gideon said. "It was a shock to him to lose the nephew who had taken the place of a son to him, as you might imagine." He could not resist the rider, being certain that Jervaulx must be grief-stricken over Jack's death; however, as was the marquess's custom, he had let nothing show. Nor did he now.

"You have been all this time at Tattersall Green?"

"Yes, sir, until today." He had not planned to divulge his visit to Tuscombe Park, but having had enough of allowing his baser instincts to rule, he added bluntly, "I'd promised Penthorpe I'd take word of his death to the young woman to whom he was betrothed. I stopped there on my way here."

"Anyone who reads *The West Briton* or the *Royal Cornwall Gazette* knows of that betrothal," Jervaulx said evenly. "Do you mean to say that you have been to Tuscombe Park?"

"Yes, sir."

"No self-respecting Deverill has set foot there in forty years, but no doubt you simply chose to overlook that fact."

Gideon returned Jervaulx's look steadily. "I believed my promise to Penthorpe outweighed such personal considerations."

"A conscientious man would put honor of family above a request made by an outsider, but one supposes that you will go your own road even when your actions provide distasteful grist for the local rumor mills."

"I am sorry to have displeased you, sir, but I had to do what I thought was right, and frankly, since I last saw you in Gloucestershire, I had not expected you to be here."

"The winter Assizes begin soon. In order to achieve fairness, one must have spent some few weeks here, particularly now when there will be many cases involving local miners because of the food shortages and the many mines shutting down—including the Mulberry mines, which employ many men in this very district."

"I am aware that you served as magistrate here for many years, but surely, sir, that is no longer one of your duties."

"And just who do you suppose is capable enough to assume the position?"

"I'm sure I don't know, but—"

"Precisely," Jervaulx said. "If that is all for now, there is more correspondence to be dealt with before dinner."

"Certainly." Gideon bowed and left the room, telling himself that the sooner he straightened things out at Tuscombe Park, the better it would be. The last thing he wanted was for Jervaulx to discover that the local tattlemongers were avidly discussing, not the surprising visit of a Deverill to Tuscombe, but that of the deceased Penthorpe.

Thus it was that the very next day he took courage in hand and returned to Tuscombe Park, determined to make a clean breast of the whole even if it meant ruining himself with the beautiful Lady Daintry. Giving hat, whip, gloves, and cloak to a footman, he was politely informed that Lady St. Merryn was not receiving.

"I will see the Lady Ophelia then," he said.

"Certainly, my lord. I will take you up directly."

Following the young man to the drawing room, Gideon saw with relief that Lady Ophelia's only companion for the moment was Lady Daintry. He waited only until Penthorpe's name was announced and the footman had gone before drawing breath to speak his piece.

Lady Ophelia said abruptly, "Your charade amused me for a time, sir, but before you make any more pretty speeches, I think you'd better stop this foolish pretense and open the budget to my niece. You look a great deal like your grandfather, you know, so unless I am much mistaken, you are Deverill, not Penthorpe."

Five

U ntil Lady Ophelia spoke, Daintry had been doing her best to conceal her unexpected delight in seeing him again, delight that had surged into being the moment the young footman announced him. She was certain—though she was likewise quite well aware that many members of her family would scoff at that certainty—that she had never before felt such an interest in a gentleman.

Not only was he handsome and well formed, but his warm, low-pitched, melodic voice was the sort that sent tremors radiating through a maiden's breast (and other portions of her anatomy), if she allowed her thoughts to dwell upon it. She had spent hours the previous night attempting to keep her own thoughts from doing so, or from considering his extremely attractive smile.

Her ride along the seashore with the two little girls had seemed rather flat after he had left them; and she had wasted a good deal of her time later, when she might better have been sleeping; trying to imagine what it would have been like had he ridden with them, sharing the pleasures of the crisp sea breeze, the haunting echoes when they had ridden right inside the largest cave, the splashing of horses' hooves as they chased retreating waves, and the thrill of fear when Charley had ridden too far in pursuit of one wave and had nearly been claimed by its successor.

Lady Ophelia's words acted upon her now like a bucket of ice water, for the chill sweeping over her was the same. It brought her to her feet, which had the effect of shifting his gaze from Lady Ophelia to her, and had she been asked to describe her feelings just then, she would have found the task impossible, for it was as if she were falling with no one to catch her and yet had become suspended in time between the moment of his entry and the moment her aunt's words had turned him into a stranger again.

The moment passed. Looking directly at her, he said, "It is true. I am Gideon Deverill."

Her numbness disappeared in a blaze of anger, and closing the distance between them in a few short steps, she slapped him hard across the face before she had realized what she meant to do. From a great distance, she heard Lady Ophelia's exclamation of dismay, but she paid it no heed.

"How dare you even cross the threshold of this house!"

"I came because—"

"Don't speak to me," she snapped. "You are an unprincipled, deceitful scoundrel, and you have no business to set foot on Tarrant land. The Deverills represent all that is reprehensible, and you ought to be ashamed of yourself even to belong to such a felonious family, but to try to pass yourself off as Penthorpe in order to insinuate yourself into my—"

"That's enough," Deverill said grimly.

"It is by no means enough! I have much more to say to you, and though you may suppose that because you are a marquess's son I will not dare to say it, you will, by heaven, hear every word!"

"Do not raise your voice to me."

"Don't give me orders! This is my house, and you have no business to be in it, and therefore I will say what I please."

"If you will just listen to me for a moment," Deverill said, reaching a hand out to her, "I can explain—"

Whirling away from him, she cried, "I do not want to hear glib explanations. You are a liar and a deceiver, and I will not believe anything you say to me, so—Don't touch me!"

But he had caught her by the shoulders, and he turned her back to face him, giving her a sharp shake as he said roughly, "Be silent,

I tell you, or I will not be responsible for my actions. I allowed you to slap me because I deserve your anger, but if you do not wish to be treated in a like fashion, I'd advise you not to shriek at me like a fishwife or call me names."

Daintry stared at him, caught off her guard as much by the look of fury in his eyes as by his words. Nearly everyone of her acquaintance tried to placate her when she lost her temper, but he had done nothing of the sort, and she began to think he might make good his threat if she pushed him to it. Refusing to be daunted, however, she narrowed her eyes, tightened her lips, and said with what even he ought to recognize as truly dangerous calm, "You would never dare to strike me in my father's house with my aunt to bear witness to your violence."

"You'd do better to believe what I tell you," he said curtly. "You did not hesitate to define my entire family as reprehensible, though I defy you to tell me anything anyone in it has done—until now, at all events—to deserve such a description from you. To the best of my knowledge, you do not know me or my father, and I doubt very much that you ever had the pleasure of meeting my brother, so what can you know of Deverills, my lady?"

Daintry stared at him, put off her stride by his questions for the simple reason that she had no answers to give him. Never in her life had she encountered anyone like him.

If her father lost his temper, he shouted and carried on, and he had occasionally been known to snatch up a switch or a strap to wreak vengeance for impudence, but he did not confront one or demand answers to unanswerable questions.

Lady Ophelia did not lose her temper. Nor did Lady St. Merryn. Daintry took some pains not to provoke either of them simply because the former had a needle-sharp tongue and the latter a distressing habit of employing tears, reproaches, vapors, and other such iniquitous resources when her fragile sensibilities were even the least bit agitated.

Susan had never tried to set her will against Daintry's. Nor had their brother, Charles. She had been a match for any governess, and had never been sent to school. Added to all this was the fact that she had been influenced by her aunt to have little opinion of worldly rank. Thus her experience of persons with wills stronger than her own was severely limited, but she recognized in Gideon Deverill a man whose temper at least matched hers, and she rather envied him his air of rigid control.

His grip on her shoulders was tight. She could feel his fingers digging into her flesh, and he continued to look down at her, waiting for her to reply. She wondered what Lady Ophelia thought of it all, but much as she would have liked to glance at that lady, she could not seem to drag her gaze away from his.

Glaring back at him, determined to appear as controlled as he was, she said between her teeth, "You're hurting me. Let go."

"I am not hurting you," he retorted. "I just want you to listen to me."

His grip slackened nonetheless, and she ripped herself free, crying triumphantly, "I will not listen to you! You lied to me before, and you will no doubt he again. It is all of a piece and just what a Tarrant expects from a Deverill. And do not dare to tell me I can know nothing of Deverills. They are enemies of my family, which is all I need to know. And as for you, sir, I just hope that when Penthorpe does get here, he thrashes you to within an inch of your life for what you have dared to do!"

"He will have to rise from the grave to do it," Deverill said bluntly. "He was killed at Waterloo."

"He is dead?" Daintry's hand flew to her mouth, and she stared at him in shock.

"Damn," Deverill said, moving toward her again, but this time his expression showed only regret. "Forgive me."

"Not the best way to break such news, young man," Lady Ophelia said dryly, speaking for the first time since greeting him. "Distressingly tactless, in fact. No, no, I pray you, do not lay hands upon her again. My niece's reaction to such treatment is entirely unpredictable, as you have seen."

"I am sorry to have spoken so abruptly, ma'am," he said, shooting a glance at Lady Ophelia. "I came here today to make a clean breast of things, and to tell you of Penthorpe's death, which I ought of course to have done yesterday. When his lordship mistook me for Penthorpe, I . . . that is, I—"

"Your curiosity about our family is no doubt as great as that of some members of ours about the Deverills," Lady Ophelia said helpfully. "One cannot help but understand your impulse to take advantage of the opportunity to learn more when it was no doubt thrust upon you by St. Merryn himself."

"That . . . that was it," he said, looking at Daintry.

Though she had been aware of their exchange, she had paid no heed to it. The news of Penthorpe's death was a shock, but though she was certain she ought to feel grief at this appalling turn of events, she could not feel more than she felt for the thousands of other young soldiers who had given their lives at Waterloo. Her strongest emotion was still anger with Deverill, underscored by a powerful sense of having been betrayed by him.

"You are despicable," she said at last, "to take advantage in the basest manner of a man's death, to try to take his place merely to satisfy vulgar curiosity. Such contemptible behavior must be thought offensive by any right-thinking person. To take the place of a man who died valiantly, fighting for his country against the most dreadful odds—"

"I would remind you that I also fought at Waterloo."

"Oh, to be sure," she retorted, her voice dripping with sarcasm, "but you survived, did you not, no doubt because braver men, men like poor, unfortunate Penthorpe—"

"This has gone far enough," Deverill said grimly, his voice carrying easily over hers. "You have not the least notion what you are talking about, so just sit down and be silent while I explain a few facts of life to you."

"Don't give me orders! Do you hear me? I told you bef—"

"If you do not sit down, I will sit you down."

His tone of voice and the hard look in his eyes told her that if he had been angry before, he was furious now. Shooting a glance at Lady Ophelia and seeing from her expression of placid interest that there was not the least hope of rescue from that quarter, Daintry took a step backward, saying tensely, "If you dare to lay hands upon me again, sir, I will—"

"You will what?" He had taken step for step, and he was much too near now for comfort. She could tell from the look of purpose in his eyes that he was going to grab her again, and no doubt he would shake her as he had done before. She waited, lips parted, her breasts heaving with suppressed emotion.

Very close now, he said softly, "What will you do, my lady?"

She stared up at him. "I . . . I . . ."

The look in his golden hazel eyes was warm now, inviting. "Tell me," he murmured, holding her gaze. "I want to know."

Lady Ophelia cleared her throat, and they both stepped back as if they had been bitten. Daintry, seeing him flush, felt an answering warmth in her own cheeks, and looked quickly away.

Lady Ophelia said, "You know, Dev—Dash, just what is your proper title, young man? I've not the least notion what styling your brother took after that poor young cousin of yours died so unexpectedly and your father became Marquess of Jervaulx."

"Deverill is sufficient, ma'am," he said. "My cousin being a posthumous child, there have been only heirs presumptive for years, and although I am told that my brother had applied for the heir apparent's styling, which is Earl of Abreston, it had not yet been conferred. There will be time enough to sort that out once I have learned my new duties, but in the meantime, as the new heir I've changed only from Lord Gideon to Lord Deverill."

She nodded with satisfaction. "I own, I am glad you are not out of reason puffed up by your new consequence, but I have been thinking, sir, and if you came here to tell us young Penthorpe had fallen in battle, surely that somber duty ought to have outweighed idle curiosity. What is more, I am rarely mistaken in my judgment of people, and my first impression of you was an unnaturally favorable one, considering your sex, so perhaps you had better confess your true reason for this pretense of yours."

Flushing more deeply than ever, he straightened, ran his fingers through his thick hair, and said, "When I accepted your own suggestion, ma'am, as to why I'd behaved so reprehensibly, I did so out of base cowardice because I realized quite suddenly that I had no desire to reveal the truth."

Instantly Daintry said, "So you are not only a plain and simple liar, sir, but a compulsive one. Can one ever believe what you say?"

His eyes flashed, and she saw with satisfaction that his tight control was slipping, but his voice was steady when he said, "I acted impulsively. I do not generally do so, but when your father declared that I must be Penthorpe, I had already decided—for reasons it would serve no purpose to reveal now—that I wished to become better acquainted with members of your family. Having no doubt that if I revealed my true identity, St. Merryn would instantly order my departure, I took advantage of his mistake in, as you have noted, the basest manner. If I regret having done so, it is because my action has served only to nourish the previous ill feeling between our families."

Before Daintry could point out that his words scarcely constituted an apology, he added, "I do not share that ill feeling, by the way. Indeed, if you know the cause of the infamous feud, you know more than I do, for I have not the least notion what began it, nor do I care. Such a petty conflict pales in my mind by comparison to the bloodbath at Waterloo."

For once in her life she could think of nothing to say. No more than he did she know the cause of the discord between their two families. She knew only that she had grown up hearing that Tarrants and Deverills were not and never would be on speaking terms, that Deverills were beneath contempt, that any contact with them was abhorrent. Trying to remember how she had come to believe such things, she looked inquiringly at Lady Ophelia.

Deverill's gaze followed hers, and Lady Ophelia, blinking owlishly back at them, said finally, "Dash it, do not look to me to explain it to you. I am sure I have never had the least idea what caused the feuding."

Daintry said, "Then the feud dates back even farther than I had thought, Aunt. Is it a truly ancient one?"

"No, of course it is not, though Tarrants have resided in this part of Cornwall for generations. The Deverills . . ." She raised her eyebrows at Deverill.

"Deverill Court has been part of the family holdings for nearly five hundred years, ma'am, though to be sure, it has never been the primary seat for the Marquesses of Jervaulx. I know that in my great-grandmother's time, it was the dower house, where my grandfather grew up and where he continued to reside after his brother succeeded to the title. My father was born in that house, as were my brother and I. I believe the feud originated in my grandfather's day, but if that is true, surely you would know . . . that is to say—" He broke off, clearly trying to think of a tactful way to make his point.

"You are perfectly right," Lady Ophelia said. "Tom Deverill and Ned Tarrant were the best of friends as boys. They were almost exactly the same age, I believe, and both went off to Eton together as happy as grigs, and then on to Oxford, where they shared the same tutors. And both of them made dead sets for the same females when they went to London to learn to be gentlemen."

"Then perhaps it was a female who caused the feud," Daintry suggested. "That has been known to happen before."

"Well, I do not think it can have been that," Lady Ophelia said, looking self-conscious. "You see, for the most part, they made wagers as to which could achieve success first with a chosen target. It was only a game to them, which I should know, for I was the first to whom they each dared to propose marriage."

"But then—"

"Oh, no." Lady Ophelia chuckled. "If you are seeing me as their bone of contention, it was no such thing, for although they each proposed, both knew that I had no intention of marrying any man. I believe they merely put the question to me in order to practice their courting methods, so to speak. Neither one could possibly have had serious intentions."

Deverill protested. "But surely, ma'am, no gentleman would propose marriage to a lady without being entirely serious about it. Why, where would he be if she accepted?"

Dryly she said, "Gone to his banker, no doubt, to puff off his increased estate. I was a very great heiress, you know, for although my brother inherited the title and estates, Papa divided his extremely large private fortune equally between us."

"But then, surely both men had excellent reason to pursue you, and each must have been sorry when you turned him down. Are you quite certain—"

"I voiced my opinions and intentions then as clearly as I do now, sir. There can have been no misunderstanding. Moreover, I can tell you that it would have upset your grandfather no end if I had accepted his offer, for he was one who believed, along with Mrs. Malaprop in that otherwise rather humorous play of Mr. Sheridan's, that 'thought does not become a young woman.' Most men despise learned females, you know, and your grandfather was no exception. According to Lord Thomas Deverill, an intelligent female was one who could sew, run a household properly, and produce healthy children. Your grandmother was perfectly capable of all that. I believe she produced six children for him."

Deverill laughed. "Seven, ma'am, although six of those were females, but surely—"

Tartly, Lady Ophelia said, "Well, Ned Tarrant had only St. Merryn, who now has only Charles to succeed him. And Charles and Davina, though they have been married eleven years, have only our dear Charlotte to their credit. Did you know, by the bye, that your grandmother was an aspiring authoress before she married?"

"Good God, no!" He sounded appalled.

"It is perfectly true, nonetheless. Tom did not approve, however, and so of course she gave up her ambition and devoted herself to pleasing him. Not that her sacrifice was any great loss to the literary world, for her only novel was an utterly unreadable romance—kittenish and cute, just like Harriet herself."

"Aunt Ophelia, what a thing to say!"

"Well, I know it was, for she gave me the manuscript to read, and I waded through only the first thirty pages before I told her I could stomach no more. Maudlin stuff, all morals and sweet sentiment about a sadly wronged heroine with no backbone whatever, who tried to solve her problems by poking and prying into other people's lives. Utter twaddle. Why, my own journals are more worthy of publication than that was. My point, however, is that Harriet ought to have been allowed to continue to write if it pleased her, and the fact that Tom utterly forbade it proves that he cannot truly have wished to marry me."

Deverill looked perplexed. "I collect that you were not then closely related to the Tarrant family, ma'am. How did that connection come about, if I may ask?"

"My brother's daughter, Letitia, married Daintry's papa," Lady Ophelia said. "And I can tell you, St. Merryn—Ned Tarrant, that is, not your papa, Daintry—behaved as if he had got a point more than Tom Deverill when she did. Ned always was looking to line his pockets, so I suppose that, having married a woman with an income of seven thousand a year, then managing to arrange for his son to marry into the Balterley family, he thought he'd won."

"He did marry better than my grandfather," Deverill said. "At least, if my grandmother was an heiress, I never knew it."

"She wasn't," Lady Ophelia said, "but she had always had a soft spot in her heart for Tom. I thought, myself, that Harriet hoped he would make her a marchioness, but although the senior branch of your family was never strong, it didn't die out soon enough to benefit her. In any case, Tom didn't marry her until several years after the feud began and she's been dead for forty years, so she can be of no help to you now. Tom himself has been dead for nearly thirty years. I don't suppose you even remember him."

Deverill shook his head.

"I am sorry I cannot be of more help," she said.

Deverill turned to Daintry. "You must agree now that it is absurd to ring a peal over me in the name of this old feud when I daresay everyone connected with it has just as little understanding of it as we do."

Daintry felt obliged to agree, but Lady Ophelia clicked her tongue in annoyance and said, "I gave you credit for better sense, sir. Surely you must realize that reason rarely prevails in such instances as this. If you can convince St. Merryn that there is no longer cause for a feud, I shall congratulate you, but you won't do it, for a more pigheaded man never existed unless he was a Deverill. More than that I will not say."

"We must suppose that the feud has been fueled by other incidents over the years," Deverill said thoughtfully, turning to Daintry. "If we accomplish nothing else, I say we should do what we can to end it now and become better acquainted."

He was looking directly into her eyes, and there was a light in his that warmed her. Though she had been to London and seen all the elegant gentlemen who flocked to the Marriage Mart in search of suitable brides, she had never known a man like this one. Three times she had believed she had found a man she could bear to marry—since her father insisted that marry she must—but each time she had rebelled once she had discovered the flaws of character lying beneath each handsome face and manly figure.

No doubt Gideon Deverill also had feet of clay. Indeed, he had already wickedly deceived her, but something about him made it easy just now to forgive the one transgression if there were no more. Until there were—and if she could manage to teach him that it was folly to try ordering her about—she was willing to encourage his attention. Indeed, it was no more than her duty to encourage him, for now that Penthorpe had been killed, her father would certainly make new arrangements to find her a husband if she did not find one for herself, and rather quickly.

She said, "I must apologize, sir. You were quite right to say that I ought not to condemn you and your family out of hand. In truth, I did not realize until just now that I had not the slightest understanding of what caused the feud."

He smiled. "Perhaps if you were to speak to your father, he would agree to lay the business to rest."

"He won't do it," Lady Ophelia said.

"I do not know if I can bring Papa round my thumb or not, but I mean to try," Daintry said. "He must be made to understand that there is no longer any feud worthy of the name, and once he does, I am certain he can have no objection to your paying the occasional friendly call, Deverill."

Lady Ophelia clicked her tongue, but whatever she might have meant to say was lost in a clamor of noise when the doors were opened and a number of people entered the room.

Startled by the din, Daintry whirled to discover what looked like an invasion. "Gracious, Charles and Davina are home," she exclaimed as she found herself crushed in a brotherly embrace.

"You and Susan missed a dashed good time in Brighton," Charles Tarrant said, laughing.

He was a man of middle height with a sportsman's muscular body and the dress sense of a dandy. His chestnut locks were brushed in the windswept style made popular by Beau Brummell, his snowy cravat was stiffly starched, and his shirt points were a good deal too high for any comfort of motion.

Holding Daintry in the curve of one arm, he raised his gold-rimmed quizzing-glass to peer at Deverill, and said, "By God, you must be Penthorpe. Here, Daintry, let a fellow go, so he can do the proper. Dashed glad to meet you, Penthorpe. My father has been telling us how glad . . . that is, he has been saying—Oh, good God, I shall put my foot in it if I say any more, shan't I?" Grinning broadly, he thrust out his right hand. "Pleased to meet you. There, no one can cavil at that."

Deverill shook his hand, but if he had intended to reveal his true identity, he had no opportunity to do so, for reaching out rather wildly to catch hold of the slender, darkhaired lady who had accompanied him into the room, Charles said, "Davina, allow me to present Penthorpe. Oh, and there are Geoffrey and Lady Catherine. Come and meet Penthorpe. Papa, I have stolen your thunder, by Jupiter. Hello, Mama . . . Cousin Ethelinda. Good God, it's a dashed family reunion, that's what it is! If we don't take care, we shall have the children underfoot next."

"I am here, Papa," Charley cried, hopping up and down on one foot beside him. "Wait until I show you the new tricks we have taught Victor while you were away! What did you bring me?"

"Bring you?" Charles looked dismayed. "What did you want me to bring you? Davina, did we bring her anything?"

Davina said sternly, "It is very bad manners to demand a present the minute your parents walk in the door, Charlotte."

"You promised," Charley cried. "I didn't ask for anything. You said when you left that you would bring me a lovely present to make it up to me for being away so long. You know you did."

Behind them, Sir Geoffrey Seacourt, a tall, slender, fair-haired man, said, "We have presents for you and Melissa both, Charlotte, so stop screeching like a banshee and come kiss your favorite uncle. But where are Melissa and your Aunt Susan?"

"They are coming, Uncle Geoffrey," Charley said, recovering her dignity instantly and responding to his demand for a kiss with a demure peck on his cheek. When he hugged her, she freed herself with a quick, twisting motion and said, "You know I do not like to be mauled about, sir, though I do thank you very kindly for my presents. Where are they? And who is that lady?"

"Forgive me, everyone," Sir Geoffrey said with a boyish grin. "I'd forgotten you do not know Catherine. This is a sort of cousin of mine, Lady Catherine Chauncey of Yorkshire, who was most unfortunately widowed last year. We met her in Brighton and she consented to let us carry her back with us to see the county of Cornwall. Catherine, this disheveled young lady is my wife's niece, Charlotte. Charlotte, do pull up your stockings. You look like a shag bag, and do not," he added, laughing as he tousled her hair, "ask me what a shag bag is."

"I know what it is," Charley said scornfully. "It is the bag one keeps a fighting cock in, and if that is not something I ought to know, then you and Papa and Grandpapa ought not to use the term so often. Lady Catherine is pretty," she added, making a swift curtsy without bothering to hitch up her stockings. "There is Aunt Susan, now, sir. And Melissa, too."

Sir Geoffrey turned quickly, saying, "My dearest love, I do hope you are quite well again. You missed a delicious treat by not accompanying us to Brighton. And," he added, catching her and kissing her hard on the mouth, "I missed you very much. You, too, my darling Melissa," he added, releasing his wife and catching up the fairylike child in her place.

Melissa put her arms around his neck and kissed his cheek, and still holding her, he called to Medrose to bring in the parcels he had brought with him. "All of them, Medrose."

Daintry had taken advantage of the distraction to catch Charley and pull her a little to one side. "Do pull up your stockings, darling, and stop dancing about. Grandpapa has been watching you, and so has Aunt Ophelia, so if you do not want to suffer a severe scold later, do as I say right now."

As the child bent to obey her, Daintry glanced at Deverill, and saw that he was watching the others with a somewhat bemused look on his face. Her father moved to greet him with a beaming smile, and Daintry wondered when Deverill would reveal his true identity. That he had not done so at once could not surprise her, for he would have had to shout to make himself heard, and with all the chatter, it would have taken a good deal of exertion even then to make himself understood. The matter could be set right in a trice once the others quieted down.

Charley tugged on her sleeve. "May I go and open my presents, Aunt Daintry?"

"Yes, darling, and be sure to thank your uncle and your mama and papa for being so kind as to bring them to you."

"Well, I shall thank Uncle Geoffrey, of course, for I believe he did remember them, but I shall not thank Mama or Papa, for I am just as certain that they did not."

Daintry, too, was certain of that, but she said firmly, "Thank them nonetheless, Charley. Your good manners must never be dependent upon those of anyone else."

"Very well, I will." She was dancing again with impatience, so Daintry shooed her off to open her presents. Then, seeing that Davina and Charles had moved away from the others to sit on a sofa while Sir Geoffrey passed out his gifts, and that St. Merryn had engaged Deverill in conversation near the window, she dutifully turned her attention to the stranger in their midst.

Lady Catherine, who was, as Charley had noted, very pretty indeed, was a buxom, golden-haired beauty with sapphire-blue eyes and a complexion of peaches and cream. She stood quietly near Sir Geoffrey, and Daintry, remembering that Susan had come in after the introductions and seeing how she kept glancing at the woman while she opened her gift, feared that Sir Geoffrey had neglected to present Lady Catherine to his wife.

Susan took a pair of dazzling diamond earrings from a black velvet box, and her eyes began to shine. "Oh, Geoffrey, thank you. I want to wear them now. Will you help me put them on?"

He turned with a grin to do so, and Daintry, regretting the sudden suspicion that had leapt to her mind, said politely to Lady Catherine, "Do come over here and sit down. You must be dismayed by all the uproar, but it is always the same when the whole family gets together like this. Do you mean to stay long in Cornwall? Have you other friends in the county?"

As they moved to join Davina and Charles, Lady Catherine smiled, showing pearly white teeth and full, sensuous lips, and said, "I do have friends at St. Ives. Cousin Geoffrey, the knave, led me to believe it was quite nearby, but I have come to understand during our journey—thanks to your extremely charming brother—that St. Ives is really quite some distance from here."

"Oh, yes. Cornwall is not so tall, but it is very wide, and St. Ives is much nearer to Land's End than it is to Devon. We are less than twenty miles from the river Tamar, which forms the boundary, you know, between Devon and Cornwall. That was too bad of Sir Geoffrey to mislead you."

"Well, he is determined that I shall make a long stay at—"

"*What?*" St. Merryn's roar drowned her out, and the rest of the room fell instantly silent, so that his next words, spoken in a menacing growl, carried all too clearly. "What the devil do you mean, you are not Penthorpe?"

Six

It seemed to Daintry as if someone had created a *tableau vivant*. Charley, holding the new blue Paisley silk scarf she had unwrapped, sat with her mouth agape, her eyes wide and focused on her grandfather. Melissa, caught in the motion of slipping a gold bangle on her thin wrist, was utterly still. Sir Geoffrey and Susan stared at St. Merryn; and Charles and Davina had frozen so that the former's smile and the latter's look of polite welcome as Daintry led Lady Catherine toward them, had become as fixed as if the expressions had been painted on their faces.

Lady St. Merryn, reaching for her salts bottle, was the first to move, and Cousin Ethelinda, ever vigilant, leapt to spare her even that small exertion.

Awakened from his own shock by their movement, St. Merryn snapped, "Damme, I won't have it! You must be Penthorpe!"

Lady Ophelia said, "Pray moderate your tone, St. Merryn. There are children and ladies present."

"I never raise my voice," he snarled, "and you keep your nose out of this, Ophelia. I won't tolerate any more of your damned meddling. Only look where it has got us now!"

"I quite fail to see how this imbroglio relates to me," she retorted. "It was your own impulsive assumption that began it, you know. Had you waited, as any reasonable man would have done, to allow the young man to give his name—or indeed, his calling card—to your footman, as I have not the least doubt he meant to do before you snatched the moment to yourself, as so frequently is your habit and indeed, the habit of most men—"

"Spout me no more infernal nonsense about the imperfections of men," St. Merryn shouted at her. "Men are the superior sex because we *are* superior, and that is all there is about it."

Charley said matter-of-factly, "Men are superior only in matters of muscle, Grandpapa. It has been proven, you know—or at least, it has been written," she added conscientiously, "that the female brain is quite as capable of logical th—"

"Go to your room, you unnatural child!" St. Merryn roared, rounding on her with frenzy in his eyes.

"But—"

Daintry, recognizing that the earl's love for his granddaughter was presently outmatched by his driving need of a quarry upon whom to wreak vengeance, snapped over her shoulder, "Charles, I will deal with this," as she strode forward, snatched Charley up from the floor by one arm and hustled her out of the room, pulling the door shut behind them on her father's outraged declaration, "But, damme, you must be Penthorpe!"

In the blessed near-silence of the corridor, Charley said with an air of dignity at odds with Daintry's firm hold on her arm, "I am dreadfully sorry, but he was wrong, you know."

Giving her a shake, Daintry retorted, "I don't care if he was, young lady. You have no business to talk to him that way, particularly when others are about. You will be fortunate if your papa does not thrash you soundly for such bad manners."

"He won't," Charley said forlornly. "He never does."

Worried about Deverill but caught off guard by a sudden bubble of laughter in her throat, Daintry released her, saying, "Your grandfather was right, you know; you are unnatural. Do you expect me to believe that you want your papa to spank you?"

"No, of course not." The child grimaced. "I do not approve of violence, and most certainly not when it is directed toward me. But Papa pays me no heed at all. I heard you tell him you would deal with me, but he had not begun to move, you know, so there was not the least need for you to speak to him."

"Your grandpapa had begun to move."

Charley shuddered. "I know. Honestly, Aunt Daintry, I spoke without thinking, but it was nonsense that he was speaking. Aunt Ophelia says—"

"Sometimes," Daintry said with a sigh, "I think Aunt Ophelia would have done better to interest us in needlework, like Cousin Ethelinda. Independence for women is an excellent notion, but in reality . . ." She strained her ears to make sense of what seemed to be an unceasing low roar from the drawing room.

Taking advantage of the pause, Charley said, "I'd rather teach Victor to come to me when I want him than learn to sew, and I'd much rather read history than learn to run a great house like Mama says I must, but"—she sighed—"Grandpapa once said that a female who argues facts of history might as well have a beard."

"At least he didn't quote Samuel Johnson to you, darling. Johnson believed the only virtuous woman is a silent one."

Charley giggled. "Even Grandpapa would know better than to expect me to be silent."

"Perhaps," Daintry agreed, "but you may be sure he will not want to see your face again soon. Go upstairs now, and try after this to behave like a lady of quality."

"If that man is truly not Lord Penthorpe, then who—?"

Daintry pointed toward the stairs. "Go, Charlotte."

Charley went without another word, and shaking her head, Daintry turned back to the drawing room, pausing a moment to draw a deep breath before opening the door. The first person she saw was Deverill, and when his gaze met hers, she saw both amusement and frustration in his eyes. The amusement disappeared when Sir Geoffrey said loudly over the rest, "But damme, I say *again,* if he is not Penthorpe, then who the devil is he?"

Astonished that the point had not yet been clarified, Daintry caught Deverill's gaze again. His rueful shrug coupled with the din that greeted Sir Geoffrey's question informed her that he simply had not yet attempted to make himself heard.

St. Merryn snapped, "Damme, I don't care who he is if he ain't Penthorpe, for it's Penthorpe I want to see. Where the devil is the fellow, I ask you? Stands to reason since he's sent this fellow in his stead"—he glared at Deverill—"that the young whippersnapper means to delay his visit indefinitely or to turn tail altogether. Well, I won't have it! He's betrothed to my daughter, and by God, he will marry her. I have put my foot down, and there is no more to be said about it."

"Stuff and nonsense," Lady Ophelia said.

When the earl turned indignantly to glare at her, Deverill said calmly, "I am afraid there is more to be said, sir. Penthorpe is dead. He fell at Waterloo."

"What? Upon my soul, what did the fellow go and do a thing like that for? Are you sure?"

"Perfectly sure. I saw his body. In point of fact, he had a premonition beforehand and asked me to bring the news to you if he fell. When you mistook me for him, I was dumbfounded, sir, and I behaved badly. I am entirely at fault and can do no more than beg forgiveness, undeserving though I am to receive it."

"Never mind that now," St. Merryn said testily. "What I want to know is, who is going to marry my daughter? I've got a surfeit of women in this house, as you see, and here I thought the whole business was settled and I could get rid of one of them. Now I've got to begin all over again. I say," he added with a speculative look, "you ain't a married man, are you, lad?"

"No, sir, I have not that honor."

"Honor be damned, it's the one thing the Almighty did that I'd like to call Him to account for. To declare it a man's duty to marry when he'd never done it himself was a curst bad thing!"

Lady St. Merryn gasped, "Blasphemy! Oh, how can you say such a thing? Where is my handkerchief, Ethelinda? Ring for some hartshorn at once. I feel quite faint."

As Cousin Ethelinda rushed to obey, St. Merryn snorted and said to Deverill, "There, you see, lad. Too damned many women in this house, and now your friend Penthorpe has left Daintry on my hands. Damme, but perhaps all is not lost. Who the devil are you, lad? If you're eligible, by God, you may have her!"

Seacourt laughed, but Charles exclaimed, "Father, really!"

Daintry saw Deverill frown and, holding her breath, looked quickly at her great-aunt, whose eyes were alight with expectant laughter. Daintry could see nothing funny in the situation.

St. Merryn, hands on his hips, was waiting for Deverill to speak. The others, too, were silent, waiting.

Looking from one to another, Deverill straightened, and for the first time Daintry thought he looked like a marquess's son. His very size was intimidating, for he was taller than any of the other men, and broader, and much better looking.

"I am Deverill," he said with quiet dignity.

There was a different quality to the silence now, as if the room held its breath, and suddenly she became aware of Catherine Chauncey, not only as a stranger in their midst but because the woman looked utterly fascinated by the scene she was witnessing. The thought passed through her mind in the split second before St. Merryn, nearly choking on the word, repeated, "Deverill?"

"Yes, sir."

"Jervaulx's son?"

"Yes, sir, his younger son. I've been abroad since leaving Oxford, with Wellington. I was a brigade major under Uxbridge at Waterloo. Penthorpe was my best friend, sir."

"Don't mention him to me again," St. Merryn growled. "What the devil are you doing in my house?"

"I explained that. Penthorpe asked me—"

"Damme, I won't have a Deverill in my house! Get out!"

Daintry, seeing that Deverill was about to obey the unjust command, said quickly, "Papa, he does not even know about the feud. That is to say, he knows, but he does not know what caused it, and nor do I, or—"

"Upon my soul, girl, it is not necessary for you to understand anything. Such matters are the business of men, and such business they will remain. If you have nothing of more interest to contribute to this conversation, keep silent."

"But I have a great deal to say," she insisted. "You cannot throw him out merely because of some outdated squabble between our grandfathers. That makes no sense at all."

"Silence," St. Merryn snapped. "You know nothing about it. We Tarrants have had nothing to do with Deverills for more than sixty years, and I do not propose to alter that fact today. Leave my property at once, sir, and never dare cross onto it again."

Daintry, furious now, cried, "You are unjust, Papa! Even if the cause of the feud was something dreadful, Deverill had nothing to do with it, and if Lord Jervaulx never even thought the finer points important enough to pass on to him, there can be nothing to warrant such enmity now."

"Deverill only recently became the heir," St. Merryn said. "Stands to reason he don't know everything yet. Jervaulx ain't had time to tell him."

Turning on her brother, Daintry said, "Do you know the facts, Charles? Has Papa told you? Well, has he?"

Charles, caught off guard, looked dismayed. "Here, I say, it's none of my affair. Davina, tell her. Not my affair at all, but dash it, Daintry oughtn't to talk to my father in that dashed impertinent fashion. Tell her."

Davina, pressing her lips together, said nothing.

Looking around for allies, Daintry realized that Susan and Melissa—neither of whom she would have expected to fill that role—had vanished. Sir Geoffrey looked annoyed. Lady Catherine still looked fascinated. Lady St. Merryn was engaged with her salts bottle, and Cousin Ethelinda was engaged with Lady St. Merryn. Only Lady Ophelia appeared at all likely to back her.

"Aunt, please."

But Lady Ophelia shook her head. "I can do nothing to prevent your father from making a fool of himself if he wishes to do so, my dear. Tuscombe Park does belong to him, after all, and he can deny anyone he dislikes the privilege of setting foot upon its soil." She smiled at Deverill. "It has been extremely stimulating to make your acquaintance, young man."

"Never mind that," St. Merryn snapped. "Must I call my servants to escort you from the premises, sir?"

"That will not be necessary. I can find my way. Your servant." Deverill bowed, his dignity apparently intact, and strode from the room, nodding at Sir Geoffrey, who held the door open for him, as though he had been a lackey.

Daintry waited only until Geoffrey shut the door again before rounding on her father. "Papa, you are mistaken—"

"Silence, I said!" St. Merryn bellowed, advancing on her with menace in his eyes. "How dare you speak to me as you did? Have you no manners? Is this what your precious education has produced? You see, Ophelia?" Pausing in his advance, he glared at Lady Ophelia, who gazed imperturbably back. "You see what you have created with your foolish nonsense? At least Susan has had better sense than to—" He broke off, looking around the room in sudden bewilderment. "Where is Susan? And Melissa? Not that I want them, mind you, but where the devil did they disappear to?"

Seacourt said blandly, "I sent them away, sir, when it became clear that this discussion was no concern of theirs."

"You did?" St. Merryn blinked at him owlishly. "Blessed if I know how you manage that sort of thing, lad."

"A man is master of his own household, surely."

"Oh, surely," St. Merryn agreed, grimacing, "but how the devil he convinces the women of that fact is what I should like to know. I am master here at St. Merryn, right enough." His glare swept the room, as if he dared anyone in it to challenge his declaration, and came to rest upon Daintry. "You still here? Thought I sent you to your bedchamber, girl."

"No, Papa, you did not," she said. "You ordered me to be silent and then demanded to know if I had any manners. Since I could not reply to the second statement without disobeying the first, and since the question was clearly rhetorical, I did not attempt to answer. But you did not tell me to leave the room."

"Well, I'm telling you now, and I'll tell you another thing, too, my girl. You are to have nothing more to do with that lying jackanapes Deverill. Do you hear me?"

"I hear you, sir, but unless you mean for me to send regrets to Mount Edgcumbe and the other places to which I have accepted invitations for house parties, and to remain here throughout the entire London Season, I cannot promise to have nothing to do with him. When I encounter him, as I am extremely likely to do, good manners will demand that I be civil to the man."

"Damn it, don't quibble! Go away!"

She went, hearing Sir Geoffrey say as she passed him, "I do not know why you put up with her impertinence, sir. I am sure I should never tolerate such behavior from Melissa."

On her father's "Ha!" she closed the door, only to hear it open and shut again seconds later as she was nearing the stairway to the upper parts of the house. Turning, she beheld her sister-in-law, and stifled a sigh of annoyance.

"Really, Daintry," Davina began before she had even caught up with her, "I cannot understand why you persist in stirring up such commotions. I had hoped, just this once, to come home to a little peace and quiet. Life amongst the *beau monde* is exhausting, and I had looked forward to finding at least a modicum of tranquility here at Tuscombe Park."

"I suppose that means that you and Charles are at outs again," Daintry said. "Who is the lovely Lady Catherine Chauncey, Davina? Is she Charles's retaliation for your indiscretions in Brighton, or Geoffrey's latest conquest?"

Davina stiffened. "You never cease to amaze me, Daintry. Such vulgar accusations are entirely unwarranted, I assure you. She is a cousin of Sir Geoffrey's, just as he said, a widow for whom he feels a natural, even admirable, sense of responsibility. Her husband fell at one of those dreadful places on the Continent. You should be ashamed of yourself."

Daintry did feel slightly chagrined, but she saw no point in admitting as much. Instead, she said, "Is that a new gown? Did you have some new things made up for Charley, too?"

Davina's gray eyes lit with laughter. "Goodness, are you going to tell me Charlotte wants new dresses? It must be for the very first time. I am persuaded she would liefer have a new riding habit, but I did not see any reason to have one made up at London prices or in Brighton, I can tell you. It was bad enough having to discover a new governess, but we did find an acceptable woman, who promised to come to us at once. I would like to know, however, just how Charlotte frightened away Miss Pettibone."

"She asked her more questions than the good lady was able to answer," Daintry said bluntly. "Miss Pettibone, my dear Davina, expected to teach her to do fancy needlework, to speak a few fashionable phrases in French, and to play the pianoforte in elegant style. She was not prepared for a child whose French surpassed her own and who reads Latin and a bit of Greek as well. Nor was she a match for Charley when it came to persuading her to practice deportment or her music lessons, things in which she has not the smallest interest. I only hope this new one is better."

Davina shuddered. "I do not know how your aunt expects us to find a husband for such a child."

"Well, you scarcely need think about it at this early date," Daintry said, her ready sense of humor stirred by the thought.

"Oh, you may laugh," Davina said bitterly, "but you, of all people, ought to understand the difficulty she will face. I am not the only one to suspect that it was not you who gave the *congé* to your various suitors, but they who fled in dismay. What gentleman wishes to marry a woman as well-educated as himself?"

Daintry said sharply, "I'll have you know, Davina, that not one of my suitors feared my education, for not one of them had sufficient understanding to fear it. Indeed, all three proved to be little more than fashionable fribbles. I am going up to Charley now," she added, striving to moderate her rising tone, since Davina was looking increasingly wary. "Will you come?"

"No," Davina said hastily, "I must see that my woman is attending to my unpacking. Charlotte will be allowed to come down to dinner this afternoon, in any event, will she not?"

"I daresay she will," Daintry said, sorry now for her brief outburst, knowing Charley would be waiting hopefully for her mother to come up and see her. "She has missed you, you know."

"Has she, indeed?" Davina's tone was skeptical. "We had no more than three letters from her the entire time we were gone."

"And how many did you or Charles write to her?" Daintry demanded, her temper rising again.

Flushing, Davina turned away. "I must see to my unpacking."

Sighing, aware that she had not handled Davina well, Daintry went to the upper west wing of the house, where the schoolroom and Charley's bedchamber were located. Not much to her surprise, she found Susan and Melissa with Charley in the schoolroom. The two little girls got politely to their feet when she entered, and she saw that Charley wore Melissa's gold bangle on one wrist and had been admiring the way the sunlight from the window reflected from its highly polished surface.

"That bracelet is lovely," Daintry said. Grinning at her sister, she added, "And your ear bobs are dazzling, Susan. I seem to be the only one for whom Sir Geoffrey did not bring a gift. Even Cousin Ethelinda got a new silk scarf."

"I daresay he simply forgot to give you whatever it is he brought you," Susan said placidly. "Things did become a trifle unsettled down there, did they not?"

"That is certainly one way to put it."

Susan grimaced. "Did Papa forbid Deverill the house?"

"He did. He was most unfair."

"Oh, Daintry, do not tell me you have formed a tenderness for that deceitful young man! It will never do, for Papa will shout himself into a seizure, or worse."

"Nonsense, Susan. He said he never raises his voice."

Charley giggled, and even Melissa smiled. Hugging them both, Daintry told them they might sit down again, and took a seat beside Susan, saying, "Melissa, darling, did your papa bring you anything else?"

"This," the little girl said, producing a flaxen-haired china doll from beneath a fold of her skirt, which had concealed it when she sat down. She handed it to Daintry.

"Oh, how pretty! She looks just like you, my dear."

"Dolls," Charley said scornfully, "are for babies. Melissa would much rather have had a new riding whip."

"*You* would rather have had a riding whip," Daintry said, smoothing the doll's pink silk gown and admiring the roses and cream complexion of its exquisite face.

Melissa said, "You can keep that bracelet since you like it so much, Charley. It looks very pretty on you."

Susan exclaimed, "Oh, no, darling, your papa would be so extremely disappointed if you were to give away his gift. He will want to see you wear it frequently, you know. Gentlemen are very observant about such things."

"Oh," Melissa said. "I just thought that since Charley so rarely likes feminine gewgaws Papa would not mind if—"

"No," Susan said with uncharacteristic firmness.

"Very well, but you may wear it this afternoon, Charley."

"Well, I will wear it if we are allowed to go downstairs for dinner," Charley said, "but since I mean to ride Victor this afternoon, perhaps you had better keep it until then."

Susan said quietly, "I am sorry to sound disobliging, Charlotte, but when the two of you go downstairs, Melissa must wear her bracelet, for it will be the first time she sees her papa after receiving his gift. Moreover, you forget that you are in disgrace. Your grandpapa ordered you to seek your bedchamber, you know, and in all truth, though I did not like to say so, that is where you ought to be right now, not here with us."

Seeing that Charley was about to say something impertinent, Daintry intervened. "Aunt Susan is right to remind you that your credit is not very good at the moment. You must make your peace with Grandpapa before you do anything else, certainly before you go out to the stables again."

"But—"

"No," Daintry said. "It is as important for you to learn that limitations exist as to learn to think and to speak for yourself. Part of thinking for oneself is learning to recognize obstacles when they present themselves, and understanding that one must confront those obstacles, not merely ignore them in the mistaken hope that they will disappear."

"But I already sent an order to the stables," Charley said stubbornly, "and I promised Melissa she could go too, so you are punishing her if you forbid me."

Daintry stood up, but before she could administer the reproof the child so richly deserved, there was an interruption.

"Begging your pardon, Lady Susan," the maid at the door said, "but Sir Geoffrey requests your presence in the drawing room at once. He said . . ." The maidservant paused, swallowed, looked at the floor, then murmured, "He said to tell you, you be neglecting your guest, ma'am."

Daintry's temper, checked mid-breath by the entrance of the servant, found welcome relief in an even more worthy target than Charley. "If that is not just like a man," she snapped, "to blame a woman for not being where he wants her when he is the one who sent her away!" Turning on the quaking maidservant, she said, "Did he order you to say those exact words to her ladyship? Come, Millie," she added, forcing herself to speak more quietly. "I did not mean to terrify you, but do answer my question."

Still looking at her feet, Millie said, "In truth, m'lady, his lordship told Jago to say it, and Jago told me. Said it warn't his business to be coming up to the schoolroom, that he'd go to Lady Susan's bedchamber, and I were to come up here in case she had come up to visit the young ladies, which she had."

"Just as I thought," Daintry said. "You may go, Millie. And I hope you, Susan, will give Geoffrey a piece of your mind for sending such an impudent message to you by a servant."

Susan smiled. "Oh, no, for it would do no good, you know, and I believe poor Lady Catherine must by now be quite bewildered by all the commotion, and yearning for someone to take her away for a quiet respite. Why, she has not even seen the bedchamber that has been allotted to her. We have been quite remiss."

"In my opinion, she was highly entertained by it all," Daintry said, "though I cannot doubt that she will be glad of a chance to get away from Papa's ranting and Geoffrey's absurd advice to him on how he ought to manage things. Even Davina abandoned her, for she followed me out of the room to speak her mind to me. She called the proceedings a commotion, just as you did, but she blamed me for creating it, if you please."

"Well," Susan said, getting to her feet and smoothing the front of her skirt, "you did little to pour oil on the troubled waters. No, no, pray do not bite my head off! I am sure that even you could not have stopped Papa from ordering that poor man off the premises. In any case, I must go downstairs at once."

She was gone on the words, and Daintry turned back to attend to her errant niece.

The two little girls had their heads together, but Charley looked up just then and said quickly, "I'm sorry, Aunt Daintry. I should not have spoken as I did, and I ought not to have talked to Grandpapa as I did either. I will apologize to him when we go down for dinner. And," she added with a sigh and a glance at Melissa, "if you truly forbid it, I suppose I can send a message telling them we won't want our horses after all." The look that accompanied this noble statement was both melting and hopeful.

Daintry, her sense of humor tickled and her temper eased by the opportunity to express her opinion of Sir Geoffrey's behavior, nevertheless forced herself to remain firm. "An excellent notion," she said. "If you do make your peace with your grandfather, then you and Melissa may go to the stables after dinner to take sugar lumps to Victor and Tender Lady."

"Very well." Charley sat down again, looking rather put out but resigned. Then a new thought entered her agile mind, for she widened her eyes and said, "And tomorrow, Aunt Daintry, will you take us riding again?"

Daintry hesitated. "First we must discover when your Uncle Geoffrey intends to take his family home," she said.

Melissa said, "Mama told us that he wishes to remain here for a few days, Aunt Daintry. I think that when he wrote to tell her to look for his arrival, he wrote that as well."

Charley said casually, "We could ride up onto the moor if it is not foggy, and have a really good gallop. Although," she added with a thoughtful frown, "I daresay we ought not to mention the galloping part to Uncle Geoffrey."

Deciding that she had been firm enough for one day, Daintry refrained from pointing out the impropriety of the afterthought, particularly since she wholeheartedly agreed with it. Instead, she said that if the little girls behaved themselves and the next day proved a pleasant one, she would certainly take them riding.

Not until later did she wonder if Charley had mentioned the moor for any particular reason, but she dismissed the thought at once, for it led far too easily to others that were much more disturbing. As she tossed and turned in her bed that night, unable to sleep, she came to the unwelcome conclusion that a certain tall, broad-shouldered gentleman with speaking golden eyes, an attractive smile, and a deplorably commanding nature had made more of an impression upon her wayward sensibilities than was commensurate with the comfortable image she had of herself as an independent female.

Seven

Gideon's image of himself had been severely shaken. Riding away from the house, he had all he could manage to maintain his dignity, for the memory of St. Merryn's demanding to know if he should send for his servants to escort him out had been nearly more than his temper could bear. Bad enough that it had happened at all; much worse that it had happened before such an audience. In his mind's eye, he could still see Seacourt's expression of contempt, and it brought forcibly to mind certain incidents of his school years that he would just as soon forget.

Briefly he wondered if Jack had ever made a cast toward St. Merryn's daughters, but a moment's reflection told him he had not. He had had no interest in galloping gentility, as he called it, and since he had not yet been on the lookout for a wife, and preferred to spend his time in such manly pursuits as boxing, gambling, hunting, and shooting, he was more likely to have been found at the Newmarket races than at Almack's Assembly Rooms.

Gideon smiled, suddenly remembering the way Daintry had leapt to his defense against her irascible parent, just as if she had not torn a strip off him herself less than half an hour before. The wench had some odd notions in her head, thanks to that formidable aunt of hers, and was too much accustomed to having her own way of things, but she was nonetheless beautiful or desirable for all that.

Penthorpe would have been no match for her, of course—would have found himself living under the cat's paw within a month. She was a termagant, but a magnificent one, and his own temper could match hers any day.

It was a pity that St. Merryn's commands would make it a trifle awkward for him to pursue the acquaintance. Still, she was determined to end the old feud, and she seemed the type who, once she'd got a bee buzzing in her bonnet, would do all in her power to put it to rest. Moreover, it was the house-party season, and he had received a number of invitations. No doubt Daintry Tarrant would turn up at some of the same houses.

His thoughts remained thus pleasantly occupied until Deverill Court came into view, at which time they shifted abruptly back to the scene at Tuscombe Park. Unaccustomed as he was to the sort of Turkish treatment he had received from St. Merryn, he could not deny that he had deserved the man's anger. What his own father would have to say about it did not bear thinking about, and he had still not made up his mind whether to confess the whole to him or hope he never learned about it from anyone else—rather a forlorn hope considering the number of persons present and the fact that one of them, Lady Catherine Chauncey, was completely unknown to him. And, too, Sir Geoffrey Seacourt, having been a crony of Jack's who had enjoyed helping him make life miserable for the younger boys at Eton, was scarcely a man whose discretion he ought to rely upon now.

Sighing, he gave his horse into a groom's keeping and went into the house, removing gloves and hat and handing them, with his whip, to the footman who was the sole occupant of the hall.

"Is my father at home, Thornton?"

"Yes, my lord"

"The book room?"

"Yes, sir, and begging your pardon, my lord, but I'm afraid there has been a bit of a dust-up of sorts."

Gideon raised his eyebrows. "A dust-up?"

"Yes, sir. Mr. Kibworth and Mr. Shalton, sir."

Gideon grimaced. "I'll deal with them later. First I must see my father." His erstwhile batman and the fashionable valet his father had thoughtfully provided for him at Jervaulx Abbey had not yet managed to come to terms with each other for the simple reason that Shalton had accompanied him north while Kibworth had proceeded directly to Deverill Court, but it had become clear even before they all left the Abbey that the two men were not precisely kindred spirits. Gideon had accepted Kibworth's services because Jervaulx clearly had expected him to do so, but Shalton was more than just a servant to him, and if he had to decide between the two, it was Kibworth who would go.

In the book room, a fire crackled on the hearth, and Jervaulx was standing by the window overlooking the south lawn. When Gideon entered he turned, saying, "Thornton said you had gone out. It is a good day for a ride, is it not?"

"Yes, sir." Gideon was not generally one to charge before his defenses were in place, but he could see no reason to delay once he had made up his mind to a course. Shutting the door, he said bluntly, "I rode to Tuscombe Park, sir, to clear up some unfinished business. St. Merryn ordered me off his land."

"Precisely what one might have expected him to do. 'Tis odd he did not do so yesterday." Jervaulx moved away from the window to a wing chair near the hearth. Resting one slender, well-manicured hand on the chair back, he looked directly at Gideon. "Perhaps now you will be content to let the matter rest."

The order was clear, and Gideon experienced a sense of being swept backward in time to a period when defiance had been utterly unacceptable. Nevertheless, he said evenly, "Before I can do that, sir, I would like to know how the feud between the two families originated. The oddest thing in all of this is that no one at St. Merryn seems to know."

"There can be no good cause to rake up old quarrels. Suffice it to say that grievous fault lay with the Tarrants, and the families have not spoken since. No reasonable man requires to know more than that, and at present you would be far better occupied in putting an end to the conflict between your servants before it disrupts this entire household."

"I'll attend to that," Gideon said, accepting the snub for the moment at least, knowing from experience that it would do no good to press Jervaulx any further. "You seem to have a great many papers piled on your desk, sir. Is there anything I can do to be of assistance to you, since I am here?"

Glancing toward the desk, Jervaulx said, "An inexperienced assistant is more trouble than good, but if you wish to learn about this estate, no obstacle will be placed in your path. Put yourself in Barton's hands. He is an excellent steward and will show you what you will need to know when this house is yours. Most of the papers on the desk concern magisterial affairs. The parishes of Bisland and Alturnun request that new constables be appointed, and the poorhouse in Bodmin requires a new overseer."

"Really, sir, should you not be turning such duties over to someone else? There must be several competent men, and I own, I find it amazing that you have not already found one, particularly now that you must spend so much of the year in Gloucestershire."

"One does not shirk prior obligations merely because one ascends to higher estate," Jervaulx said coldly, "and one must understand the common people in order to serve their needs. Davies Giddy, the member for Bodmin, recently had all his windows broken because the local miners believe—understandably—that with the war over, the food shortages should likewise be over. They want higher wages, but in fact, two more mines will soon close. Pray, who would you suggest should assume the local magistrate's duties at such a dangerous time? St. Merryn?"

"Have you reason to believe him incapable?"

"There is a good deal to be accomplished here before the Assizes begin next month," Jervaulx said abruptly, moving to the desk. "Whilst you remain at Deverill Court, you will best serve your interest by submitting to Barton's instruction. A sensible man will attempt no more until he has gained experience. Once you have learned all Barton can teach you, you may apply to Shilcroft at the Abbey—a very good man in his way—and no doubt Lynmouth will wish to add his mite. But more than likely, you will have found more amusing pursuits before then."

The marquess took his seat at the desk as he spoke, and Gideon accepted his dismissal. He had little desire to submit to his father's stewards for instruction, but since the estates would one day be his,

he supposed that soon he would have to do just that. As to applying to Lord Lynmouth, the previous marquess's maternal uncle and
primary trustee, he had a strong sense of resistance to the very idea.
Deverill Court was one thing. It was his home, and the thought of
owning it one day was not particularly unsettling. Jervaulx Abbey
was another matter. All his life, the Abbey had been the seat of the
senior branch of the family. He had visited it only one time before
his father had inherited the title, and only once since then. He had
no sense of attachment whatsoever to the place.

As a matter of fact, he felt oddly detached from life as he had
previously known it. For as long as he could remember, he had
been the younger son, whose primary task was to find his own
niche and carve out a place for himself. He had gone from being
a quiet supporter of boys that his brother and others of the same
ilk had tried to bully to commanding a number of those same lads
in Wellington's Army. He knew he was good at organizing others'
lives and saving them from the consequences of their own folly; he
was not so confident of his ability to organize himself.

Having taken leave of Jervaulx, he went to his own bedchamber, a well-appointed and comfortable but at the moment a
rather impersonal room, and rang for Ned Shalton.

Ten minutes later, Shalton entered, a stocky man of medium
height and middle age with a soldierly manner and a shock of
grizzled curls. "Aye, Major, what's the drill?" His voice was low and
gruff by nature, but his light blue eyes twinkled.

Gideon was silent long enough to see the twinkle fade. Then
he said quietly, "I am informed that there has been some sort of a
ruckus, Ned. I won't tolerate that."

Shalton straightened to a parade ground posture. "No, sir."

Amused, Gideon said, "Enough, damn you. I'm not going to
eat you, as you know very well. What was it all about?"

Relaxing, Shalton ran a hand through his grizzled curls, shook
his head, and said, "It's that horse-faced fopdoodle Kibworth,
Major. Man talks like he's got a mouthful of buckshot, and if he
don't drown in the first squall from holding his nose so high in
the air, I'll eat my hat, and that's a fact. Can't be in the same room
with him for ten seconds without wanting to draw his cork, much

as I *try* to mind my temper, and when he said he don't know what incompetent fool's been looking after your traps, 'n all, well, it was more than mind and heart could stomach, and that's the truth of it. I tipped him a wisty castor, I did. Aye, and I'm glad of it, too," he added belligerently.

No longer amused, Gideon let the silence lengthen again until Shalton looked defensive, then said, "I won't have this sort of thing, Ned. It annoys my father and unsettles everyone else in the house, so in future you will keep your temper. Kibworth has his uses, you know. He wields a mean iron and knows just what he's about when it comes to seeing my shirts and other linens properly laundered and starched. "You, on the other hand," he added when he saw Shalton's face tighten with indignation, "have an unmatched talent for putting a gloss on a pair of boots and for looking after my leathers and other traps. The two of you can sort things out if at least one of you will exert a modicum of tact. Is that clear?" His voice hardened on the last words, and the look he bent upon his henchman was implacable.

Shalton had heard the tone and seen the look before. "Aye, sir, it be as clear as daylight."

"Good. Now, find that rascal Kibworth and send him to me."

Looking instantly more cheerful, Shalton went to do as he was bid, and it was not long before the valet appeared.

"You rang, sir?"

An entirely different sort of man from Shalton, Kibworth was precise to a pin and carried himself with a good deal more dignity than even Jervaulx did. His face was long and narrow, his lips thin and unyielding, and he did seem to look down his nose at the world. Gideon felt a stirring of sympathy for Shalton. Again he let the silence lengthen, but it seemed to have no effect upon the valet. He merely waited patiently until it should be his master's decision to speak.

At last Gideon said, "I won't have discord between my servants, Kibworth. Is that clear?"

"Certainly, my lord."

"Excellent. No, no, don't go. I have more to say to you. You are new to my service, and there are a few things you ought to know in order to serve me well. First of all, Mr. Shalton has been with me for some years and knows my ways better than anyone else can ever know them."

"Shalton is no doubt an excellent man, in his way, to serve a military officer, my lord, but surely now that you are come home and will be meaning to go about in society—"

"Mr. Shalton is still an excellent man, Kibworth, and if there is any more of the sort of uproar there was today, he will be the only man. I trust I make my meaning clear." He could see that the valet was struggling with his feelings, but training stood the test, helped by the knowledge that he would be unlikely to find another position of such enviable stature in his world.

"I will see that you are not disturbed by such discord again, my lord. Will your lordship be riding again today, or shall I order your lordship's bath and lay out fresh raiment?"

Satisfied, Gideon said, "I intend to meet with Mr. Barton for an hour or so, but then I shall want to change. You may go."

Hoping he had scotched the rivalry between the two men and forced them into a semblance at least of unity, he went to find his father's steward.

Barton, a bald little man with a habit of rubbing his hands together when he was pleased, was uncommonly delighted to see him. "Excellent, my lord," he said when Gideon had stated his purpose in seeking him out. "I hope this means you intend to take some of the burden from his lordship's shoulders. He goes a mean pace, sir, and he ought to be taking matters more at his ease these days."

"Well, he isn't handing over the reins, Barton, but he did say that I should look to you for schooling."

"Then you intend to remain here for a time, sir. I had thought you would be leaving soon, what with all the house parties and other activities of the autumn to look forward to. 'Tis what young Master Jack would have been doing, I can tell you, God rest his soul. I see you've put off your mourning."

Gideon recalled that his father had been wearing a black coat and pantaloons, but Jervaulx nearly always wore black, and he had not thought much about it. Jack had been dead for less than four months, so he supposed he ought to be wearing a black waistcoat at least. He had not known him well and had not liked him at all, and what with all the deaths at Waterloo and the tacit understanding that the entire nation would not smother itself in black after such a great victory, despite the enormous losses, he had somehow neglected this admittedly important mark of family duty. Odd, he thought now, that Jervaulx had said nothing to him about it.

To Barton, he said only, "I mourn for my comrades in the field as well as for my brother, Mr. Barton, but I believe in getting on with life rather than pondering our mortality. Tell me, sir, where will I find any old letters that might lie amongst the family papers? I am particularly curious to learn more about the feud between the Deverills and the Tarrant family of Tuscombe Park. Perhaps you know what began it all."

Barton shook his head. "Before my time, that was, my lord. All I know about it is that when your father and St. Merryn had a dispute some years ago about a piece of land, St. Merryn was very mifty. Nothing much came of it, as I recall, but it seemed to me that Lord Jervaulx was displeased even to have had it brought to his attention, and I soon realized that the less he had to deal with the earl, the better. As to old letters, things of that nature would be in the muniments room. I don't know what all you might find there, but the whole lot could stand a sorting."

Gideon nodded, agreed to setting a time to allow Barton to begin his instruction, and went to have a look at the muniments room in the northwest tower. He could not remember setting foot in it before, and he soon formed the opinion that no one else had done so for some time other than to add another record book or pile of papers to the litter in the room. His was an orderly mind, and the sight of books piled on shelves lining the walls, scrolled documents, stacks of papers, and general clutter everywhere else both irritated and dismayed him. A writing table near the window overlooked the peaceful home wood, however, so gathering a pile of what appeared to be miscellaneous records, he soon made himself comfortable and began to sort through them.

An hour later, he gave it up for the day. There were records of every sort imaginable in the pile, but it was just as Barton had warned him. They would require careful sorting and examination before he would be able to make any sense of them.

Remembering that Daintry Tarrant liked to ride, he sent orders to the stables to have Shadow saddled for him first thing in the morning, then went to have his bath and change for dinner.

Eight

The following morning dawned bright and sunny, but Charley's plan to ride on the moor nearly failed at the outset. Knowing that at least one of the little girls would want to get an early start, Daintry went downstairs nearly an hour before her usual time, expecting to have the breakfast room to herself. But to her annoyance, she found Sir Geoffrey there before her, halfway through the large plate of food in front of him.

Daintry smiled at the footman Pedrek, hovering helpfully nearby, replied to his usual query that she would take tea and some hot buttered toast, then turned to the sideboard where enticing odors escaped from a number of covered dishes.

Sir Geoffrey, speaking around a mouthful of food, said, "Good morning. Got your habit on, I see. Good color for you. Matches your eyes, and makes you look almost like a proper lady."

Reining in her volatile temper with difficulty, she replied over her shoulder, "Thank you, Geoffrey. I believe you meant that as a compliment. I generally do not eat a full breakfast until I return from my ride, but this ham smells delicious."

"As tasty as if it had come from Yorkshire," he said, wiping his lips with his napkin and eyeing her speculatively. "Still go dashing all over the countryside on your own, I suppose. I own, I hope you haven't taught such independent ways to my daughter while she's been staying here with you."

Well aware that her response might determine whether Melissa would be allowed to ride with her or be forced to remain at home, Daintry swallowed the retort that sprang to her lips and said as she set her plate on the table and took her seat, "Melissa is an excellent rider, sir. You ought to be proud of her ability. I take both girls riding frequently and have been in the habit of giving them a lesson each morning if the weather permits. There is nothing in that, I hope, to warrant disapproval."

"Certainly not," he agreed, smiling at her. "In fact, I'll give myself the pleasure of attending your lesson this morning, for I'm curious to know how one female goes about teaching another to ride. You won't object, I hope."

Fearing that her expression had already made her misgiving plain, Daintry greeted the entry of the footman with her tea and toast with relief, thanking him before she said mendaciously that Sir Geoffrey was certainly welcome to join them.

Fifteen minutes later, when the two little girls came running to find her, she saw her concern reflected in their expressions when they discovered she was not alone. Catching Charley's gaze and holding it with what she hoped was a warning look, she said cheerfully, "Here is a treat for you, girls. Sir Geoffrey has decided to watch your riding lesson this morning. He will be surprised to discover how well you both ride now."

With a sinking feeling, she saw that Melissa was unable to conceal her dismay, but before Sir Geoffrey had taken note of it, Charley stepped in front of her cousin and said lightly, "I daresay you will be very surprised indeed, Uncle Geoffrey. Melissa is hardly ever afraid anymore."

He laughed, reaching out to pinch her cheek. "I do not concede that to be necessarily an improvement, Charlotte, for you must know that I do not consider intrepidity an asset to a female on horseback. Good, healthy fear will keep her much safer."

"Oh, no," Charley said, "for she is certain to communicate her fear to the horse, you know, and—"

"Charley, for goodness' sake," Daintry interjected, "your uncle does not require a lecture on horsemanship. If you are ready, we will go to the stables now."

"But you have not finished eating," Sir Geoffrey protested.

"I told you, I rarely take much food before I ride. Come along, girls," she added, hoping she would have a few moments alone with them before he followed, to warn them to say nothing about their erstwhile plan to ride on the moor.

She was not given the chance, however, for Sir Geoffrey followed at once, shouting to Pedrek to fetch his hat and coat, and clearly expecting them to wait until these articles had been brought to him.

The last thing Daintry wanted was for him to order a horse saddled for himself when they reached the stables, and although he was not wearing riding breeches, she suspected he might do so if it appeared that they meant to leave the yard. Therefore, when Clemons brought out the three horses, she said, "You forgot to bring their lead reins. Please, go and get them at once."

The wiry groom did not so much as blink but handed over the reins he held to a nearby stableboy and turned on his heel. Daintry held her breath, hoping neither of the two girls would be so foolish as to mention that they had not suffered the indignity of a lead rein in weeks.

They remained obediently silent until Clemons had attached the leads, but when he bent to lift Charley onto her saddle, Daintry saw the spark of mutiny flare in the child's dark eyes, and said, "Wait, Clemons. Miss Charlotte would prefer to show her uncle that she can mount unaided."

Sir Geoffrey laughed. "Daintry, don't encourage such folly. No child can mount a full-grown horse without assistance."

"Charley can. Watch."

Charley, grinning now, moved up beside the bay gelding and patted its muzzle. "Now, Victor, my lovely fellow, show Uncle Geoffrey how clever you are." She touched his shoulder, spoke softly to him, and to Sir Geoffrey's visible astonishment, the gelding folded his front legs beneath him, kneeling so that the little girl could put her left foot in the stirrup. Accepting her reins from the stableboy and holding firmly to pommel and hind bow, Charley made no attempt to seat herself until the gelding had obeyed her command to rise, but then she settled herself with dispatch, grinning triumphantly.

Melissa said, "Is Charley not amazingly clever, Papa?"

"Amazingly," he agreed, "but I hope you never attempt such an indelicate method, my dear. It is not at all the proper way for a young lady of quality to mount a horse."

"Oh, I could never teach a horse to do such clever things," Melissa said naively, "but Charley and Aunt Daintry have taught all sorts of tricks to Grandpapa's horses."

Daintry said, "That is quite true, Geoffrey. Charley has a real gift for training animals to do the most amazing things, but I promise you, she has taught Tender Lady nothing alarming. Put Miss Melissa up, Clemons, and then lead them both to the end of the stable yard, if you please. You may assist me, Geoffrey."

He was still watching Charley, but he turned obediently and formed a cup with his hands so that she might put her left foot in it. Holding reins and whip in her right hand and resting it on the pommel, she put her left hand on his shoulder and sprang lightly into the saddle, putting her right knee over the pommel to secure her seat. Then, arranging her skirt, she shifted her reins to her left hand and turned her attention to her charges. Clemons held the long lead reins, and the two girls had already begun to ride circles around him. Daintry saw that Charley, having knotted her reins and left them hanging on Victor's neck, had her hands folded demurely in her lap.

"Don't panic, Geoffrey," she said when she saw him frown. "I believe that too much dependence on the reins is one of the most common faults in riding, so I have taught both girls to ride without them, depending on their balance to keep them in the saddle. They will come to no harm, Clemons is very careful." She saw no reason to mention that Clemons generally had no lead rein and could thus do no more than chase after the girls when they rode in this fashion, which Charley at least had been known to do on occasions when it was less than sensible.

"Bring them to a trot, girls, and show me that you can rise without benefit of your stirrup. I daresay it has not occurred to you, Geoffrey," she added, seeing him frown again, "but on a side-saddle, an amateur has a tendency to push up from the stirrup instead of employing the muscles of her right leg. That will not do for any girl who learns from me, I can tell you."

He turned toward her when she said his name the second time, but she doubted he had heard what she said, for his attention was fixed upon a point behind her. Turning, she saw her brother striding toward them with Lady Catherine Chauncey at his side. Lady Catherine was dressed for riding.

Charles, waving, shouted, "There you are, Seacourt. I have been searching the house for you. Good morning, Daintry. Lady Catherine here tells me it is her habit to ride each morning, and I said you'd be delighted to take her out and about, so I hope you don't mean to spend the whole morning giving the girls riding lessons. They ought to be in the schoolroom, oughtn't they?"

"Nothing will be gained by forcing them to remain locked up with Cousin Ethelinda, Charles, particularly when she feels guilty if she has to abandon Mama to look after them. Melissa has only a few more days before she must go home, and Charley's new governess will be here soon enough. In the meantime it will do neither of them harm to get some extra fresh air and exercise. If Lady Catherine wishes to ride," she added before he could debate any portion of her statement, "I will be happy to take her over some of the nearby countryside. I had promised the girls an outing after their lesson, in any event, and by the time a horse can be saddled and bridled for her, they will be ready. Are you an expert or a mere hacker, Lady Catherine?"

"Why, I have frequently been told that I am a born rider, Lady Daintry, with a natural seat on any horse." She fluttered her long eyelashes at both men, adding with a pout, "but surely, my dear, you do not ride without a proper male escort."

Sir Geoffrey said instantly, "Tarrant and I will be happy to accompany you, won't we, Charles?"

Daintry, glancing apologetically at Charley and Melissa, saw that the former was watching her father expectantly, and turned back just as Charles replied, "No, dash it, we won't. "You don't think I was turning the house upside down looking for you so that we could join the infantry on an amble around Cornwall, do you? We are going shooting, Geoffrey, my lad. Medrose tells me there are woodcocks and coots in the home wood, and dash it all, I haven't been out with a gun in six months. You don't want to play the dashed knight errant to four females, do you? Clemons can take some of the other stable lads if you're in a fret about their safety. No need for that, though. Bruising riders, all of them. At least, Daintry is, and the girls, I daresay, and Lady Catherine just said she's perfectly at home in the saddle, too, so come on with me. I'll show you some real sport."

Sir Geoffrey looked doubtful, but Daintry knew her brother would prevail and, her spirits rising, called to a stableboy to fetch out a lady's mount at once for Lady Catherine.

"Which one, my lady?"

Before she could reply, Charley shouted, "Bring the Duchess, Teddy. She will be perfect for Lady Catherine."

Opening her mouth to protest, Daintry encountered a fierce glare from her niece, and fell silent. Common civility dictated that one ought to provide one's guest with the best riding horse at one's disposal, but Lady Catherine had said she was an expert, so no doubt the Duchess's frequently peculiar gaits and odd habits would not trouble her.

Lady Catherine was watching the gentlemen's departure, but she turned just then, looking not quite so much as before like a lady expecting to enjoy an exhilarating gallop across the moor. But when Teddy emerged from the stable, leading a lovely little white mare, her countenance brightened. "Oh, how pretty," she exclaimed, walking up to stroke the Duchess's rosy muzzle.

Charley, having removed her lead rein the moment her Uncle Geoffrey's back was turned, rode up beside Daintry and muttered, "I don't believe she really wants to go with us at all, you know. In my opinion, she saw Uncle Geoffrey and thought he meant to ride with us, and so she came out, too."

Realizing that her niece suffered from much the same misunderstanding that she had suffered the day before, Daintry said, "I doubt that, darling. She is a cousin of his, you know. Moreover," she added, remembering that Lady Catherine's bedchamber did overlook the drive leading to the yard, "if she saw him, she must have seen that he was not dressed for riding."

Charley looked doubtful, but Lady Catherine was mounted and though she still was arranging her skirt and had not yet even taken her reins from the stableboy, there was no further opportunity for private conversation. When Clemons asked if a second groom ought to accompany them, Daintry replied quickly in the negative before Charley could commit another impertinence.

Daintry had seen from the way Lady Catherine mounted that she was not the expert rider she had claimed to be, and soon realized that the case was even worse. Not only did the woman persist in clucking to the mare, a habit that would soon make her unpopular with anyone riding a skittish horse near her, but she held her reins in both hands as if she were rowing a boat and sat much too far forward in her saddle. Glancing at Charley, Daintry tried to remember if the Duchess had any really dangerous habits.

Their ride progressed without incident for nearly half an hour, and Daintry exerted herself to maintain a conversation with Lady Catherine while the girls rode a little ahead of them.

"I am surprised that your brother and Sir Geoffrey allow their little girls to ride such big horses," Lady Catherine said when they were barely out of the stable yard. "My own dear papa refused to put me on one until I was sixteen, for of course, no younger female is strong enough to ride really well."

Daintry replied vaguely but as politely as she could.

When Charley and Melissa increased their pace to a trot and she followed suit, Lady Catherine said, "Surely, this pace is too fast for them, particularly since the road is beginning to rise. All this bouncing about cannot be good for tender little bodies!"

This time, Daintry said only, "*They* do not bounce."

Lady Catherine certainly did bounce, and knowing that only a very good rider might have a hope of matching her rises to the Duchess's notion of a trot, Daintry soon called to Charley to canter instead. "I know you must be longing for a real gallop, Lady Catherine," she said, raising her voice to be heard above the hoofbeats, "but I insist that the girls increase their paces slowly, and only after they are certain the ground is safe."

Lady Catherine did not respond, and not long afterward Daintry took pity on her and shouted for the girls to draw rein, knowing the incline would soon increase significantly, in any case. As they came up to the others, she heard Charley begin to whistle rather tunelessly and saw Melissa look sharply at her.

Saying that they would walk the horses now that they had run the fidgets out of them, Daintry prayed that Charley would behave herself, since it would do neither of the children any good to have Lady Catherine telling tales of them when they got back to Tuscombe Park. Charley's odd whistling continued.

"What is that child doing?" Lady Catherine said. "Ladies do not whistle, Charlotte. Gracious, what is wrong with this mare?"

"Sorry," Charley said, falling silent.

Daintry looked at the mare, which appeared to be walking just as it should be. Catching sight of Clemons, riding behind them, she saw the man wipe a smile off his face, and grew alert.

As if absentmindedly, Charley began the tuneless whistling again, and Daintry, still watching the mare, saw at once what was happening. The Duchess had developed a limp.

"There," Lady Catherine cried, "what is it? She nearly had me off that time. There *is* something wrong with her!"

Drawing rein and struggling to control her unreliable emotions, Daintry said, "Check the Duchess's right hind shoe, Clemons. Perhaps she has picked up a stone."

Wooden-faced, the groom dismounted and painstakingly checked all four of the mare's shoes, one after the other. "Nothing, my lady. Like as not she's strained that rear hock again."

Charley said instantly, "That's it, Aunt Daintry! We thought it was completely healed, of course, but I daresay it was still a trifle weak, or else she simply twisted it again. You will have to go back, Lady Catherine. How dismal for you!"

Remembering her duty, Daintry said firmly, "We must all go back, of course. What a shame."

"Oh, no!" Charley cried.

Lady Catherine said grimly, "I am sure I would be perfectly able to go back alone, you know, only I do not know the way, and I would not for the world deprive you of your groom."

Surrendering to her baser instincts, Daintry said, "Oh, we do not care for that, ma'am, I assure you. Indeed, if it were possible, I should simply tell Clemons to lead the mare home and change your saddle to his horse. But unfortunately, that animal is not trained to carry a female or even a sidesaddle. If you are perfectly certain you do not mind, I confess I would prefer not to disappoint the girls after promising them this outing."

"I do not mind at all," Lady Catherine retorted, "so long as you do not expect me to walk the whole distance back."

"Oh, there is no need for that," Charley said. "You must just let Clemons lead her and not permit him to go too fast."

Daintry scarcely waited for the pair to ride beyond earshot before saying sternly, "You abominable girl, I do not know what you deserve for that ill-mannered trick."

"You know? How did you know? Oh, isn't it famous, Aunt Daintry? I've never tried it when I wasn't actually riding her, you see, and I was not perfectly certain she would do it when she hadn't yet begun to do it on her own, but she always limps when she thinks she has been away from her stable too long."

"Charley, you are . . . I don't know a word bad enough that I can repeat to you."

Charley laughed, unrepentant. "Can we gallop when we get to the top of the road, Aunt Daintry?"

Daintry agreed, and when it leveled out a few minutes later, she led the way, leaving the hard-packed roadbed at once for the softer footing of the moorland. The two little girls were close behind her. Since she was concentrating on the terrain ahead, knowing there might well be muddy spots, even some deep puddles still, it was Charley who first saw the rider two fields ahead of them. Her cry alerted Daintry.

She had not the least doubt who it was, although at first he was no more than a dark shadow galloping against the horizon and looking, she thought, just like the centaurs of ancient days must have looked. Animal and man moved as one, their pace so smooth, yet so swift, that they seemed almost to fly.

He saw them and turned so quickly that the great horse reared, pawing the air. Then, heading Shadow straight toward them, soaring high over the stone walls that marked the field boundaries, Deverill closed the distance rapidly.

Daintry reined Cloud in to wait for him, and as the little girls did likewise, Charley waved her whip and cried, "View halloo," adding in a lower tone, "Lord Deverill is a bruising rider, isn't he, Aunt Daintry?"

"He certainly is," Daintry agreed.

"That's how I'd like to ride," Charley confided.

"Then you must practice a great deal more, my dear," Daintry told her absently, still watching Deverill. He certainly could ride, she thought, and he was an excellent judge of horseflesh, as well. Shadow's forward action was as smooth as could be, though no one could mistake his power.

Deverill slowed the great horse before he reached them, and approached at a decorous walk. "Good morning, ladies," he said as soon as he was within speaking distance. "Have you murdered your groom and buried his body beneath the heather?"

Daintry wrinkled her nose at him. "I did not think you, of all people, would dare to preach propriety," she said.

He laughed. "Just shows how wrong you can be, does it not? Bodmin Moor is no place for any female to be without male escort, and certainly not three very young ladies."

"I am more than twenty, sir," she said, stiffening, "and I have been riding on Bodmin Moor all my life."

"But not, I'll wager, without a groom in attendance."

Charley said quickly, "Pray, do not scold Aunt Daintry, sir. It is all my fault that Clemons is not with us at present."

"So *you* murdered the groom."

Melissa cried, "Oh, no, sir!"

Charley only chuckled. "You know very well that I did nothing of the kind, but I did arrange it so that he would have to go home. You see, we had company, and we did not want her."

Deverill looked at Daintry, then back at Charley. "I cannot imagine that you would wish to send your Aunt Susan home, so it must have been the lovely Lady Catherine Chauncey. Was her company so objectionable to you?"

"She clucks at her horse, sir," Charley said, disgusted.

"Definitely objectionable then," he agreed without so much as a twitch of his lips.

"Well, I knew you would think so, and she saws at the reins, too, and bounces all over the saddle. Although that," she added conscientiously, "might easily have been the Duchess's fault."

"And which duchess is that?" Deverill asked, casting a smile at Daintry as he maneuvered Shadow next to the silver dun.

Daintry, enjoying the exchange and wanting to see how he would deal with Charley, remained silent but returned his smile.

Charley said, "Our Duchess, of course. She is the prettiest little white mare you ever saw, absolute perfection. Very showy and precisely the sort of animal to appeal to Lady Catherine, just as I thought she would be. Only from some cause or other—"

"Charley," Daintry interjected, "if you are going to tell the tale at all, you would be wise to tell the whole truth and not merely the bits of it that suit you."

"Well, I was going to. Lord Deverill is not one who will give me away, and certainly not to Papa or to Grandpapa."

"No, indeed," Deverill agreed instantly. "Tell me."

"Well, the real reason I wanted Lady Catherine to ride the Duchess is that I can make her limp by whistling at her, and that is what I did, and so Clemons had to take her back to the stable, on account of Lady Catherine thought she had strained her hock again, which she never really did in the first place, only Clemons said she did, and so of course I said the same thing. Only Aunt Daintry knew all along it was me."

Deverill looked at Daintry in astonishment. "Is that the truth? Has she really taught the mare to limp on command?"

"Don't encourage her to boast of the tricks she has taught the horses in our stables," Daintry said, laughing. "I began it by showing her some simple schooling methods, but she left my teaching in the dust long ago, and I fear that any number of the things she's taught them since must be entirely reprehensible."

"No, they aren't, Aunt Daintry. Well, only that one, maybe, but I did it because Duchess limps so often anyway that I thought it would be easy to teach her to do it on command, and so it was.

Aunt Daintry says I have a knack, sir, though I still have not managed to teach Victor here not to be afraid of thunder."

Deverill said, "You terrify me. I have schooled any number of horses, and I cannot remember a single time I have been the least bit tempted to teach one to limp on purpose."

"Well, but we have taught them lots of useful things as well," Charley assured him. "May we ride on ahead, Aunt Daintry? Melissa wants to try jumping the walls."

Daintry, noting the quickly masked look of dismay on Melissa's face, said, "You may certainly ride where you like, girls, so long as you do not go where I cannot see you, and so long as you are careful. You may jump the gates, Charley, but not the stone walls. One day when we can take time to examine them carefully first, we will see about attempting them, but not today when you two want to ride on ahead of us."

When the little girls gave spur to their horses and dashed away, Deverill said, "They ride extremely well for their ages. Two of the firmest seats I've had the privilege of seeing."

Pleased that he recognized their skill, and even more pleased that he had not qualified his praise by adding the infuriating words *for little girls,* or worse, *for females,* Daintry said with a smile, "They practiced their balance by riding without relying on reins or stirrups until they could sit on handkerchiefs and hold bits of paper between their legs and the stirrup leather. They have become quite skilled indeed."

He nodded but made no reply. Charley had set Victor at a timber gate, and he watched alertly until horse and rider sailed smoothly over. When Melissa had followed Charley's lead without mishap, he said, "I wondered if the little one might be a bit tentative. She seems less confident than her cousin, but I suppose I have done her a grave injustice by saying so."

"She has implicit faith in Charley, sir. The difficulty was to induce her to look for her own route and not always to depend upon Charley to give her the lead. I finally convinced her by pointing out that she would be teaching Tender Lady always to require a lead horse, so now she makes it a habit to take turns with Charley. There now, you see, she will come back first."

They continued to watch until the two children rode into the next field, when Deverill grinned at Daintry and said with a hint of challenge in his voice, "You will not want them to leave us too far behind, I suppose."

She knew that Charley would do nothing of the kind, but she had been wishing she might join in their fun, and she did not hesitate now, giving spur to Cloud and riding to leap the nearest gate. Deverill, riding beside her, opened the distance between them and took Shadow over the wall at the same time.

Drawing up a few moments later, Daintry glanced at her two charges to see that once again, Melissa was taking the lead. To her experienced eye, it was evident that Tender Lady was going too slowly, but she relaxed when she saw Melissa touch the mare's flank with her whip. Tender Lady seemed to jump cleanly, with the little girl leaning back just slightly, the way she had been taught, and all would have been well had the mare not stumbled on the landing. Melissa collected her without falling, but as the mare recovered and broke into a run, it quickly became clear that the little girl had lost at least one of her reins.

Looking frantically over her shoulder, she cried, "Charley!"

Muttering an epithet, Deverill urged Shadow forward, but Daintry drew rein, knowing Melissa was in no danger.

Before Shadow had taken half a dozen steps several piercing, gull-like shrieks rent the air, and Tender Lady slowed to a trot, then to a walk, before she stopped altogether. Melissa leaned forward, clinging to the mare's mane and trying to snag the loose rein with her whip. "It's broken," she called to Charley.

Deverill had reined in the black, and looked back now at Daintry, raising his eyebrows. "Another of her little tricks?"

"An extremely useful one, you will agree," Daintry said. "The only drawback is that well-nigh every horse in our stables responds the same way that Tender Lady just did. It would have been no use my trying to dash after her like you did until after Charley had whistled. However, that is one reason Melissa has become a confident rider. She was terrified to ride at Seacourt, because she cannot control her pony. The little beast has the worst manners in the world, and there are times when I think Geoffrey must have been mad to purchase him. But once Charley proved to her that Tender Lady would not run away with her, she became much more interested in learning to ride well. Now, I daresay even that awful pony won't frighten her anymore."

Charley had joined Melissa, and as they approached, both girls looked at Daintry. Charly said, "She knows she ought not to have relaxed her hold on the rein, Aunt Daintry."

Daintry smiled at Melissa. "I am sure she does. You kept your head very well, my dear. I was proud of you."

Melissa flushed a little but said, "The rein is broken. She must have stepped on it."

Deverill, dismounting, said, "I have just the thing, ladies. I, too, know a few tricks, having spent more months campaigning than I care to remember." He reached into a leather pouch attached to his saddlebow and took out a coil of leather. "I always carry an extra rein, because one never knows when a mishap will occur, only that when it does it will be most inconvenient."

Charley exclaimed, "What a good idea! I shall begin to do that myself. If saddles were properly designed with notion bags, one could carry as much as Aunt Ophelia does in that great traveling reticule of hers. But how does one attach that, sir?"

He showed her how to attach the new rein to the broken piece. "It is only makeshift till your tack man can repair it properly, and we must attach it so the broken end will not flap around. If I had a knife with me, I could cut it off, but that will serve you until you get home."

Melissa thanked him prettily, and Daintry said, "We all thank you, sir, but I do think we had better return now."

"I will not offer to accompany you," he said, frowning. "That is, unless your esteemed parent has changed his . . . No, I didn't think he had. However, perhaps I will see you at Mount Edgcumbe's house party on the twelfth."

Her spirits rose considerably. "We have been invited, sir."

"All of you?"

She chuckled at his dismay. "My father does not attend such parties, sir. He likes shooting parties, of course, but not mixed hunting parties, theatricals, or dancing, so I believe our group at

Mount Edgcumbe will consist of only my aunt, myself, and Charles and Davina, for Geoffrey's tastes are similar to Papa's."

"And there will be no children," Charley said with a sigh.

Deverill laughed. "Your day will come soon enough, Miss Charlotte, and I doubt that the *beau monde* will ever be the same afterward." The two little girls broke into delighted laughter, and under its cover, he turned to Daintry and said warmly, "I look forward to advancing our acquaintance, my lady."

Unable to resist looking over her shoulder as she rode away with the children, Daintry saw that he was still where they had left him, watching. Smiling, he raised his hat, and she turned quickly away, but she could not so easily dismiss him from her thoughts. He could be charming and delightful, but he could also be extremely vexatious and at times even stuffy, as when he had taken her to task about her groom. In point of fact, there was no place in her life for a man like Deverill. At best he would provoke her; at worst he would rob her forever of the independence she sought.

Gideon stayed where he was until the three riders had disappeared over the rise. He had enjoyed himself enormously and wished he might repeat the experience soon, but he knew he would gain nothing if St. Merryn discovered his daughter meeting the enemy at his gate. Mount Edgcumbe would be soon enough to learn if he could stir the little termagant's passions.

In the meantime, he enlisted Shalton and a pair of sturdy footmen to help with the chaos in the muniments room, and the four of them attacked the mess with ruthless efficiency, their labors undisturbed since Jervaulx had received word that his presence was required at once at the Abbey and had journeyed post into Gloucestershire. Though Gideon was interested only in the years shortly before his grandfather's marriage, the records and papers dated back to the fourteenth century, and his orderly nature required that all of them be at least sorted if not catalogued. Even that much proved to be a Herculean task, but before long order began to emerge from the chaos, and he decided that when he returned from Mount Edgcumbe, he would be able to proceed with a more thorough search.

Nine

The Tarrant family accomplished the fifteen-mile journey to Mount Edgcumbe in four carriages, the first and most elegant one carrying Lady Ophelia, Davina, and Daintry, who occupied the forward seat with Lady Ophelia's traveling reticule. Their maids and Charles's valet followed in the next coach, and the enormous amount of baggage required by four members of the *beau monde* for a week's visit to one of the county's most fashionable houses more than filled the last two vehicles. Charles disliked being confined and had chosen, despite the threatening skies, to ride.

Rolling thunder accompanied them along the way, causing carriage horses and Charles's mount to skitter nervously from time to time, but there were no unfortunate incidents, and the rain most generously held off until after their arrival.

The house at Mount Edgcumbe, perched on its promontory at the entrance to Plymouth Sound and surrounded by picturesque parkland, was compact and symmetrical, a golden three-story mock castle with four octagonal corner towers and a broad rectangular central tower at the front. The carriages approached it by way of its gardens. Long considered to be some of the most beautiful in England—though not at their best at this season—they were adorned with temples and a ruined folly, which loomed in turn out of the dusky gloom. Above the sound of the distant thunder could be heard the nearer sound of guns overlooking the harbor as they roared their host's welcome to arriving guests.

From the east front, they could see across the mouth of the River Tamar to the city of Plymouth, a view touted by many but deplored by more discriminating persons who disliked gazing down upon dockyards. Daintry, who had been to Mount Edgcumbe before, enjoyed the sense of being on top of the world looking down at the ships and yachts, and she particularly enjoyed the lights of Plymouth at night. On a clear day one could see the Eddystone Light, fifteen miles out to sea, a beacon to ships entering Plymouth Harbor, as well as a warning to ships proceeding toward Southampton and London not to venture too near without care. The lamp had been lit early because of the gloom, and looking back as she followed Lady Ophelia into the hall, Daintry could see its friendly, sweeping glow in the distance.

In the lofty, candle-lit front hall, which was as large as a courtyard since it had been built two hundred years before to replace one, the sound of their heels on the tessellated marble floor echoed from the high ceiling and distant walls despite the heavy, magnificent tapestries with which the latter were hung.

Liveried servants scurried to deal with baggage while a pair of tall, handsome footmen led the way to the guest bedrooms in the east wing, one stopping to attend to Charles and Davina while the second went on with Lady Ophelia and Daintry, who were given adjoining bedchambers near the southeast tower.

Though Daintry was curious to know if Deverill had arrived, she knew better than to make a gift to any servant of information that might provide grist for the ever-active rumor mills. Moreover, it was already time to dress for dinner. If Deverill was present, she would see him soon enough.

In fact, he was practically the first person she did see when she and Lady Ophelia joined the other guests in the first-floor saloon, a noble, gilded white chamber with a high, coved ceiling and a magnificent pink and gray Axminster carpet. Judging from Deverill's expression—and from the way he instantly detached himself from the gentleman he was speaking to—that he had been watching for her, Daintry felt a glow of satisfaction and greeted him with a smile.

"I was afraid this dismal weather might put you off," he said, then turned guiltily to Lady Ophelia, as if he had just recalled his manners, and added, "Good evening, ma'am. I hope your journey was a pleasant one."

"It was," she replied, her eyes twinkling, "but if you consider this to be dismal weather for Cornwall, young man, you have been away much longer than I had thought."

He chuckled. "I have been away a good many years, but in my own defense, let me point out that we are practically in Devon, where the weather is thought to be considerably more temperate."

She smiled. "As a recovery, that was not too bad, but close as Devon might be, we are still in Cornwall, where they say sunny days are so few as to be worthy of underscoring in one's journal, though I rarely bother noting the weather in mine at all. However, I daresay that having spent so many years on the Continent, you are more accustomed to sunshine than we are."

"It was certainly warmer than England," he said, "but here is our host bearing down upon us. There will be dancing after dinner, Lady Daintry. May I hope that you will honor me?"

"Certainly, sir," she replied, wondering what her brother would have to say about it and deciding that Charles, loath as he was to endure dissension, would say nothing whatever, nor would he carry tales of her activities to their father.

Deverill bowed and left them as the Earl of Mount Edgcumbe approached. In his fifty-first year, he was a neat little beau and an accomplished flirt, having been a widower for twenty years. Since his hostess for these occasions was his cousin Albinia Edgcumbe, he did not hesitate to greet Lady Ophelia as if he would like to add her to his long string of conquests. They had known each other for years, and as Daintry knew, her aunt, despite her oft-expressed prejudices against the strong sex, enjoyed these encounters as much as his lordship did. Daintry came in for her own share of winks and compliments, but she was feeling charitable to all men at the moment, and did not mind.

Her pleasure in being at Mount Edgcumbe suffered a slight set-back when Davina, whose opinion generally counted for little with her, met her on the way into the dining room and, as the two of them fell back to allow Lady Ophelia to precede them, pulled her to one side in the corridor and demanded to know what she meant by setting the whole company agog.

"I don't have the least notion of what you are talking about," Daintry replied, irritated by Davina's air of criticism but genuinely at a loss to understand her.

"I have heard from at least four persons, including Sally, that you have set your cap for Deverill," Davina said in an angry under-tone at odds with the smile she kept pinned to her face for the ben-efit of passersby, "so don't play the coy lamb with me. If you shake everyone by the ears before we have been here a day, only think what a temper your father will be in when we return!"

"Oh, pooh," Daintry retorted, nodding at an acquaintance who passed them to enter the dining room. "He will hear nothing about it, and even if he did, he can scarcely expect me to be uncivil to Deverill. That really would cause a scandal."

"Civil? Do you call it civil to run to him the minute you arrive and to stand talking to him, fluttering your lashes and blushing as if he had been the only man in the room? I am only glad I did not actually see you myself."

"Well, I wish you had," Daintry said with asperity, annoyed that anyone had described her in such a ridiculous manner. "It was nothing like that, Davina. He came to pay his respects to Aunt Ophelia when we joined everyone else before dinner. We exchanged a few comments about the weather, and then Mount Edgcumbe chased him away so he could flirt with Aunt, just as he always does. Whoever was unkind enough to speak such nonsense to you was exaggerating the situation beyond all reason."

"Well, it was Sally, so I do not doubt that you are telling me the truth," Davina said, stepping back as yet another group went by, "but it just goes to show, Daintry, how easily the smallest thing can be made into scandal."

"Well, you are scarcely one to talk," Daintry said grimly, "and nor is Lady Jersey. How anyone can call her 'Silence' quite astonishes me, for a greater chatterbox I do not know." She was not on such terms with the fifth Countess of Jersey as to call her Sally like Davina did, but she had decided opinions about the woman. "Her family has provided more than its share of scandal, what with her mama eloping with her papa and her sister-in-law running to Scotland to divorce Lord Uxbridge and marry Argyll, so your precious Sally should not criticize others. She may be a great heiress and a patroness of Almack's, but she is *not* kind."

Davina looked swiftly around. "Merciful heavens, Daintry, do not let anyone else hear you! One fatal word from Sally and you will be sunk beyond reclaiming. Your flirting with Deverill merely amused her, for she knew him in Brussels, and of course, everyone knows all about the feud between your two families."

"Well, if they know *all* about it, I wish someone will tell me what caused it," Daintry said frankly, "for from all I can learn, it must have been the veriest piece of nonsense. Even Aunt Ophelia does not know how it began."

"We must go in," Davina said. "Nearly everyone else has done so. Charles ought to be here to escort us." She looked around for her husband. "My goodness, there are Geoffrey and Catherine, and Susan, too. I did not know they were coming."

Daintry had not known they were coming either, but since everyone else had been seated, and since her place was at the opposite end of the long oval table from the others, there was no more opportunity for private conversation, and she turned her attention to her dinner partner, a young man with whom she was slightly acquainted from her visit to London the previous Season.

Lady Ophelia was seated on his other side, and Deverill was across the way beside Lady Jersey, who was flirting shamelessly with him. Not that he minded. Daintry, her attention straying from her dinner partner's cheerful discourse, could see that much easily enough. Turning back, she batted her lashes at her dinner partner, who was describing a newly purchased horse to her.

The young gentleman swallowed wrong, and for several moments was unable to speak. Finally, however, after being vigorously pounded on the back by the footman behind his chair, he recovered sufficiently to say, "Dashed if I hadn't thought I must have offended you in some way, my lady, by talking of horses at the dinner table. Glad to know I haven't. Beg you will honor me with a dance later. A waltz, perhaps?"

A little startled by the result of her casual flirtation, Daintry agreed at once, then glanced back at Deverill to see to her chagrin that he was amused. Lifting her chin, she shifted her gaze down the table toward her sister.

Susan looked up from her plate, and Daintry, thinking she was looking at her, smiled, but her sister stared straight ahead, her gaze unfocused. Sir Geoffrey, farther down the table, was talking with Lady Catherine, but there was nothing in that, for husbands and wives rarely were seated next to each other at such parties. Charles was flirting outrageously with Miss Haversham, whom Daintry had met in London, and Davina was behaving in much the same way with a dandified gentleman whom she also recognized but whose name she could not at the moment recall.

After dinner, the ladies retired with Albinia Edgcumbe to the crimson drawing room, leaving the gentlemen to enjoy their port and what Daintry knew they would describe as intelligent conversation. The crimson drawing room was warm and comfortable with a cheerful fire blazing in its white-marble fireplace, and Albinia Edgcumbe was a comfortable woman of Lady Ophelia's generation who knew precisely how to involve her guests in amusing conversation. Nonetheless, Daintry noted that she was not the only one who glanced frequently at the door through which the gentlemen would come after they had imbibed enough port.

Lady Ophelia murmured under cover of the general chatter, "Do not look so impatient, my love. Sally is looking this way and is bound to misconstrue your lack of interest in this chitchat. Albinia will have made it clear to Mount Edgcumbe that he must not allow the gentlemen to linger over their wine."

Daintry, deciding that her great-aunt knew perfectly well she was on the watch for Deverill, collected her wits and said, "I do not know what it is about that man, ma'am, but I confess, he affects me in a way that no other gentleman has ever done."

"So I have noticed," Lady Ophelia said dryly. "Do not distress yourself, however, for I daresay it is nothing more than the lure of forbidden fruit, which will soon pass."

Much struck by the suggestion, Daintry wondered if it were possible that the strong attraction she felt for Deverill had its beginnings in nothing more than that. A second, even less palatable thought followed the first. "Is that why he pays heed to me, Aunt Ophelia, because I am forbidden fruit to him?"

"Very likely," was the placid response, "though it may be no more than habit with him, you know. He was, I am told, actually a member of Lord Hill's staff before Bonaparte escaped, and you know the sort of things they said about those young men."

"I do," Daintry said, her spirits sinking even more.

Thus, when the gentlemen entered a quarter-hour later, she had herself so well in hand that not even Lady Jersey, who was no doubt still watching closely, could have read anything untoward in her expression. The party adjourned soon after that for dancing in the large saloon at the rear of the house, and Daintry gladly accepted the invitation of her dinner partner for the opening set of country dances.

She had seen Deverill approaching, but she did not think he could accuse her of breaking her word to him, since she had said only that she would allow him a dance. She had not promised him any one in particular.

Susan was dancing with Lord Alvanley, a plump, rather witty member of the dandy set and a particular friend of Mr. Brummell, the man who had for a number of years fixed the standard for that set. Alvanley was a favorite of Daintry's, and she was glad to see him with Susan, for he would be certain to cheer her up.

When Sir Geoffrey claimed Daintry's hand for a cotillion, complimenting her on her lavender, lace-trimmed gown and generally behaving with all his customary gallantry and charm, she took advantage of a pause in the pattern to ask him if anything was amiss with his wife.

He smiled. "She is tired, I think. Traveling always exhausts her, and although we had only a short distance to come, and in a well-sprung carriage, she insisted upon taking the forward seat so my cousin would not be forced to ride with her back to the horses. It was generous of Susan, but I think that may be the reason she seems a trifle out of spirits now."

"Does Lady Catherine make a long stay with you, Geoffrey?" Daintry asked bluntly. "I thought she intended to go on to St. Ives, to visit other relations of hers."

"Oh, yes, she will certainly do so after Christmas," he said, "but Susan prevailed upon her to extend her visit to us. My poor little wife was not looking forward to being the lone adult female in the house again, as you might guess, after first enjoying the gaiety of a London Season and then a lengthy visit to Tuscombe Park. I am sure you must understand how she feels."

Daintry thought she did understand, and since, when Geoffrey escorted her back to Lady Ophelia, Deverill was standing beside her with a look of definite purpose in his eyes, she put Susan out of her mind altogether for the time being.

"My dance, I believe," he said as the band struck up the first waltz.

"Is it, sir?"

"It is," he said firmly, taking her hand in his.

His hands were large. Indeed, she thought, looking up at him, all of him seemed larger than she remembered. As he drew her onto the floor, she experienced a sudden, not unpleasant thrill of danger, and looking up at him, said, "Ought you not to have asked me first if I am permitted to waltz, sir?"

"I was under the impression that you do not seek permission for anything you wish to do. Was I mistaken?"

Twinkling, she said, "I am quite capable of making my own decisions, certainly, if that is your meaning, sir."

"It wasn't." But he smiled as he took her right hand in his left and, placing his right firmly in the small of her back, drew her closer. The commanding way he held her made her aware of his strength, not just of body but also of personality, and although she had danced the waltz many times in the few years since its acceptance in fashionable ballrooms, she had never before been so conscious of the vitality and penetrating warmth of her partner's touch. When her body responded with a spreading warmth of its own, she understood for the first time exactly why so many people still disapproved so strongly of the controversial dance.

As Deverill whirled her into the pattern of dancers, he murmured provocatively, "In my opinion, you simply have not yet been broken to bridle, but that day cannot be far off now."

Forcing herself to ignore the delicious sensations stirred by his touch and the sensual warmth of his voice, she looked up at him in what she hoped was a challenging manner and said, "Do you think I can be so easily mastered, sir? I warn you, I have yet to meet a man to whom I would willingly submit."

"Not yet?" He was looking directly into her eyes, his gaze holding hers hypnotically, daring her to look away. "Are you so certain of that, my lady?"

She swallowed, unable to look away, following his lead as automatically as Tender Lady followed Charley's Victor over a leap, without conscious awareness of her surroundings, her attention focused on her partner's face, not trusting her traitorous emotions any more than she trusted those she saw written on the countenance so disconcertingly near her own.

He chuckled, and discerning satisfaction in the sound, Daintry pulled away, the spell broken. "You hold me too closely, sir. It is not seemly and will be remarked upon."

"Very well," he murmured, relaxing his hold, "but you will not so easily escape your feelings, my dear, for you have met your match. You may believe that if you believe nothing else."

She could think of nothing worth replying to such an impudent statement, and decided to leave it to the future to prove his error to him. He was certainly more fascinating than the three other young men who had so fleetingly attached her interest, but he was entirely too sure of himself and deserved a sharp lesson for daring to challenge her in such a manner. It would serve him right if she flirted with him for a time, merely to amuse herself, and then snapped her fingers under his nose.

When he returned her to Lady Ophelia's side, she thanked him politely and turned away at once to look for Susan, having still had no opportunity to speak with her since her arrival. She spotted her at last nearby, talking with a friend, and to Daintry's fond eye, she appeared still tired and out of spirits. Excusing herself to her great-aunt, Daintry moved to join them.

Hugging her sister, she waited only until Susan's friend had moved away to speak to someone else before she said, "I have not even had a chance to say hello to you, and you did not so much as tell us you were coming to Mount Edgcumbe, you silly goose."

Susan smiled. "I did not know myself until a few days ago, and then it was all flurry and uproar to prepare. Geoffrey had got the invitation in Brighton and, just like any other man, had forgotten to mention it to me until Catherine chanced to do so. She had been invited, too, you see, but had cried off, thinking she would be in St. Ives. As soon as Geoffrey heard her say so, he insisted we must come. You may imagine my surprise."

"Yes, indeed, for he rarely brings you to such parties, but it is no wonder you look so fatigued. You ought to be in bed."

"Oh dear, do I look as bad as all that?"

"You do."

Susan laughed ruefully. "Only a sister would be so blunt. Very well, as soon as I can manage it without drawing attention to myself, I will retire."

"You will go now, my love, and no one will be the wiser, for I will go with you and anyone who notes our departure will simply think we have gone to the ladies' withdrawing room. By the time anyone chooses to wonder why we have not returned, they will no longer care. Unless, of course, you think we ought to tell Geoffrey," she added, looking toward the floor where Sir Geoffrey was dancing with a bright-eyed miss in a stunning pink gown.

Susan followed her gaze and shook her head. "Oh, no, I daresay he will not notice if I go now. We do not live in each other's pockets, after all, and Geoffrey enjoys this sort of entertainment much more than I do."

"Why, I thought it was he who disliked it," Daintry said in surprise as they made their way toward the door to the corridor. "You used to enjoy all manner of parties."

Even Susan's smile was tired. "I did, I suppose, in the old days. I daresay it is a sign of old age creeping up on me."

"Don't be nonsensical, and for heaven's sake don't go about saying such silly things to anyone else, or people will think you are sinking into a deep decline." They were on the stairs now.

"Don't scold," Susan said. "You sound like Davina."

Daintry smothered an improper exclamation. "If Davina has been scolding you, just tell her to mind her own affairs and leave you to yours. She is not your sister—well, only by law."

"It's all the same, for you both have a habit of telling me what I ought and ought not to do. No one considers my feelings in the least, Daintry. Doesn't anyone ever think about what I might want? Why does everyone insist he knows what is best for me when I am perfectly capable of deciding matters for myself?"

Hearing a note of near hysteria in her voice, Daintry ruthlessly repressed an urge to reply in kind, to tell her that no one was attempting to tell her what to do. Instead, as they approached Susan's bedchamber, she said calmly, "I know you are capable of anything. Are you not my big sister, the person to whom I so frequently go for her excellent advice?"

"Well, no," Susan said, but her eyes were twinkling now. "You go to Aunt Ophelia, of course, and have done so ever since I got married. You rarely even ride over to visit me anymore."

"You know very well it was Geoffrey's joking that I was underfoot all the time that made Papa forbid me to visit so frequently," Daintry said, opening the door to the bedchamber. "That was only at first, of course, but then somehow we all seemed to get out of the habit. Now that Charley and Melissa have become such friends though, I daresay you will see more of us in future." Finding Susan's maid awaiting her, she added, "You may go, Rosemary. I will attend to Lady Susan tonight."

As the door shut behind the maid, Susan sighed. "You see that, she did not so much as ask my permission to go."

"Don't be foolish, love. She has been acquainted with us both nearly all our lives and knows you would never contradict an order of my giving—at least, not while I stood beside you. You may be very certain she will be listening for your bell and will return in a trice if you want her. Do you?"

"No, but I wish . . . Oh, pay me no mind. I am—"

"You are exhausted," Daintry said, beginning to unfasten the row of buttons down the back of Susan's gown. As the gown fell open, she saw, above the lace edging of Susan's shift the dark shadow of a bruise. Clicking her tongue, she said, "What have you done to yourself this time?"

Susan laughed. "Nothing that will entertain you in the least, I assure you. Just my usual clumsiness, tripping over my own feet. I don't recall precisely what I did, but if it's the one on my shoulder, I believe I backed into my wardrobe at home. At all events, it is nothing. I can dress myself now if you have undone all those dreadful buttons."

"There is warm water waiting for you in the basin yonder, with a fresh towel, and your nightdress is laid out on the bed." Daintry said no more until Susan was tucked beneath the covers, but she had been thinking. Pulling the dressing chair up beside the bed when Susan was settled, she said, "Look here, is anything amiss? You really have not seemed at all yourself tonight."

"No, of course there is nothing—" She broke off when the door opened and Sir Geoffrey entered the room, the frowning look on his handsome face turning instantly to an anxious one.

"There you are, my love! I turned away for a moment, and when I turned back, you had disappeared into thin air." Grinning at Daintry, he said, "Did you abduct my wife, lovely sister-in-law, and carry her bodily off to bed? For I swear no one else could make the foolish child admit her exhaustion."

"I suppose I did carry her off," she said, smiling back at him and moving her chair to make room for him nearer the bed.

Susan sat up at once to put her arms around him when he sat on the bed, and he hugged her, still smiling at Daintry. "You have done her an excellent service, little sister. I am in your debt." He smoothed Susan's hair back from her face and kissed her gently on the lips, then said, "You did not plait your hair, sweetheart. It will be all tangles in the morning."

Daintry said, "I was sitting in her dressing chair, Geoffrey, and her hair never tangles very much, anyway. Rosemary will deal with it in the morning."

"Ah, but it will be better to attend to it now," he said, "and as it happens, I am an expert at such matters. Hand me her hairbrush there on the dressing table, will you, before you go?"

Accepting her dismissal, Daintry did as she was asked. As she handed him the silver-backed hairbrush, she smiled at Susan, who was blushing furiously and avoiding her gaze. "Very well, I can take a hint. I will see you in the morning, Susan."

"Late in the morning," Sir Geoffrey said.

Shaking her head in amusement, Daintry left them, and when she saw Susan the following day, though they scarcely had time to talk, she was impressed by the change in her spirits. Susan appeared to be much more cheerful. Her movements were animated, and her conversation was lively. It was, Daintry decided, a definite improvement. Clearly Geoffrey did have his moments.

The weather had not improved. Rain beat down steadily on Mount Edgcumbe's verdant gardens, so the entertainment was of a necessity limited to the confines of the house, but there was no lack of amusement. By day there were roles to be learned for amateur theatricals, and a host of indoor games to play. Rooms had been set aside for correspondence, reading, cards, or merely for conversation, and the evenings sparkled with the theatricals, as well as with musical performances and more dancing.

Daintry saw a good deal of Deverill in the course of these events, and she rapidly came to the conclusion that Lady Ophelia had been perfectly right in her assessment of his intentions. He had only to meet her gaze across a room to flirt with her, and if she was with someone else, he showed a flattering determination to cut out the other gentleman. It soon became clear that, like the capable soldier he was, he counted her as yet one more military objective to be achieved. Enjoying herself now, certain it would be only a matter of time before he betrayed himself, and knowing she would gain more by frustrating him a little than by seeming to leap like a hungry salmon to his lures, she forced herself to pay his attentions as little heed as possible.

When he asked her to dance, she made much of examining her program as if to be sure she could spare one for him. When he suggested a stroll in the long gallery to look at the pictures there, she declined on the grounds that such a stroll would be too remarkable to others. But on the fifth morning, when the sun came out at long last, and Daintry, rising early, entered the breakfast room to find Deverill there alone, dressed for riding, her spirits leapt with pleasure at the sight of him.

"I knew you would come," he said.

"How long have you been waiting?" she demanded.

He made a big thing of looking at his watch. "Two hours."

"You have not!"

"Perhaps only one then, but I was sure you would come down. I have ordered horses for us both."

"I have ordered my own horse, thank you."

"Do you think your order will provide you with as good a mount as mine will?" he asked lazily.

She knew the answer to that. Lord Mount Edgcumbe's people did not know her well, and no doubt would provide a meek and gentle ladies' mount for her, but if Deverill had ordered a more spirited animal, he would get it. And if she rode with him, she would not have to match her pace to a groom's or concern herself with whether the groom would report her to be a too-daring rider for a female, which was a thing that had been known to happen in the past when she visited houses where her skill was unknown.

As it was, she had risen early, hoping to enjoy a gallop without being forced to plod along with a party of ladies. Riding with Deverill would be much better than either course. So swallowing her lofty attitude, she smiled warmly at him and said, "I will not pretend to be ungrateful, sir, for I am very much obliged to you."

"Excellent," he said. "Very much obliged is exactly what I'd intended you should be."

Ten

Sunlight sparkled on the bright blue water of Plymouth Sound, and as they rode along the cliff edge toward Rame's Point, the view across the Channel was so clear that they could see not only the Eddystone Light but the distant, shadowy shoreline of France as well. A soft breeze blew wisps of Daintry's hair into her face, and the warmth of the sun touched her skin like a caress. High overhead, wispy white clouds floating on the breeze looked like white muslin gowns freed from a clothesline.

They rode silently for a time, enjoying the fresh sea air and the sounds of nature—the crying of the black-backed gulls and kittiwakes as they swooped and dove through the air overhead, the soft thuds of the horses' hooves on the sandy turf, the song of the sea drifting up from below, and the nearby chirping of birds in the garden shrubbery. For propriety's sake, one of the grooms accompanied them, riding a discreet distance behind.

Yellow gorse blossoms peeked cheerfully through the masses of dull bracken and bloomless heather that covered the cliff slopes, and away to their right the Mount Edgcumbe gardens gave way to scrub woodland, but the melody of the birds continued, accompanied occasionally by the scratchy chirp of a bush-cricket fooled by the warmth of the sun into thinking it was spring.

Daintry looked at her companion. He seemed utterly relaxed, not at all as if he had spent the past minutes wracking his brain for something clever to say, as she had done. He seemed content to ride in silence, and she wondered what it was about him that made her want to say something witty to impress him. The urge was a new one, for she rarely concerned herself with such things, assuming people she met would either like her or not like her as they chose, and not much troubled about it one way or the other. But with Deverill it was different. Even though he was, unfortunately, much like any other man, it had become a matter of importance that he continue to like her.

He looked at her and smiled, and she marveled again at the warmth of that smile, the way it fired a glow through her whole body. The corners of his golden eyes crinkled upward, making him look not only harmless but downright trustworthy, the sort of man to whom one could confide one's innermost thoughts. Had she not known that such men simply did not exist, she might well have been fooled by that look.

"A penny for your thoughts," he said suddenly.

"My thoughts are worth a great deal more than that, sir, but if you must know, I was wondering what life would be like in a world where one could say precisely what one thought without any concern for the consequences."

He grinned. "One can do so now, if one truly does not care about consequences."

Wrinkling her nose at him, she retorted, "You know that is not what I meant. I just think it would be gratifying to know one could speak one's mind without having one's opinions laughed at or dismissed as inconsequential."

Deverill was silent for a long moment, long enough that she wondered if she had somehow offended him, if he might be turning over previous conversations in his mind, searching his memory for something he might have done or said to make her think he had laughed at her or dismissed her opinions. Deciding it would be good for him to wonder, she held her tongue.

At last he said, "I suppose people often do such things to each other, although I hadn't thought about it before and certainly wouldn't have expected such concerns to silence you. In my experience, you say precisely whatever you want to say whenever you want to say it. Words just seem to tumble from your brain out through your mouth without so much as a pause for reflection along the way."

His tone was so matter-of-fact that she was not certain whether she had just been insulted or complimented, but decided it did not much affect the point at hand in either case.

"I have been raised to believe I might generally say what I please," she said, "but that is not by any means the same as knowing that what I say is respected. More often than not, when I speak to my father, my brother, or to Geoffrey, I am asked to repeat myself for the simple reason that they did not bother to listen to me the first time and only really acknowledged the fact that I had been speaking once I had finished. Can you imagine how infuriating that is, always to be asked to repeat oneself?"

He shook his head. "No, I doubt that I can, for I rarely am asked to repeat myself."

She nodded vigorously. "That is precisely what I mean. When you speak, people listen because the consequences of not listening can be most unpleasant. If my father fails to pay heed to my words, however, how unpleasant can the consequences be?"

He chuckled.

"It is *not* funny!"

"No, I do not suppose that it is, but I am sure you exaggerate the difficulty, and I know for a fact that you are complaining to the wrong person. I don't believe I have ever once asked you to repeat yourself."

Realizing that he was right and, moreover, that they had arrived at this point because she had not wanted to tell him exactly what she had been thinking in the first place, she decided she would be wiser to change the subject. Smiling sunnily she said, "You are perfectly right, sir, and I apologize for leading you to believe I was accusing you of any such thing. Have you managed to learn any more about our dreadful feud?"

He replied as if he were perfectly accustomed to abrupt turns of conversation, "I have not, but not from lack of trying. Not only have I begun a search of our family papers but I also asked my father for information; however, he snubbed me, making it clear that to press for answers would prove not only fruitless but would seriously annoy him, something I try never to do."

"Goodness, do you fear your father, sir? I should never have guessed it."

Deverill chuckled. "You've never met him, so I cannot think why you might expect to guess what he is like, but I assure you, I do not fear him. I just make it a point not to annoy him."

"But this matter is an important one. We can do nothing to mend the rift if we do not know what harm was done at the start."

"Do you want to mend the rift?" he asked gently.

"You know I do." Seeing the warm look in his eyes again, she added hastily, "It is most uncomfortable being at odds with one's neighbor, and I can see no good cause to continue a feud that has no known cause. It's plain silly, sir."

He nodded thoughtfully. "I agree, it seems that way, but of course, we do not know for a fact that our respective sires are not well aware of such details as would explain it perfectly and are simply refusing to tell us. Have you asked St. Merryn?"

"Of course I have, but he will tell me nothing. And my Aunt Ophelia, who knew both my grandfather and yours, insists she knows nothing at all about what caused them to quarrel."

"She knew them both well?"

"Well enough that both of them proposed marriage to her."

"But does she not keep a journal? I seem to recall her speaking of one when we discussed the weather the other day."

"Yes, she does keep one."

"Then, perhaps she would allow you to read it, or would take some time to read it over herself," he suggested.

"But what purpose would that serve?"

"I should think that would be obvious," Deverill said. "If something occurred between them, and if she knew them both, surely she must have noted it down in her journal at the time."

"But she has said she knew nothing about it."

"It was a long time ago." His tone was patient. "She is elderly. She might well have forgotten."

Daintry laughed, then said contritely, "I beg your pardon. It is most unfair to laugh at you, but although you have had the pleasure of meeting my great-aunt, you cannot know her yet if you can believe she would have forgotten such a thing, or indeed anything at all. She has a most remarkable memory, sir, not just for her age, but for any age whatsoever."

"I see." His expression was enigmatic for a moment, but then he seemed to shake himself, and he said, "I believe that making your acquaintance is going to prove a salutary experience for me, for I recall now that I once knew precisely what it is like to have one's opinions dismissed as inconsequential. Both my father and my brother, Jack, once made a habit of deflating all my pretensions. When Jack left Eton things became different there, of course, and in the Army, I soon had my own command, so I am no longer accustomed to being put so firmly in my place."

Seeing no point to be gained by trying to make him see that he had just equated the general treatment of women by men with the treatment of children by adults, she said only, "I know one should not speak ill of the dead, sir, but your brother does not sound like he was a very kind man."

He smiled. "No, 'kind' is not a word one would apply to Jack. He was a sportsman and thought himself the devil of a fellow, especially after my father came into the title. Jack couldn't wait to be Marquess of Jervaulx. I certainly never thought to find myself in his shoes, and I'm not at all sure I like it, for it's as if my life had abruptly shifted course, almost as if I had suddenly ceased to be myself and become another person altogether." Straightening in his saddle and giving himself another one of those odd shakes she had noted before, he said, "There's a long straight stretch ahead. Shall we gallop them?"

In reply, Daintry lowered her hands, leaned forward, and touched her mount with spur and whip. The spirited bay gelding Deverill's order had provided for her gathered itself and leapt forward, settling rapidly into a smooth pace that covered the distance with speed. She had caught Deverill off guard with her quick reaction, but it was not long before he drew up alongside her, his big gray horse easily keeping pace with the bay.

She was reminded of the first time she had seen him on horseback when she had thought that he and Shadow moved as if they were mentally and physically one. Now, his grinning face and laughing eyes showed that he loved riding as much as she did.

To gallop was exhilarating, but soon there were woods ahead, their edges bare and weatherworn where the winds from the sea had battered them, the dim interior filled with elder, ash, sycamore, and hawthorn trees, their trunks wrapped in bryony and the clinging ivylike stuff known as broomrape. As they passed beneath the first branches, Daintry slackened the gelding's pace, and the gray slowed beside her. Minutes later they were deep in the woods, where the air was cooler, though still not chilly. The path was easily wide enough for them to ride abreast, and firm enough underfoot to let the horses canter until they came to a wide stream, where they slowed again to a walk.

About to urge her horse into the stream, Daintry caught sight of two swans displaying in a nearby sunlit pool, and reined in instead to watch. Like mirror images, the birds stretched their necks upward, then curved them and dipped their heads under the water before repeating the movements. They were magnificent, like sensuous dancers, and she watched, mesmerized, scarcely noting that Deverill had drawn up the gray beside her.

The dance continued, the swans teasing each other, then moving in unison. After several minutes, they added the rubbing of their sides with their beaks and heads to the first movements, moving faster and faster till finally they were touching each other. Then, possessively, the cob put his neck over the pen's when he immersed his head. Shortly after that he mounted her, and when it was over, they both seemed to stand right up in the water, facing each other, rubbing heads affectionately.

Daintry said quietly, "It is intriguing to see how much interest they show in one another after mating. So many birds part immediately afterwards and just fly away."

"People, too," Deverill said in an oddly strained tone.

Glancing at him, she saw that he was not watching the swans. He was watching her, and the look in his eyes brought heat to her cheeks. She could not look away. "Swans," she said in a voice not at all like her own, "mate for life, you know."

"Do they?" He was still watching her, his expression making her unusually conscious of his nearness. The woods were silent.

"Yes." She licked suddenly dry lips. "Yes, they do."

The groom behind them coughed, reminding them of his presence, and Deverill said in a normal tone, "Although that pool is warm and sunny, this is certainly not spring. What do they think they are about to be mating in the middle of October?"

Recovering with more difficulty than he had seemed to experience, she said, "Aunt Ophelia calls it bonding behavior, a renewal of their loyalty to each other. We have a number of swans on the river at Tuscombe Park, and they molt in July, August, and September, you see, so in October they . . ."

"I do see," he said quickly, turning the gray's head and urging it across the stream. Flashing a look over his shoulder, he said, "You really are an amazing young woman."

"Nonsense, I am perfectly ordinary." She followed him, bringing the gelding alongside the gray.

Deverill's eyes glinted. "A perfectly ordinary girl would have blushed and gone all fluttery, coming upon that little scene, and would undoubtedly have sputtered a great deal of nonsense at me about how we ought to ride on very quickly."

"Oh." She thought about that. "I suppose you may be right. Many people nowadays would think it improper for me to watch swans mating, I suppose, let alone to watch them in the presence of an unmarried gentleman, but Aunt Ophelia has always said such prudish behavior is ridiculously missish and absurd."

"Quite so," he said. His eyes were twinkling now. "Have you no sense of propriety, Lady Daintry?"

"Of course I have. I just do not happen to agree that watching an act of nature is improper."

He chuckled. "I would like very much to put that to the test, but I have a strong feeling that the act of nature I have in mind is not one that you would include in that declaration."

She knew she was blushing, because she could feel the fire of it in her cheeks, but she did not want to give him the satisfaction of knowing how greatly he had discomfited her. Managing to look him straight in the eye, she said evenly, "No doubt, when you were a member of Lord Hill's staff, you found seduction to be a lively game as natural to you as breathing, sir, and looked upon the females you knew at the time as no more than quarries to be hunted; however, I am not such easy prey. You will have the goodness to remember that, Deverill."

To her annoyance, he chuckled and said, "You are almost as skilled with words as you are with a horse, my dear, and if you will permit me to tell you so, you have the finest seat—"

"If you say 'for a female,' sir, I will hit you."

"I am afraid that is just what I was going to say, but perhaps I can make a small recovery by pointing out that it is hard to compare you with, say, the men of my brigade—or other men for that matter—when you ride sidesaddle and they do not."

"If you think riding sidesaddle is one bit easier—"

"I don't. Good God, to tell the truth, I don't know how you women stay on those things, and when I watched your little nieces jumping timber and even thinking of jumping stone walls, it turned me cold with terror one moment and filled me with awe the next. I doubt that I could do it without considerable practice, and I am thought by most to be an expert in the saddle."

"You could do it easily. It is all a matter of balance, you know, nothing more."

"Oh, certainly. I remember when you said those two children learned to ride without so much as holding the reins or putting their feet in the stirrups. Something about handkerchiefs and bits of paper, too. I thought you were quite mad."

"Well, I wasn't. That is how they were trained. Charley can ride sitting on a handkerchief and never lose it, and Melissa is nearly as skilled. I taught them both, you know, and," she added with a challenging look, "I can teach you to do it as well, if you really want to learn."

"That will be quite enough of that, you little cat."

"Coward."

Deverill stiffened, then looked straight at her with an uncharacteristic look of indecision on his face. They had emerged from the woods and were once again riding on the sandy grass, their path leading toward a timber gate in a hedged field. Beyond it the garden hedges of Mount Edgcumbe could be seen, and she saw him look toward the house, the windows of which were perfectly visible now. He looked back at her.

"I dare you," she said provocatively.

His lips twitched as if he was suppressing laughter, and he relaxed. "You don't believe I can do it. Confess now, you simply hope to watch me make a fool of myself."

"On the contrary, I am perfectly certain that you *can* do it, but I also believe that it will teach you to have more respect for women who ride well, particularly for those of us who hunt."

He looked intrigued. "Do I ride your horse, or do we attempt to put your sidesaddle on mine?"

"You ride mine," she said, surprised but oddly pleased. "That way you can't blame the horse if you do fail."

"You misjudge me," he said, dismounting. "I should never employ so paltry an excuse for my own failure."

Chuckling, she waited until he had tossed his reins to the astonished groom, then allowed him to help her down. His hands at her waist were a minor distraction, his nearness a worse one, but she managed to ignore both and keep her mind on the lesson at hand. When he moved to the gelding, she said quickly, "Before you mount, there are certain things you should know."

"Patience, my dear. I am merely going to adjust the leathers for my longer legs. That saddle," he added, eyeing it askance, "is too big and too cluttered up with pommels and such."

"You will get used to them, and you will be glad of its greater size. Are you ready?"

He looked back at the groom. "One word of this, my man, to anyone, and I will see you get turned off without a character."

The groom grinned at him. "Do you require assistance to mount, my lord?"

"I do not. Speak your piece, worthy instructress."

"Very well. There is nothing at all odd about mounting, but instead of beginning with your left hand on the pommel, as you are accustomed to do, you must use your right. Your reins and whip must be in your right hand, too," she added.

Deverill gave her a speaking look. "My dear girl, I have no skirt to manage, and I am perfectly capable of climbing onto that saddle without the aid of a groom's shoulder. It's what I am to do after I get there that concerns me."

She watched doubtfully, but he was right, and she envied him the ease with which he put his left foot in the stirrup and still managed to slip his right leg past it into the proper position to lift himself onto the saddle. He grimaced as he pressed his left knee into place, and she recalled that the leaping horn had been specially fitted to her much less muscular leg, but a moment later he was settled, looking only a little uncomfortable.

He called the groom to adjust the leathers again, and Daintry held the man's horse and the gray while he did so. When she saw him hide a smile, she glared, and he sobered at once.

Even knowing Deverill to be highly skilled, she was astonished at how easily he managed the strange saddle and how quickly he found his balance. She had only to tell him to keep his left knee firmly in the angle between pommel and saddle flap, with his thigh and calf close to saddle and stirrup leather.

"Don't just hook your right leg over the pommel, Deverill. Sit well back on the saddle with your shoulders square to the front and press down from hip to knee until your leg is as close to the saddle as possible. One rises from the right knee, so it is essential that the leg below the knee be held as firmly against the horse as the left one is."

"This is not so easy as I thought," he said, grimacing.

"You ought by rights to be wearing a skirt."

The look he cast her that time sent a shiver up her spine, and she knew Susan had been right to say she would be unwise to anger him, but the look was gone in an instant. He said only, "I think not, thank you. How on earth do you ride with half your body facing one direction and the other half facing another?"

"Really, it is not so different from the way men ride. You are making far too much of having both feet on one side of the horse. One simply shifts one's weight so that it is evenly distributed. That's it exactly," she added, when he made a minor adjustment in his position.

In what seemed to her to be only moments, he looked as if he had ridden sidesaddle all his life. First he walked the gelding in circles, then urged it to a trot, nearly unseating himself before he grew accustomed to rising from his right leg, but not long after that he was riding easily. He grinned at her.

A shout from the direction of the woods caught them both off guard, for so absorbed had they become in the lesson that the intruders were upon them before they saw them coming. Daintry turned, stifling a groan of dismay when she recognized her brother-in-law and Susan, Lady Catherine, Lord and Lady Jersey, Lord Alvanley, and her brother, Charles. Casting a glance back at Deverill, she saw that he was still grinning at her.

Seacourt, riding up first and reining in with a flourish, shouted, "What the devil are you doing here, my dear Daintry?"

"We went riding, Geoffrey, and Deverill decided to see what it was like to ride a sidesaddle, that's all."

"You ought not to be here alone with him," Seacourt said, eyeing her with disapproval. "Your father will be most displeased to learn of this, will he not, Charles?"

"He will," Charles said unhappily, not looking at Daintry.

"Only if someone is mean-spirited enough to tell him," Daintry said. "I am not alone with him, after all. The groom has been with us every moment." Remembering the brief period before the man had rejoined them at the stream, she salved her conscience with the fact that nothing had happened.

Lady Jersey, looking from one rider to another, said, "My goodness me, I do not think anyone here would carry tales even if there were any to carry, which in view of the groom's presence, there cannot be. I daresay even the most finicking patroness of Almack's would not look askance at a lady and a gentleman riding through an open field in the company of the lady's groom. But pray, why are you riding Daintry's horse, Deverill? I will most obligingly pretend not to see that sidesaddle."

Seacourt laughed. "Well, I certainly will not be so obliging, for this tale is far too rich not to be repeated. What an ass you are, Deverill, to put yourself in such a ridiculous position, let alone to allow yourself to be found out."

Deverill's eyes glinted with that look of danger Daintry had come to recognize. "Ridiculous, is it? Have you ever tried to ride with a sidesaddle, Seacourt?"

"Don't be stupid. Of course I have never done such a ridiculous thing."

"Then do not be so quick to condemn it. I'll wager anything you like, within reason, that you cannot stay on one."

"Good God, if a *woman* can stay on one, of course I can!"

"Would you care to put money on that statement?"

Seacourt laughed again. "I see how it is. You merely want someone else to look as ridiculous as you do."

Lady Jersey's tinkling laughter rang out. "Do you think it is truly so easy as all that, Sir Geoffrey? I am here to tell you, it is not. Is it, Susan?"

"Oh, I am certain Geoffrey could do it easily," Susan said, smiling at her husband. "He is a very fine rider, you know."

"Of course, he could," Lady Catherine said, adding with a teasing look at Seacourt. "Geoffrey can ride anything."

Sally laughed again. "As you say, my dear, but not on a sidesaddle. Alvanley, have you ever ridden on a sidesaddle?"

"Not on purpoth, Thally," the plump little dandy lisped. "Not on purpoth. There wath one time when the thaddle thlipped. I believe the animal—or, no, it wath me—had had too much wine and failed to tighten the girth properly. But otherwithe, no, I have not. But I'd like to watch Theacourt attempt it."

When the laughter had faded, Deverill said, "Well, Seacourt? I'll wager a monkey that you cannot trot this horse twice round the field without either losing control of it or falling off."

With the others urging him to take Deverill's five hundred pounds, Seacourt, his face reddening, said, "Very well, I suppose I must show you all how easy it is. Good God, my little daughter rides one of those things. How difficult can it be?"

Deverill jumped down and handed him the reins. When Daintry moved forward to tell Sir Geoffrey what he should do, Deverill said quietly, "He knows all about it, my dear. There can be no need to offer him assistance."

Seacourt, hearing him, shot him a look of disdain. "What, take direction from a female? I should say I don't need any such thing.

Stand back, Daintry," he added as he hoisted himself into the saddle. His attempt was not so smooth as Deverill's, but he accomplished it easily enough, finding difficulty only when he tried to settle himself. The gelding fidgeted nervously, dancing and refusing to stand as quietly as it had with Deverill. Seacourt held onto the pommel, trying to get his knee around it, clearly finding the position an awkward one.

Lady Catherine said, "Hold the reins in both hands, Geoffrey, not one. "You will find it easier to sit properly."

And Susan said, "Sit back a little farther, Geoffrey. You forget you are accustomed to a much smaller saddle."

"I am doing perfectly well on my own, ladies, thank you," he said, his tone grim.

Deverill glanced at Daintry, his amusement clear, and she held her tongue, waiting for the inevitable. Geoffrey deserved his fate. He still had not found his balance, for he was too far forward in the saddle just as Susan had said, and his weight was too much to the left. It was a common error, easily corrected, but if Geoffrey did not want correction, who was she to offer it?

He was using the stirrup to balance himself, a thing she was certain he would never do riding astride, and he managed to get the gelding to walk, then to trot, but he had not the least notion of how to rise, and the gait nearly unseated him. Reining the horse in, he tried again, not looking at anyone now, and ignoring the good advice Lady Jersey and the others offered him. When the gelding began to trot again, he sawed on the reins with his left hand and hit it with the whip in his right. Daintry cried out to him to use only the reins but it was too late. The gelding reared, and Seacourt, already off his balance with his left leg nowhere near the horn, tumbled over backwards and landed on the sandy grass with a thud that knocked the wind out of him.

The groom leapt to help him up, but Sir Geoffrey, still holding the reins and recovering quickly, snatched up the whip and moved purposefully toward the gelding.

Deverill intercepted him. "I think not," he said calmly. "It was not any fault in the animal that caused you to fall."

Seacourt looked at him angrily but did not argue. Thrusting the reins at him, he snapped, "I've no money on me now. You'll have to wait." Then, striding to his horse, he snatched the reins from Alvanley, mounted, and rode off at a gallop without waiting for the rest of his party.

Watching him jump the gate in the hedge surrounding the next field, Lady Jersey shook her head. "My goodness me, but men are sensitive. You must go after him, Susan dear, and soothe his lacerated feelings. The soft, comforting touch of a female, you know, can work wonders on the beasts. Only ask Jersey if that is not true." She grinned saucily at her husband, then cried, "Come on, everyone! We will go tell Seacourt that Deverill was quite mistaken. The horse is clearly a brute." And with a last tinkle of laughter, she rode after Seacourt, followed by her husband.

Susan had been staring at Deverill as if she were not certain what to make of him, but now, looking down at Daintry in disapproval, she said, "How could you let him do such a thing to poor Geoffrey? I am most displeased with you." And on these words, she rode after the others.

Daintry turned to Lady Catherine, who had said nothing at all since Sir Geoffrey's fall. "Are you angry with me, too?"

"Good heavens, no. Why should I be angry? Geoffrey will be in a pet, of course, but there are any number of others to talk to, and even to dance with. Geoffrey's moods are nothing to me, I'm sure. Charles, Alvanley, shall we join the others or remain here to play propriety to these two?"

Alvanley, exchanging a look with Deverill, said, "We will go on, I think, Lady Catherine."

Deverill said to the groom, "You ride on, too. Lady Daintry and I will follow soon enough, and since we are in plain view of the house, I think I can assure you I will do her no harm."

The groom looked at Daintry, and though she wondered why Deverill was sending him away, she nodded, whereupon he handed the gray's reins to Deverill, mounted his own horse, and rode off in the wake of the others.

Watching them go and not at all certain what to expect next, Daintry hesitated even to look at Deverill. Suddenly she felt vulnerable and isolated, as though she were being abandoned. At the same time, she was only too well aware of his presence. She thought that so strong was his personality and his intrinsic determination to dominate her that she would be aware of his nearness even if she had not known he was there.

"Will Seacourt try to make trouble for you?"

The gravity in his voice made her turn at last. "I don't know," she confessed. "He has never done so before."

"He lives very near you, after all."

"Yes, but he does not visit. Even Susan does not visit often. We see more of her in London than we do during the rest of the year. We invite them, of course, and although the distance by road from Seacourt Head is absurdly long, it is much shorter to ride around the bay, and I was used to visit them frequently. From some cause or other, the habit died, but as I told Susan, now that Charley and Melissa have become friends, I daresay we will visit more frequently. In any event, as you see, I doubt that Geoffrey will carry tales of me to my father."

"He will not have to carry tales. Your brother saw as much as he did." He moved nearer. He was standing right in front of her now, looking down at her.

"Charles won't say anything," she murmured, looking at the middle button of his waistcoat. She let her gaze drift upward past his broad shoulders and strong chin to his face. His jaw was taut. His lips were pressed together in a straight line, but as she watched, they softened. His nostrils flared. His eyes—

She saw his intent, but it was too late to stop him. Later she would ask herself, more than once, why she did not resist, but at that moment, caught in his strong embrace, it did not occur to her to do so. And when his lips touched hers, she dropped the reins she was holding, put her arms around his neck, and pressed her body against his, savoring the sensations that coursed through her, delighting in his taste, his strength, and the way his kisses sent hot flames rushing through her veins.

She was aware of his hands moving over her body, caressing her, pulling her closer, and she knew she ought not to allow such liberties, but she did not want to stop him. No other man had ever dared treat her to such a display of passion, not the men to whom she had been betrothed, or any other. Then, as if her body had taken command of her good sense, her lips suddenly parted beneath his, and she could feel him tasting her, exploring her mouth with his tongue. She had not known such sensations existed, had never suspected that a man might wish to learn what the inside of a woman's mouth tasted like. But without giving the matter another thought, she pressed her tongue against his, teasing him, then pushing his tongue away so that she might thrust hers between his strong white teeth, to learn why—

Deverill set her back on her heels with a thud that jarred her entire spine, and looked down at her in consternation.

"Either you've had more experience than I thought, sweetheart, or I am the worst scoundrel unhung." He drew a ragged breath. "Damn, I deserve to be flogged."

Staring at him, paying little heed to his words, she wondered what on earth had possessed her to submit to his embrace in such a wanton manner, particularly when—not an hour before—she had declared herself more than a match for him. A lowering reflection, to be sure, since not only had she submitted, she had responded. But more lowering still was the undeniable awareness that she very much wanted him to do it again.

Eleven

Gideon was silent on the way back to the stables, and he was glad that Daintry made no effort to draw him into conversation, for he needed to think. The guilt that had nearly overwhelmed him as a result of her instant response to his kisses was a new experience for him. Having had little to do with innocent young ladies in his years on the Continent, and accustomed as he was to casual flirtations with women who understood the rules of the game as well as he did, he had been completely unprepared to meet with such passion. He realized that he had begun to relax with her in the same way he had with his more experienced friends, and in his wish to prove he could overcome her independence, he had in fact taken base advantage of her innocence.

Escorting her back to the house, he kept up a flow of small talk, hoping to avoid any discussion of what had occurred until he had had time to sort out his feelings. She seemed to have withdrawn, and he was sorry for that. If he were any sort of a decent fellow, he would apologize for the whole and let her think he had simply let his detested male urges get the better of him. The problem was, he didn't think it had much to do with basic urges. It had seemed so natural to kiss her, not a game at all. Lord knew, he had wanted to do it since the day Penthorpe showed him her miniature. But what kind of a fellow would he be to try to attach her interest before he had sorted out his own life?

The damned feud was the least of his worries. Before Jack's death it might well have been a major impediment, but he could not believe that even St. Merryn would deny his daughter the opportunity to become a marchioness. Jervaulx would prove more of an obstacle if the feud were not laid to rest, but if worse came to worst he was of age and could do as he liked. Still, to offer for any young woman before he had come to terms with his place in the new order of things would be unfair, and in truth, he was not ready to put his belief that she cared for him to the test. He had seen enough of her to know that she would not let herself be led by any mere physical attraction to believe she was madly in love. She blew hot and cold, and he thought it would be far wiser to scout the territory ahead with care before he committed all his resources to an uncertain victory.

They parted in the entry hall, and he spent the afternoon riding out with a shooting party. At dinner, he was seated again beside Sally, whom he knew from her visits to the Continent during the peace celebrations before Bonaparte's escape and to Brussels before Waterloo, and whose flirtatious manner amused him. When the dancing began, he made a point of searching out another old acquaintance for the first set. Later, he danced twice with Daintry but saw by the distant look in her eyes that she was holding herself aloof, and, understanding that she was protecting herself, he made no effort to break down her shell.

Daintry was mystified by her own behavior and not a little confused by Deverill's. The incident in the field had caught her off her guard, for she had never expected to react to any man's kisses in such a passionate way, and she had spent the afternoon trying to make sense of what made no sense at all.

He had kissed her as if he really cared about her, but when she responded, he had stopped and had even talked as if he wished he had not done it. Well, she too wished it had never happened, or if not that precisely, at least that it had not affected her the way it had. Clearly he had singled her out for conquest and then had experienced second thoughts once he suspected that she might be developing strong feelings for him. And thanks to her faithless passions, she had behaved like a fool.

He had certainly proved he could stir those passions as no man had ever done before. But did she have feelings for him, or was she being fooled by her own love of a challenge and the lure of forbidden fruit into suspecting she had them?

Dinner brought a reminder of his past when he flirted outrageously with Sally Jersey—whose husband clearly lived under the cat's paw—and afterward he had asked several other women to dance before he had asked her. Moreover, when they danced, he had treated her with extreme civility. Had he already gained what he wanted from her? Had he wanted only to prove he could attach her interest, and now wanted nothing more to do with her?

She looked for Susan but did not see her, although she saw Sir Geoffrey dance with several women, including his cousin. He seemed to be behaving with all his customary charm again, but Daintry was not even tempted to ask him about Susan, for she was certain he would enjoy nothing so much, after his humiliating afternoon, as to snub her soundly.

She went up to her bedchamber earlier than had been her habit at Mount Edgcumbe, stopping along the way to bid good-night to Lady Ophelia in the card room, and to tap at Susan's bedchamber door. There was no response, and when she tried the door handle and found it locked, she decided her sister must have also decided to retire early.

The following morning, although she and the other members of her family were ready to depart early, they discovered that the Seacourts had gone even earlier. There was no sign of Deverill either, and as the carriage rolled away down the gravel drive, Daintry fought to keep from looking back at the house in hopes of catching a glimpse of him. Instead, she looked across the bay, at Plymouth, where rays of sunlight through gray clouds gathering overhead glistened on marble buildings and slate roofs, making the town look as if it had been frosted with snow.

As their journey progressed, Daintry waited for Davina to mention the previous day's incident, even to scold her for allowing Deverill to single her out in such a manner for his attention, but Davina was uncharacteristically silent, replying in monosyllables to those conversational gambits initiated by Daintry or Lady Ophelia. She had not even objected to taking the forward seat, which she generally disdained to occupy, deeming it fit only for servants, children, or Daintry.

Charles rode alongside the carriage, and even when it began to drizzle some distance from Tuscombe Park, he insisted that he preferred to ride. Daintry thought there must have been a falling-out between her brother and his wife, but she was too preoccupied with her own affairs to think much about theirs.

The more she thought, the more confused she became, but one perception stood out from the rest, that so long as she continued to wonder if Deverill's interest in her stemmed from the fact that he was forbidden to approach her—or if her interest in him might stem from that same fact—there could be no progress in their relationship. Thus, the feud was now an encumbrance that must be removed. But if she could disarm it, what then?

It was possible, of course, that she might discover their attraction to be a mutual and lasting one; however, it was more likely, particularly in view of his past and the faults she had already discerned in him, that the same whimsy of fate that had resulted in three broken engagements would cast its shadow again. In any event, she decided, staring out at the mist swirling down from the moor to envelop the carriage, if she were to keep her distance and concentrate on resolving the mystery of the feud, she would be giving her thoughts a more proper direction, and although Deverill might continue to view her as an objective, at least the path to the future would be less cluttered.

Abruptly, she said to Lady Ophelia, "Have you kept a journal all your life, ma'am?"

The old lady had been watching the descent of the mist outside the window. Turning, she said, "Not my entire life, certainly. One generally does not attempt such things until one has been released from one's leading strings."

"You know perfectly well what I meant. When did you begin?"

"Oh, I suppose I must have been about Charlotte's age when I first decided to keep a journal. Mostly foolishness then, what I wrote, but very earnest and self-important. I had not yet come to realize at that time that my prospects for a brilliant future were limited. I have no particular gift for writing, so I did not aspire to become a second Eliza Haywood or Fanny Burney."

"But you tell stories as delightful as theirs, ma'am. It seems a great pity that more people cannot enjoy them."

"They would not be the same written down. I talk better than I write, for I am able to judge the effect by watching my listener's face. When one writes, one must hope one's readers understand, and I never had much faith in them. Indeed, that is one thing I always admired in Harriet Deverill. She had no gift either, you know, nothing that made her work stand out or even that made anyone desire to publish it—and of course Tom Deverill would not—but she did try. I became a student instead, and should have done very well at Oxford, I expect, had it occurred to anyone to allow me to enter there."

Daintry chuckled at the thought of her formidable aunt assailing the hallowed gates of Oxford University, but she did not want to dwell on that topic. Gently, she said, "Would you object if I read your journals? I know I would be fascinated."

The old lady's eyes narrowed but there was amusement, not displeasure, in her expression. "I suspect, you have no interest in the earlier journals, miss, merely in the ones beginning before, oh, let us say sixty or so years ago?"

Daintry could feel warmth in her cheeks but she said firmly, "I would be honored if you would let me begin at the beginning and read every single one, Aunt Ophelia, but I will not conceal from you the fact that I hope to find a clue to the roots of that ridiculous feud somewhere within them."

"You won't do it," Lady Ophelia said flatly. "How can there be a clue when I never knew the least thing about it? Men do not confide in their wives, let alone in the women they only hoped to wed. Whatever it was that set those two at odds, it was nothing that they confided to me.

"But still, Aunt, I might learn something about the men themselves, don't you think? You must have written down your impressions of them."

"Oh, yes, I am quite sure to have done that," Lady Ophelia said, chuckling. "Nincompoops, the both of them." She hesitated, then said, "My journals are reservoirs of my private thoughts, you know. I never meant them to be made public."

"Nor would I do such a thing," Daintry said indignantly. "You know I would not. I do understand that I am asking leave to invade your privacy, ma'am. Pray, if you do not like it, say no more. I shall not take offense."

She meant it, but when her great-aunt made no effort to continue the conversation, she found it difficult not to demand to know if she did not trust her. Later she was glad she had held her tongue, however, for that evening when she was preparing for bed, Lady Ophelia came to her, wrapped in a flowing robe of sky blue wool, and carrying two slim volumes beneath her arm.

"These are my journals for the year of my come-out and the one following it, the years I first came to know Lord Thomas Deverill and your grandfather. As you will see, they figured no more prominently than a dozen other gentlemen. I was," she added, lifting her chin, "rather a popular young woman."

"I do not doubt it, ma'am."

"Well, it was due only to my vast inheritance, I can tell you, for I doubt I ever met a new acquaintance without hearing the amount whispered by someone nearby, and I know for a fact that there were wagers made in the London gentlemen's clubs on a weekly basis, as to whom I would choose. But, thanks to Papa and Sir Lionel Werring, I fooled them all," she said placidly. "Your grandfather thought Papa was crazy, for he could never believe any woman capable of managing her own money. He coveted it in the worst way and was always giving me advice that I did not want or need. Years later, of course, he saw that it would be far easier for him—or for his son, I suppose—to manage your mama."

Lady Ophelia did not linger, and Daintry, shooing Nance out the door as soon as she was dressed for bed, opened the first volume. But within an hour, she had come to the conclusion that her great-aunt was right. The journals would be of little help in her quest for information about the feud.

The writing was detailed, but its focus was not the social world or even the personalities of people her aunt had met. The journals had formed an outlet instead for her feelings about a society that wanted its women to be silent and decorative, and that denied them even the simplest of the rights it granted to men. There were frequent references to novels written by women of the mid-eighteenth century, novels that Daintry knew were scarcely ever read by young women of the present day.

She had read most of the books, though had her father ever read them, he would have forbidden her to do so. Their heroines did not behave in the manner now expected of a young lady of quality. Closing the first journal and blowing out her candle, she lay back against her pillows and tried to imagine Eliza Haywood's once famous heroine, Miss Betsy Thoughtless, stepping across the threshold at Almack's or being accepted by members of the *beau monde* into their homes.

She failed, for despite the fact that Betsy had been shown the error of her thoughtless ways and, after many adventures, had married Mr. Trueworth, Miss Haywood's boldly expressed views of such sexual and social concerns as abortion, divorce, and marriage laws, not to mention the double standards governing men's and women's behavior, simply did not bear discussion in most polite gatherings of the present day. Indeed, as Daintry knew well, the so-called polite behavior of even *twenty* years before—when men and women had been more outspoken than they were now—was now thought to have been remarkably uncivil.

It took her nearly a week, reading whenever she found time to do so—frequently in a small unused back parlor, so as to remain undisturbed—to finish the two volumes and learn that although the particular information she sought was not there, Lady Ophelia had described the two gentlemen, albeit briefly, in just the manner one might have expected. Deverill's grandfather she had liked well enough, while deploring his politics. He was a follower of Tobias Smollett, who believed in retaining a strong monarchy, undermining Parliament, and using citizens like pawns in a chess game. According to Lady Ophelia, Tom Deverill, while professing to love her, had seen himself as a monarch and her as a woman to be mastered. Daintry decided that if old Deverill had truly been the man her great-aunt described, he must certainly have been infatuated ever to have considered marrying her.

She wondered if the present Deverill saw her in the same way his grandfather had seen Lady Ophelia. Remembering that he had said she needed breaking to bridle, she rather thought that was the case, though she doubted that he was infatuated with her.

Lady Ophelia had dismissed the fourth Earl of St. Merryn even more flatly as a man who cared only for money, who counted her dowry in his mind as he prated sweet nothings in her ear. From the succinct notations of the social events she had attended, Daintry realized her great-aunt had been extremely active during both London Seasons covered by the journals, but since she had hoped to read lovely gossipy bits about the famous people of that time, she was sadly disappointed.

Closing the second volume at last and setting it aside, she wondered if there was any point in reading another, and decided there was not. Her time would be better spent, she decided, attempting to compile a list of those persons most likely to know anything about the feud, whom she might question. Nance entered the little parlor while she was considering these possibilities.

"Miss Charley is looking for you, my lady."

Daintry smiled. "And, being Charley, I suppose she has got every servant in the house searching high and low for me."

Nance chuckled. "That she has. Says she has leave from that new governess of hers and wants to ride over to Seacourt Head to visit Miss Melissa, and she's that certain you will go that she's already ordered the horses saddled. Shall I go up with you to fetch out your habit?"

"Yes, please," Daintry said, getting up and putting away her list, "but first, tell me something, Nance. Do you know anyone hereabouts who might remember the beginnings of the feud between the Tarrants and the Deverills? About sixty years ago, I think."

Nance frowned. "Before my time, that was, but my old granny might recall the Tarrant side. She were a housemaid here at the time, and what Granny Popple knows about this family would fill volumes, did she know how to write it all down. Not that she would ever do such a thing, even could she write her letters," Nance added hastily. "Knows her place, does Granny."

Nodding, Daintry gathered her things and preceded Nance to her bedchamber, where she found Charley waiting. Smiling at the child, she said, "Are you not supposed to be with Miss Parish, studying your lessons?" The new governess, a vast improvement on the old one in Daintry's opinion, had arrived at Tuscombe Park during their absence, and seemed to have settled in nicely.

"Miss Parish said Aunt Ophelia wished to discuss my lessons with her, and gave me leave to go riding. Of course," she added with a calculating gleam in her eyes, "I did not tell her I mean to ride to Seacourt Head."

"Nor shall you do so," Daintry said, turning so Nance could undo her buttons.

"But I told Melissa I would ride over frequently, and I've not been over once since she went home! Please, Aunt Daintry."

"No, and there is no use in widening your eyes at me, for I am not to be won over by such tactics. You may ride with me to visit Granny Popple in the village."

Nance said, "She is not in the village, my lady. She's gone to stay with my sister Annie on the moor, at Warleggan Farm."

Daintry nodded. She knew Annie's husband, Feok Warleggan, for he was one of her father's tenants. "Is your granny ill?"

Nance laughed, helping her into her habit skirt. "No, miss, she's meddling, is all. Feok has a brother, and Granny's took it into her head that he'd make me a fine husband if he gets hired on at the mine again. But I've no use for Dewy Warleggan, though I do have to be civil to him now if I'm to visit Granny. He's in a fidget because he's got to work the farm now, but he ought to be grateful he's got any job at all, to my way of thinking."

Charley said, "I'd rather visit Melissa. May I not go alone, Aunt Daintry? I am quite old enough to ride a mere seven miles by myself—with my groom, of course."

"I said no," Daintry said, looking at her in such a way that the child grimaced again and sighed in defeat. "Will you ride with me, or do you prefer to return to the schoolroom?"

"With you, of course, only don't let Granny Popple pinch my cheek and tell me how plump I am getting. I am not fat, and she makes me think of a witch testing a child for the oven."

Nance said, "That will be enough of your sauce now, Miss Charley. My granny never was no witch, and she'd not thank you to be going about saying she were one."

"Good gracious, no," Daintry said, laughing. "You mind that impudent tongue of yours, or we'll have Feok Warleggan throwing us right off his farm."

"As if he would," Charley and Nance said in unison. They looked at each other then and laughed, and Daintry, shaking her head at both of them, shooed her niece out the door, following as soon as she had snatched up her whip and hat from the dressing table. She and Charley found Clemons waiting with the horses, and were soon on their way, the groom following placidly behind.

Three-quarters of an hour later, they arrived at the farm cottage, a haphazardly built, two-story building of whitewashed cob with a thatched roof. As they approached the front door, Annie, as buxom and rosy-cheeked as her sister, opened it with a beaming smile, and bobbed a curtsy. "Saw you from the kitchen winder my lady. Good day to you, Miss Charley. You'll be stepping into the hale, you will, and I'll be fetching me granny, for she'll not want to miss bidding you a good day."

"It is Granny Popple we have come to see," Daintry said, following Annie into the tiny hale, or parlor. The room was used only on very special occasions, and it smelled of soap and beeswax. The furniture consisted of three painted wooden chairs against the whitewashed cob walls, a large table kept beautifully clean by constant scouring, and a corner-cupboard with a glass door, containing numerous knickknacks. A pair of china spaniels and two brass candlesticks decked the mantelpiece.

They were not left long to wait before Granny Popple, a wizened little woman with eyes that looked like tiny polished lumps of coal, came in hobbling on her stick and pulling her shawl more tightly around her scrawny shoulders.

"Greetings to ye, my lady," she said. "Chilly in here. Ought to light the fire, Annie."

Daintry, knowing that turf for the fires had to be cut out on the moor and hauled to the house, said quickly, "That is not necessary, Mrs. Popple. We are not chilly, I assure you."

"Bless ye, lass, 'twarn't you I were thinking of. These old bones o' mine need a fire to keep 'em warm."

Annie smiled and said, "We can light the fire, Granny."

Charley said, "May we go into the kitchen instead, Annie? I like your kitchen." Looking at Daintry, she said, "Remember the last time we came here, when Annie gave us saffron cakes?"

Annie laughed and said, "Come you in, lassie. The kitchen is where we entertain our closest friends, after all."

The kitchen, much larger and more comfortable than the parlor, was clearly the real living room of the house. Its ceiling was low with dark oak beams, and strips of wood had been nailed to them to make a sort of rack overhead where Annie's herbs were stored along with all sorts of other odds' and ends.

While Annie laid out a comfortable snack of saffron cakes and tea, Daintry explained the reason for their visit.

"Don't know nothing about that old feud," Granny said flatly. "His lordship's pa weren't a man to encourage idle chatter about his personal life, no more than his lordship be."

"But surely you heard things."

"We did, but nothing a body could sink her teeth into. We heard he and Lord Thomas had a falling-out over a lady in London, but didn't nobody know the rights of it, not then nor after."

Daintry persisted but discovered nothing more, and soon took her leave, though not before the men came in for their dinner at noon. Greeting Warleggan, she found herself looking his younger brother over carefully, trying unsuccessfully to imagine the slim, broody middle-aged man married to her Nance.

As they were riding away, Charley showed that her thoughts had followed the same track. "He is not my notion of a good man for Nance. He is too sullen. Nance laughs all the time."

"Then Nance would be just the person to cheer him up."

"Perhaps." But Charley did not sound convinced. They rode in silence for a time before she spoke again. "Aunt Daintry, we have come at least eight miles today, have we not?"

"We have, but don't get to thinking that means you can go alone to visit Melissa. Your Uncle Geoffrey would be most displeased, I think, if I were to let you do any such thing."

The child was silent for a moment, then said rather abruptly, "I don't like Uncle Geoffrey."

"Good gracious, darling, why don't you like him? He has been kind to you, and even brought you a present from London."

"Oh, yes, and I know it is my duty to love him because he is family, but he is so sticky smooth. Being with him is rather like having a jar of honey spilled all over one. He likes such smothery hugs, and he tickles people who loathe to be tickled."

"You?"

"And Melissa, too. I know she is required to love him; he is her papa, after all. But I do not think it is precisely mandatory for me to do so, is it?"

"No, darling, certainly not." Daintry replied, chuckling at the phrasing as much as at the sentiment.

Charley sighed. "I do not want to displease Uncle Geoffrey, because he can get very angry, but I still don't see that there can be any harm in my going by myself. If you don't want me to ride over and back in one day, perhaps I could stay overnight."

"That is something you must talk over with your parents, darling, not with me," Daintry said, realizing that she ought to have pointed out that fact rather sooner.

"But Papa and Mama never listen to me. They just say no and go on about their business, or they tell me to run along to the schoolroom. At least you listen."

"Nevertheless, now that your papa and mama are at home, you should not ask my permission to do things that they must approve. You must make them listen, and," she added swiftly, "you will not do that by being impertinent. Make a plan of what you want to say, then go to them and say it."

Charley would no doubt have continued the argument, but at

that moment her attention was diverted, and she exclaimed, "Is that not his lordship riding toward us, Aunt Daintry? Oh, it is! I would know that stallion anywhere!"

Daintry, too, recognized horse and rider, and the rapid beating of her heart informed her that she had not yet managed to deal with her wayward passions. Only with great effort was she able to restrain the impulse to urge her mount to a faster pace to meet him. Had he perchance been on the lookout for them? She had not thought about the likelihood of meeting him—or at least she had not allowed her thoughts to dwell upon the possibility—but now, as she watched his approach, she could not fool herself into believing she was not very glad to see him.

Deverill looked tired, she thought, but he smiled and greeted them, saying politely when Charley told him where they had been, "I hope your visit was a pleasant one."

"Aunt Daintry asked Granny Popple a lot of questions about that old feud between our families," Charley said, "but Granny doesn't know how it got started."

Deverill looked at Daintry. "Nothing new?"

"No, and I've read Aunt Ophelia's journals, too."

"Well, I've spent the week searching, and I've asked anyone I can think of who might remember it, but I've done no better."

She had been watching him carefully. "Is something amiss, Deverill? You look as if something had vexed you."

He was silent for a moment, turning the stallion and falling in beside them. "I am confused rather than put out," he said, then added with a wry smile, "No, in truth, I am very much put out, but since I do not know what lies at the root of the business, it seems more accurate to claim confusion."

Charley, chuckling, said, "You must know what vexed you, sir. I always know."

He looked at her, then at Daintry, and Daintry knew he was choosing his words with care. "I received payment of a wager," he said, "from someone who is angry with me. And while I know that he has some cause to be angry, the contents of the letter he wrote have nothing to do with the matter that I recall."

Daintry said, "I believe I understand, sir, if you mean—"

"I do," he said quickly, with another glance at Charley. "He has warned me away."

"But he has no right!" He spoke of Geoffrey, she was certain, but although the man was her brother-in-law, he had no business to be ordering Deverill to keep away from her. Her father had already done that. The thought brought another, more unwelcome one. "Do you think he has also written to Papa?"

Deverill shook his head. "You misunderstand me. He would have every right to protest if what he writes were true, and no reason to complain to your father."

Daintry could stand it no longer. "Charley, ride on with Clemons. I must speak to his lordship in private."

So abruptly did she speak that for once, though Charley had been listening with unconcealed curiosity to their exchange, she did not question the command but touched Victor at once with spur and whip. Calling to Clemons to catch up with her, she rode on.

The moment the child was beyond earshot, Daintry said, "What is it, sir? Of what has Geoffrey accused you?"

"Only of trifling with his wife," Deverill said grimly, watching her with narrowed eyes. "I would not blame you in the least if you believe—"

"I don't." She tried to think of what he might have done to make Geoffrey suspect him of such a thing.

"Don't be so quick off the mark, my dear," he said dryly. "You once accused me of trifling yourself, and I confess, your accusations were not altogether undeserved."

She waved his words away with a gesture. "Susan would not respond to such advances," she said. When his eyebrows rose ludicrously, she laughed and said, "Does that prick your vanity, Deverill? Are you so certain of your charms?"

"Certainly not."

"It would not matter if you were, for Susan, as you have seen for yourself, is in love with her husband. Even if she were not, she likes protective men, the sort who like her to flutter her lashes and tell them how wonderfully strong they are."

He reached out and caught Cloud's bridle, pulling the silver dun to a halt, and Daintry suddenly found his face disturbingly near her own. "Do you think I don't like such women?"

Her breath stopped in her throat, and all she could think of was that the last time he had been this close to her, he had kissed her. Determined not to allow her passions to betray her into unbecoming behavior a second time, and drawing upon every resource at her command to control her voice, she said, "*Do* you like them, Deverill? I should not have guessed it."

"Why not?" His face was inches from her own.

Fighting an impulse to lean forward just enough to press her lips against his, she murmured, "In truth, I believe you are tempted by anyone with bosoms, sir, but I also think you would find a lot of fluttering and fawning downright bothersome."

"Do you?" He held her gaze for a moment longer, and she fancied he was somehow both amused and a little shaken. But then he straightened, released her bridle, and added in a more natural tone, "We have drifted from the point, however, which is that your brother-in-law accuses me of trifling with his wife, and insists he has his information from an unimpeachable source."

"But that must be nonsense." She wished he had not released her bridle. She did not want to talk about Susan or Geoffrey.

"It is nonsense, but I am not altogether certain what I can do about it, though I doubt he'll make the accusation public."

"No, for that would damage Susan's reputation and his own, too. But you may be wrong about his not telling Papa. He might do so just to add fuel to the feud, and it would, you know."

He said, "Your niece is waving. If you don't want her riding back here, I suggest you smile and wave back. Whatever Seacourt does, I must tell you I do not like this cocksure attitude of his very much, and I'd like nothing better than to have a private chat with him to tell him so."

Smiling and waving at Charley, she said nonetheless firmly, "You must not, for it would only make matters worse. Let me see what I can discover first. Charley has been begging me to let her visit Melissa, and while I have refused to let her go alone, perhaps if I go with her, I can learn more about this matter and put in a good word for you at the same time."

"Much obliged to you," he said dryly.

She grinned at him saucily. "At least you must agree, sir, that doing it my way is less likely to result in all-out war."

"I agree to nothing of the sort."

They caught up with Charley a few moments later, and not long afterward he left them, saying it was not advisable for him to ride too near Tuscombe Park. Daintry, listening to Charley's chatter with only half an ear, spent the remaining time trying to think of how she could discover what had led Geoffrey to believe the worst of his own wife. She said nothing to Charley about the intended visit to Seacourt Head, which was just as well, for as they rode up to the house, a chaise drew up before the front entrance, and two figures descended. Charley recognized them first, shouting, "Melissa! It's Melissa and Aunt Susan!"

Daintry recognized Melissa, but she was still not certain that the veiled figure who emerged from the chaise after the child was her sister. Jumping down from her horse and throwing the reins to Clemons, she cried, "Susan, is that you? Why on earth are you wearing that veil? Did someone die?"

"Go inside with Charlotte, Melissa. We will be right behind you." The voice was Susan's, but she was clearly not herself, for she held her arm tight against her waist and moved with unaccustomed stiffness. "Take in our things," she said to Jago when the young footman came down the steps to meet them.

"You are staying a while then," Daintry said, surprised.

"Don't chatter. Just come with me," Susan said, looking down the drive as though she expected to see someone approaching.

Her curiosity nearly overwhelming her, Daintry followed her sister into the house and up to her own bedchamber. Only when that door had been shut did Susan raise her veil.

Daintry gasped with shock. Her sister's beautiful face was a mass of livid bruises.

Twelve

Daintry stared at Susan in disbelief. "Who did this to you? Here, sit down," she added quickly when her sister swayed. Taking her by the arm, she led her to the dressing chair and pushed her down upon it. "Tell me now. How did this happen?"

Susan opened her mouth, then closed it, squeezing her eyes shut at the same time. When she opened them again, tears glistened on her lashes and spilled down her cheeks. "I thought it would be easy to tell you," she whispered, "but it isn't."

Sudden, unwelcome suspicion leapt to Daintry's mind. "But surely it is not true that you and Deverill—"

"Oh, no! Never!"

"But he received a letter from Geoffrey that said—"

"I know. I had received a letter, too, unsigned but saying Deverill cared for me and wanted to look after me. Geoffrey read it before ever I saw it, of course. He reads all my letters." A wracking sob shook her body. "H-he was f-furious with me."

"He did this—beat you like this—and accused Deverill of trifling, all because someone told you Deverill wanted to look after you? But how could he believe you were a party to such a thing? He must know you are the most dutiful of wives."

"Oh, yes," Susan said, looking away. "I am dutiful, and obedient, and submissive to all of Geoffrey's wishes." Her tone was exceedingly bitter.

"But then how could he believe—"

"Geoffrey believes what he chooses to believe."

"But to have done this, he must have gone quite mad."

"He was certainly enraged," Susan said wearily, swallowing another sob. "He is frequently enraged."

Daintry stared at her. "What can you mean? He has never been so angry as to beat you before."

Susan was silent. Her shoulders slumped. She stared bleakly at the carpet.

"Has he?" Daintry touched her shoulder, meaning to make her turn and look up at her so that she could see her expression more easily. When Susan winced and jerked away, she exclaimed, "Good God, what else has he done to you?"

"No more than it is his legal right to do," Susan muttered. "I displeased him. I frequently displease him, though God knows I try very hard not to do so. Even when he brought his mistress home and informed me that she was going to remain as our guest, I tried my best to be the perfect wife."

"His mistress! Lady Catherine?"

"Oh, yes, dear Catherine. It is done in the best families, you know. Duchess Georgiana put up with Devonshire's mistress for years before his death, and Lady Chelsea has put up with Caro What-not these past ten years and more. At least Catherine can be pleasant when she wishes to be. She is practical, too," Susan added with a grimace. "She made it perfectly clear—to me, at least—that it is because she has so little money of her own and dislikes Yorkshire that she finds it convenient to live with us."

"But . . ." Daintry remembered her suspicions and how easy it had been to dismiss them. "But I don't understand. Your marriage always seemed so happy. *You* always seemed so happy."

"Did I? Perhaps that is because I was terrified to seem otherwise." Susan looked directly at her for the first time. "Remember when Geoffrey interrupted our *tête à tête* at Mount Edgcumbe, how solicitous he was about brushing my hair? He even asked you to hand him that dreadful hairbrush." She shuddered. "H-he was displeased that after being forced to take second place to his mistress at home, and then in the coach all day, I had dared to behave in such a manner as to draw attention to myself."

"He hit you when I left?" Daintry felt a fury rising within her unlike any she could remember feeling before. "I am more sorry than I can say if I said or did anything to cause him to hurt you," she said, struggling to keep her voice under control.

"It was not your fault. It was mine. It is always mine. I should not have come here." She looked around the room much, Daintry thought, like an animal in a trap. "He will come after me, and when he does . . ." Her face grew white.

Daintry moved to pull the bell, and when Susan protested, said, "I am sending for Nance to sit with you while I find Aunt Ophelia. She will know what to do. I don't, but I promise, I will do everything in my power to see that Geoffrey never hurts you like this again."

When Nance entered and gasped at the sight of Susan's face, Daintry said crisply, "Take care of her, and say nothing to anyone about her condition. She will stay here in my room until I can talk with Lady Ophelia. And, Nance, I mean not one word about this below stairs. Do you understand me?"

"I do," Nance said grimly, still staring in shock at Susan, "but you are mistaken if you think you can interfere in this business, Miss Daintry. If those bruises mean what I suspect they do, Sir Geoffrey will be hard upon her heels. How is it he did not catch you up on the road, Miss Susan?"

"He went riding with his cousin," Susan whispered. "They did not mean to return until late afternoon."

Daintry, not waiting to hear more, left them and went in search of Lady Ophelia, whom she found in the drawing room with Lady St. Merryn and Miss Davies.

Before she could think of a tactful way to draw her great-aunt away from the others, her mother said, "Jago tells me Susan and Melissa have arrived, but if that is the case, where are they, my dear? Surely Susan must know that I want to see her."

"She is . . . she is ill, Mama," Daintry said, inventing swiftly and casting a beseeching glance at Lady Ophelia. "I came down to ask

Aunt Ophelia if she would recommend one of her remedies that might be of some help."

Miss Davies said brightly, "Oh, I'll go up to her at once, shall I, Letitia dear? I am sure I will know precisely what to do for her. Perhaps a hot brick to her feet, or a soothing tisane. I concoct a very fine tisane, you know."

Lady St. Merryn reached for her salts bottle. "Is she very ill, Daintry? Are we likely to catch something from her? If you go to her, Ethelinda, you must be careful not to carry her illness back to me. I am in no fit state—"

"Cousin Ethelinda need not go upstairs at all, Mama," Daintry said. "I don't want her, only Aunt Ophelia."

"Oh, my dear," Lady St. Merryn said faintly, "is that how little you care for my health? You must know that Aunt Ophelia will not be at all cautious and, if Susan is truly ill, will not even admit the possibility that I might contract her illness."

"Oh, for goodness sake, Mama," Daintry said, exasperated, "you will not catch anything from Susan."

"And just how can you be so certain of that, miss?"

"Because she is not really ill, or not . . . not in the way you mean," she added, hoping to cover the slip.

But it was too late. "What do you mean?" Lady St. Merryn said, sitting up. "Is she with child? Is that it? Oh, Geoffrey will be so pleased. He has wanted a son so desperately, and it has seemed so unnatural of Susan not to provide him with one."

"Geoffrey is not pleased," Daintry retorted. "If you must know, Mama, Susan came to us for sanctuary because her odious husband beat her so that she can hardly stand. Her face is bruised beyond recognition. I just hope he has broken no bones."

Lady St. Merryn moaned and fell back against her cushions, her salts bottle firmly clutched beneath her nose. "Oh, what has Susan done?" she moaned. "She was always such a good, obedient child. What dreadful thing can she have done?"

"She did nothing at all," Daintry said angrily. "Some wicked person wrote her a disgusting letter, claiming Deverill had singled her out for his attentions. Geoffrey read it, of course, and although he must have known perfectly well it was all a sham, he used it as an excuse to beat her. Moreover, if I am not greatly mistaken, he has beaten her many times before now with even less cause to do so."

"But he must have had cause," Cousin Ethelinda said reasonably. "Why else would a gentleman do such a thing? And it is not as if Deverill were a saint, you know, for he *was* a member of Lord Hill's staff, after all, and we all know what those—"

"I don't know what would make any man beat his wife like Geoffrey has beaten Susan," Daintry interjected, unwilling to hear anything more against Deverill, "but if you think my sister, of all people, has done such dreadful things that . . . Oh, I have no patience for this. The whole notion is absurd."

"Where is she?" Lady Ophelia asked, getting to her feet.

"In my bedchamber, ma'am," Daintry said gratefully. "If you will go to her, I will find my father. He must be told about this if he is to protect her. She fears Geoffrey might be hot on her heels, and I for one don't doubt that he must be."

Lady St. Merryn sniffed. "Well, I do not believe a word of this. Sir Geoffrey Seacourt is a perfectly charming man who would never lift a finger to harm anyone, let alone a defenseless female. If he has punished Susan, she must have deserved it, and that is all there is about it. It is a husband's right—indeed, his duty—to punish his wife if she misbehaves."

"Well, if any man did to another what Geoffrey has done to Susan, he would be thrown in prison," Daintry snapped. "Even my father will agree to that much, once he sees her poor face."

And with that, she left the room to search for St. Merryn, finding him in his library, where he was reading his afternoon post. He was none too pleased to be interrupted.

Looking up at her over his wire-rimmed spectacles, he said, "What is it, girl? I'm busy."

"Papa, Susan is here."

"What? Surely, we were not expecting them again so soon."

"No, sir, but she has been dreadfully hurt, and she wants to stay here."

"Stay here! What nonsense is this? Got a perfectly good home of her own and a husband to look after her, don't she?"

"Geoffrey hurt her," Daintry said, striving to remain calm so as not to arouse his temper. "She has run away from him."

"What's that you say?"

"She has run away, Papa, because Geoffrey beats her."

He shrugged. "If she has run away, she must go back."

"Didn't you hear me, sir? Geoffrey has beaten her black and blue, and what's more, he's keeping his mistress in their house."

"What business is that of mine—or yours? His mistress is his own business, and he has every right to discipline his wife. Stupid of her to run away. Only forces him to punish her again."

"How can you say that when she is your own daughter?"

He removed his spectacles, gesturing with them to emphasize his words. "More to the point, girl, is that she is Seacourt's wife. I have no power to prevent his reclaiming his property, you know. Nor would I want to prevent it. It is his duty to chastise her if she disobeys him, so you tell Susan not to bother to unpack her things. If Seacourt don't show up to claim her, I'll pack her right back to him tomorrow."

"You can't do that!"

He stood up, dropping his spectacles onto the desk and leaning over it to glare at her. "I not only can, I will. As for you, I've had enough impertinence. You go to your bedchamber and stay there till I give you leave to come downstairs again. You've got much too far above yourself, what with your aunt's stuffing your head with her fool notions." Moving around the desk, he stopped in front of her and, when she did not move, put his face close to hers to say menacingly, "Did you hear me, girl? First you tell that sister of yours what I said, and then you—"

"I won't," Daintry cried. "If you won't help her, then I will, but I won't let you send her back to that bul—" Her words ended in a sharp cry when he slapped her, and her hand flew to her cheek. She stared at him in shock. Through a mist of tears she saw him lift his hand again, and stepped back, saying angrily, "I'll go, but I won't forgive you for this."

"By God, Seacourt's got the right way about it," he growled. "Just remember, girl, a female can always spare herself the indignity of punishment. She need only obey."

Hurrying upstairs, determined to ignore her stinging cheek and the resentment it stirred, she remembered that St. Merryn had expressed admiration for Geoffrey's methods before, and realized she would have to take care in future not to stir him to such a pitch as she had today. He generally had given wide berth to her temper, so that she had come to believe herself immune to his blustering, but the painful slap warned her that if she was going to help Susan, she must do so without inciting him to violence again. So deep in thought was she that she nearly tripped over Charley, lying in wait for her in the gallery corridor.

"Aunt Daintry, what are we going to do?" The child's eyes were wide, and Daintry knew that Melissa had confided at least some of the truth to her.

"I don't know, darling, but keep Melissa out of Grandpapa's way. He has said Aunt Susan must go home in the morning, and I do not know what she will want to do about Melissa."

"But Melissa said Uncle Geoffrey—"

Daintry put a finger to the child's lips, silencing her. "I know, darling, but we cannot talk about that now. I will speak with Aunt Ophelia, and we will think of something, so you go back to Melissa now and tell her she is not to fret."

"I already told her that," Charley said. "She knows I will look after her if I can, but what are we to do?"

"*You* are to do nothing," Daintry said firmly. "Just keep Melissa calm. I will do the rest."

Wishing she were half as confident as she had sounded, she went on to her own bedchamber. Opening the door, the first thing she heard was Lady Ophelia's voice with a note in it indicating that she was very near to losing her patience.

"Cease your wailing, child, and just be grateful you do not live in ancient Rome, where a husband could kill his wife, not only for adultery, but merely if he caught her drinking wine."

Certain the old lady had added the last bit only to see if Susan was listening, Daintry forced a laugh. "Not just for drinking wine, ma'am!"

Lady Ophelia sniffed. "A woman who drank wine was believed to have closed her heart to every virtue and opened it to every vice. What happened to you? Your cheek is all red."

"Nothing to speak of." Daintry glanced at Nance, standing as still as a mouse near the wardrobe, then back at her great-aunt. "Papa won't help. What are we going to do?"

Lady Ophelia looked hard at her, as if she wanted to ask again about her reddened cheek, but in the end she said only, "I see how it is. Very well, don't talk to me. I must think."

Daintry turned to her sister. "How often has Geoffrey done this, Susan? Why do you allow it?"

Susan sighed. "You are so foolish, Daintry. What, pray, do you think I can do to stop him? What could any woman do?"

"Well, I for one—"

"You would not fare any better against such a man than I have," Susan said grimly. "You are even smaller than I am, and though you like to think yourself such a firebrand, your temper would mean no more to him than a flame to be beaten out."

Daintry opened her mouth to deny it, but a vivid memory of the recent scene with her father made her shut it again, and Susan misunderstood, saying, "Oh, you are shocked, I know. So was I, the first time he struck me. The offense was such a small one—I do not even recall it now—but he knocked me down, and I could scarcely believe it. Then, afterward, he was so remorseful. He promised it would never happen again, and I believed him."

"Geoffrey always seemed so charming, until Mount Edgcumbe."

"He is almost always charming in public, but at home he has temper tantrums like a little boy, and at such times, I can do nothing right. Usually, he shows that side of himself only at home, but at Mount Edgcumbe, first after he found us talking together and realized that my behavior was causing concern, and then after he fell off that stupid horse—"

"That is why you did not come down to dinner that last night! When I found your door locked, I thought you had merely gone to bed early because you were tired."

"He was humiliated," Susan said. "To have fallen at all was bad enough, but to have fallen in front of Alvanley and the Jerseys was worse. He was beside himself, and though I tried my best to placate him, I could not. I could not let anyone see me afterward for fear that they would guess something was wrong, and we left

early the next day for the same reason, because Geoffrey was afraid
people would see that something was wrong with me."

"I should think they would! Is that when he did all this?"

"No, the first letter came two days after we got home, and there
was a second one this morning." Susan looked away.

"Two! But who would do such a dreadful thing?"

Susan was silent.

Lady Ophelia said abruptly, "What about Annie, Nance? Would
she take them in?" Daintry had forgotten the maid's presence.

Nance nodded her head but looked wary. "She might, my lady,
but I don't know about Feok or Granny. They mightn't like it much,
particularly if his lordship says they mustn't."

No one had to ask which lordship she meant; there was only
one at Tuscombe Park. Daintry exchanged a look with her aunt,
then said firmly, "His lordship won't know anything about it,
Nance, so he won't say they mustn't. What shall we tell them?"

Susan seemed to have withdrawn from the conversation, but
Lady Ophelia and Nance were willing to discuss possibilities with
Daintry at length, and they finally decided to tell Annie only that
Susan wanted to stay at the farm for a time with Melissa. That,
they agreed, would leave the erstwhile housemaids to draw their
own, no doubt accurate conclusions, but Lady Ophelia said grimly,
"That may do us more good than harm in the end."

"We'll go first thing in the morning," Daintry said, "unless you
think, Nance, that you ought to go over at once and tell Annie to
expect us."

"No," Lady Ophelia said. "Better to make it a matter of mercy,
when Feok and Dewy are in the fields and Annie must speak face
to face with Susan. She won't ask questions then, of you or Susan;
however, she and Mrs. Popple would certainly demand answers
from Nance if they had her all to themselves beforehand."

Nance nodded. "I'd have to tell them the whole truth, I would,
and like as not Granny would cut up a mite stiff."

Susan said miserably, "I don't want anyone else to see me like
this."

Daintry turned, her temper perilously close to snapping, and
said, "You will do as you are told. Keep your veils if you must, but

you cannot stay here, for Papa has said you cannot. He means to send you back to Geoffrey, Susan. He will do nothing to help you. There, don't cry. I don't know why I am snapping at you, but I want to help and I cannot if you put foolish obstacles in my way. Annie knows you and loves you as much as we do, and she will do what she can. There is nothing else we can do. Nance will look after you now, and I will go tell Melissa what we have decided. Unless you would prefer to leave her here. Perhaps Geoffrey will not be so angry if—"

"No!" Susan sat bolt upright. "She mustn't go back alone. It isn't safe for her."

"Merciful heavens," Lady Ophelia exclaimed. "Does he beat the child, too?"

Susan shook her head but said, "He disciplines her, of course, when she is naughty, but it isn't that. He . . . oh, I am speaking foolishly, I know, but it seems to me that he . . . oh, pay me no heed. I am merely being jealous, I suppose, and there has been nothing really, except . . ."

When her voice trailed away, Daintry looked at her in vexation and said, "I do wish you would speak plainly, Susan. What on earth are you trying to say?"

"Pay me no mind," Susan said. "I don't know why you must always behave as if you were the elder sister, Daintry. You make me forget your youth and inexperience. It's nothing. I am upset, and I want Melissa to stay with me, that's all."

She moved to the washstand to bathe her face, and Daintry went to tell the two little girls what she could. When Charley assumed that she would accompany them to Warleggan Farm, Daintry said, "No, darling, that would not be wise. For a large group to descend upon poor Annie when she has not the least notion that anyone is going to visit her would be most impolite."

"Pooh, Annie will not care if I am there, and Melissa will care very much if I am not. Won't you, Melissa?"

Melissa turned her huge blue eyes toward Daintry. Tears sparkled on her lashes. Her lip trembled, but she said nothing.

Daintry sighed. "I suppose there will be room for you in the carriage if you do not mind being squeezed up with us on the forward seat so Aunt Susan and Aunt Ophelia can be comfortable."

"In my opinion," Charley said thoughtfully, "the carriage is not a good idea at all."

"Then just how do you think we are going to transport your Aunt Susan to Warleggan Farm?"

Charley shot an oblique glance at Melissa, then said with seeming innocence, "I should think that a peaceful ride across the open moor would suit Aunt Susan much better than being rattled along in a carriage on the *public* road."

Daintry drew breath to point out that Susan would certainly not wish to ride, but before she had said a word, she realized that Charley was afraid Seacourt would come after them on the road. If he did, he would catch them, even if he were not riding but driving his own rig. And Lady Ophelia could do more good by staying to deal with him at Tuscombe Park—if the chance arose for her to do so—than by going with them to Warleggan Farm.

So instead of snubbing Charley, she said quietly, "I will have to discuss that with Aunt Susan, darling, but perhaps you are right. I'll leave you now, and trust that you will not leave the house. Have your supper, and get a good night's rest."

The evening would be the most dangerous time, she knew, for Geoffrey could arrive at any moment. As the hours passed, she grew more and more nervous, and could only imagine that Susan's nerves were in a worse state than her own. Neither of them went down to dinner, knowing it was best not to remind St. Merryn of Susan's presence in the house, and when Daintry remembered belatedly that she had been ordered to stay in her room, she had their dinner served to them there. Lady Ophelia assured them that she would send a warning up at once if Seacourt arrived.

Once the two young women were alone together, Daintry tried to maintain a cheerful conversation, as much to keep her own mind off the probability of Geoffrey's arrival as to distract Susan. But her sister was singularly uncooperative, remaining silent, unusually so, until finally Daintry's patience snapped.

"Look here, Susan, I know you are upset, but you have no cause to behave as if I have offended you. I have already apologized for what happened at Mount Edgcumbe, though in truth it was not my fault that Geoffrey behaved like such a beast."

"No. It is not that," Susan said. Glancing at her, she looked away again.

"Well, don't stop there," Daintry said. "If it is not that, what is it? You look exactly like Melissa looks when she has let Charley drag her into some mischief or other. What is it?"

"I don't know why you should instantly assume I had done something wrong," Susan said, still staring into the distance.

"I did not assume it," Daintry said, but her thoughts had taken another tangent, and although she told herself the notion was an absurd one, she could not help saying, "*Was* there something between you and Deverill at Mount Edgcumbe?"

Susan shook her head, but still she would not look at her.

"But there must have been something, even something very small, to make someone think he was—"

"No, how many times must I say it? There was nothing!"

"Then who would write such stuff to you, and why?"

Susan flushed to the roots of her hair, and bit her lip. After a long moment, she whispered, "No one."

"Well, someone did, and I for one would—" She broke off, staring, as the meaning of Susan's words grew clear in her mind. "You wrote them yourself." She saw the truth in Susan's expression and, outraged, demanded, "Why? What possible reason could you have to blacken Deverill's reputation, or your own?"

"You mustn't tell," Susan said as tears spilled down her cheeks again. "Oh, please don't tell him. Don't tell anyone."

Reining in her temper, Daintry said calmly, "Why, Susan?"

"I saw how Geoffrey backed down, and I thought . . ."

"Backed down? What do you mean?"

"After he fell, when he was going to beat that poor horse, Deverill just stepped in front of him, and he put down the whip. I hoped, if he thought Deverill had an interest . . . Oh, I see how stupid I was. I never spared a thought for Deverill or for anything but making Geoffrey afraid to hurt me again. Instead, it just made him furious, and . . . and I knew the second letter was coming, because

I'd given it to a housemaid to post after we left, and . . . Y-you see the r-result." She burst into tears.

Daintry did what she could to comfort her, assuring her that she would tell no one and that Deverill could take care of himself. At last Susan stopped crying and agreed to go to bed.

She said, "I'll sleep here with you. Geoffrey will look for me in my old room, but he will not come in here."

But to their surprise, morning came without a sign of him.

Rising early and partaking of no more breakfast than the rolls and chocolate Nance brought to them, Daintry and Susan donned habits, packed a few necessary items in a pair of bandboxes, collected the little girls, and went to the stables, where Clemons soon had horses saddled and ready for them.

The groom had looked surprised to see Susan heavily veiled, and Daintry realized that his company might prove awkward, so she said firmly, "You need not come with us today, Clemons. Lady Susan and I will look after the girls."

"His lordship don't like it much when you go out on your own, my lady," the groom reminded her.

"Then do not tell him," she said. She thought of saying that they did not mean to go far, but realized that would only stir his curiosity more, since he had just finished tying two bandboxes to her saddle. Instead, she said nothing, giving him a look that warned him not to pursue the matter.

Despite the fact that both Charley and Daintry had done their best to get their charges out at a very early hour, it was nearly nine o'clock by the time they were ready to mount their horses. Charley, dancing with impatience, kept looking across the stable yard, as if by doing so she could see through the house to the front drive.

Susan, adjusting skirt and whip to her satisfaction once she was seated, noted her niece's anxiety and said sharply, "Calm yourself, Charlotte. You are making a spectacle of yourself."

Daintry bit back the sharp words that rose to her tongue, knowing she would not help matters by pointing out that concern for Susan's safety was making Charley nervous. It was plain to see that Susan cared even more for maintaining an appearance of propriety than for the need to get away before Seacourt arrived.

They rode out of the stable yard at last, avoiding the main road as much as possible, but while it was easy to ride in the shadow of the hedges while they were near the house, once they turned toward the moor and the ground began to rise, Daintry knew the danger of their being seen was greatly increased.

Charley, too, was aware of the danger, for she kept glancing over her shoulder, and it was she who cried, "There he is! He is driving up to the front gates now. Oh, I think he has seen us, for he checked just then, and there is no other cause to do so!"

Daintry looked the moment she cried out and, seeing the curricle, knew at once that Geoffrey must have seen them, too. He seemed to experience momentary indecision but then drove right past the front entrance to the stable yard. It would be no time at all before a horse could be saddled for him to follow them.

Susan reined in her horse. "We had better go back, I suppose," she said dismally.

"Don't be absurd," Daintry snapped. "He can't catch us in an instant, and if we can be away across the moor before he gets to the top of the road, you can be safe and sound at Warleggan Farm before he has the least idea which way we have gone."

"But he'll see us on the moor. There is no place to hide!"

"We need only get beyond the first rise," Daintry said calmly. "There are granite tors and plenty of scrub. The land is not flat, for heaven's sake, so collect yourself, Susan, and ride." Urging her horse to a lope, not daring to go any faster uphill for fear the animals would be blown, she cried, "Come on!"

Susan turned to look back again, then followed. At the top of the rise, Charley looked back, and called out, "He's got a horse, Aunt Daintry. It's Grandpapa's hunter, Celtic Prince."

Prince was the fastest horse in their stable and so powerful that Daintry feared even the steep rise near the top of the road would not slow him. She could not see Susan's expression because of the heavy veil, but she could tell she was tired, and she knew that the pace they had set must have been painful for her.

Charley rode up beside them. "There's plenty of scrub here, Aunt Daintry. I'm going to stay behind for a bit. I know the way, so I can catch up with you. You know I can."

They were off the road now, but they would not be out of sight of anyone coming over the rise until they had got beyond the next hill. Then there would be any number of directions they might have taken, and Daintry was certain that Geoffrey, with his low opinion of women's capabilities in the saddle, would assume they had followed the road—at least until he had gone far enough to be sure they had not. But he would only do that if he saw no sign of them when he reached the top of the hill.

The thought of leaving Charley behind was worrisome, but the little girl looked perfectly sure of herself.

"He will see you riding away."

"No, he won't. I can slow him down, Aunt Daintry, until he dismounts to see if something is wrong with Prince. He will not dare ride farther until he looks, for Prince is Grandpapa's favorite horse. I was afraid he would bring one of the grooms with him, but since he has come alone . . . Let me. Please!"

Susan had ridden ahead but looked back now and cried, "Don't slow down! We must hurry." There was panic in her voice now.

Daintry made her decision at once, telling herself that even if something went wrong, Geoffrey would not dare to harm Charley. Nodding at the child, she gave spur to her horse, urging Melissa and Susan to ride as they had never ridden before, and hoping Susan would be too concerned for her own safety to notice that Charley was no longer with them.

Moments later, over the low thunder of the horses' hooves, she heard in the distance a familiar whistle. Kicking Cloud hard when he tried to slow, and praying Charley's plan would work, she shouted at the others to use their whips, but not till the ground beneath them began to slope downward and Charley's faint whistles were lost in the distance did she dare to breathe normally again.

Charley, grinning, caught up with them at the entrance to the farm twenty minutes later. "Had to do it three times," she said, chuckling. "Poor Prince's sides must be smarting, and Uncle Geoffrey probably believes there are banshees hiding in the heather, but it worked."

"What are you talking about, Charlotte?" Susan demanded.

Charley winked at Melissa. "Why, nothing, Aunt Susan, nothing at all."

Thirteen

Daintry and Charley did not linger at Warleggan Farm once they were assured that Susan and Melissa were welcome to stay and that Feok Warleggan was not there to object.

"Gone to Truro," Annie explained, "with a herd of sheep for slaughtering, and won't be back for two days. Dewy's not here either. Gone off on some business of his own, but it's no manner of use thinking I can tell him or Feok that Lady Susan prefers a small room abovestairs in a farmhouse to the comforts of Seacourt Head," she added bluntly, "and they are no more likely than any other men to want to help a female defy her lawful husband."

"Less than some," Granny Popple added tartly.

"Never you mind," Charley had said cheerfully. "We shall think of a much better plan before Feok gets back."

Daintry wished she shared Charley's optimism. Riding back across the moor, she found herself scanning the horizon, hoping to see the figure of a centaurlike horseman, but aside from the occasional twitter of a meadow pipit, the flock of migratory lapwings Charley startled into flight, and a column of smoke in the distance where someone was burning heather to stimulate new growth, the moor appeared uninhabited that morning.

Charley chattered all the way, telling Daintry in detail just how she had hidden behind a small tor at the top of the road and whistled to make Prince slow to a halt, not once but three times, until Seacourt had dismounted to examine the horse's hooves. "Then I ran and got back on Victor—for I had got down and crept closer so that I could see Uncle Geoffrey to whistle, you know— and then we just galloped off like lightning was after us. I stopped again behind another big pile of rocks to be sure Uncle Geoffrey stayed on the road. He did."

Daintry was afraid they would see him all too soon, but they reached Tuscombe Park without encountering him, and she sent Charley at once to Miss Parish, warning her that if her mama or papa were to ask where she had been, she must be truthful without revealing their precise destination.

"They won't ask," Charley said with a sigh. "I've scarcely laid eyes on them since you all returned from Mount Edgcumbe, and they are getting ready now, if you can call it that, to go to Cothele. They were shouting at each other the last I saw. Would they pay me more heed if I were a boy, Aunt Daintry?"

Daintry touched the child's flushed cheek and smiled at her. "If you were a boy," she said gently, "they would have packed you off to Eton or Harrow two years ago to have a grand education flogged into you. In my opinion, miss, you are much better off here with me and Aunt Ophelia."

Charley grinned at her. "I am glad you are my aunt."

Daintry watched her run off, and wished her own spirits might be lifted so easily. She wondered once again what was amiss between Davina and Charles, but with Seacourt likely to descend upon them at any moment, she did not spare them more than a brief thought, hurrying instead to find Lady Ophelia.

That worthy dame was sitting placidly in the drawing room, her journal, pen, and inkwell pushed to one side while she gave her attention to Cousin Ethelinda, who, when Daintry entered the room, was explaining in tedious detail, just how it was that Lady St. Merryn had not yet chosen to come downstairs.

"I am really quite concerned about your mama," she added, seeing Daintry. "She is that vexed over Susan that she seems to have no spirit at all today. Why, she did not even want me to read her a chapter from her Bible this morning, which she generally likes, for it makes her feel as if she had had enough energy to attend morning prayers with the servants, which, of course, she never has. But today she just wanted to sleep."

Lady Ophelia made an unladylike noise. "All Letitia needs is some responsibility. She is like a plant with no one to water it. She droops."

Cousin Ethelinda stiffened. "I am sure I water her . . . that is to say, if she were a plant, which she is *not,* I am sure I should take just as good care of her as I do now. There is nothing at all she needs that I do not provide for her."

"Oh, my dear," Lady Ophelia said, shaking her head, "if only that were possible. But though you do your best for her, every woman has needs that cannot be met by another woman, or by a man, for that matter. One must have inner resources as well, and I fear Letitia has none. I have given orders," she added, looking significantly at Daintry, "for any visitors to be directed to us here. There have been none."

"I see," Daintry replied, meeting her gaze.

Cousin Ethelinda said brightly, "I hope Susan got away early this morning and that she will quickly make amends with Seacourt. A woman ought not to be at odds with her husband."

Daintry, having been taken aback by the first part of the statement, realized what was meant and was briefly at a loss for something to say. Glancing at Lady Ophelia, she said, "Susan left at nine, Cousin. Is that a new bit of tapestry you are working?" she added, sitting down beside her on the sofa.

"Oh, yes, is it not a pretty pattern?"

Daintry was able to keep Cousin Ethelinda's mind occupied with matters other than Susan until they heard the unmistakable sounds of male voices on the gallery. Stiffening, she looked again at her great-aunt to see that Lady Ophelia had picked up her pen and appeared to be concentrating on her journal.

The door was thrown open, and St. Merryn entered, followed by a furious Seacourt.

"Where the devil is Susan?" St. Merryn demanded.

Daintry got to her feet, striving for calm. "She is not here, Papa. Since you would not help her, she has gone away."

Seacourt took two steps toward her. "Damn it, you young—"

"Language, Seacourt," St. Merryn snapped. "Ladies present."

"Sorry, sir, but this is enough to make anyone forget his manners. Susan came here, prating of abuse because she is a trifle put out with me at the moment, and Daintry, if I am not much mistaken, has assisted her to do something very naughty."

Daintry glared at Seacourt. "I daresay Papa told you he refused to see Susan. You would not be pretending it was no more than a foolish little squabble if you knew he had seen her face."

Flushing, he kept his gaze pinned to hers. "You will regret it if you have tried to come between me and my wife, my girl."

"I am not your girl, thank heaven," Daintry said, "nor am I much impressed by your threats, Geoffrey. Papa, please," she added, turning to face him, "you must not listen to him."

St. Merryn returned her look angrily. "What are you doing in here, anyway? I distinctly remember ordering you to stay in your bedchamber until I gave you leave to come out of it."

"Well, yes, you did, but I knew Geoffrey would come, and—"

"She was out on the road with Susan, sir," Seacourt said.

"Upon my word," St. Merryn growled, "I ought to take you across my knee to teach you obedience, girl."

"Not," Lady Ophelia said evenly, "if I have anything to say about it." She looked him in the eye, and St. Merryn was the first to look away, glancing at Seacourt, then balefully at Daintry before muttering, "Anyone who thinks it's easy for a man to command a houseful of women has never done it, that's all."

Lady Ophelia said quietly, "Daintry, you did not tell me you had been confined to your room. You ought not to have left it. Apologize to your papa at once, if you please."

"I do apologize," she said. "Truly, Papa, I did not really mean to disobey, but Susan needed me, and I just did not think."

"Never mind that," Seacourt snapped, clearly disgusted. "Where the devil have you taken Susan? And do not bother denying that you took her somewhere, for I saw you, all four of you, and if that damned horse I took from the stables here had not suddenly taken it into his head to slow to a walk—not once, mind you, but three times—I'd have caught up with you on the road."

"What horse is that?" St. Merryn demanded, diverted.

"The one they call Prince, sir. A big bay hunter."

"Upon my word, Seacourt, if you've hurt that horse—"

"I haven't He was startled by some wild birds, I think. At all events, he recovered and was fine when I brought him in."

Not daring to look at Lady Ophelia, who had often heard Charley describe her training, Daintry said, "I have sworn to say nothing, Geoffrey, so do not ask me. I always keep my word."

Seacourt, still watching St. Merryn, said, "Order her to tell me, sir, or send for young Charlotte, and I'll soon have the truth out of her if I have to shake it out."

"Careful, Geoffrey," Daintry said. "You will reveal rather more of your delightful personality than you mean to reveal."

He shot a furious look at her but kept his attention focused on St. Merryn. "Well, sir?"

"Tell him where Susan is, Daintry."

"No, sir."

"What's that you say?" St. Merryn's mouth dropped open.

"I won't tell him. You may lock me in my room, or beat me, Papa, but I will still refuse to tell you. I promised Susan I would not betray her, and I mean to honor that promise."

"Then get Charlotte," Seacourt said. "I'll talk to her."

St. Merryn frowned, and Daintry held her breath, fearing he would send for Charley; but before he could speak, Lady Ophelia said in the same even tone she had employed before, "You may ask Charlotte, of course, but if I know her—and I daresay I know her very well—she too will refuse to tell you, and she will enjoy the scene she creates by refusing very much more than you will."

"Get Charles," Seacourt snapped. "Surely, he is not so cowed by you that he will refuse to force his daughter to speak."

Daintry sighed. "You really do not know Charles very well, do you, Geoffrey? Davina might help you if she wanted to do so, but I daresay she might have more sympathy for Susan than for you, and at all events, she would not try to beat an answer out of Charley. Nor, to his credit, would Charles ever do so."

St. Merryn shrugged. "Daresay there ain't much you can do, lad, if they refuse to speak. Take my advice and just wait a day or two for the chit to go home. She will, you know. They always do, and you can teach her then to mind you better."

"She has taken my daughter from my house," Seacourt said, his voice tight. "I will not simply sit and wait for her to decide what to do next."

St. Merryn shook his head. "Now that was wrong of her, very wrong. Man's child belongs at home. So does his wife, for that matter. Susan's done wrong, Ophelia. Even you must see that."

Lady Ophelia, looking straight at Seacourt, said, "Susan has done what she thinks best and will live with the consequences, whatever they may be; but understand me, young man, when I say that I believe every word she told us. Bad enough that you treated her roughly, but to force her to accept your mistress into your household, and to be carrying on such a relationship under the innocent eyes of your own child—"

St. Merryn interrupted angrily, "What nonsense are you prattling now, Ophelia? Mistress? What the devil's his mistress got to do with any of this?"

Daintry said, "She is living in his house with him, Papa—Lady Catherine Chauncey. I told you—"

"And I told you then, as I tell you now, that such things have nothing to do with you. A pretty pass we have come to when females begin cutting up stiff over a man's private affairs." He looked at Seacourt with new respect. "Actually got one living in your house with you, you say?"

"My cousin is making an extended visit," Seacourt said stiffly. "Whatever Susan might think of her, that is all it is."

"Upon my word," St. Merryn said, almost reverently, "I don't know how you manage it, lad. I truly don't."

Seacourt turned to Daintry. "You may think you have won, but you are dead wrong. I have every right to take legal action, and I shall. In fact, if I am not much mistaken, taking such action might prove interesting." Looking at her now as if he expected to catch her off her guard, he said softly, "The nearest magistrate, according to your father, is presently to be found at Deverill Court, and now that I come to think of it, that may even be the likeliest place for Susan to have sought refuge."

"You are mad, Geoffrey."

Shocked, St. Merryn said, "Deverill Court! Now, look here, Seacourt, don't you be saying I told you to lay your dirty laundry at Jervaulx's feet. I won't have it! We've kept our business well away from him all these years. I won't have you—"

"You cannot stop me," he snapped. "I can see that Daintry is none too pleased by this turn of events, so I daresay I may have guessed aright. But in the event that I have not, you will see me here again within the day, all of you, and I shall have the law on my side by then." And with that, he was gone.

Daintry, her eyes wide, turned to Lady Ophelia. "Is it true that Deverill's father is the nearest magistrate?"

Lady Ophelia nodded, watching St. Merryn. "Yes, he is. Has been for years, though many people expected him to hand over the duties to someone else once he became a marquess. But does Seacourt expect to find Susan at Deverill Court? He must know his so-called suspicions were utter nonsense."

"What suspicions?" St. Merryn demanded.

Daintry said calmly, "There were letters accusing Deverill of trifling with Susan, but they were not true, Papa. Susan is not the sort of woman to allow such behavior, nor Deverill the sort of man to attempt it."

"Well, if you think he wouldn't attempt it, you haven't paid heed to what those lads of Hill's got up to on the Continent, but it don't matter one way or another. Susan is Seacourt's problem, and he will soon have her sorted out."

"Not if I can stop him," Daintry said. "And what's more," she said to Lady Ophelia when St. Merryn had gone, "I would very much like to be present when Geoffrey storms Deverill Court and demands the return of his wife."

Deverill was sitting at his ease, his feet propped up on the fender before a crackling fire in the book room, reading a book. He had finished his midday meal less than half an hour before, and was enjoying a postprandial glass of wine and a few moments' leisurely reading before turning his attention to the pile of papers his father had left on the desk. He meant to sort them, and to put away what he could before he returned to his labors in the muniments room, but first he would read for a while.

When a footman opened the book-room door and said, "Sir Geoffrey Seacourt, sir," he thought for a moment that he must have misheard the man. But, looking up, he observed Seacourt himself, looking as red as bull beef, and primed for a fight.

Deverill put down his book. "Come in, Seacourt. Pour Sir Geoffrey a glass of wine, Thornton." He smiled at his visitor. "My father's selection is extremely large. What will you have?"

"I want my wife," Seacourt said, his eyes gleaming with spite. "If she's here, Deverill, suppose you trot her out."

Raising his eyebrows, Deverill said gently, "I believe that means Sir Geoffrey declines refreshment, Thornton. You may go. Fortunately," he added when the footman had gone, "my father trains his servants well. You need not fear that Thornton will repeat what he heard you say."

"I don't give a damn if he does repeat it," Seacourt snapped. "Where is she?"

"You know," Deverill said, stretching one leg out to ease a kink in his calf muscle, "I received your absurd letter and was not much impressed by it, but now I see that you are completely unhinged, which may explain a good deal. When, my good fellow, do you suppose I've had the time to attach Lady Susan's interest, let alone to do anything of which I seem to stand accused?"

"How do I know what you have done?"

"Oh, come, come, it is not what I have done that need concern you, but what your wife has done. From what I am given to understand, she rarely leaves Seacourt Head and then only in your company."

"I was in Brighton for more than two months without her."

"So you were. I, on the other hand, was in Belgium through those same months—or near enough—and when I returned, I went straight to my father's house in Gloucestershire before going north for a fortnight. I met your wife for the first time when I stopped at Tuscombe Park on my way back. You came home the next day. Sit down, man, have a glass of wine, and tell me what the devil this is really all about."

"No, thank you," Seacourt said stiffly. "I cannot prove that you are lying, but I have no way to know you speak the truth, either. Oh, I know you were at Waterloo; who does not know that? But as to the rest—Waterloo was in June, after all; I came home in late September. In point of fact, however, I came here today looking for Jervaulx. I heard he was here."

"He returned a few days ago, but he is away again now."

"I will wait."

Deverill sighed. "You begin to annoy me, Seacourt. I have purposely remained seated, because if I get up to you, I am likely to lose my temper. You will not wait here. If you did, you would be obliged to wait for some time, because the winter Assizes are in session. His lordship is in Launceston."

"Thank you," Seacourt said, adding curtly, "I will seek him there. You need not ring for your man. I can find my way out."

"No doubt, but I think I shall ring for him all the same," Deverill said gently, reaching to pull the cord near the mantel.

Flushing, Seacourt strode from the room, nearly colliding with Thornton, who was already responding to the bell.

With the door shut again, Deverill got up from his chair and moved to the desk, pushing aside his father's papers to write a letter. Then, ringing again for Thornton, he folded the note and sealed it, imprinting the warm red wax with his signet.

When the footman returned, Deverill smiled and said, "Seen him well away?"

"Yes, my lord."

"Good. Now, find Ned Shalton and send him to me. Oh, and Thornton," Deverill added as the man turned away.

Thornton turned back. "Yes, my lord?"

"I'd be most obliged if you could contrive to forget everything that occurred here within the past half hour."

"Certainly, my lord."

When Shalton arrived, Deverill said, "Take this note to the stables at Tuscombe Park, Ned, and give it into the tender keeping of a groom named Clemons to be delivered to his mistress at his earliest opportunity. And, Ned, don't get yourself run off the premises if you can help it."

"Aye, Major," the batman said, grinning. "A *billet doux*, is it? I'll see it to the wench safe enough."

"Not a wench this time, Ned. A lady, so mind your tongue."

"Oh, aye, Major. Mumchance it is then, sure enough."

"How are things with Kibworth?"

"Got a truce, Major. He don't sniff at me; I don't knock him into the middle of next week. Seems to work just fine."

"Out, Ned. Have a care with that note."

When the man had gone, Gideon turned his attention to the pile of papers on the desk and soon discovered that there were as many pertaining to business in Gloucestershire as to Jervaulx's affairs in Cornwall. He began to sort them into orderly piles.

Late that afternoon, when Daintry went down to the stables with Charley to feed carrots to Victor and Cloud, Clemons approached them, looking carefully around as he did so.

"What is it, Clemons?" Daintry demanded. "You look as if you had got smuggled goods hidden under your coat."

He put a finger to his lips, glanced around again, turned so Charley could not see what he did, then slid a hand inside his jacket and pulled out the note. "Mum's the word, Miss Daintry. I were told to slip this to you on the sly. Didn't know the man what brung it. You got yourself a beau now? That it?"

She was staring at the bold black letters forming her name, and she did not speak. Turning it over, she saw the seal, and though it was not one with which she was familiar, she knew whose it must be. Carefully, so as not to damage the wax, she slid her fingernail beneath it; loosening it so that the seal came away whole. Then, carefully unfolding the note, and ignoring Clemons's urgent suggestion that it would be better to wait until she need not fear being seen and reported, she read Deverill's words. Calling to Charley that she was going back to the house, she hurried inside to find Lady Ophelia.

Her aunt was in her bedchamber, beginning the important business of dressing for dinner.

"Look at this, Aunt," Daintry said, holding out the letter.

"I cannot look at it," Lady Ophelia said, observing the fall of her skirt in the cheval glass. To her maid, hovering nearby, she said brusquely, "I'll have the gray sarcenet instead, Alma. This gown don't become me today, and Sir Lionel is coming to dine with us." When the woman had turned away, she said in the same tone, "Well, don't keep me on tenterhooks, child. I can see that letter came from a gentleman. Who is it?"

Daintry glanced at the maid.

"Oh, for pity's sake, don't heed Alma. Close as an oyster, as you ought to know after all these years. Who's it from?"

"Deverill." Daintry waited for a reaction.

"Most improper, but one supposes that if he had sent it over with a footman to be delivered in the front hall, the servants would have taken it straight to your father, and we should have heard his reaction echo through the whole house. Read it."

Daintry said, "He wrote only to tell me that Geoffrey has gone to Launceston to find Lord Jervaulx."

"The Assizes are in session," Lady Ophelia said wisely. "Summer ones at Bodmin; winter at Launceston. That's why Lionel has come down from London just now, which I thought providential, but I wonder what Geoffrey thinks Jervaulx can do for him."

"I don't know, and Deverill does not say. He writes that Geoffrey was most put out by Susan's disappearance, and that if I had anything to do with it, I ought to advise her to come to her senses as quickly as possible. If that isn't just like a man, to make such a judgment before he has discovered all the facts! At least I know that when he does hear them, he will understand, and then he won't be so quick to take Geoffrey's side."

"You have no business to be telling anyone your sister's private business, Daintry, and for that matter, if he should learn the facts, you ought by now to have learned better than to expect any man to see any matter from a woman's point of view. They don't do it and never will. I doubt it's even possible."

"Deverill will," Daintry said confidently, remembering that he was unafraid even to be caught riding a sidesaddle. Surely, a man like that would examine both sides of an issue and then have the good sense to see which side was right. Deciding, improper or not, to reply to his note directly after dinner and explain to him just how matters actually stood, she soon took her leave to change her own dress for dinner.

Her hope that Seacourt's mission would prove futile lasted only until his return late the following afternoon, when he and St. Merryn, accompanied by Charles, entered the drawing room where she sat with the other women. Seacourt looked pleased with himself; St. Merryn and Charles looked extremely put out.

Her father said testily, "See what you've done now, girl. All over the county it will be within the week that my daughters have gone mad. How do you imagine that sits with my pride, eh?"

Davina had been reading aloud from a Gothic romance for the entertainment of the others. She closed the book, saying, "What is it, Papa St. Merryn? What have Daintry and Susan done?"

When St. Merryn only continued to glare at Daintry, Charles said, "Susan has run away. Seacourt is trying to find her."

"Dear me," Davina said on a note of sarcasm, "why would any woman want to run away from her husband?"

Daintry, realizing that Davina had not been present to hear Susan's story, said, "I will tell you about it later. Papa, I am sorry you are vexed, but whatever Geoffrey has done now, or threatens to do, I still will not help him find Susan."

Seacourt reached inside his coat and withdrew a rolled bit of parchment. "Oh, yes, you will, much though you will dislike it. I told you the law would support me, and so it has."

"What can the law do? It cannot make me tell you anything."

Seacourt looked at Lady Ophelia. "What of you, ma'am? Do you also refuse to tell me where my wife can be found?"

"I do," Lady Ophelia said firmly.

"Do you know the meaning of *habeas corpus*?"

Lady Ophelia grimaced. "I do. Is that what you have in your hand, sir, a writ of *habeas corpus*?"

"It is."

The old lady nodded, and Daintry, unable to stand the suspense a moment longer, cried, "But what is it, Aunt Ophelia? What can a piece of paper have to say to any of this?"

"Only this, my pet," Seacourt said smugly. "If you do not tell me where Susan is, then you must produce her at the Assize Court in Launceston by Thursday next, or the magistrate—in this instance, the Marquess of Jervaulx—will take great pleasure in throwing you and dear Lady Ophelia into the Launceston jail."

"He can't do that!"

"He can and he will. Now where are my wife and child?"

Daintry looked pleadingly at Lady Ophelia. "I won't tell him. I would rather go to prison."

Lady Ophelia's lips tightened, and she was silent for a long moment before she said, "There is no need yet to speak of prison. You say the writ demands their presence on Thursday, Seacourt?"

"Yes, but surely you won't suffer the indignity of showing your-self in a courtroom, ma'am. Just tell me where they can be found, and there will be no need to subject yourself to that."

"Nothing undignified about a proper English courtroom," the old lady said. "You forget one thing, young man. Once we get there, we will have our own tale to unfold."

"But to what purpose, ma'am? No court will rule against a hus-band in a case like this one. If you and Daintry want to make fools of yourselves, I cannot stop you, but warn Susan that the angrier she makes me, the sorrier she will be when Jervaulx orders her home again."

When he had gone, Daintry took the first opportunity to con-fer privately with her aunt. "What are we going to do, ma'am? Must we give Susan up to them?"

"Do you imagine your sister will allow you to go to prison on her behalf?"

Daintry had not thought of that. She sighed. "No."

"Do you mean to ask Annie to put herself, Granny Popple, and Feok at risk on Susan's behalf? Or do you suppose that Seacourt, once he finds out, will forgive them for helping Susan?"

"Oh, this is dreadful! Very well, then, we must do as you proposed, ma'am, and lay Susan's case before the court. Papa will not like it, but Jervaulx must be fair, after all, and we will have Deverill to speak to him for us. I will write at once to tell him what Geoffrey has done now."

"Proper young ladies do not correspond with unmarried gentlemen, and certainly not about private family affairs."

"Oh, pooh, as if I cared a straw for that. Besides, after he wrote to warn us of where Geoffrey was going, I thought it only sensible to write back—explaining the truth, you know—and now it is only courteous to let him know about that . . . that what-not Geoffrey managed to get from Lord Jervaulx."

"'Tis a writ of *habeas corpus*."

"You may have the body," Daintry said, remembering long-ago Latin lessons with her aunt. "But what does it mean, precisely."

"Just what he said. I confess, Lionel Werring warned me that this might well be the next step, but I could see no good to be accomplished by putting you in a fidget when he might still be proved wrong. We must produce Susan, either to Seacourt, since he was awarded the writ, or to the magistrate."

"Then Jervaulx it is," Daintry said, drawing a long breath. "Geoffrey Seacourt will rue this day, ma'am."

"I hope so," Lady Ophelia said doubtfully. "I must write to warn Lionel that we shall have need of his services."

Fourteen

Gideon received Daintry's letters with only a small degree of surprise, for he had long since understood that she did not concern herself much with notions of propriety. Nonetheless, he did not reply to them. Her father did not share her notions, and he had no wish to figure, since he had written the first letter, as the instigator of a clandestine correspondence.

That she and the other ladies meant to confront Seacourt and expected Jervaulx, not to mention himself, to support them, he found disquieting. He smiled at her naive assumption that he could influence his father, and though he knew he could not, decided he must certainly attend the Assize Court on Thursday, so that she should not think he had basely deserted them. And, too, despite all her independent airs and graces, she was vulnerable and all too likely to make a fool of herself if he were not there to protect her from the consequences of her own impulsiveness.

What his father would make of his presence, he could not imagine, nor did he attempt to do so, but Thursday morning found him at Launceston Castle in the ancient county capital, where Dukes of Cornwall still came to receive their feudal dues, and where assize courts had been held since the twelfth century.

There was a great deal of traffic since Thursday was a market day, but he was able without much difficulty to pass through the town gate of the castle and drive his curricle straight inside, past the jail and onto the castle green, where the Assize Court building was located. Court was already in session when he entered, but although Sea-court was seated near the front, he saw no sign of the ladies or St. Merryn before he found a place in the second row. Jervaulx, the sole magistrate, was seated behind the high bench, and looked sharply at him for a brief instant before returning his attention to the case at hand.

Once Lady Ophelia's carriage had passed the Launceston sheep market and made its way down the hill, Daintry could see the ancient south gate of the castle ahead.

"There it is, ma'am."

"Yes," Lady Ophelia said. "We will go round to the north gate and right in, too, for I've no mind to present myself or you gels to the populace at large as a spectacle. I do wish your father had seen fit to accompany us, or even your brother."

Susan had been silent, as usual, but at these words she murmured, "Papa is so angry with me. 'Tis a pity Melissa cried so when we wanted her to stay with Annie, and insisted upon going to stay with Charlotte, or we need not have seen him today."

Daintry said pacifically, "He agreed to allow Melissa to stay at Tuscombe Park until this business is settled, which must mean he expects Jervaulx to decide in your favor, love, so cheer up. We will have Deverill on our side, at all events, and Aunt Ophelia has arranged for Sir Lionel Werring to plead your case. Sir Lionel is most eloquent, is he not, ma'am?"

"He'd better be," Lady Ophelia said grimly.

Susan fell silent again, and when they rolled through the castle gate, Daintry realized they were passing a prison. The sight of a man in chains being led inside by a burly jailer reminded her of how casually she had said she would go to prison rather than give Susan up. The thought made her feel sick now.

The huge round tower of the castle rose up on her left, and ahead on the castle green she saw the Assize Court building. The carriage rolled to a stop, and the footman riding behind leapt down to open the door and let down the steps. Daintry got out first, accepting the footman's hand when she realized her knees were weak. There were people standing around, but she did not see anyone she knew. For some reason, she had expected to see Deverill, but she told herself now that he must have expected St. Merryn to accompany them and had decided it would not be tactful to make his presence known at once.

Her father had flatly refused to come. In fact, he had agreed to allow Melissa to remain at the house only when Lady Ophelia had pointed out that the child would not be allowed in the courtroom and could scarcely be left in the carriage. "Only think what people would say about a man who forced his innocent little granddaughter to sit outside a courthouse in plain view of all the riffraff, only because he was too puffed up in his own conceit to look after her properly himself," she had said.

Though he had given in on Melissa's account, nothing they had said would induce him to accompany them to Launceston. "Susan's made her bed and must lie in it," he said flatly. "It is no doing of mine, and I'll be damned before I'll set foot in Jervaulx's court and let him smirk at my misfortunes."

When Daintry had pointed out to him that it was Susan's misfortune and Susan's future that was at stake, he snarled, "Stuff and nonsense. All Susan has to do is to obey her husband, and she will get on perfectly well with him."

"And what about Lady Catherine Chauncey?" Daintry demanded. "Is Susan expected to get on well with her, too?"

"More stuff and nonsense. If Seacourt's taken a mistress, it is plain that Susan has not been a good wife to him. She must strive to do better, and that's all there is about it."

"She is not going to go back to him, Papa."

"Of course she is. Jervaulx will order her back simply because a wife belongs with her husband."

Remembering those words now as she entered the courtroom with her great-aunt and her sister, Daintry prayed he would be proved wrong. Looking swiftly around, she saw that there were few women present, and not one to whom she would wish to be seen speaking. At first she did not see Seacourt or Deverill, but then, as if drawn, she found herself looking at a head of dark auburn hair set above a pair of broad shoulders. Deverill shifted in his seat and turned, his gaze locking with hers. He did not smile, but so certain was she that his intent was to protect her sister that she smiled at him to show him she was grateful for the support of his presence. She had never expected to look to any man for protection, but she had to admit now that it was rather pleasant to be able to do so.

She glanced at Lady Ophelia and Susan, but the former was searching the crowded room for her solicitor, and Susan, white-faced, was staring at the floor and trembling.

Sir Lionel, a small, wiry gentleman dressed with quiet good taste, approached them, nodded at Lady Ophelia, touched Susan's arm, and said in low but carrying tones, "This way, Lady Susan. I've seats for you near the front so you will not have to walk the full length of this place when your name is called."

"Are you quite prepared for this business, Lionel?" Lady Ophelia demanded over the rumble of noise around them.

"As prepared as possible, Ophelia, but as I warned you—"

"Yes, yes, I know. Just do your best. No one can expect you to do more than that."

Daintry looked at her aunt in dismay. "Does he think Susan cannot win, ma'am?"

"Take your seat, my dear."

Sir Lionel indicated space on one of the polished oak benches near the front, and Daintry, realizing that they had begun to draw attention, quickly took her seat. She could see Deverill ahead of her, at the end of the next row, and taking comfort from his nearness, turned her attention to his father.

The marquess, though harsh of countenance, much thinner, and nearing his sixtieth year, looked a good deal like his son, she thought. He was seated high above everyone else in the court, wearing the black robes and a full-bottomed powdered wig of a magistrate, and he had noted their presence, for Susan's case was soon called. Daintry had no notion what to expect, but when Sir Lionel began to explain that Lady Susan sought permission from the court to live apart from her husband, she saw Susan begin to tremble more than ever, and prayed hard that the solicitor would be eloquent indeed. He was not a barrister, after all, but Lady

Ophelia had assured them that merely to present their position with regard to the *habeas corpus* did not require one, and that to engage one would serve only to annoy the magistrate.

Sir Lionel began persuasively enough by explaining that he spoke on behalf of an innocent woman who had been grossly mistreated by the very man sworn to protect and cherish her. But that was as far as he got with his rehearsed periods.

"One moment, Sir Lionel," Jervaulx said suddenly. Daintry noted that his voice was low like Deverill's but contained more of a growl. The sound was not comforting. "The man you speak of is Lady Susan's husband, is he not?"

"He is, my lord."

"Then one fails to comprehend your point, sir. The law of England attributes general dominion of a husband over his wife, so she must always be better off in his custody than elsewhere, regardless of how he treats her. By entering into marriage, she consents to submit to his will, so he may keep her by force and he may beat her—within reason, one hopes—if she disobeys him. In any event, the law disapproves of separation, since a much greater amount of happiness is produced in the married state when the union is known to be indissoluble than could be enjoyed if the tie were less firm. Lady Susan must return to her husband."

"No!" Daintry was on her feet, crying out the word before she had any notion that she was about to do such a thing, but even the chorus of gasps from the courtroom audience was not enough to silence her. "You cannot send her back to him! It would be too cruel!"

Jervaulx's cold gaze came to rest upon her, and although she was conscious of a sudden movement ahead and to the right of her, she could not look away. The magistrate's thin lips tightened, and for a moment she had an awful premonition that he was going to cry, "Off with her head!" Licking suddenly dry lips, she waited for summary execution. The courtroom was deathly silent.

"Who, pray, are you?"

"Daintry Tarrant, sir. Lady Susan is my sister."

"Is that so? Then perhaps you may be forgiven for your unseemly outburst. Reasonable persons will attribute it to a female's natural inability to control her sensibilities."

"My sensibilities have nothing to do with it, my lord. You have not even heard her case."

"She has no case."

"If she were a man who had been assaulted—"

"She is not a man. She is a wife. And according to the laws of England, a wife has no civil status at the bar—"

"Then the law is unfair to women!"

"Daintry, sit down," Lady Ophelia hissed.

Daintry ignored her, but Lady Ophelia's words had clearly carried to the high bench, for Jervaulx glanced at her. His gaze flickered toward his son, then came to rest again upon Daintry. "This discussion had better be continued in the magistrates' chamber. Sir Lionel, bring your party. Sir Geoffrey, you come along too, of course." Jervaulx got to his feet and, robes swirling, descended from the high bench to make his exit, barely pausing long enough for a minion to snatch open the chamber door.

Daintry stood in shock, wondering what on earth she had done. She saw Susan move ahead with Sir Lionel and felt her aunt tug her sleeve but could not seem to move. Then a firm hand grasped her other arm, and she looked up to see Deverill, looking more like the stern-faced marquess than she had thought possible.

"Come on," he said. "He does not like to be kept waiting."

"You will come, too, won't you? What will he do?"

"He won't eat you." His tone was brusque.

"It is not myself I'm worried about. You must make him listen to all the horrid things Geoffrey has done to Susan!"

Giving her a little push toward the others, Deverill escorted her past the fascinated onlookers to the door through which Jervaulx had disappeared. It led into a medium-sized chamber used generally for robing, but there was a large desk at one end near a window, and Jervaulx had seated himself behind it. He indicated chairs for Lady Ophelia and Susan.

"There seems, unfortunately, to be an insufficient number of chairs for everyone, but the gentlemen will not mind standing. Step forward, Lady Daintry, and perhaps these matters can be made plain to you. No, no, Sir Lionel," he added when the solicitor stepped forward with her. "You are an excellent advocate, but she has no need of you just now." To Daintry's surprise, his tone was nearly benevolent.

"I should not have shrieked out at you like I did, sir," she said, aware that although Sir Lionel had stepped away Deverill was still behind her. Grateful for his presence, she took a deep breath, adding, "I do apologize if I behaved badly."

"You did, and to no good purpose."

"But the law *is* unfair."

"My dear young woman, so great a favorite is the female to the laws of England that a good many of them are specifically intended to protect and benefit her. By marriage she becomes one person in law with her husband. That is to say, her very being, her legal existence, is consolidated with his, and she is perceived to act at all times under his command and protection."

"Protection," Daintry said scornfully, "is not what my sister has received at the hands of her husband, sir."

"Consider the many advantages granted a woman," Jervaulx said as if she had not spoken. "She does not lose her rank on marriage, a privilege of which Lady Susan has taken advantage. She is allowed to testify on her own behalf if she is raped, and she cannot be imprisoned for debt. She is not even obliged to pay her debts. Her husband must pay them. He is obliged to support her as long as she shares his bed and board, and he is answerable for her actions. In fact, since she is presumed to act under his command and control, she is excused punishment for offenses committed in his presence unless it can be proved that she did not act under his influence."

"But none of that applies to Susan. She has committed no wrong. She does not even have any debts. What she *has* got is a great many bruises!"

Patiently, Jervaulx said, "But you see, a husband has a vested interest in keeping his wife under his control and out of mischief. Not only is he responsible for her actions but—you will forgive some plain-speaking here—England is the one country in all the world which gives a woman an extraordinary opportunity to palm off a bastard child on her husband. If an Englishman cannot prove his wife's adultery, any child she has is assumed, under law, to be his full responsibility, however improbable the circumstances of that child's birth."

Seacourt snapped, "That's right, by God."

Jervaulx shifted his chilly gaze. "As to you, sir, pray recall that, under law, a husband *can* be punished if he mistreats his wife in ways *not* acceptable to the community. No one questions his right to chastise her, but he must not go too far."

Seacourt looked directly at Susan and said, "The community will hear no complaints from my wife, my lord."

"Excellent," Jervaulx said, beginning to rise.

Desperately, Daintry cried, "Please, my lord—"

"No, Lady Daintry," Jervaulx said sternly. "There is no more to be said. Extraordinary measures have been allowed today, because of the history existing between the Tarrant and Deverill families. You were not to suppose that your sister could not receive justice from this court. But now that the matter has been fully explained to you, there are other cases that must be heard without further delay." He got to his feet, nodded at the others, and swept from the room.

Daintry, turning to watch him leave, found herself face to face with Deverill, and all the rage she had had to suppress boiled over in that instant. "You betrayed us," she snapped. "We depended on you to help, and you did not speak one word in Susan's defense. It is just as I'd feared, and you are no better than any other man. In fact, you are worse, for you led me to suspect that you had a heart, Deverill, and you have none!"

"It is not a matter of heart," he retorted, "but a matter of law. You heard him." He shot a glance at Susan, still sitting by Lady Ophelia but staring at Sir Geoffrey with much the same look on her face as a rabbit mesmerized by the approach of a fox.

Daintry's glance followed Deverill's, and impulsively she stepped in front of Seacourt. "If you dare to hurt Susan again, Geoffrey, so help me, I will see that you pay dearly."

Seacourt smiled, but the expression was not pleasant. "So fierce, little sister-in-law, but you have no power to stop me, you know, and nor does Deverill." He shot a triumphant look at the latter. "Whether or not there is truth in the accusations against him,

Susan has not behaved well at all and deserves to be punished. Come along, my dear," he added, pushing Daintry out of the way and holding out a commanding hand to his wife.

Still with that mesmerized look on her face, Susan stood up. Her cheeks were pale, her lips parted, her eyes wide with fear.

Lady Ophelia stood up too, briskly shaking out her skirts. She said, "See here, young man, you may have won this skirmish, but the war is far from over, and it would behoove you just now, I think, to recall the source of your wife's expectations."

Sir Geoffrey looked sharply at her.

Lady Ophelia's smile was grim. "Ah, yes, that has brought you up short, has it not? You have always gone out of your way to be charming to me before, but you have seriously blotted your copybook now, and I should like to make you aware of a thing or two. First and foremost is the fact that Susan's inheritance is merely a matter of my will, which can easily be altered. At present, she is co-heiress with Daintry, but it might be more sensible to put her share in trust for Melissa instead. And lest you think that would make no difference to your control, sir, let me make it plain to you that Sir Lionel here will arrange the whole business for me, not through the common court, but through a Court of Chancery, where it can be arranged so that you will have no access to the money. I should be reluctant to humiliate you so, since at Susan's own request I did not arrange it that way from the outset, and the news would get round quickly, but if you antagonize me, do not think for a moment that I will not."

Seacourt's cheeks were red, and his outstretched hand had fallen to his side. He said in a tightly controlled voice, "You misjudge me, ma'am, but I cannot blame you, knowing how much inclined you are always to support the members of your own sex against mine. Indeed, that part of your character is what I have most admired in you. But in this instance, I believe you have carried it too far. I love my wife, not her expectations, so you may do as you please with your money. I own, I behaved more like a beast than a lover when I thought Susan had been involved in a clandestine affair with such an acknowledged rake as Deverill."

Lady Ophelia's glance shifted abruptly to Deverill, but Sir Geoffrey did not pause long enough for her to speak.

"Perhaps no one chose to mention it to you, ma'am, but Susan received two letters accusing her of misconduct with him. I let the first pass, accepting her assurance that there was no truth in it, but we had all been guests at a large house party where, as you know, any number of things might have happened of which I was unaware, and thus, the second letter was more than I could bear. I lost my temper, and if I was rougher than I'd meant to be, I doubt I did more than any angry husband would. It was no cause for Susan to run away, and surely none to complain to you of abusive treatment. I give you my word, I have never been so cruel to her before. Have I, Susan?" he added, looking directly at his wife. "Come now, it is time for the truth, my dear."

Susan seemed frozen where she stood, her only movements a darting of her tongue to wet her lips and a flickering of her eyes as she glanced first at Deverill, then back at Lady Ophelia, as if she were measuring their reactions to his words.

Sir Geoffrey said gently, "Come, come, love. You cannot want dear Lady Ophelia to think so ill of me as she does now."

"N-no," she said, her voice catching on a sob.

Lady Ophelia said, "Tell the truth, Susan, whatever it is."

"Yes," Seacourt said. "This is no time for more lies, my dear. Tell everyone the truth."

Daintry cried, "Can't you see that he is terrifying her? She knows she must go with him afterward. She dare not speak!"

Seacourt smiled ruefully at her. "I had not realized you despised me so, little sister. What have I done to draw such ire? Had you more experience of this world of ours, you would understand that husbands and wives—the people who care most for one another—frequently say dreadful things that they do not mean in the least when they are angry, only to hurt each other and cause trouble. I think Susan was as angry with me as I was with her, for similar reason. Has not some wicked person suggested an illicit relationship between me and my poor widowed cousin?"

Susan gasped.

Lady Ophelia said, "You know that accusation has been made, for you heard it yourself. Do you deny any such relationship?"

"Of course I deny it," Seacourt said indignantly. "I did at the time, and good God, ma'am, would I be so cruel as to keep my mistress under my own roof, to flaunt our relationship before my wife's very eyes? Of course not. Indeed, who but an insanely jealous wife could believe such a thing of any man? But some wicked person put the notion in her head, no doubt a person as cruel as the one who wrote letters accusing her of misconduct, knowing that, like anyone else, I read all letters addressed to those living under my protection. Perhaps it was even the same person, for now that I see them together, I find it difficult to believe Susan could encourage advances from a man like Deverill."

"Much obliged to you," Deverill said dryly.

"No doubt," Sir Geoffrey went on earnestly, "that very same person wrote similar accusations about me to Susan, or else in her own imaginings . . . Was that it, my dear?"

Susan said, "But you—"

"What you thought about me is not the truth, love. I swear it to you before these witnesses. Now, can you forgive me for being so angry when similar accusations were made against you?"

Susan flushed, glancing away from him to the others, looking as guilty as a child caught in mischief. When no one else said anything, she turned back to her husband and said in a small voice, "Are you still angry with me?"

"You deserve that I should be," he said, "for putting us all through this dreadful ordeal, but if you will come home with me now and promise to think better of me, I promise not to be angry. Come, my love," he added, holding out his hand again.

This time Susan put hers in it at once, and he drew her close and kissed her gently on the forehead. "That's my good girl." Over her head he said to Lady Ophelia, "I'd take it kindly if you will arrange to send my daughter home tomorrow."

Daintry, who was growing more wrathful by the moment, had opened her mouth to protest when a large hand clamped like a vise on her arm. She turned indignantly, and Deverill shook his head at her, the look in his eyes warning her in no uncertain terms to keep silent. Before she could tell him what she thought of his interference, or warn her aunt not to agree to Geoffrey's demand, Lady Ophelia said, "Your arguments are persuasive, Geoffrey, but they do not altogether convince me. I shall escort Melissa home myself, and I shall expect to see Susan looking the picture of domestic tranquility when we arrive."

"That is precisely what you will see," he replied, looking lovingly at Susan. "I have missed her very much, and as to your fortune, you may leave it as you please, in trust or not. I hope yet to have sons as well as a daughter, you know, and the more secure Melissa's future can be made, the better I shall like it."

"There is no need to alter anything just yet, I think."

Seacourt smiled. Then, tucking Susan's hand into the crook of his arm, he turned to Deverill. "Is there a way out of this building other than through that courtroom? Susan will not want to create a further spectacle for the riffraff."

Deverill had released Daintry's arm as soon as Lady Ophelia had spoken, and he said now, "That door at the rear leads to a corridor, and another at the end leads outside. You can send one of the lads hanging about outside to fetch your carriage."

"Obliged to you. Come, my love."

Daintry scarcely waited until the door had shut behind them before glaring at Sir Lionel and Deverill in turn and saying, "I suppose you both believed that drivel Geoffrey was spouting!"

"His argument was plausible," Deverill replied calmly.

Sir Lionel nodded his head. "It certainly was."

Wildly, she looked at Lady Ophelia. "You did not believe him, did you, ma'am? Oh, please, say you did not! In the first place, that business about the letters . . ." But even as she said the words, she knew she could not explain, not without betraying Susan to Deverill, and that she could not do, not after he had proved so unworthy of the trust she had placed in him.

Lady Ophelia reached for her large reticule. "I have never known Susan to utter an untruthful word," she said. "On the other hand, since one cannot doubt that husbands and wives do frequently hurt each other, Geoffrey's argument was certainly plausible—most fortunately so, perhaps."

"Not to me it wasn't! He was lying in his teeth. I only hope he does not beat Susan senseless the moment they get home."

"He will not do that," Deverill said flatly.

His calm assumption of something she could not believe for a minute ignited her temper again, and she whirled on him, snapping, "What can you know about what he will do? How could you stand there and let him accuse you? Or did you, in fact, have nothing to say because you had done something to make her look to you—" She caught herself, adding hastily, "That is to say, to make someone accuse you of trifling? You certainly did nothing to protect her! I trusted you to help, and you just stood in that courtroom and let that horrid old man cite idiotic laws as cause to order her home with Geoffrey again."

"I remind you that the horrid man you speak of is my father," he said curtly. "As to the rest, it was out of my power to do anything even if I had wanted to."

"There! I knew it. You didn't want to."

"Damn it, stop ripping up at me like a shrew. Your voice will carry into the courtroom and bring him down on us again if you're not careful, and you won't fare as well a second time, I promise you. You're damned lucky he didn't clap you into jail for your outburst earlier. He was extremely patient with you, uncharacteristically so, but press him further and—"

"Oh, do not talk to me!" Clapping her hands to her ears, she turned away from him, meaning to leave by the same door her sister and Seacourt had used.

Before she had taken a step, Deverill caught an arm and spun her around to face him. Taking her hands from her ears, he held them tightly, saying, "If you do not want to be well shaken, you will stand still and listen to what I tell you. That's better," he added when she froze in fury. "I made no attempt to influence my father, even when I knew you meant to fight the writ, because it would have done no good. Not only would he have refused to listen to me—and rightly, since I have no business interfering in matters coming before him for judgment—but it is likewise no business of mine to interfere in another man's marriage. I do not expect you to understand that, since women simply cannot know as much about matters of law as men do; however—"

In a single swift movement, Daintry snatched her right hand from his relaxing grip and flung it up to slap him as hard as she could, but he caught it a hair's breadth from his cheek, his grasp so tight that she winced.

Grimly he said, "I do not deserve to be slapped for telling you the plain truth, and until I deserve it, you will not do it. As for what you deserve from me for that little exhibition—"

"Enough," Lady Ophelia snapped, startling them both. "I have been plagued by enough histrionics this past fortnight to last me a lifetime. Unhand my niece, sir, and send for my carriage. I want to go home."

Deverill released Daintry at once, leaving her to rub her sore wrist while he went to send for the carriages. Gazing resentfully after him, she said, "Men! How can any woman stomach the creatures?"

When there was no response, she turned to see that Lady Ophelia was regarding her with a quizzical, enigmatic expression on her countenance, and that Sir Lionel was still in the room.

Feeling warmth invade her cheeks, she said, "I beg your pardon, Sir Lionel, but why do you look at me so, Aunt Ophelia? Most men *are* dreadful."

"To be sure they are, my dear, but some are occasionally less dreadful than others, you know."

Fifteen

The journey back to Tuscombe Park seemed a particularly long one to Daintry. Once they had seen the last of Sir Lionel and Deverill, and were alone in the carriage and back on the main road, she tried several times to discuss what had happened in the courtroom, but she found Lady Ophelia singularly unwilling to enter into her feelings upon at least one topic.

When she muttered, "Deverill is the greatest beast in nature," Lady Ophelia replied simply, "I do not agree." And when, some moments later, she said, "A *gentleman* worthy of the name ought to feel obligated to aid a lady in distress," Lady Ophelia replied placidly, "Deverill holds by his own principles. There is a good deal to be said for that, you know."

"Not when he was our strongest hope, ma'am. Why—"

"It is done now," the old lady interjected flatly. "We must look ahead, not dwell on the sorrows of the past."

"I know that, but what lies ahead for Susan except more of the same sorrow? I know you believed Geoffrey—"

"I did not believe him," Lady Ophelia said, "but what I believe and what he thinks I believe are two different matters, as Deverill was trying to explain to you before you flew out at him like the shrew he named you."

"Are you taking Deverill's side against mine, ma'am?" she asked in astonishment.

Lady Ophelia sniffed. "I take no side at all," she said. "I merely point out to you that he saw what you did not, that it was important for Geoffrey to believe he had convinced me."

"But that will only make him more arrogant than ever," she protested. "He will think now that he can continue to get away with treating Susan as badly as he has in the past."

"On the contrary, I hope he will be less likely to harm her if he believes he still has his charming facade to protect, and having been reminded that her inheritance depends on his good behavior, surely he will tread more lightly now." Clearly deciding these words clinched the matter, she reached into the large reticule she always carried when she traveled—and which she said contained anything anyone might ever need on the road—and withdrew a book by one of her favorite female authors. Opening it, she found her place and began silently to read.

Daintry had not paused to consider the effect that Lady Ophelia's threat might have on Seacourt, but she saw now that it was the one thing that could weigh heavily enough with him to insure his good behavior, at least for a while. Still, the situation was unstable, and since Deverill had not helped in the least, she was entirely out of charity with him. In fact, she was furious with him, because she had dared to trust him and he had let her down with a vengeance. Looking at her aunt, she wished she could discuss the matter more fully with her, but Lady Ophelia's gaze remained riveted on her book, making it clear that she did not wish to talk about Deverill or anyone else.

It was dark by the time the carriage rolled up before the front entrance of the house, and golden light spilled down the marble steps when the tall doors were flung wide and the butler stepped out to see if they required assistance.

Lady Ophelia's footman leapt down from his perch to open the carriage door, and as Daintry accepted his help to alight, she saw her nieces peeping around the front door. "Hello, you two," she called. "Why are you not upstairs where you belong?"

At this small encouragement, and with Melissa trailing like a shadow in her wake, Charley ran out and down the steps, crying, "What happened, Aunt Daintry? Where is Aunt Susan?"

Lady Ophelia, emerging from the carriage, said tartly, "Mind your tongue, Charlotte, and go straight back into that house. The very idea of running out here without so much as a wrap to cover your bare arms! You will catch your death. You, too, Melissa. Back inside at once, the pair of you!"

Charley looked mutinous, but Daintry said quietly and with a warning glance at the servants, "We must not talk here, my dears. I will come to you as soon as I can, to tell you everything."

Biting her lip, Charley gave her a long look, then turned and went back. Melissa had already slipped back into the house.

Daintry meant to go straight up to the schoolroom, knowing the little girls would be impatient to know what had occurred, but no sooner had she and Lady Ophelia entered the hall than Medrose said, "His lordship desires you both to go at once to the drawing room, my lady. He has ordered a light repast to be served to you there."

"Excellent, for we are famished," Lady Ophelia said gratefully, allowing him to take her cloak and reticule. "I suppose everyone else is in there with him."

"Yes, ma'am. That is to say, Lady St. Merryn, Miss Davina, and Master Charles are there, and Miss Ethelinda, of course."

Daintry, realizing that she had no choice in the matter, said to the butler as he took her things, "Please send someone up to the schoolroom, Medrose, to tell Miss Charlotte and Miss Melissa that I shall be a trifle delayed in coming to them."

She was more than a trifle delayed, however, for by the time she and Lady Ophelia had described the courtroom scene and its aftermath to the others, and had their supper, a considerable amount of time had passed.

Lady St. Merryn appeared to think the entire episode had been devised to distress her, Charles and Davina were diverted, and Cousin Ethelinda exclaimed her dismay after nearly every statement made by either Lady Ophelia or Daintry, until the latter at least was ready to strangle her. St. Merryn, on the other hand, declared with obvious satisfaction that he had never looked for such a sensible decision from Jervaulx.

"Sensible, Papa? How can you say so?" Daintry demanded.

"Just did, didn't I? Can't think why you females make such a piece of work about it when there was no other legal course the man could take. Not that I didn't expect him to pull some damned foolery or other just to spite me, mind you. Only saying his action was proper. Don't do to interfere between a man and his wife, don't do at all. That Jervaulx didn't try to do so makes me think the better of him, upon my word."

"Well, I do not think better of him," Daintry said.

Davina, chuckling, said, "By the sound of it, I should say you were fortunate not to have vexed him beyond reason. Did you really cry out at him right there in his courtroom?"

Flushing at the memory, Daintry said, "I spoke without thinking, that's all. He made me too angry to think."

"When I think that Charles accuses me of making a spectacle of myself when I do no more than smile at another gentleman, I shudder to think what he would say if I were to behave as you did," Davina said, sending her husband an arch look.

Charles grimaced but said nothing.

When Lady St. Merryn moaned, reached for her salts, and lay against her cushions, holding the back of her free hand feebly against her forehead, Cousin Ethelinda said, "Pray, do not distress your mama with more of this talk, for now that Susan has returned to her family, all will be well. How thankful Sir Geoffrey must be to have her at home again where she belongs."

Daintry's fingernails dug into her palms, and she wished it were possible to tell one's cousin precisely what one thought of her foolishness. Since it was not possible, she held her tongue, but she did not hold it later, when she was finally able to go to the children and Charley's indignation at both the fact that Susan had returned to Seacourt Head and that Melissa was to return the next day led her to be impertinent.

"I won't let Aunt Ophelia take Melissa back!" she cried when Daintry had explained matters.

"You have no more to say about it than I had," Daintry said, holding her sorely tried temper in check with difficulty.

"Then we'll run away."

"You will do no such thing."

"We will so!"

Daintry had been sitting between the two little girls on the schoolroom sofa, but she rose now and looked sternly down at Charley. "Stand up."

Slowly Charley obeyed. There were tears in her eyes, but she did not make the mistake of trying to defend herself.

"How dare you speak to me in such an improper manner?" Daintry said. "Had you spoken so to your papa or grandpapa, you know exactly what would befall you. As it is, you may take yourself off to bed at once and you will spend the entire day tomorrow attending to your lessons with Miss Parish. I had hoped to arrange matters so that you could go with us to take Melissa home, but you do not deserve such a treat now. Have you anything at all to say for yourself?"

"No, Aunt Daintry." The tears spilled down her cheeks, and she added with a sob, "I-I'm sorry."

"I suppose you are, now," Daintry said, steeling herself to remain firm. "Go to bed. You, too, Melissa."

When they had gone, she went to her own bedchamber, thinking of the blissful moment that lay ahead when Nance would have gone to bed and she would be alone at last after the long and trying day. But when she entered her room she found not only Nance but Davina awaiting her.

Her sister-in-law said cheerfully, "Got the children all tucked up in bed?"

"Yes, but I had to scold Charley. She is very upset that she can do nothing to prevent Melissa's return. And she's your daughter, Davina. You ought to do the tucking up, not me."

Davina shrugged. "Charley does not care. I daresay she is closer to you than she is to me, and if she was impertinent, I doubt she was any more so than you were with Jervaulx, and with much the same cause. In any case, these days I should be thought an odd sort of mama if I hovered over her."

"Perhaps, but you are wrong about her not caring. She misses you both when you are away so often."

"So you have said before, but I did not come to talk about Charley, you know. Do you think Susan lied about Geoffrey just because she was angry with him?"

"I do not think she lied at all," Daintry said, holding her temper now on a slender thread. "I have said that all along."

Davina sighed. "Men are very difficult, aren't they?"

"I wouldn't know," Daintry said, but the image of a tall, broad-shouldered one leapt to her mind's eye and she knew at once that she was equivocating. Men were loathsome creatures.

Davina said, "Well, I do know. Your brother is a puzzle, Daintry, and that is plain fact."

"Charles?" Daintry was astonished.

"You needn't sound as if I had just said something absurd," Davina said crossly, "for it was nothing of the kind. He seems to expect me to know what he is thinking, as if I had a crystal ball. Can you tell when he is angry, Daintry? I promise you, I cannot—not until he explodes, at all events."

"And has he exploded?" Daintry asked, thinking she knew now where the conversation was leading.

"Twice in a fortnight," Davina said with another sigh. "At Mount Edgcumbe because I smiled more than once at Lord Aston, and two days ago at Cothele just because I borrowed a few rouleaux from Alvanley. It was no great thing, so do not look at me that way. I won on the next turn and paid him back. At all events, I do not know how Charles thinks I can live on the pittance he gives me each month—as if a woman did not require a new gown from time to time, not to mention money for trinkets and loo."

"But it is not just loo, is it, Davina? At Mount Edgcumbe you were plunging rather deep."

"And what else was there to do, with Charles playing cards himself or drinking himself into a stupor? I wore a brand new dress that I thought he would particularly like, and he just demanded to know what it cost. Right in front of everyone, too. I wanted to sink through the floor. And if I so much as smile at anyone, he sulks, but he has no romance in him, Daintry, and I like to be courted and made much of. Is that so dreadful?"

"I suppose not, but would it not be better to tell him how you feel, rather than me?"

"I did tell him but it was as if I spoke a foreign language. I said I wished he would recite poetry to me, and he quoted some non-sensical thing about a flea on a lady's bonnet on a Sunday."

Daintry laughed. "It was a louse, not a flea. Charles has always liked Mr. Burns's poems." The frustrated look on Davina's face caused her to add quickly, "I beg your pardon, but I cannot imagine him reciting any other type of poetry, you know. He is not a romantic man. He's sensitive, but he tends to be like Papa and bluster when he's angry, and he loathes strife. At all events," she went on, too tired to be tactful, "you don't really want my advice. You just want me to agree with you."

Davina looked angry for a moment, but then she smiled ruefully and said, "I suppose you are right, but can you imagine what it is like for me, Daintry, living here where everyone is on Charles's side and no one ever takes mine? If I had to stay here all year, I'd go mad. At least Susan, with all her problems, has a home of her own."

"Is that what you want?" Daintry asked, thinking it would not be if Davina truly understood what Susan's home was like.

Davina hunched a shoulder pettishly. "Oh, how does one know what one wants? What one thinks is desirable generally turns out to be nothing of the kind. I just never realized Charles would want to bury me alive in Cornwall, that's all."

"But he doesn't. You just returned from Cothele, in fact, and are you not leaving tomorrow for Wilton House?"

"Yes, although Charles has been complaining that it is too far to go for only four days. If I had my way, we'd not come home till Christmas, but perhaps if you tell him you want to go to Wilton with us . . ." She paused hopefully,

"I already sent my regrets," Daintry said. "Moreover, I promised Melissa that both Aunt Ophelia and I would see her home again tomorrow, and it would not do to disappoint her. And, in point of fact, Davina, you will go whether I do or not, and so will Charles. He nearly always does what you want him to."

"I suppose he does, but he would do it more gracefully for you," Davina said.

Daintry wondered if Deverill would be at Wilton House, but told herself it did not matter in the least, and soon managed to be rid of both her sister-in-law and Nance. Once she was in bed with the quilt pulled up to her chin, however, thoughts of Deverill's anger that afternoon came flooding back to haunt her.

She did not know what to make of him. He intrigued her and he fascinated her. He had been kind to her; he had certainly flirted with her; and, at one point, before she had known he was not Penthorpe, he had even said he wanted to marry her. No doubt that had been but part of his play-acting, but he had certainly wanted to get to know her better, and he certainly had a knack for stirring her passions. He had shown her consideration and warmth. He had even pretended to respect some of her opinions. All in all, it was no wonder that she had finally come to trust him, though she had certainly been foolish to do so.

It had been amazingly easy to ignore the fact that he had begun their acquaintance with a deception, that he had all too clearly decided after that to see if he could steal a kiss—or worse, heaven knew—but even when she had taken his measure, it had proved nearly impossible to keep the man at arm's length—witness the speed with which she had agreed to help him put to rest the ridiculous accusations Seacourt had made. And now, when he had betrayed her beyond all chance of forgiveness, she still could not seem to banish his image from her thoughts.

She remembered her last view of him, standing on the castle green. He had not spoken another word to her, nor she to him, although he and Sir Lionel had lingered, chatting with Lady Ophelia until both ladies were safely in the carriage. Deverill had been particularly charming to her aunt, almost as if he had meant to engage her support. And judging by Lady Ophelia's conversation in the carriage, or lack of it, he had succeeded.

After Daintry had replayed the events of the afternoon in her mind's eye several times more without being able to fix upon the exact cause of his anger, she finally realized that her own wrath had stirred his. He had thought her anger irrational, outrageous, even shrewish. But had his accusations been justified? And why was it, she wondered, that women who lost their tempers were shrews, while men who did—like Seacourt—were reasonably angry? If angry men were compared to members of the animal kingdom, they were generally compared to bears or dogs—dangerous animals—not to small, pestiferous rodents.

The fact was, she had somehow made herself believe Deverill was different from other men, more understanding, more sensitive to the difficulties faced by women, more willing than most men to listen and to comprehend female frustrations, and even, perhaps, willing to love a woman on her own terms. In fact, she had begun to think she had found a man whose feet were not made of clay. She had been wrong, and she began to see now that her anger had not been directed at him but at herself. She had let her guard down again, only to be brought up short by reality.

Previously, once she had discovered flaws of character in her suitors, it had been easy to dismiss them from her thoughts. But that night, each time she told herself that enough was enough and turned over again, determined to clear her mind and go to sleep, the unbidden image of Deverill would rise up to unsettle her. It did not seem to matter if she saw him smile or frown. Either way, he filled her thoughts and murdered sleep.

One moment she wanted never again to see the man or speak to him; the next, she wanted to explain matters so he would understand and agree with her. Sometime in the middle of the night, it occurred to her that perhaps she did not know him at all, that she had attributed characteristics to him based solely upon her own needs and wishful thinking. Nonetheless there had been something about him that led her to believe it was safe to trust him, to believe in him, and remembering his touch brought an unexpected wave of desire such as she had never experienced before, that stopped her train of thought cold in its tracks.

Was it possible that she had talked herself into trusting him simply because he stirred feelings that had never stirred before, because he could make her knees weak by looking into her eyes, or send flames shooting through her body just by kissing her? Was it possible that a mere physical attraction could influence her to such a point that she would forget all that experience had taught her about men, or was it merely part and parcel of what her aunt had called the lure of forbidden fruit?

Remembering what Lady Ophelia had said reminded her of the feud, and believing that a far safer subject for contemplation than the other, she managed to fix her mind upon it. She had been distracted for a time by Susan's predicament, but if any good might be said to have come of its resolution, it was that Jervaulx's decision had made St. Merryn think the better of him. Outrageous as that was, there could be no better time to ask her father about the feud's origin. And this time, she would keep her temper. One did not want to be thought a shrew, after all. Moreover, the next time she lost her temper, she would put the fear of God into someone or know the reason why.

Dozing at last, she nevertheless awoke early the following morning and, feeling restless, both at the thought of confronting her father and at what they might discover at Seacourt Head, she went for a solitary ride on the moor, leaving Clemons in the dust when he attempted to keep up with her. But even Cloud's fast pace, and the exhilaration of the moor wind blowing through her hair did nothing to erase thoughts of Deverill from her mind. She could not seem to stop searching the horizon for a centaur.

Returning to the house, determined to take some action, if only to allow herself a pretense of accomplishment, she was glad to find St. Merryn alone in the breakfast parlor. Taking a seat opposite him, she said to the footman who came to discover her wishes, "Nothing now, Jago. I will ring when I want you."

The footman vanished, and St. Merryn said, "What the devil are you about, girl? I wanted more herring."

"I'll serve you, Papa," she said, getting up and looking under lids on the sideboard until she found the kippered herring. Putting a generous portion on a fresh plate, she handed it to him, saying, "I want to know about the feud, sir, and I hope you will not try to fob me off again, because it will be easier for me to respect your dislike of the Deverills if I can discover what caused the dissension in the first place. Do you know?"

"Upon my soul," he exclaimed, smearing jam on his toast with lavish abandon, "what can that matter now?"

"Aunt Ophelia says no one knows the cause," she said, hoping he would respond as he would to any sporting challenge if the matter was put to him this way.

He sneered. "No reason that dratted female should know. No business of hers. She wasn't even a part of the family in those days, not that she probably wasn't as damned nosy and interfering then as she is now. Probably was. I don't know. Wasn't born yet, was I? Only thing I know is that my father said when old Tom Deverill quoted Smollett about making the monarchy stronger, he was not speaking of the present royal house."

"He was a Jacobite?"

"So they say. Can't really have blotted his copybook, though. Those who did lost most of what they owned. Then, too, most folks around here held by the true line then. Not that it did them any good. We're all stuck with the same mad king and his precious offspring now, aren't we?"

"Was my grandfather a Jacobite?" Daintry asked.

"Upon my word, girl, how should I know? He would not have told me. All secrets and plotting, it was. I just mention it because since the feud began when your aunt was young, it must have begun when there were still a few Jacobites hanging about, and I remembered that bit about Tom Deverill."

"But surely your father told you something about the feud."

He shrugged. "When I married your mama, he said it put him ahead of Deverill, but what the devil he meant, I can't tell you, for he never told me."

"Then why do you persist with the feud?" she demanded.

"That you can ask such a fool question just proves what I've said all along," he said with a snort. "Females don't understand simple facts of life. A feud grows, girl, and it's a matter of family loyalty. Just look at what happened in Launceston—my daughter calling down a magistrate in his own courtroom. Jervaulx probably thought you held him cheap because of the feud, so then he bent over backward to show he wasn't cut from the same bolt of cloth. Gave him a point to the good, that did. Once before, when we battled it out over a boundary line, I won the point. It all feeds into the whole."

"It's ridiculous, and the pair of you ought to mend matters," she said bluntly.

"You don't know what you're talking about." He got to his feet and threw down his napkin. "I've business to see to. All these mines shutting down have made difficulties for my tenants." He paused at the door. "Mind you don't forget to take Melissa home today. Charles and Davina ought to have done it on their way to Wilton, but Ophelia insisted she was taking her. In any case, I want to hear no more complaints from Seacourt about your interference in his family affairs. You understand that?"

"Yes, Papa." She ate her breakfast and went up to change out of her riding habit, knowing her great-aunt and Melissa would soon be ready to depart for Seacourt Head.

They did not leave until ten, but the roads were dry, and they arrived at Seacourt Head shortly after noon. Melissa passed most of the journey staring out of the window, responding politely when she was addressed by either of her companions, but initiating no conversation of her own. Daintry chatted with Lady Ophelia about the book the older lady was reading, but soon gave up any attempt to draw the child into the conversation and began to wish they had brought Charley along, after all.

Their reception was warmer than they might have expected, for Geoffrey, apparently on the lookout for them, came to the door while his servants were still collecting Melissa's baggage. "Come in," he called. "Susan was hoping you would arrive in time to take a light nuncheon with us. Hello, darling. Come and give Papa a big hug."

Melissa ran to him at once and put her arms around his neck, whereupon he lifted her, whirling her so that her skirt billowed around her slender legs. Then, setting her on her feet again, he kissed her cheek and said, "Let us go find your mama and Cousin Catherine. They have been anxiously awaiting your return."

Surprised by his easy manner, Daintry wondered if he truly believed he was in everyone's good graces again. He seemed to do so, and to her own amazement, she found herself automatically smiling back when he turned his flashing grin in her direction.

Lady Ophelia allowed her footman to help her down from the carriage, and they went inside to find Susan in her pleasant drawing room, looking perfectly well and happy to see her daughter again. Daintry searched her sister's face for any sign that she had been hurt again, but although her earlier bruises could still be detected, she could see nothing newly amiss.

Lady Catherine Chauncey, standing near one of the two tall windows and looking as beautiful as ever in a pale green, flowing robe of India muslin, smiled and greeted them. "We were just gazing out at the sea," she said, gesturing toward the magnificent view. Sunlight sparkled on the foam-crested waves of the Channel, while gulls darted and drifted on capricious breezes. "Hello, Melissa, did you have a pleasant journey?"

"Yes, ma'am. Mama, may I be excused now?"

Seacourt said, "Of course you may, darling. You will want to put all your things back where they belong and tell Miss Currier all about your visit to Tuscombe Park. She has missed you, you know. She had little to do when you were not here."

The little girl ran away without another word, and Seacourt said to Lady Ophelia, "Her governess is very fond of her, you know, though I daresay she has begun to wonder if Melissa really lives here or not; however, we shall say no more about that."

He continued to converse cheerfully with Lady Ophelia, and Daintry moved to stand by Catherine at the window. The view was spectacular, for the house was perched out on the headland, and she could see across St. Merryn Bay, all the way to the park, but she could not see the house. Some windows of its upper stories had a partial view of the sea, but by and large, Tuscombe's views were of its parkland. Realizing that Catherine had spoken, she said, "I'm dreadfully sorry. I was not attending."

"That view is hypnotic, is it not? My bedchamber faces the sea, and I get up early in the morning just so I can look out and see what sort of day the sea is having. Usually," she added with a sigh, "it is as gray as any day in Yorkshire."

"I had forgotten you come from the north," Daintry said.

"Well, I don't really, but my husband did. My family is from Lincolnshire, which is much the same—fens in place of the moors, but very bleak. My parents are dead, and my brother and his wife have too many in their own family to welcome me. I simply couldn't stomach the thought of Yorkshire at this season. Gray days notwithstanding, Cornwall is much more pleasant."

"I believe you said you had cousins in St. Ives," Daintry said, hoping the remark was not too pointed.

Evidently it was. Flushing, Catherine said, "You are thinking of the dreadful accusations Susan made, and believe I *ought* to leave, but she has apologized to me, you see, and I am quite willing to forgive her, for she must have been utterly furious with Geoffrey. I have told him he mustn't look to me for sympathy, either, for in my opinion, he was much too harsh with her. Men do tend to forget their own strength, do they not?"

Susan was smiling at her husband, and just then he put an arm around her shoulders and gave her a hug. For the first time, Daintry's convictions were shaken.

"You see," Catherine said softly. "He loves her very much and is truly sorry to have hurt her. He will not do so again, for he has promised us both that he will not."

At the table, Daintry saw nothing to indicate that Susan was not content in her marriage. Nothing at all was said about the day before, and when she said Charley had been disappointed not to be allowed to accompany Melissa home, Seacourt said she could visit whenever she liked. "And you must come often yourself," he added. "Here we are, so near, yet so far that Susan sometimes begins to think she lives in quite another county altogether."

Later, as they were driving away, Lady Ophelia said with satisfaction, "That looks to be going well now, very well indeed. We have taught Sir Geoffrey a valuable lesson, I think, my dear."

"Perhaps," Daintry said, but she decided to put him to a more severe test. In the weeks left before Christmas, instead of attending house parties as she had planned to do, she would visit Seacourt Head often, with or without Charley, to discover for herself if what they had seen today was truth or illusion.

She had turned to confide this simple plan to Lady Ophelia when the first shots rang out.

Sixteen

The carriage slowed rapidly, and Daintry heard the driver shouting at the horses to "Whoa." Looking out the window, she saw several masked horsemen approaching, pistols drawn.

"Highwaymen!" she exclaimed.

"Villains," Lady Ophelia said grimly. "Dash, I must take off my gloves!"

Daintry, startled nearly as much by these words as by the approaching highwaymen, turned sharply to see that Lady Ophelia was struggling to tug a pistol from her large reticule. The old lady snapped, "Don't sit gaping, child. Your father never thought it right to mount proper holsters in his carriages, on account of you girls and then Charlotte, but no sensible person travels the moors these days without a weapon at hand. We have just been fortunate enough never to need this one before."

Daintry stared. "But do you know how to use it, ma'am?"

"Certainly. Papa taught me. Like this." She put down her window and a deafening shot rang out. Daintry looked out again just as one of the villains yelled and clapped a hand to his shoulder. "Got him," Lady Ophelia said with satisfaction.

"Goodness, ma'am, that was an excellent shot!"

"Would have been if I'd been aiming at him," the old lady said.

"Dash, the others are still coming! I believe this thing fires twice. Let us see if it will."

It did. "That does for them," she announced happily, banging with the butt of the pistol on the forewall of the coach. "Drive on, Cotter, drive on! I hope those men are not greater nincompoops than I think, and have sense enough not to follow."

But the men had retired, evidently believing themselves defeated, and the rest of the trip was without incident. At Tuscombe, the earl chose to make light of the matter.

"Disgruntled miners, no doubt, looking for easy pickings," he said when they told him what had happened. "Lots of that sort of nonsense going on hereabouts, what with the bread shortages and so many of the mines closing down. But upon my word, Ophelia, it's lucky you didn't blow your fool head off with that damned popgun. If you must go gallivanting over the countryside, take care that Cotter and your footmen are armed from now on."

Thus it was that the first few times Daintry took Charley to visit Melissa, they went by carriage, making the journey over and back a full day's business, but though they heard of other incidents occurring elsewhere, they saw not the least hint of danger to themselves and soon began riding the cliff path instead, which made the journey much shorter.

Daintry was determined to make her presence felt at Seacourt Head, and Susan's delight in the frequent visits was obvious, making her certain that they forced Seacourt to keep his promise to control his temper. Lady Catherine Chauncey was still with them and clearly had no plan to depart until after Christmas. Her cousins at St. Ives, she said, had gone to visit friends in Devonshire, and she had no notion when they meant to return.

Daintry heard nothing from Deverill, nor did she see him, although it had become her habit to ride on the moor any early morning that it was not fogbound. By mid-December, with an increasing hint of snow in the air, such mornings became rare, but she did not want to leave matters as they were, because she was still determined to end the feud between the two families and knew she could scarcely make any progress toward that end if she remained at outs with Deverill.

She thought about writing to him again, but although she sat down to do so several times, she could not bring herself to send the letters. Now that she knew he was simply a traditional male with traditional values and attitudes about female behavior, she was certain he would think less of her if she committed the social solecism of writing to a man not only unrelated to her but whose family was at outs with her own. Moreover, each time she picked up her pen, the words flowed from its nib as if she wrote to an intimate friend, and since she was well aware that she wrote to the mysterious stranger she had concocted in her imagination and not to the real Deverill at all, she was certain that to send any such letter would be utter folly.

Thus, when she did meet him one fine afternoon, she instantly recalled letters written with an intimacy that had no place in their real relationship. Moreover, she and Charley were not alone, for Davina, home from her most recent house party and forced to remain for a few days before attending another, had chosen to accompany them. It was she who first saw Deverill.

"There is someone riding yonder," she cried as they galloped together toward Dozmary Pool, that ancient haunt of King Arthur and his knights of the Round Table. "Perhaps it's the ghost of Sir Bedivere, riding to throw the sword Excalibur into the pool."

Daintry, seeing the rider and recognizing his form at once but determined to give Davina no cause for teasing or comment, said lightly as she slowed Cloud, "More likely it is the ghost of that wicked fellow who was forced to empty the pool with a perforated limpet shell to atone for his sins."

Charley, hearing them, laughed. "It is Lord Deverill, Mama, on Shadow. A most magnificent animal!"

"Yes," Davina said, her eyes twinkling as she exchanged a look with Daintry, "he certainly is."

Daintry said nothing, drawing rein and pretending to keep her interest focused on the dark and lonely lake that for centuries had fascinated local inhabitants and visitors alike. Though its shores were said to have been inhabited before any other inland area of Cornwall, the place had been desolate for years, peopled only by ghosts and legends. "Hard to imagine now that it was once thought to be bottomless," she said casually.

But the others were paying her no heed. Charley had waved to Deverill, who was riding straight toward them, and Davina's interest was clearly riveted upon the magnificent figure he made.

He was with them in moments, greeting them politely, then saying, "And where are your grooms today, ladies?"

Charley said, "Oh, we didn't want them. Mama said we should bring them, but Aunt Daintry said we needn't. What can they do that we cannot do ourselves?"

Deverill was looking at Daintry, and she felt telltale warmth enter her cheeks. Having so frequently imagined his presence and herself making peace with him, she discovered now that he was with her that she could think of nothing to say. She wished her body were not so aware of his presence. She wanted to glare at him, to let him know she was still angry with him for refusing to help Susan, but she could not even seem to look at him. Perversely, it occurred to her just then that regardless of what had happened at the Assize Court in Launceston, he had stood beside her to face Jervaulx, and for the first time she wondered if she had been unreasonable to resent the fact that he had not then danced to the tune of her choosing. Now, confronting him, she felt like a schoolgirl, and a shy one, which she had never been even at the age of twelve or thirteen.

He said, seemingly in response to Charley, though Daintry knew he was still looking at her, "My dear child, this part of the moor is not safe for females traveling alone. The three of you ought to know better than to come so far without escort."

Was that why he had ridden here, Daintry wondered, because he had not expected her to do so? Had he hoped to avoid just such an encounter as this one?

Davina said lightly, "We did not mean to come so far, sir, I assure you, but these two just seem to forget where they are once they throw themselves atop a horse, and whoever is with them either rides along or is left behind. Not that anyone could blame them on such a beautiful day. We seldom see so much sun at this time of year in Cornwall, you know."

Collecting her wits, Daintry said in what she hoped was as light a tone as Davina's, "It can be nothing to you what we do, sir. My father did not forbid our coming here."

"The miners are restive," he said, his voice still even but with a note in it that reminded her suddenly of how quickly his temper could rise. "Even I have been fired upon twice, for there is widespread discontent, which no doubt will continue until such time as they can more easily feed and clothe their families."

Nodding wisely, Charley said, "That is just what Grandpapa said, sir, when Aunt Daintry and Aunt Ophelia were shot at one time, coming home from Seacourt Head."

Daintry glanced at him then and the look on his face sent a shiver racing up her spine. Certain that it would be wise to divert him before he could respond to Charley's naive revelation, she blurted out the first thing that came into her head. "Do you know the legend of Excalibur, Deverill? When we first caught sight of you, Davina thought you might be the ghost of Sir Bedivere riding away after the battle with Mordred, after he had thrown the sword into Dozmary Pool."

His hard expression did not alter. "Bedivere at least understood obedience and sensible behavior. Who fired at you?"

"Why, we presume now that they were some of those miners you mentioned, although we did not see them closely enough to identify them. At the time, we thought they were highwaymen."

"Since you are unharmed, I suppose your people were armed."

"Not then, although they are always well armed now." Saying the words, she realized they really had been foolish to ride so far from home without their grooms, but it had been just as Davina had said. They had meant to go only a short distance, but the mixture of sunshine, idle conversation, and a tremendous urge to let the horses stretch their legs had carried them much farther than they had intended to ride. She saw the thought form in his mind as clearly as if it had been her own and said quickly, "Aunt Ophelia carries a pistol in that huge reticule of hers, and she managed to injure one and frighten the rest off."

"The redoubtable Lady Ophelia," Deverill murmured, but the stern look disappeared from his face just as she had hoped it would. "If you are returning to Tuscombe Park now," he added, "I will do myself the honor to accompany you."

Charley and Davina accepted with alacrity, and the latter managed to manipulate matters so that Deverill was soon riding beside her. Daintry saw that he was perfectly willing to respond to Davina's flirtatious manner, and when Davina mentioned that she and Charles were to be guests the following weekend at a house party in Truro, and hoped to see him there (as indeed they seemed, from the conversation, to have seen him at numerous other such parties), Deverill said he looked forward to seeing them again, too. Daintry had also been invited to the Truro house party but once again had sent her regrets, believing it was far more important to continue her visits to Seacourt Head. Now she tried to convince herself that she was glad she had done so.

Deverill reined in when the road began to descend toward Tuscombe Park. "It would be unwise for me to accompany you farther," he said, "and since you can now be seen from the stable yard, you will be perfectly safe."

Charley said bluntly, "Why do you not tell your papa to stop fighting with my grandpapa, sir?"

He smiled. "Do you tell your papa or your grandpapa what to do, Miss Charlotte?"

She shook her head. "No, but I am just a child. No one listens to me except Aunt Daintry and Aunt Ophelia."

Davina, laughing, said, "Unnatural girl, would you have him think your own mother pays you no heed? And to think I even exerted myself to come riding with you today!"

"But it is the first time in ages you have done so, Mama," Charley pointed out, "and you mostly talked with Aunt Daintry. I wish you would do it more often, however." Turning back to Deverill, she said, "I do not think that for you to tell your papa is at all the same thing as for me to tell mine, sir."

"Perhaps not," he agreed, "but I must warn you that parents rarely forget they are parents, and continue to treat their sons and daughters like children even after they are grown up." He shifted his gaze to Daintry, saying ruefully, "I confess, though I did search the records for the years before my grandfather's marriage, I have done no more to the purpose, for I've come to believe there is no one left who knows what began the feud."

She nodded, meeting his gaze, surprised to learn that he had not stopped thinking about it altogether. Quietly, she said, "I too have had no luck, though I did talk with my father. He said there were rumors, albeit no proof, that your grandfather was involved with Jacobites, and he mentioned petty incidents that have occurred, but even he seems not to know what began it all."

"But that's plain silly," Charley said. "Really, sometimes I think children are more intelligent than grown-ups are."

Davina said sharply, "That will be enough of your impudence, miss. If you really wish me to ride with you more often, you must take better care not to put me to the blush when I do."

Charley, flushing deeply, fell silent, but Deverill said dryly, "She makes a good point, you know. Since our families are neighbors, it seems ridiculous that we cannot mend the rift. Perhaps we can manage to bring our fathers together once everyone is fixed in London for the Season. When do you mean to go?"

He was looking at Daintry again, but Davina answered, "We go in late February, sir, just before the opening of Parliament. Lady Ophelia has already begun to complain that she will get no sleep, but I just hope we do not find ourselves buried alive here in Cornwall from Christmas until London like we did last year!"

"There will be shooting parties, and hunting, to amuse you."

"To amuse the gentlemen, you mean," Davina retorted. "If you think a house party where the gentlemen retire immediately after dinner in order to be up at cockcrow to scramble through bushes and briars after elusive birds and rabbits—or to fling themselves onto horses to chase a fox—holds much amusement for their ladies, sir, you are mistaken."

Shooting a provocative look at Daintry, he said, "But ladies frequently hunt too, ma'am, and in any case, surely we are but carrying out our ancient masculine duty to put food on the table for those living under our protection."

Charley said, "Oh, but sir, Aunt Ophelia says—"

"Lord Deverill," Daintry said at the same time, grateful for an opportunity to vent at least some of her feelings, "surely you do not believe that any society, ancient or otherwise, has had to depend upon its hunters for food. Nowadays, most Englishmen take their guns out only when game is plentiful, and even in the old days it was more likely that such kills provided seasonal treats, just like they do now, while the family's daily dependence was on the bounty of orchards and gardens planted, tended, and harvested by its womenfolk. Moreover, sir—"

"No more," Deverill said, laughing. "You had been so quiet that I found myself unable to resist casting a fly to see if I could get a rise. I look forward to Truro, ladies. Good day."

Gideon rode away with a smile on his face. She had been glad to see him, and she had not liked it one bit when he had flirted with her sister-in-law. Realizing now that she had been singularly silent on the subject of Truro, he wondered if she would be at the house party. He hoped so, but then he had assumed that she would be present at many of the other parties he had attended, which, if the truth were told, had been the primary reason he had attended as many as he had. It had been fine to renew old friendships again, to be sure, and to see men with whom he had served on the Continent, but everywhere he had gone, he had found himself searching for one face, and with the exception of the Mount Edgcumbe party, he had searched in vain.

Charles and Davina Tarrant had been at many of those same parties, and though he had not wanted to make an issue of asking after Daintry, he had once approached Davina in hopes of leading casually to his point, only to encounter a savage look from her husband that made him change his mind. It made him wonder, too, if perhaps St. Merryn had forbidden his daughter to attend any more house parties simply because she might encounter him again.

He no longer questioned his feelings but conceded that he had been drawn to her from the first. The young woman intrigued him, surprised him, outraged him, and delighted him. She made him feel protective one moment, exasperated the next. She flatly refused to see any point but her own, her temper was frequently as ungoverned as Charley's, and she was a darling. He had set out to tame her. Now he just wanted her. Winning her would be difficult, certainly, but he had never yet run from a challenge.

As they watched Deverill ride away, Davina said with an arch look at Daintry, "I believe I am going to enjoy London this year. What a delightful man he is, to be sure! I quite look forward to each house party, though I had begun to find such events rather insipid. It is a pity you have missed so many this year."

Daintry returned a polite response, but try as she would, she could not easily dismiss Davina's flirting with Deverill. It was not jealousy, she told herself many times in the next few days, but justifiable fear that, with Deverill's reputation and the fragile relationship between the families, any response he made to Davina could stir the coals of the feud to unquenchable flames. Nevertheless, she was grateful that she was not called upon to explain the strange urge she had, each time Truro was mentioned, to scratch out her lovely sister-in-law's eyes.

She could not seem to stop thinking about the house party, and when Charley looked disappointed to see Davina and Charles depart for Truro three days later, she immediately invited the child to accompany her to Seacourt Head the following day.

"It has been nearly a sennight since we both visited Melissa, and she will be expecting us, I think."

"Oh, yes, and you promised to take us riding on the shingle again, from Seacourt this time."

"So I did. Very well, pray for good weather then, and we will leave first thing in the morning by the cliff path."

The following morning, however, she awoke to find clouds gathering overhead, and had she not been so determined to give Charley a treat to make up for her parents' absence, she might well have changed her mind about going. As it was, she took the bright blue sky in the west as a sign that the weather would clear without subjecting them to more than a shower or two, and they set out for Seacourt Head soon after breakfast.

The breezes were brisk and chilly, and the water of the Channel was gray, with foam edging its scudding waves and an occasional wall of spray flying before a gust of wind. The shoreline of France was hidden in mist, and Daintry, glancing around warily as they rode, noted unhappily that the western sky, which had been clear earlier, was rapidly growing dark.

Calling to Clemons, who rode placidly behind them, she said, "What do you think? Will it hold off until we get there?"

Casting an experienced eye skyward, the groom called back, "Going to spatter within the hour, my lady, but nothing heavy for a few hours yet. Ought to have listened to me earlier when I told you we was in for a storm. We'll not get back today."

"It didn't look so bad before," she said, "and furthermore, I had promised Miss Charley."

"A little rain won't hurt us so long as there is no thunder to terrify poor Victor before we get there," Charley shouted, giving spur to the gelding, "and if it gets too bad to go home again, we shall just have to spend the night. There is nothing to fret about in that! It will be an adventure, that's all."

Exchanging a smile with Clemons, Daintry followed the child, urging Cloud to a faster pace to keep up. They made good time, and though it did begin to sprinkle before they reached Seacourt Head, they escaped a real wetting.

When they were shown into the drawing room overlooking the Channel, the lamps had already been lit against the darkening sky, and Susan, sitting near the fire with Lady Catherine, greeted them in some surprise. "Melissa said that you would visit today, but when we saw what the weather was like, the rest of us were sure you would not come."

"The weather was fine when we left home," Charley said, giving her a hug. "A little cloudy, but that was all."

Daintry chuckled. "She is an optimist. I ought to have known better, but from some cause or other, I was restless and could not be content to remain at home. Moreover, I knew that if I refused to come, Charley would become impossible to live with."

"But surely," Sir Geoffrey said from the doorway into the stair hall, "Charlotte does not yet run things at Tuscombe Park."

"No, of course not," Daintry said, keeping her tone matter-of-fact, albeit with difficulty. "Truly, I did not think it would rain before we arrived here, Geoffrey, and I knew we might depend upon you for shelter if it grew too stormy for us to return this afternoon."

"To be sure you can," Susan said cheerfully.

Charley said, "May I go to Melissa now, Aunt Susan?"

"Of course, dear. She is in the schoolroom with her governess."

"Where you ought to be," Seacourt said with a grin, tousling her hair as she slipped past him. Then, looking at Daintry and no longer smiling, he said, "I cannot think what ails your father that he does not take firmer hold of the reins. In a properly run household two young females would certainly not be allowed to ride out on such a threatening day. As to seeking shelter here, you can be assured that you will not leave this house until I say you may. I do not want your deaths laid at my door."

"They will not be, Geoffrey," Daintry said, giving him look for look. "I am grateful for your hospitality, but there is no need to think my father ought to have forbidden us to come, for there was not. There was no danger this morning—"

"What of miscreants?" he demanded. "Do you forget that you and Lady Ophelia were fired upon, traveling from this house to Tuscombe Park. I do not forget that so easily."

"I do not forget either, but we had Clemons with us today, and he is well-armed and perfectly able to look after our safety. Moreover, though there has been trouble elsewhere, we rarely meet anyone on the cliff path, as you must know as well as I do. All the land around the bay belongs to either Papa or to you, after all. When we were attacked before, we were on the public road."

"Nonetheless, it will be as well for you to remember that I am master here, my girl, and you will certainly spend the night, for I will not hear of you leaving before the weather clears."

Daintry said calmly, "Thank you for your concern."

He gave her a look that was, she was certain, meant to intimidate her, but she met it easily, not looking away until he did, then turning her attention to Susan and Lady Catherine. When she glanced back a moment later, he was gone.

Susan breathed a sigh of relief. "I wish you would not bicker with him, Daintry. You only make him angry."

Daintry looked at her searchingly. "Has he . . . ? That is . . ." She glanced at Lady Catherine and back at Susan. "How are you getting on these days? I have not seen you in more than a sennight, you know."

Susan said with a wry smile, "Last year at this time you had not seen me in months!"

"Nevertheless, I had hoped that the good example Charley and I have been setting might by now have encouraged you to ride over to Tuscombe Park with Melissa, and with Lady Catherine, too, of course," she added hastily.

"Please, I wish you will call me Catherine. I feel that I have become quite one of the family after so long a visit, you know, and such formality makes me feel as if you do not like me."

Even after numerous visits, Daintry had learned little more about Catherine. Seacourt's cousin seemed quiet and unassuming, and behaved like the perfect guest, pleasant and cheerful. It was impossible to dislike her, but it was equally impossible to feel that one knew her or to judge if she was in fact Geoffrey's mistress, as Susan had claimed, or not. Daintry had had no chance to talk privately with her sister, for they were rarely alone together for more than a minute. She could not say whether that was by Susan's choice or by the others' conspiracy, only that there just never seemed time to talk.

These thoughts flitted through her head now in the scant seconds after Catherine spoke and before Susan said, "Geoffrey does not like us to leave home, Daintry, even with our grooms. He says it is just too dangerous at present."

Catherine said, "You saw how he was just now. He is a very protective man, particularly where his womenfolk are concerned, and since that dreadful incident of the shooting, the local papers have reported many such tales. Geoffrey has read several of them to us, just to prove his point."

"Then come to us in the carriage and stay overnight," Daintry said. "Geoffrey can provide you with an army of outriders if he wishes, but really, Susan, we are not so far away that you cannot make more of a push to visit. Mama feels your neglect, and so do the rest of us, particularly after you were able to spend such a lovely long visit with us last summer."

For the first time that day, Susan failed to meet her gaze as she said, "I should be delighted to visit, but Geoffrey says Melissa has already missed too much time with her governess. He fears she will grow up to be as unlearned as a cottage child if she is not made to apply herself to her lessons. How does Nance go on? Does she hear from Annie? How kind they all were to us!"

Accepting the change of topic, Daintry wished again that she were able to demand an explanation of Susan's behavior. Had she really lied to them about Seacourt? It was so easy for everyone else to believe that at the least she had exaggerated her danger. Daintry knew that both Jervaulx and Deverill believed Susan had done so, that she had behaved "just like a woman." But she was not so sure. Even though her convictions had been shaken by Susan's subsequent behavior and by Catherine's casual mention of an apology, she still believed Susan had told her the truth at Tuscombe Park, and that she had behaved in the courtroom as she had because she knew Jervaulx was going to send her home, where she would be at her husband's mercy. And yet, here she was now, looking as contented as if she had never had a problem in her life, let alone one so dangerous as a husband who beat her.

There was distant thunder in the air by the time the two little girls joined them for a light repast when Melissa's lessons were done. Sir Geoffrey was not present, and the conversation was desultory, and soon turned to riding.

Lady Catherine said, "Charlotte, I understand that besides being quite a little horsewoman yourself, you are also an instructor. I paid Melissa a pretty compliment on her riding several mornings ago, and she said you were the one who had taught her to ride so well."

"Oh, it was not me, ma'am," Charley said with a grin. "It was Aunt Daintry. She taught us both."

Shyly, Melissa said, "But it was Charley who made riding feel safe, Cousin Catherine. I was used to be afraid that my horse would run away with me, even though Aunt Daintry said over and over that it would not. But Charley said she would fix it so that not a single horse at Tuscombe Park would ever do such a thing, and she did it, too."

"Goodness," Catherine said, visibly impressed, "how ever did she contrive to do that?"

"She trained them all to stop when she whistles at—Ow!" Melissa looked indignantly at Charley. Encountering a fierce glare and a warning glance toward the doorway, she turned white as chalk and fell silent, but it was too late.

Catherine frowned and said slowly, "I see." She turned

accusingly toward Daintry, and at the same time, from the doorway, Geoffrey said sternly, "It is not polite to kick people under the table, Charlotte. Such behavior might be acceptable in your grandpapa's house, but I send unmannerly children straight up to their bedchambers. Go up at once, please."

"Yes, sir," Charley muttered, getting to her feet just as a particularly loud crack of thunder exploded overhead, startling them all. "Oh," she cried, "I must go to Victor! He does not like thunder so close as that."

"You will do as you were told," Seacourt snapped.

"But you don't understand," Charley said, moving swiftly to pass him. "He panics. I must go to him!"

Seacourt grabbed her and shook her. "You will do precisely as you are told, young lady, and if I hear another word out of you, I will put you straight across my knee right here and now and spank you so hard you will not want to sit down for a week."

Daintry leapt to her feet. "Let her go, Geoffrey. She is not your daughter, and you will not lay a finger on her or, by heaven, you will answer to Charles and Davina, and to Aunt Ophelia, as well. Charley is not defying you. She is frightened for her horse, and with good reason."

Seacourt released Charley, saying sternly, "You will seek your room, Charlotte, just as you were bid. If your groom cannot look after your horse, my people will help him, but you may not leave this house. Nor will you," he added with a grim look at Daintry. "Neither Charles nor St. Merryn would dispute my right to keep you both inside on such a day as this, and what the devil are stablemen for if not to attend to the horses? That child," he added, glancing over his shoulder to see that Charley had gone, "has been grossly overindulged and needs a sharp lesson."

He left the room, and Daintry breathed a sigh of relief, hoping he had not drawn any undesirable conclusion from Melissa's comments, and that if he had, he had forgotten it as a result of the brief dispute. Sitting back down, she saw that Catherine was looking displeased and thoughtful, and remembered with a sinking feeling that she also had cause to deprecate Charley's horse training. Before she could think of anything to say to her, however, Susan said, "I wish you would not challenge Geoffrey like that. You make him angry, and he becomes very difficult."

Catherine collected herself and said lightly, "You must exert yourself, Susan, to charm him into a better mood. No doubt the weather has dampened his spirits, and indeed, it is a pity that Daintry cannot seem to be in the same room with him without putting him out of sorts, but I do not doubt that you can bring him round your thumb easily enough before suppertime."

Whether or not it was Susan who placated him, Geoffrey was perfectly amiable over dinner, relating legends of the Cornish moors for his cousin's enjoyment and making the tales so lively that Daintry wished the little girls might have dined with them instead of in the schoolroom with Melissa's governess. The weather continued to be wild, however, and when he decided they would make an early night of it, even Daintry made no objection.

The winds howled around the house, and thunder and lightning crashed and flashed till it seemed as if the place were under attack. In her bedchamber, having refused the assistance of Susan's maid, Daintry paused before undressing to look out the window at the water below. Flashes of lightning reflecting from flying spray and foam made the scene an eerie but magnificent one, and only when she began to shiver with cold did she scramble into her borrowed nightgown and jump beneath the covers.

She fell asleep at once, despite the noise, but her dreams were filled with drums and storms and pounding hooves. She was high on a mountaintop looking down into a dark, mysterious lake, watching the approach of a rider on a great thundering black horse, who waved the sword Excalibur overhead as he rode up the hill toward her, when she came wide awake, her heart leaping with terror, to feel a hand clamped over her mouth and a heavy body pressed against hers in the bed.

Seventeen

Struggling wildly, Daintry nearly failed to hear Seacourt when he growled, "You could scream yourself hoarse, you little bitch, for all the good it would do you, but I don't choose to allow that, and whether you like it or not, I am master here." Shifting his weight, he shoved the quilt aside, and when she began to struggle harder, he grabbed her left breast, squeezing it until she gasped and moaned at the pain.

"There are any number of ways for me to make my point," he said. "Stop fighting me, damn you."

The agony he caused brought tears to her eyes, but the terror was much worse. Lightning lit the room, and she could see his face close to hers, eyes glittering in anticipation of what he meant to do. She could smell brandy on his breath, and she tried to turn her face away but he would not let her. His hand, leaving her bruised breast, moved lower, and when she struggled again, he pinched the tender flesh of her abdomen, making her scream against the hard palm held tight against her mouth.

Then her mouth was free and she opened her lips to scream in earnest, but his head came down and his mouth covered hers, his tongue darting inside like an evil fat snake, in and out again so quickly that she could not react fast enough to bite it.

The quilt was gone, her nightgown rucked up to her thighs, and she felt the cold air on her bare legs. His knee pressed between them. Then his moving hand, with its long, horrid fingers, slipped between her legs, touching her where no one had ever touched her before, and when she tried to bite his lip, he jerked away and slapped her hard across the face.

Her ears rang from the slap, but she heard him clearly when he said, "That's just a taste, little sister. You think you're so very clever, with your horse tricks and your delight in making a fool of me. But now you'll pay. You'll do exactly what I tell you, or I'll hurt you like you've never been hurt before, and there won't be a sign of it afterward for anyone else to see." He chuckled, the sound utterly fiendish in her ears, then added, "Not that you'll want to show anyone, for you won't. I'll make sure of that. A woman's body is easily punished. See?"

His hand moved between her legs, pinching her hard, proving his threat a real one, for she would never willingly let anyone see the flesh he was torturing. She screamed again, trying to make the sound carry above the crashing thunder, and this time he waited until the thunder stopped before he slapped her, snarling, "No more. No one can hear you anyway, and you'll do yourself more good by obeying me. I've no intention of raping you, since that would be too easy for you to prove, but I am going to teach you a damned good lesson, and if you don't lie still and take it, I'll make you sorry you didn't. Do you understand me?"

Crying now, as much from frustrated rage as from the pain he gave her, she wanted to kill him, but she had no weapon, so there seemed nothing to do but nod helplessly, then lie stiff and still while his hands roamed at will over her body, his touch making her feel sick. Thunder crashed, so near this time that it shook the walls, and she knew she would never again hear even a distant rumble without remembering this horror-filled night.

His hand slid under the borrowed nightgown to her breast, pinching the nipple until she wanted to scream again. Only the dawning realization that her screams somehow amused him, even gave him a perverted sort of pleasure, kept her silent. He pinched harder, however, and involuntarily, she cried out.

"That's better," he muttered. "This damned gown is in the way." He shifted his weight to grab the nightdress, and quick as the lightning, she jerked her knees up to push him away with her feet. One knee grazed him between the legs, and he yelled in pain and jumped back, stumbling to avoid her flailing feet, his expression a mix of pain and fury. "By God, you little—"

The bedchamber door opened, and the glow of a lamp spilled into the room. "My lady, are you all right?"

Starting as if he'd been shot, Seacourt straightened and spun around, somehow managing to yank the quilt over her as he did. "Who is there?"

"Oh, sir! How you startled me! It is I, sir, Hilda, Lady Catherine's maid. I came—"

"You startled me too, wench. I heard Lady Daintry cry out with fear at the storm as I passed by," he added in a tone of concern. "I came in to calm her, but what brings you here?"

"Why, the very same thing, sir," she said. "Lady Catherine remembered Lady Daintry saying she has a terror of thunderstorms, so she sent me to be sure she was not frightened. Lady Catherine said if she was scared, I was to stay right here with her."

"An excellent notion," Seacourt said. "Not only has she been terrified but she's had a frightening nightmare as well. You will be glad of Hilda's company, will you not, my dear?"

"Yes," Daintry said fervently. She saw the glittering look in his eyes again and knew he was still angry, and even somehow blamed her for the maid's intrusion. He probably knew as well as she did that she did not fear the storm, but since he had been the one to suggest it in the first place, he could hardly tell Hilda now that her mistress was in error to believe such a thing. It was all very odd, and though she was grateful for Hilda's arrival, she wondered if Catherine had known he would be there.

As Seacourt moved to go, the maid said, "Oh, I nearly forgot, sir, but Lady Catherine's window is rattling so that she cannot sleep. She said if I saw anyone who could fix it, would I send them to her, but at this hour I don't know who—"

"I'll tend to it, Hilda. Good night." And he was gone.

Daintry nearly sobbed in relief, and the maid said matter-of-factly, "Can I fetch you anything, ma'am?"

A pistol, Daintry thought, *or a very large knife, or even a basin to be sick in,* but she said, "No, thank you, Hilda. Where will you sleep?"

"I believe there is a cot in the dressing room, my lady. I'll leave the door open, shall I?"

"Please." The maid said nothing about Geoffrey's presence, and Daintry, not having the least idea how much she knew about his habits or about Catherine's motives in sending her, merely breathed a prayer of thanksgiving and tried to go back to sleep.

She was unsuccessful, and although the storm finally passed, she was wide awake when the sun rose. Getting up, she went to the window, pushed it open, and inhaled the fresh sea breeze. A few lingering clouds floated over the Channel, looking serene and beautiful, as if there had never been a storm. There was no reason to stay at Seacourt Head a minute longer than necessary.

Hilda was not in the dressing room, so she assumed the woman had returned to her mistress, and turned her attention to dressing herself. Though she did not much want to go down to breakfast, she knew Susan would send someone to discover what was wrong if she did not, and she could not face the thought of telling her sister what had happened in the night.

In the clear light of day it was impossible to imagine telling anyone about it, for although she was certain Hilda would confirm Geoffrey's presence in her room, his seemingly casual declaration that she suffered from nightmares made it probable that he would insist her belief that she had been molested to be no more than a reaction to a particularly vivid dream. In any event, she shrank from the thought of describing to anyone precisely what he had done to her.

The only people present in the breakfast room when she entered were Catherine and Susan, and both greeted her as they normally would, but the incident seemed somehow to have isolated her from them. Though she felt as if they ought to be able to know everything Geoffrey had done simply by looking at her, she could read nothing in their expressions but innocent welcome, so when Catherine said nothing about sending Hilda to her in the night, Daintry also said nothing. She had no wish to add to Susan's troubles, and Catherine was certainly not a woman in whom she could confide. In fact, she did not even know that Catherine had sent Hilda to her, only that the maid had said she had.

Servants often knew even more about what went on in a house than their masters or mistresses did, and the fact that Hilda had left the dressing room before sunrise might mean that Catherine had done no more than send her to find someone to stop the window's rattle, and knew nothing of her absence afterward.

As soon as Daintry had eaten, she sent for Charley, and taking leave of Susan and Catherine, the two left at once for the stables. They were crossing the muddy yard, approaching the stable door when they heard the unmistakable scream of a horse, followed by two shots fired in quick succession.

Daintry's heart thudded, and she saw that Charley had stopped still in her tracks, her face turning white. Before Daintry could think to stop her, the child came to life and darted into the stable. Daintry rushed after her, terrified to think what they would find. Inside, she stopped, sudden tears blinding her at the sound of Charley's sobs.

"Oh, Victor," the child cried, "I thought it was you!"

Dashing a hand to wipe the tears from her eyes, Daintry saw that Charley had flung open the door to Victor's stall and was hugging the gelding's neck as it nuzzled her, searching for sugar or carrots. Cloud's silvery head appeared over the gate to the next stall, and he whinnied, recognizing his mistress.

Clemons spoke before she realized he was beside her. "Right sorry about that, my lady. I'd have told the lads to hold off had I knowed the lass was so nigh, but one of Sir Geoffrey's hunters panicked in the storm and broke a leg. The lad looking after it thought it were nobbut a bad sprain, but now the farrier says as how it's broke, and we had to put the poor beast down."

"It was not your fault, Clemons," she said, realizing she was trembling. "If our horses are saddled, let us go at once."

In those brief fear-filled moments before she had seen that Cloud and Victor were safe, she had remembered Melissa's words of the day before and Geoffrey's angry comment about horse tricks, and she had not doubted for a minute that the man was capable of vicious, petty revenge, even against a child.

There was still no sign of him, and she did not inquire as to his whereabouts, not having the least notion what she might say to him or how she would act, but knowing full well that if she never laid eyes on the man again, she would not regret it. They rode out of the stable yard, and as they approached the cliff path, she glanced at Charley, who had been unnaturally silent. "A penny for your thoughts," she said gently.

Charley met her gaze but did not speak for a long moment. Then she said, "I thought . . . That is, for just a minute, until I saw him, I thought maybe it was Victor. You know how scared he gets when it thunders, Aunt Daintry, and . . ."

"I know," Daintry said, not waiting for her to try to complete the thought.

Soberly, Charley said, "What makes some houses comfortable and others not, Aunt Daintry? I don't mean their furnishings; I mean the way they make a person feel."

"The people in them, I suppose."

"Uncle Geoffrey is horrid."

In full agreement but aware that it would not do at all to enlarge upon the topic, she said, "You were in the wrong yesterday, you know. He was right to be displeased with you."

"I know, but does he always want to hit people when he's angry with them?"

"Some men are like that, darling."

Another long silence fell, and Daintry did not break it. She had no desire to discuss Seacourt and thought it best to let Charley think her feelings through for herself.

The bright sunlight and the ocean scents wafting upward on the sea breezes cleared her head, making it a little easier to put the incident of the previous night behind her. When the silver dun tossed its head, its dancing pace indicating that it was ripe for a run, she took herself firmly in hand. "Shall we let them out? Cloud is champing at the bit."

Their return journey was without incident, but Daintry's

interest in continuing the frequent visits to Seacourt Head had died. So, it seemed, had Charley's, for the child said nothing about returning to visit Melissa again before Christmas. And however well intended their visits might have been, Daintry knew now that they might well have made matters worse for Susan in some ways. Certain as she was now that Seacourt knew how Charley had helped his wife and child escape him that day on the moor, she thought it would be better for all of them if she and Charley played least in sight for a while. And, in any case, with Christmas approaching and winter setting in with a vengeance, there was little opportunity to ride anywhere.

Davina and Charles returned from Truro barely speaking to each other, but Daintry discovered not only that Deverill had been one of the guests but that he and Jervaulx had left Cornwall for Gloucestershire, and she wished more than ever that she had gone to the house party rather than to Seacourt Head.

Lady St. Merryn seemed to take it for granted that her elder daughter's family would join them for the holiday, but the harsh weather provided an excuse for Seacourt to keep his family home, and Daintry, though she missed Susan and Melissa, was not sorry. A number of other guests did join them, however, including Lord Alvanley and Sir Lionel Werring, both of whom soon admitted that they had been invited to see the New Year in at Jervaulx Abbey.

Lady Ophelia took instant exception to the news. "Into the enemy's nest, Lionel, that's where you're going," she declared, fuming. It was the day after Christmas, and everyone had gathered in the drawing room after dinner.

Lady St. Merryn, sitting upright for once, suggested plaintively that the weather still was not suitable for travel.

"Not to worry, ma'am," Werring retorted, holding out his wine glass for Medrose to refill. "Daresay we shan't fall into a snowdrift, shall we, Alvanley?"

Alvanley's eyes twinkled, and his cherubic smile lit his face as he said to Lady St. Merryn, "I doubt we shall get lotht on the main road to Gloucestershire, you know, ma'am."

"I hope you do," Lady Ophelia said tartly. "Serve you both right, going over to the enemy like that. You heard that wretch

Jervaulx in court, Lionel, saying a woman must be better off with any husband, even one who tortures her, than on her own."

"But, my dear Ophelia, that scarcely makes him your enemy, I hope," the solicitor said blandly, "for I have said similar things to you on any number of occasions."

"That is not the same thing," she said. "One debates such things as a matter of course, but that courtroom was real. And prating utter drivel, Jervaulx dared to call it law!"

Sir Lionel swirled the amber liquid in his glass and said gently, "It is the law. Moreover, Jervaulx believes, as many do, that man is woman's natural protector and defender, and one can scarcely blame him when the notion is as old as the Bible."

"Very true," Alvanley said. "Ever thince poor old Adam gave up hith rib to make Eve. There are great differences between the thexes, Lady Ophelia. You cannot dithagree with that, you know."

"Try and see if she cannot," St. Merryn said bitterly. "Must you prattle of our affairs to all and sundry, Ophelia?"

"Oh, pooh," she said. "Lionel was there, and Alvanley has already heard the whole, for I told him myself. As to the drivel about Adam's rib, any sensible person must disagree, since the Bible clearly was written by men as a fable to entertain other men. Simple logic tells us God must have created woman first, since women, not men, give birth, but the writers of the Bible had to make up a way for a man to give birth in order to create an importance for him that otherwise he did not possess."

Lady St. Merryn gasped in shock, and Cousin Ethelinda twittered, "My dear Ophelia, such blasphemy! What would Reverend Sykes think of your saying such dreadful things about the Bible?"

"Reverend Sykes knows exactly what I think," Lady Ophelia said. "We have had more than one stimulating discussion about those very things, and he, I might add, has even admitted that women ought to have a good deal more say-so in this life. I hope someday to convince him that we ought to be allowed the same political and economic rights that men have."

Testily, St. Merryn said, "Upon my word, Ophelia, what will you say next? Women are not equal to men and never will be. Even to suggest they should have such rights implies they are fit to assume power." He laughed, and to her evident disgust, the other men laughed too. "Talk about something sensible, woman!"

Daintry wondered what Deverill would say, and decided he would most likely agree with her father. Still, remembering some of their discussions, she thought he might at least be willing to discuss the matter, and at all events, it would be interesting to ask him. She thought it was a pity he had left Cornwall.

Their guests departed for Jervaulx Abbey the next day, and heavy, intermittent rains settled in for several weeks. St. Merryn and Charles departed for Leicestershire, however, for the hunting season, leaving the ladies to their own devices.

Davina did not hesitate to make known her disgust at being left behind, but when Daintry asked if she would rather have accompanied the earl and Charles to their neat little hunting box at Melton Mowbray, Davina stared at her. "Merciful heavens, no! I cannot imagine anything more uncomfortable, but it astonishes me that your great-aunt and her friends have not yet devised a way for ladies to enjoy themselves while all the men go hunting."

The weather remained inclement for nearly two months, making everything gloomy, but at last it cleared to dull gray skies, and St. Merryn and Charles returned to escort their ladies to London. Leaving Charley with her governess as was their annual custom, they departed the final week of February; however, the two-hundred-and-fifty-mile journey took two weeks to accomplish, because Lady St. Merryn insisted upon stopping frequently, either to recoup her strength with food and drink or to spend a night or two with friends along the way. St. Merryn grumbled at the delays but made no attempt to countermand her instructions.

They reached the outskirts of the metropolis at last on a drizzly March afternoon, and Daintry, occupying the forward seat of the carriage opposite Lady Ophelia and Davina, was profoundly grateful to hear the carriage wheels rattle onto the cobblestones of Kensington High Street. Her mother and Cousin Ethelinda occupied a second carriage all to themselves, while St. Merryn and Charles either rode or traveled in a third. The fourth and fifth carriages contained their personal servants, and several other vehicles followed behind with all the baggage.

As the cavalcade rolled past the magnificent brick facade of Kensington Palace and turned into Knightsbridge, Daintry saw that the bare branches of the trees in the gardens and adjoining Hyde Park were shrouded with mist, and dripping, but on sunnier days she knew the spacious gravel roads would be crowded from two until five each afternoon with horsemen and carriages, and the fashionable walks would be so crowded with well-dressed people, passing to or returning from the gardens, that it would be difficult for one to proceed. Only the Hyde Park turnpike remained to be passed, and then they would be in Mayfair.

Twenty minutes later, the carriages drew up on the west side of Berkeley Square before the tall, brick, stone-dressed house that William Kent had built the previous century for the second earl. The scale of its architectural elements was impressive, for it was designed in a plain Palladian style with wide window spacing and pedimented, balustraded windows. Though the facade was restrained, it had a decided sense of ceremony, and Daintry thought the house looked enormously self-assured.

They passed through the entrance hall, a modest, stone-flagged room that gave no hint of the magnificent staircase soaring up through the center of the house. A breathtaking example of Kent's best work, though its oak treads were no more than four feet wide, the curved flights swept upward, splitting and turning back on themselves, and bridging the landings as the upper flights disappeared behind screens of Ionic columns. The domed ceiling above was like the interior of a jeweled casket, the panels between the heavily gilded ribs having been painted by Kent himself in grisaille on dark red and blue grounds. And, as was frequently the case with Kent, the coffering and modeling of the ceiling was real and not an optical illusion.

Daintry loved the house and, as she always did when she first arrived, left the others to their own devices and went quickly upstairs to the great drawing room with its rich blue fabrics and curtains, and beyond to the twin saloons and smaller parlors, then up another flight to her own yellow and white bedchamber. Seeing that all was in order, she returned to the drawing room level to be sure Lady St. Merryn was comfortably settled in her boudoir at the rear of the house.

She was looking forward to the new Season with greater joy than usual, and thought Davina, too, appeared to be in excellent spirits. Davina had missed Charles during the weeks he had been in Leicestershire and had been delighted to welcome him home again, and Charles seemed to be more in charity with her as well.

London was still thin of company, but Parliament had opened, and once the knocker was on the St. Merryn House door again, its inhabitants did not lack for visitors. Ladies Melbourne and Cowper called the day after their arrival and were soon followed by Lady Jersey and a number of others, including many of Lady Ophelia's particular friends. It was also necessary to find time for all the fittings required by their seamstresses before the Tarrant ladies could be rigged out in the latest fashions.

There were gentleman callers as well, and after an evening at Covent Garden, and another at a rout given by Lady Jersey, a steady stream of gentlemen began to leave cards and posies, all asking if Lady St. Merryn was at home to visitors when what they really wished to know was if her daughter was at home.

Daintry was accustomed to such attention in town, but though in previous years she had basked in it, wanting to see which of her many potential suitors would intrigue her most, this year, she found herself starting alertly each time Medrose entered the drawing room to announce a caller's name. Then, with an unusual sense of disappointment, she would exert herself to greet the new arrival, and to make pleasant small talk until they had gone.

She knew Jervaulx was in town and had taken his seat in the Lords, for she had heard his name mentioned more than once, but she heard nothing of Deverill and did not ask. Nor did she hear from her sister until shortly before the first subscription ball at Almack's Assembly Rooms, which auspicious occasion marked the true beginning of the London Season.

Since Lady St. Merryn had begun to fret about Susan's continued absence, it was just as well, Daintry thought, that Susan sent a note at last to say she and Geoffrey had arrived at their house in Brook Street. It would have been better had they called in person, however, and when yet another day passed without further word, Daintry took her courage firmly in hand and decided to visit her sister.

Susan greeted her warmly when she was shown into the drawing room of the elegant little house, and said apologetically, "I had meant to call at once, but there just has not been an hour to spare. We were so late arriving, and there is so much to do before we shall be fit to be seen. I wonder where Geoffrey can be. He will pop in to say hello before you go, I am sure."

Reassured that her sister appeared to be in excellent if rather fidgety spirits and that Lady Catherine Chauncey appeared nowhere at all, Daintry was nonetheless glad that Geoffrey did not pop in during her visit. She had no wish to see him and had not the least notion of how she would manage to speak two words to him without succumbing to strong hysterics. Knowing she would have to face him sooner or later, and well aware that to create a scene when she did would be to call down remonstrations upon her own head rather than upon his, she tried to imagine a way to deal with the incident when it should arise.

The exercise was not particularly successful, for she was well aware that Geoffrey would not behave according to plan. Thus, as she dressed for the opening of Almack's the following Wednesday night, she found herself hoping that he, like her father, would elect to remain at home. Her hopes were not high, although Susan had declined an invitation to dine that evening with the family before going on to Almack's together.

Ready at last, she joined her great-aunt and Davina in the hall to wait for Lady St. Merryn, who had said there was no good reason for her to miss the opening of Almack's, since she would be expected to do no more than sit and watch the dancing with the other mamas, or perhaps take a hand of whist in the card room.

The assembly rooms in King Street looked the same as they had every other year Daintry had visited them, neither grand nor elegant. The refreshments, she knew, would be mediocre; however, to be denied entrance was to be shunned by the first circle of London society, a fate considered worse than death by any ambitious young lady or gentleman. The balls were governed by a group of patronesses, who bestowed vouchers upon the few persons they considered eligible to purchase tickets. Their word was law, and they had ordained that no one, not even a royal duke, might be admitted after eleven, and that gentlemen must wear knee breeches, white cravats, and carry *chapeaux-bras.*

Daintry and the others were welcomed at the door by Mr. Willis, who owned the assembly rooms, and soon afterward, the orchestra, directed by Mr. Colnet as it had been for many years, struck up for the grand march. The London Season had begun.

Daintry kept her eye on the entrance to the ballroom, telling herself it was in hopes of seeing her sister, but when the Seacourts arrived just as the opening set of country dances came to an end and her partner moved to return her to her mother's side, she experienced a strong reluctance to go.

From across the room Geoffrey smiled at her as if nothing had ever happened, and she froze, certain that any words she might try to speak to him would choke her. When Lord Alton stepped up to her, asking if he might have the next dance, she turned to him in relief, congratulating herself on thus deftly avoiding a sordid confrontation. Therefore it came as a shock to her, when the dance was over, to find Geoffrey at her side.

"I will escort my sister-in-law back to her mama," he said.

Alton bowed and turned on his heel.

"How dare you, Geoffrey!" she said in a low voice.

"I want to talk to you," he said, smiling in a perfectly normal fashion. "Come with me to that anteroom yonder."

"I won't. You must be out of your wits."

"I want to apologize, Daintry, and I'll be damned if I'll try to do it in a sea of people trying to make up new sets."

Looking at him, she thought he looked sincere, and knowing that if good relations were ever to be restored, she must at least hear him out, she allowed him to escort her to the little room but insisted that he leave the door ajar.

"Anything you like," he said. "I do want to apologize, for I was over the mark with brandy and I behaved like a pig."

"If you are hoping for instant forgiveness," she said, "you will not receive it. I shall do my best to forget what you did, Geoffrey, but that is the best you can hope for now." Moving to pass him, she stiffened in alarm when he caught her arm and swung her back to face him. "Let me go, Geoffrey."

"Wait, Daintry, you don't understand what I'm—"

"Release her."

Despite Seacourt's grasp, Daintry turned at once, her eyes aglow with pleasure.

Deverill stood in the open doorway, looking grim.

Seacourt said, "Get out of here, damn you. This is a family affair and no business of yours."

Stepping into the room, Deverill said curtly, "Release her now, or answer to me, Seacourt."

"Gentlemen, please," Daintry said. She did not want this.

Seacourt shoved her behind him and confronted Deverill. "I am ready any time you are, by God," he said, jutting out his chin and putting up his fists. In the blink of an eye, with a crack of bone on bone, he dropped to the floor at Daintry's feet.

Deverill grasped her by an arm and moved her away from the unconscious man, saying anxiously, "Are you all right?"

Pulling her arm free, she said, "Of course, I am. Good God, Deverill, what have you done? He was attempting to apologize to me, and although he was not making a very good job of it, and was annoying me instead, I am perfectly capable of dealing with that sort of thing myself. There was no reason to knock him down." Hearing Geoffrey groan, she added quickly, "Go away at once. If you are still here when he comes to his senses, there will be a brawl, and it will not be either of you who suffers for that, I can promise you. Did you consider that before you struck him? No, not in the least!"

"Wait just a minute. What the devil do you want me to think he was apologizing for? I saw how he had hold of you, and I saw your face and his. He was threatening you, and you were afraid of him. And you were glad to see me, so if you think—"

"Oh, go away before I lose patience with you," she snapped. "Perhaps I was glad to see you at first, but you seem to believe that every female needs an overprotective male to fight her battles for her. Well, I do not. Now, for heaven's sake, go away and let me deal with him before someone comes through that door you so stupidly left ajar. Nothing can happen a dozen feet from hundreds of dancers that I cannot handle!"

"Handle this," he said angrily, pulling her into his arms and kissing her as if he had been starving for the very taste of her. When she tried to free herself, he stopped at once. Then, looking stern, he said, "There are many things in life that you can't handle alone, sweetheart, not because you're a woman but because you refuse to recognize your limitations. I'll go, but you have certainly not seen the last of me." And he was gone.

Daintry stood for a moment, staring after him, until a groan reminded her of Geoffrey's presence. Moving quickly, she took the flowers from a bowl on a side table and dashed the water over his head. "Get up, Geoffrey." As he struggled to a sitting position, she added grimly, "Your lip is split and your hair is wet. That door yonder leads to the gallery, and you can get to the street from there. I will make your excuses to the others."

He glared at her but did not speak, and she left him, making her way as quickly as possible toward the others, searching the crowd for Deverill and trying to sort out her feelings. He had grabbed her against her will, and she had resisted, but odd though it seemed now in view of her terrifying experience with Seacourt, she had not been afraid, and if the truth were told, she was glad he had kissed her. She knew she had overreacted to his confrontation with Seacourt, that although her anger had been genuine, it had manifested itself against the wrong man.

Gideon left Almack's with a strong sense of ill-usage, but he was even angrier with himself than with Daintry. She had been right to berate him for striking Seacourt, and though he could not really regret it, he was not by any means certain why he had done it. He had seen her go into the anteroom with the man, and knowing she did not like him, had wondered if Seacourt had forced her. Then, coming upon the scene, he had been certain Seacourt had, and had reacted instantly and without the slightest thought. Such behavior was unlike him. He was better trained than that.

As he strode west along King Street to the walkway leading to St. James's Street, he remembered her fury and smiled. Other young women of his acquaintance would at least have pretended to be grateful for being rescued, but not that one. She had been furious. Her eyes had sparkled, and her breasts had filled out her muslin gown magnificently. Shaking his head at himself, he saw that the torches lighting the alleyway ahead had gone out, making it unnaturally dark. As the thought crossed his mind, three figures loomed out of the black shadow, cudgels raised.

Deverill fought hard, but he was outnumbered, and though he knocked down two of the villains, the third got in a single, decisive blow with his club. The last thing Deverill heard before losing consciousness was a chorus of angry shouts from the King Street end of the walkway.

He came to slowly, feeling hands lightly slapping his face and chafing his hands. A flask was held to his lips and tilted. Choking on a mouthful of raw, fiery brandy, he tried to push the flask away and opened his eyes. The torches had been relighted, and he found himself staring into an anxious, freckled face that he had never again expected to see.

"Thought you were a goner for sure," Viscount Penthorpe said cheerfully. "Dashed glad you ain't."

Eighteen

One of Penthorpe's companions hailed a hackney coach in St. James's Street, and Penthorpe climbed in beside Gideon, bidding his friends good night. Gideon, leaning his aching head against the squabs and feeling a little sick, nonetheless could not contain his curiosity a moment longer. "Where the devil did you spring from? I thought you were dead."

Penthorpe chuckled, but before he replied, he put down the window and shouted, "Hey, there, jarvey, there's no need to rattle us along at such a pace. Take it slow, man."

The rocking of the coach eased somewhat, and Gideon let out a breath of relief. "Thank you, Andy. Now, answer my question."

"No use giving me orders anymore, old son. You've sold out, if I haven't, and I needn't listen to 'em anymore. What's more, you're sick as a horse, so you'd best keep mum till we reach Jervaulx House if you don't want to disgrace yourself all over this coach. Not," he added with a fastidious sniff, "that anyone would notice much difference if you did."

"But I saw you on the field," Gideon murmured. "I found the miniature and saw your red hair." The memory of what else he had seen nearly undid him, and for a moment his attention was fixed upon calming his stomach. Penthorpe's chuckle sounded heartless.

"Not mine, you didn't," he said. "Some other poor stiff it must have been. Can't tell you what a turn it gave me to learn I was supposed to be dead. A friend had the *Times,* all the way from London, and there it was that I'd fallen at Waterloo. Had to look in the glass and pinch myself to be sure it wasn't true."

"But your uncle put that in months ago! How the—"

"Not now. Take a damper, will you, till we get you home and I can have a good look at that lump on your head. Daresay you ought to have a bloodsucker to take a look as well."

"Not necessary," Gideon muttered. "I don't need a doctor."

But when they reached the huge mansion on the banks of the Thames that had been the London home of the Marquesses of Jervaulx for two hundred years, it was Jervaulx himself who decreed that a doctor should be fetched, and Gideon, whose head was aching more by the minute, did not argue. But when he had been helped to his bedchamber, and Penthorpe would have left him there, he said with a grim note in his voice, "Don't you dare stir a foot out of this room until you have explained yourself to me, Andy, or by heaven, when I get up—"

"Oh, very well, don't distress yourself," Penthorpe said, grinning at him. "I'll stay if your father don't throw me out."

Jervaulx, who had accompanied them upstairs, said, "You must do as you please, of course," and left them alone.

"Still a dashed cold fish, I see," Penthorpe said when the door was safely shut. "Talks like a book. Never known anyone like him. Don't mind telling you, he frightens me to death."

"Speaking of your death," Gideon said, ignoring his pounding head in his determination to get the story, "what the devil—"

"Oh, very well, I daresay the sawbones won't get here for a good while yet. Like as not your father's man will have to roust him out of bed at this hour. Fact is, I wasn't killed."

"I can see that, damn you. What happened?"

"Horse fell on me," Penthorpe said. "Had a ball in my shoulder, too, but the horse was much worse, and the devil of it was that I couldn't get free. Cannonballs flying all around me, and a lot of screaming and yelling that seemed to go on for hours, but I couldn't see a thing. Could scarcely breathe, for that matter. Someone fell on top of me—on the horse, that is—and I was in the deuce of a lot of pain. I must have blacked out, for the next thing I knew it was morning, and much more quiet. Not that I could hear birds, or anything pleasant like that, mind you. Just a lot of moaning and more screams, though nothing like before. Then I heard a female's voice, calling for someone named Jean-Paul, and I remember wishing I were Jean-Paul and someone would come and get me. My brain must not have been working because it was the devil of a time before it occurred to me to shout to the wench to get the damned horse off me, but I did it at last, and she got someone with a wagon to help."

"Who was she? A Frenchie?"

"No, Belgian woman, name of Marie de Larrey, looking for her husband. Found him, too, if you can believe that. Wounded, like me, but still alive and kicking. She got us both into the wagon and rattled us home to her village. Worst ride of my life, I can tell you, for I had a broken rib, I think, and the damned ball in my shoulder. I picked up some infection or other afterward, so it was a good long while before I was fit, but here I am."

"It's been months, Andy," Gideon said sternly.

"Well, I was delirious for a time, you know—didn't even know I wasn't in England. And later, well, the village was a pleasant place, and the people very friendly, and no one seemed in any hurry for me to leave. Didn't see that dashed paper until January—no season for travel then, of course—and I kept meaning to write to someone here, but . . ." He shrugged ruefully. "You know how I am about that sort of thing, Gideon."

"None better," Gideon said sourly. "Why come back now?"

"It was spring, and I got restless," Penthorpe said simply. "I ask you, Gideon, would you like to be stuck in a Belgian village when you might be in London for the Season?"

"Your reappearance is going to shock a good many people, I should think. Does Tattersall know yet?"

"Well, he's in town, I think, but I haven't quite got round to seeing him yet. I'll do it tomorrow, of course. Have to arrange to sell out properly, too, I suppose. Just got here late this afternoon, you see, and straightaway went looking for you. Went to the clubs—to

Brooks's and White's, at least—before someone chanced to mention that it was opening night at Almack's. Not dressed for it but came round anyway, hoping to get a message in to you if you were there. Just pure dumb luck I came along in time to be of any help. Didn't even know it was you at first. Wouldn't have expected you to escape the place so early."

Gideon gave him a look. "Your betrothed told me to leave."

"My betrothed?" Penthorpe's expression altered rapidly from bewilderment to a blank look. "I'd hoped . . . that is, I'd feared that was all off by now. Didn't you tell her I was dead?"

"Yes, but since you are not, and since no other arrangement has been made for her, I have a feeling her father is going to welcome you back with open arms. Not that you seem so delighted, Andy. Did Mrs. de Larrey have a pretty little sister?"

Penthorpe shook his head. "No, no, not at all. I ain't such a paltry fellow as all that, dash it, though I did get to thinking what a good thing it was that I hadn't got married before Waterloo—and left a grieving widow, don't you know?"

Gideon started to nod, remembered his headache, and said, "I do know, but you'll have to keep your vow, you know."

"Well, of course, I will. Good God, what else can I do? If I'd realized—What's she like, Gideon?"

"As beautiful as her picture," Gideon said. "She has a mind of her own though, just as you were told."

Penthorpe eyed him uneasily. "What do you mean, exactly?"

"She holds a sadly unfavorable opinion of our sex, Andy."

"She don't like men? Good God, what sort of female is she?"

Gideon hesitated, thinking of all the words he might use. Finally, watching Penthorpe closely, he said, "She's aggravating, exasperating, and too damned hot at hand for her own good, but with a light hand on the rein I think you'll like her, Andy."

"Good God." Penthorpe looked appalled, but he rallied quickly, saying hastily, "That is . . . well, I say, I hope you haven't been trying to bridle her yourself, Gideon." His laugh was forced. "What I mean to say is, I'd find myself ditched if you were to wave your expectations at the lass, don't you think?"

Gideon did not answer at once, but when Penthorpe began to look rather hopeful, he said quietly, "She's a woman of her word, Andy. She won't cry off."

"Well, you needn't make it sound like I want her to do any such thing," Penthorpe said quickly. "Couldn't say so if I did, not even to my best friend, not without looking like a dashed scoundrel, but you're talking fustian, you know. Cried off three times before, didn't she? My uncle told me so."

Gideon smiled. "The other times were different, or at least she would say they were. This time she gave her word of honor to her father and that, in her view, will make all the difference."

"Oh." He was silent for a moment, then said, "I suppose St. Merryn is in town. I'll have to see him at once."

"The whole family is in town," Gideon said, shifting his position. His headache was easing, so long as he did not move without caution.

"Lady Susan and Seacourt, too?"

"Yes. You might as well know before you hear it from the tabbies that there was an unfortunate turn-up in that household before Christmas. Lady Susan ran away from her husband."

"Ran away? Why?" Penthorpe's gaze sharpened.

Instead of answering directly, Gideon said, "Seacourt was forced to apply to a magistrate for a writ of *habeas corpus* to get her back."

"Don't babble Latin at me. What the devil does it mean?"

"That she had to return to him or appear before the same magistrate to give cause for not doing so. She said Seacourt beat her. She was heavily veiled, so we did not see her face, but he did not deny it."

"The devil, you say! Good thing she left him if you ask me. He was a Captain Hackum at school, too. Where's she living now?"

"The magistrate sent her home."

"What? How could that be?"

"It's the law, Andy, even when the fellow's a bully."

"Damned fool law," Penthorpe growled. "Damned fool magistrate, too. What a devilish thing to do! But how do you know all this? Surely, it was not all in the papers."

"I was there. The magistrate was my father."

"But, look here, he's a marquess now," Penthorpe said. "What's he doing still playing at being a magistrate?"

"He cannot seem to let his old duties go. They were part of his life for so long and the title came to him so unexpectedly that I daresay it's difficult for him to leave old obligations behind for the new ones. He's been trying to do both."

"It don't sound as if he's making a good job of either one. If he could make such a dashed silly decision in Lady Susan's case, just think what a muck he'll make of being a marquess!"

Gideon was spared the necessity of a reply by the arrival of the doctor, who greeted him cheerfully, demanded to know what he had done to knock himself up, and announced that he would just bind up his head and cup him, and he would be right as a trivet in no time. Penthorpe fled, but not before promising on his oath to visit both his uncle and St. Merryn the very next day.

The following afternoon, when Penthorpe's name was announced Daintry dropped the teapot she had been using to pour out tea for several lady callers, and it smashed to pieces, taking a number of china cups and saucers with it.

Lady St. Merryn, clasping a hand to her bosom, cried out in dismay, "The best Sèvres china, Daintry! Whatever were you thinking! And tea stains all over your lovely gown. They will never come out. My salts, Ethelinda!"

Miss Davies complied at once, and Lady Jerningham, who sat beside Daintry and had been entertaining the others with her opinion of the Prince of Saxe-Coburg, newly arrived in England and now known to be the Princess Charlotte's intended bridegroom, snatched her skirts out of harm's way and said austerely, "Very careless of you, my dear Daintry."

Lady Ophelia said calmly, "Clear away the mess, Medrose, and give Miss Daintry a napkin to blot up the tea on her gown. You might have sent to warn us that you were still alive, young man, rather than bursting in upon us in such dramatic fashion. Since you are here, however, pray let me make you known to Lady St. Merryn, and to Ladies Jerningham and Cardigan. I," she added, "am Daintry's great-aunt, Ophelia Balterley."

Daintry was still staring in shock at the lanky, freckle-faced young man who had entered the room in Medrose's wake, and had paid little heed to the introductions. In the brief moment after Lady Ophelia fell silent, before he could reply, she said, "Did they truly say you are Penthorpe? But surely . . ."

He smiled and obeyed her gesture to take a chair near her. "Not put to bed with a shovel yet, my lady, promise you. Beg to apologize for any confusion the announcement of my death may have caused you. Came at once to put matters right."

Lady Ophelia said dryly, "At once? The battle of Waterloo was fought eight months ago, young man."

"As long as that, was it? Just goes to show. I was pretty well knocked up, ma'am, out of my senses for a good long while, and slow in mending even after that."

"But surely someone could have written to your people here!" exclaimed Lady Cardigan, a plump, motherly woman, and Lady Jerningham's bosom bow.

"Suppose someone should have," Penthorpe agreed, "but there's only my uncle, you know, and by the time I'd collected my wits it seemed easier to wait and tell him myself once I got home. Then, from one cause or another, I just never quite seemed to get started on the journey."

Lady Ophelia said sternly, "I don't mind saying you behaved disgracefully. Did you not think it incumbent upon you to inform your betrothed wife that the news of your death was untrue?"

"I thought she might have made other arrangements by the time I came to my senses, ma'am, and if she had, the news would have put her in a dashed awkward position." He gazed innocently around the room. "I wasn't fit to do anything more than swallow a dose of rhubarb occasionally for more than six weeks—didn't know my own name for days at a time—you can see how it was."

"I do see," Lady Ophelia said with a grimace. "Daintry, don't sit staring like a want-wit. Go and change your gown. Penthorpe will not mind waiting while you do."

Still in a daze, Daintry stood up as Penthorpe said, "In point of fact, I'd hoped to see St. Merryn, but his man said he had gone out. When do you expect him to return?"

Lady St. Merryn put down her vinaigrette and said, "Why, he has gone to the House of Lords, sir, and might not return till all hours. I am sure I cannot think what they can find to talk about for so many hours each day."

Lady Ophelia said tartly, "They ought to be talking less and doing more, for goodness' sake. You might not know it yet, young man, but times are dark in this country right now. What with heavy taxation, bad harvests, and downright selfish legislation enacted by those who ought to know better . . ."

Daintry did not wait to hear more, but slipped out the door and ran to her bedchamber to change her gown, trying to collect her scattered wits as she did. When she returned, freshly garbed in a gown of pale-pink sprigged muslin with ribbon knots and a wide sash of darker pink silk, she met her father coming upstairs from the hall. "Papa, I thought you had gone to the House."

"And so I had, but what with the back-benchers shouting at the front, all bickering over a dozen things they find of more interest than the price of corn, I could not stand it any longer. Thought I'd step round to White's this afternoon instead, and just came along home first to see if Charles wanted to go."

"He went out an hour ago," she said.

St. Merryn looked at her sharply. "He and Davina at it again, are they? Dashed if I ever saw such a pair."

"She went out earlier," Daintry admitted. "We had just finished writing all the invitations for the ball we are to give when she suddenly looked at the clock, jumped up, and told me to tell Charles she was meeting some friends for a drive to Richmond Park and that he should not look for her return before dark."

St. Merryn grunted. "Hope he went to fetch the lass straight home again, but if I know Charles, he'll end up at some gaming hell or other instead. Between them, they mean to ruin me, for if she isn't purchasing some extravagant kickshaw or other, he's losing a monkey at the tables. Well, that's neither here nor there. If he's out, I'll just take myself off."

"I am afraid you cannot go just yet, Papa."

"And why not? Look here, miss, if you think you are going to start telling me what I can and cannot do, you'd better—"

"Of course, I would not do that, sir, but Viscount Penthorpe is in the drawing room with Mama and Aunt Ophelia, and several others, and I thought you would wish—"

"Who?"

"Penthorpe, Papa. Apparently, he was not killed after all."

"The devil you say!" And, brushing past her, he hurried to the door of the drawing room and flung it open. "Penthorpe, my dear lad, what a miracle this is, to be sure. Upon my word, but you are a sight for sore eyes, my boy. Thought I'd never marry the lass off, but here you are, so all's right and tight again."

Penthorpe leapt to his feet when St. Merryn erupted into the room, and Daintry, entering on her father's heels, saw him grab the viscount's hand and pump it enthusiastically up and down.

"Just a minute, Papa," she said abruptly.

St. Merryn glanced at her over his shoulder, then turned back to Penthorpe, saying, "Upon my word, but I'm glad to see you. To think I'd be grateful for a bunch of chowderheads wanting to talk only of the great profits they make by keeping foreign wheat and corn out of England. And here was a grand surprise just waiting for me on my doorstep."

Daintry kept silent. Her first impulse, to point out that the viscount could not possibly have taken their betrothal very seriously since he had not so much as sent word of his good health to her but had let her continue to think him dead, gave way to the realization that she could say no such thing, and certainly not before such gossips as Lady Jerningham and Lady Cardigan. She felt trapped by convention, but the last thing she wanted was to create a scandal, and in any case she was given no opportunity to speak.

"Lady Susan and Sir Geoffrey Seacourt, and Lady Catherine Chauncey," Medrose intoned from the doorway.

Despite her own predicament, Daintry stared to see Catherine, but St. Merryn turned to the newcomers with delight. "Just see who is here," he said. "Penthorpe ain't dead, after all, and the wedding is right on again. We can leave for Cornwall just as soon as the session ends next week."

There was a chorus of objections to this impetuous plan, but

Daintry's carried above the rest. "Papa, how can you suggest such a thing? We cannot pack up and leave when we have just invited upwards of four hundred people to a ball to be held a fortnight from now. The invitations went out this morning!"

"Lord, what a kickup there was!" Penthorpe told Gideon an hour later, having gone straight to Jervaulx House upon making his escape from Berkeley Square, "I never saw anything like it. Females have changed since Waterloo, and that's all there is about it. You never saw such a row, what with the tabbies all lighting into St. Merryn when he said he was going to take them back to Cornwall in a sennight, and Daintry and her great-aunt—Lord, what a dragon that one is!—both telling him to his head that he could do no such thing."

"Who won?" Gideon asked curiously, though he had little doubt what must have been the outcome of such an encounter.

Surprising him, Penthorpe said, "I think you'd have to call it a draw, but if Seacourt hadn't put in his mite, St. Merryn would have been routed. First Daintry tells her papa she can't leave before the St. Merryn ball—Oh," he added, scrabbling in his pockets and drawing out a crumpled gilt-edge card, "nearly forgot. Odd way to invite a fellow to a ball, but Lady Ophelia slipped this to me as I was going and told me to give it to you."

"Did she now?" Gideon said, smoothing the card. Then, grinning, he added, "I think you will like Lady Ophelia, Andy."

"Well, I don't think it," he said roundly. "It's my belief the old dragon is responsible for Daintry's dashed odd notions."

"Oh, yes, you are quite right about that," Gideon said, rubbing a hand across his aching brow.

"Sore head?"

"A little," he admitted, "but Kingston left me several packets of headache powders to take until they go off. I'd take one now, but the damned things send me right off to sleep."

"Don't let me keep you up," Penthorpe said with a sigh. "Dash it all, Gideon, I never meant to put everyone in an uproar, but what's a fellow to do? It's plain as a pikestaff St. Merryn means to have me in the parson's mousetrap before the cat can lick her paw, and what's more, so does Daintry."

"Does she?" Gideon regarded him more alertly.

"Just told you she did. Not that I'm complaining, of course, but I did hope for time to find my feet again before I got riveted, and I won't deny she ain't what one would expect Lady Susan's sister to be. Not that she's not well enough, and not that Susan's looking her best these days either," he added. "Looks pinched, and she's a dashed sight too thin for my liking."

"You've seen her then."

"Oh, aye, they came in while St. Merryn was flying into alt over my rise from the dead. She was too pale, and skinny as a broom straw. Does Seacourt starve her as well as beat her? And who the devil is Lady Catherine Chauncey?"

"Ah, so she is back in the play, is she?"

"Don't know about any play, but she was there right enough. Thought at first she must be some relation to Susan, because she kept hovering over her, begging her to sit down and rest as if she were recovering from an illness or some such thing, then sat down right beside her, telling Captain Hackum to fetch his wife a pillow and to ask the footman to bring her a glass of water. She seemed kind enough but a bit odd. Who the devil is she?"

"According to your betrothed, she is Seacourt's mistress."

"Do stop calling the wench my betrothed, Gideon!" He flushed, adding, "Your tone ain't at all polite, dash it, so if you don't want to answer to me, old son, mind your lip."

Gideon smiled lazily. "Well, if you think you can—"

"I don't mill down cripples," Penthorpe said with a crooked grin. "Oh, sit still, or you will have to be taking those dashed powders of yours. What did the sawbones say in the end?"

Chuckling, Gideon said, "That's right, you milk-livered turn-tail, you ran off and left me to his damned untender mercies, didn't you? By heaven, I *ought* to get up to you."

"Cupped you, did he?"

"He did not. I've too great a desire to keep my blood in my veins after Waterloo. We had a bit of a discussion about it, but the result was that he predicted a high fever for me, which never came about, and headaches, which did. He ordered me to keep to my bed until the headaches pass."

Penthorpe made much of looking around the well-appointed library. "Lots of furniture in here, of course, but I don't see a bed anywhere. Got it hidden behind one of the bookshelves?"

"If you must know, I came in here to escape a pair of my servants who insist upon competing with each other to nursemaid me, but never mind about that. "You were telling me the encounter was a draw. Are they returning to Cornwall?" He glanced at the card he still held in one hand. "They cannot be if Lady Ophelia is sending me an invitation for the twenty-sixth."

"They go directly afterward," Penthorpe said, "but that's on account of Captain Hackum. Said he never could fathom how it was St. Merryn had so little control over his household. He made a joke of it all, but I could see Daintry did not think it was so dashed amusing, and nor did St. Merryn. Seacourt told him, the first thing they knew, she'd be advising the Princess Charlotte to begin as she meant to go on and never let poor old Prince Leopold get the upper hand, and St. Merryn blustered back as to how she would do as she was bid. Don't see the problem, myself. Dash it, what would Daintry have to do with advising a princess?"

"Nothing, of course. It is just Seacourt's way of making mischief. He doesn't like her much, you see."

"Well, the feeling is mutual if you ask me," Penthorpe said. "If looks could kill, that man would be dead, but I don't think she likes you much either, my lad, although when I first chanced to mention your little accident last night, I thought she cared a great deal—went paper white, and I'd swear her hands trembled and she had to catch them together and hold them in her lap—but the next moment I knew I must have been mistaken, for as soon as I said you'd be as right as a trivet in a day or so, she turned to Lady Jerningham—Did I mention the old gossip was sitting smack in the middle of all this with the Cardigan woman, and both of them soaking it all up like sponges, I'll wager, while pretending to tell Lady Catherine all about this Prince Leopold fellow and how he means to visit the Regent at Brighton? Well, Daintry turns to her and says"—he raised his voice an octave—"'And what did you think of Prince Leopold when you met him, ma'am?'" Dropping his voice back to its normal tone, he went on, "Five minutes later she had them all talking politics, of all ridiculous things, though even St. Merryn seemed willing enough to listen to her spout off about the wickedness of the Corn Laws. Only Seacourt disagreed with her—said it was important to keep the corn prices up so the landowners didn't lose their shirts—but she snapped his nose off, said she'd expect just such nonsensical talk from him and that he was a fool."

Gideon chuckled again. "She did, did she? That young woman is bound for disaster."

"Well, you needn't look so dashed gleeful about it," Penthorpe said with asperity. "Like as not, she'll take me straight along with her. Look here, Gideon, if St. Merryn does insist upon pushing this wedding business forward, you won't desert me, will you? What I mean is, if I do have to go down to Cornwall, you'll come along to support me, won't you? I suppose I shall need a best man, after all."

"I will certainly do what I can to help you, Andy," Gideon said, "and I can go back to Cornwall with you since I've nothing much better to do, but I doubt I should serve as your best man."

"I forgot that dashed feud."

"Well, St. Merryn hasn't. If I had my way, I'd end the thing at once by any way that would satisfy him, but my father wouldn't like it, and I don't want to infuriate him."

"A most dutiful attitude, dear boy," Jervaulx said from the doorway, his voice bringing both men instantly to their feet in a manner that made Gideon's head begin to pound and left him dizzy. Neither he nor Penthorpe had heard the door open, and they both regarded the marquess in some dismay as he moved into the room and laid a pile of papers on a side table. Turning back to them and extracting an enameled snuffbox from his waistcoat pocket, he added with apparent complaisance, "Your return, Andrew, has caused a few flutters of uncertainty at the defense ministry. Apparently you have encountered a minor obstacle to selling out."

"Don't I know it, sir?" Penthorpe said with a sigh. "Went round there this morning, thinking I'd best get things in motion, and dashed if they didn't tell me that since I've somehow managed to become officially dead, I can't sell out. A dashed nuisance, that's what it is." An arrested look entered his eyes, and he added thoughtfully, "I say, what if the parson should refuse to call out the banns for a dead man?"

Jervaulx took a pinch of snuff. "There can be no trouble about that, dear boy. There are reasonable men in the present Government, you know, and a word has been dropped in a few helpful ears. Your next attempt will no doubt prove much less frustrating for you."

Seeing that Penthorpe had not understood, Gideon said, "I believe he means he has cleared the way for you, Andy." He eyed Jervaulx curiously, wondering why he had exerted himself. "Much obliged to you, sir. Your influence must be of help to him."

Jervaulx nodded, restoring his snuffbox to his waistcoat pocket. Then, looking directly at Penthorpe, he said, "The sooner you take advantage of that more reasonable attitude, Andrew, the better it will be. Moreover, Gideon is supposed to remain in bed, and there is a great deal more for a busy man to attend to here before this day will be over, as you see." He gestured toward the papers on the side table, then added gently, "Of course, if you prefer to put the matter off in your usual custom, you are quite welcome to stay here as long as you like."

Penthorpe stammered his thanks, mixing apologies with assurances that as soon as he had seen Gideon safely up to his bedchamber he would go directly to the defense ministry, assuring the marquess that he had given up his habits of procrastination once and for all, and that Jervaulx need not concern himself further with his few trifling difficulties.

Jervaulx said in the same gentle tone, "One of the footmen will assist Gideon upstairs in a few moments, Andrew."

Penthorpe hesitated, but at Gideon's slight nod, he took himself off, and when the door had shut behind him, Gideon turned warily toward his father, bracing himself and ignoring the pounding in his head, but wishing the simple act of standing had not made him feel so dizzy.

Jervaulx frowned. "When was the last time you took one of Kingston's powders?"

"Hours ago," Gideon said, still watching him. "I'm all right, sir. In fact, I daresay I feel better than you do. You look worn to the bone."

"Nonsense. Don't try to change the subject."

Gideon sighed. "I know I spoke out of turn, sir, but may I sit down for this lecture? I warn you, I'm a trifle too dizzy to maintain a parade posture for longer than a minute or two."

"You are a trifle old for lectures, too. Moreover, there can be little cause for vexation, in that the sentiments you expressed—the last ones, at all events—were entirely appropriate. A dutiful son ought not to infuriate his father."

Despite the reasonable nature of these words, Gideon did not feel that he had been given permission to sit. He said carefully, "If I cannot feel as you do about that feud, Father, it is because I have no understanding of it. To my mind the damned thing ought to be laid to rest once and for all."

"That will, of course, be your right when you succeed to the title," Jervaulx said. "One would think that a certain amount of family loyalty would prevail, but that is no more than a matter for conjecture at present, and until you are recovered from your injury, you will be much better off in your bed."

Gideon, having little enough energy even to stand, let alone to debate the matter, said, "As you wish, sir," and moved toward the door. When he reached it, he paused with his hand on the handle and, turning back, said, "What brought you back so early? Usually, you do not return from the House until after nine."

Jervaulx's frown deepened. "There will be no vote for days, and one begins to find the interminable dissension intolerable since it is perfectly plain to anyone with sense that the economy of this country depends upon keeping the price of corn high enough to ensure a profit for the farmers who grow it. Moreover, as you see—" He gestured once again toward the stack of papers.

"Does it not concern you to know, sir, that in Cornwall, miners cannot afford to feed their families because they cannot afford the price of a loaf of bread?"

"Certainly it does, but one votes for Gloucester not for Cornwall, and in point of fact, if the economy of the corn and wheat growing counties can be improved—as it should be now that there is peace—there will be a greater call for tin and other Cornish products, so the mines will open again and the economy of Cornwall will improve. Do not argue what you do not know, lad."

"What I know, sir," Gideon said doggedly, "is that there is great distress at home, caused I think, by this sudden return to peace after twenty years of war and by the return of great masses of men hitherto employed at sea and in the army. People cannot even travel in safety. Why, I have been fired upon twice."

"Such unrest must be firmly put down."

"I should think the problem would be better resolved if the distress of the people were alleviated," Gideon said.

"You should perhaps join the Whigs," Jervaulx said gently.

"And alienate you to the point of never speaking to me again? I think not, sir." A particularly sharp pain shot through his head, and though he fought to keep it from showing in his countenance, he saw Jervaulx's expression sharpen.

"Go to bed, Gideon. You are fitted neither physically nor mentally for this discussion. When you are on your feet again, perhaps you will find time amidst your many social engagements to learn more about such matters as these."

Gideon smiled ruefully. "I confess, I do not know much about them, sir, but I do intend to return to Cornwall soon to continue my lessons. Before that date, however, I have been invited to attend a ball and I do not intend to miss it."

Nineteen

In the fortnight before the St. Merryn House ball, Daintry was very busy, for the Season was in full swing, and since she frequently had as many as four engagements in a single night, she soon began to feel as if she had no time whatever to think. Penthorpe's return and the resuming of her betrothal—though not worded in quite that manner, of course—had been announced in the London *Gazette,* and she had come to accept the fact that there was nothing she could do to avoid her fate.

She had approached St. Merryn only once to ask if he would consider releasing her from her word of honor, explaining that she had come to the melancholy conclusion that she was not cut out to be a proper wife to any man, let alone to one who could forget her very existence for months at a time. Her father's reaction was exactly what she had feared it would be.

"You gave me your word, girl, and not another one will I hear," he had roared. "*This* betrothal will end in marriage, and until it does, you will pretend to be delighted with it, for I'll not have this family made the talk of London all for the whim of a capricious young chit. By God, I'm putting my foot down!"

The gossips were certainly out in full force, she knew, for not only was there Princess Charlotte's new betrothal to discuss, as well as a host of the latest *crim con*stories but the Duchess of Argyll and her husband had come to town.

Daintry saw the duchess a week before her own ball, at Lady Cardigan's great assembly, which she attended with members of her family, escorted by Penthorpe. The announcement of the duke and duchess's arrival soon after their own caused a noticeable stir.

Watching the noble couple descend the broad marble steps into the ballroom, Lady Ophelia said, "Dash, what is Penelope Cardigan thinking of? There is sure to be a scene, for Anglesey and Wellington are both here tonight, and Anglesey won't relish meeting his erstwhile wife when she has not only the higher rank of duchess but her adoring new husband by her side as well."

Daintry, watching now, as indeed everyone else was too, said, "There is Lady Jersey, ma'am, hurrying to meet them."

"And Wellington yonder, looking as blue as a megrim," Penthorpe said. He had dined in Berkeley Square with the family, as had the Seacourts, Lady Catherine Chauncey, and Lord Alvanley. Afterward, everyone except St. Merryn had journeyed together to Cardigan House to attend the assembly.

Daintry had managed to be polite to Geoffrey for Susan's sake, but he seemed to have put the past out of his head, for he treated her just as he had before the horrid night at Seacourt Head, clearly assuming that she had forgiven him.

"The Argylls won't stay," Charles said. Turning to watch his wife perform the minuet with a dashing young blade who had rushed up to claim her hand the minute they had arrived, he added, "The rest of the females will make it a dashed sight too uncomfortable for her, even with Sally to give her a lead."

He was proved right, for despite Lady Jersey's display of family loyalty—the duchess being her husband's sister—the rest of the company treated her grace as if she had been invisible, and the Duke and Duchess of Argyll stayed less than half an hour.

"It is too bad," Daintry said with disgust when she saw that they had gone. "Lord Uxbridge—that is, Anglesey—treated her with the most shameful contempt by seducing Charlotte Wellesley when he was still married, and yet there is Wellington, chatting with him as if they were the best of friends, when in fact Charlotte was his brother's wife before Uxbridge seduced her!"

"But they *are* the best of friends," a familiar deep voice murmured behind her, "and since Ux—Anglesey is also a wounded hero who is much admired, you would do better not to speak of such things where you can so easily be overheard, you know."

She whirled to find Deverill attired in a particularly well cut coat of dark blue superfine over skintight biscuit-colored breeches that set off his masculine attributes to perfection, looking amused rather than stern, but although it was the first time she had seen him since the attack on his life and her heart leapt at the sight of him, she said, "I don't care if they do hear me. She is the victim, as even the Scottish courts agreed, for they allowed her to divorce him, did they not? Yet there he stands, pompous and self-assured, the victor of the night."

Lady Ophelia said, stifling a yawn, "But so it always is, my dear, that 'tis the woman who is blamed and punished. Though she did sue him for divorce, she could only have done so in such an odd country as Scotland and will always be treated as an outcast in England; while, as you see, despite the fact that his misconduct resulted in a verdict against him for thousands of pounds and not one but two divorces, he can do as he pleases."

"Your aunt is right, you know," Deverill said quietly. "A woman has certain social rights, but she must take good care when she asserts them that she does not draw too much attention, lest she cast herself quite beyond the pale."

Seacourt said with a spark in his eyes, "Never expected to hear you preach moderation, Deverill. Turning over a new leaf?"

"But he's right," Penthorpe said. "Dash it all, the rules are clear, and it don't do to be flouting them when the only result must be disaster. Oh, I say, Lady Susan, I believe that's our dance they are striking up for."

Daintry caught Geoffrey's eye as Penthorpe slipped under his guard to whisk Susan away, and thought he looked angry and as if he meant to go after his wife, but before he could do so, Davina rejoined them and, ignoring the others, said with a flirtatious laugh, "Geoffrey, I do hope you have not bespoken a partner for this dance, for it is the most vexatious thing, but I have none. I know a proper lady must never ask a gentleman . . ." Allowing her words to trail into silence, she fluttered her lashes at him.

Seacourt's flashing grin appeared, and he said, "You need certainly not ask, my dear. I would be most honored if you would accept my hand for this quadrille."

"I like that," Charles muttered as they went off together. "The wench ought to ask her own husband if she needs a partner, though if she does, it's for the first time in her life."

Daintry smiled at him. "You detest dancing the quadrille."

"Who does not?" he demanded. "All that dashed capering about! It's all of a piece, but I'm not going to watch her make sheep's eyes at that damned Seacourt. I'm for the card room."

Daintry, seeing her great-aunt turn to sit down beside Lady St. Merryn and Miss Davies, was about to follow her example when a firm hand stopped her. "I hope you will take pity on an injured man," Deverill said with a warm smile, "and walk with me to fetch some refreshment for these ladies. They all look as if they would enjoy something cool."

"Oh, yes, please," Lady St. Merryn said gratefully, fanning herself. "I do hope our ball is not so hot as this one is. I declare, I am well nigh to fainting from this dreadful heat."

Lady Ophelia agreed. "A cup of punch would wake me up a bit," she said frankly. "Every year, I must be in London for a good six weeks before I become accustomed to the later hours and begin to sleep as well as I do in the country. Go along with him, Daintry, do, and bring us some biscuits with that punch."

Allowing Deverill to draw her hand into the crook of his arm, Daintry looked up at him and saw that he looked rather pale. "Are you fully recovered from your injuries?" she asked. "I must tell you that I . . . I felt quite dreadfully responsible when I learned what had happened—for having sent you away as I did."

"You need not have felt that way," he said quietly. "You were right to send me away. I should not have struck Seacourt." He glanced down at her, and the sudden glow of warmth in his eyes made her heart beat so hard that she wondered they could not both hear it. He said, "I am nearly my old self again, but I confess,

I still get a trifle dizzy when I stand up too quickly." Patting his waistcoat pocket, he added with a twinkle, "My servants do not agree that I should be out of my bed yet. I have discovered that two of them who delight in attempting to outdo each other in their service to me, have each bestowed upon me a packet of the headache powders the doctor left for me to take."

"Goodness, ought you not to take them then?"

"On no account. I believe I've used up no more than two doses, in fact, for once I discovered that they knocked me out more quickly than a surfeit of brandy, I decided I should do better without them. But my henchmen cannot be convinced of it, and if I were to throw the packets away, I believe they would think I had taken them, and continue to press more upon me. I hope that if I ignore them, they will soon cease to be such gudgeons. But tell me," he added as they neared the refreshment room, "is Seacourt quite restored to the family fold? He seems none the worse for our little set-to, at all events."

"No, it is the oddest thing, the way he seems always to assume he will always be forgiven, no matter what he does."

"Then he *was* apologizing for his brutality that night," he said with an arrested look in his eyes. "I wouldn't have thought it. But have you forgiven him? After what he must have done, I am not so sure I could be that generous."

His words brought a flood of unwelcome memories, and before she could think or stop herself, she exclaimed in revulsion, "Neither can I, sir, I promise you. Geoffrey is horrid!"

Deverill stopped suddenly and pulled her aside, away from a stream of other guests bent on seeking refreshment. "What else has he done?" he demanded. "Come now, tell me at once."

"It's nothing," she said, quickly realizing that she had misunderstood him, that he had been speaking of Geoffrey's brutality to Susan. Knowing no way in which she could tell him what had happened to her, she said hastily, "I-I do not like him, and I never believed Susan lied in that courtroom—or at least, not until she became so frightened that she was afraid to go on telling the truth about what Geoffrey had done to her."

"And Lady Catherine is back in the picture again."

"Yes," Daintry said, relaxing since it appeared that he believed her explanation. "I thought she had gone away because I did not see her when I called upon Susan and she was not at Almack's, but of course, I realize now that she simply was not able to obtain a voucher. They did not dine with us that night, which makes me think now that they must have stayed home to dine with her. In any case, she is very much still in the picture."

"Your sister seems friendly toward her, however."

Daintry sighed. "Susan says Catherine takes over all the details of running a large house in town, and even though Susan does not at all mind doing such things, she says Catherine is so kind and so insistent upon sparing her any exertion that she cannot bear to tell her she would as soon do the things herself, and now finds herself with almost nothing to do at all but amuse herself. Although how she can, when Geoffrey and Catherine go everywhere she goes, is beyond my understanding. But we have been standing here an age, sir. Had we better not fetch the punch for the others before they begin to wonder where we are?"

Gideon agreed, but she had given him cause to think. He did not know yet exactly what to make of the Seacourt *ménage,* but he was becoming concerned about Penthorpe. Though he had not been out and about much for a number of days, he had had visitors, and more than one had mentioned the viscount's betrothal and his obvious affection for more members of the Tarrant family than just the one he was to marry. Gideon had also spoken with Penthorpe himself, and while that young man still had given no indication that he was anything other than determined to proceed with his wedding, it was clear that he had managed to be a good deal in Lady Susan's company and was developing rather more concern for her well-being than for that of his betrothed.

He left the assembly soon after restoring Daintry to her mother's side, for although he would not have admitted it, his head was aching from the noise and bustle. He despised weakness in himself but did not doubt that Dr. Kingston had been right in warning him either to heed the signals of his body or be willing to reap the consequences of ignoring them. Much though he detested forced inactivity, he was sensible enough not to push himself too hard.

Returning to Jervaulx House, he went to the library in case his father should still be up. Entering the room, he discovered the fire still crackling on the hearth, sending a golden glow through the room, and the lamp on the desk still lit. Jervaulx dozed in a wing chair by the fire, a number of papers from his lap having slipped to the floor.

Gideon moved silently to pick up the papers and stack them on the desk. Glancing at others scattered on the desk top, he saw that the marquess, as usual, had been attending to business pertaining to the estates in Gloucestershire and Cornwall, as well as to Parliamentary matters. Shaking his head, and wishing, not for the first time, that Jervaulx would entrust some of these affairs to him, and that he could begin somehow to take Jack's place in his father's respect if not in his affection, he turned to ring for assistance to get Jervaulx to bed.

"What are you doing?"

He turned to find that the hard gray eyes were open, glinting at him with their familiar enigmatic look. "I was going to ring for someone to help you to bed, sir."

"That is not necessary. There is still much to be done. A brief nap, to restore the faculties, was all that was required."

"Father, really, you must—"

"You are in no case to be giving advice, Gideon," the marquess said brusquely. "You lack color, and the lines of pain in your face make it clear to the meanest intellect that you were ill-advised to venture out so soon after your injury. Go to bed, and take one of those powders Kingston left for you. According to that fellow Shalton, you have been neglecting to take them."

"Really, sir," Gideon said, torn between resentment and a strong desire to tear Shalton limb from limb, "I am no longer a child and can certainly decide for myself—"

"Your age appears to have had little effect on your powers of rational thought, dear boy, or you would recall that it is of little use to argue. You will do as you are bid."

Gideon's head was pounding, so he gave up, for Jervaulx was right about one thing. It was never of the least use to argue with him once he had given an order. He considered telling Shalton and

Kibworth to go to the devil when he discovered them both waiting for him, jealously vying with each other to see him safely into bed, but in the end he even accepted the glass in which Shalton had stirred a packet of Kingston's powders, knowing it was far easier to drink it than to face his father's chilly reproofs when his servants had reported his recalcitrance.

"Which I'd do in a pig's whisper," Shalton informed him, "for it's put to bed with a shovel you'll be if you don't look after yourself. That lump on your brainbox weren't nothing to snap your fingers at, if I might take the liberty to say so."

"Watch yourself, Shalton," Gideon said, feeling the effects of the powders already, "you're beginning to talk like Kibworth."

He fell asleep on his henchman's indignant retort, and woke feeling much refreshed the following morning. He did not get up at once, for it was clear from the lateness of the hour that he would be left alone until he rang, and he wanted to think.

He found himself wishing, yet again, that life might simply sort itself out to fit the pattern one most desired. But even if that were possible, how, he wondered, did one go about sorting things so that everyone had what he wanted most? For himself he would provide a lady with dusky tresses, rosy cheeks, and an irrepressible mind of her own, who would give as good as she got, and he would also arrange a position in life for himself that suited him and felt comfortable.

Though he had regretted leaving the army, he did so no longer, for although it had certainly suited him in wartime, he thought the peacetime army might well prove to be a dead bore. He would be far wiser to learn the duties that would one day be his, but that, too, was boring when it was merely a matter of attending to Barton's instruction. He wanted to do things, to have the power to make decisions based upon what he learned. But it was useless to let his mind dwell on that, for he could imagine no way in which Jervaulx would allow him to insinuate himself into what the marquess regarded as his private affairs.

The fact of the matter was that his wishes did not fit the patterns laid out for anyone else. If he were to follow his instincts and pursue the lovely Daintry, kissing his hand to the feud, to the tattle-mongers, and to Penthorpe, he would be making more trouble for her than she would likely forgive.

He thought she cared for him; he knew he cared for her and that he could stir those smoldering passions of hers; but whether she would welcome any attempt to rearrange her life was another matter altogether. Moreover, it was utterly wrong to interfere, just as it would have been wrong to interfere between Seacourt and Susan. No matter how he looked at it, it all came down to that. He had no business to make Daintry's life more difficult than it was. In fact, if he really wanted to do her a service, he would keep Penthorpe on the straight and narrow, and prevent him from making a cake of himself over Lady Susan at least until they were all safely out of London. If there was anything to be done to sort things out, it certainly couldn't be accomplished under the eagle eye of that city's busy prattleboxes.

With these good intentions in mind, he spent the next week doing his best to watch over Penthorpe and to avoid seeming to single out Daintry for his own attentions. His first task was not difficult, for it was plain that Penthorpe, too, had heard the muttering and was doing his best to curtail it. He was seen everywhere with his betrothed, attentively waiting upon her and seeing to her comfort. If Susan was often in the vicinity, it could scarcely be thought remarkable in view of her relationship to Daintry, and if Penthorpe danced with Susan, or walked in Hyde Park with her for a time during the social hour, it was always in company and always in full view of the lady's watchful husband.

Indeed, there seemed to be nothing in Penthorpe's behavior to cause comment; nevertheless, Gideon soon observed that Seacourt had begun to view the viscount with disfavor. Daintry seemed heedless of her betrothed's interest in her sister, but Seacourt was not, and on the twenty-sixth, as Gideon dressed for the St. Merryn ball he felt a tingling of anticipation such as he had not felt since last preparing to go into battle. As Kibworth shrugged him into his tight blue coat, and Shalton tucked his watch and fob into the respective pockets of his waistcoat, he wondered suddenly if he was really concerned about Penthorpe or only about what his own reception at St. Merryn House would be.

Not until he emerged from his carriage and stepped onto the red carpet that had been laid from door to flagway did he reach for his watch and realize that Shalton had slipped one of the ubiquitous packets of powders in with it. Smiling, he wondered if Kibworth had managed to conceal another in the lining of his cape or under the rim of his hat. The thought put him in an excellent humor, and he was smiling as he handed hat, gloves, cape, and stick to the waiting footman, and allowed the butler to direct him toward the line of guests entering the stair hall.

The drawing room and the two saloons behind it had been thrown together for the ball, and they were rapidly filling with guests. It was not yet a crush, for he had come early in order, he told himself, to lend his support to Penthorpe, but the family and those guests who had been honored with dinner invitations had emerged from the dining room, and at the first landing, the Tarrant family was lined up to receive their additional guests.

Bracing himself to meet the earl's displeasure, Gideon mounted the stairs behind a fat dowager and her wiry spouse, made his bow to Lady St. Merryn, greeted Daintry and Penthorpe, and held out his hand to the earl. "Good evening, sir."

"Upon my word," St. Merryn grumbled, glaring at him, "you've a nerve to set foot in this house, sir. By God, you have."

"I have an invitation, my lord, so I hope you won't order me thrown out," Gideon said calmly.

St. Merryn seemed to be of two minds about that, but their conversation had given the stout lady and her husband time to pass farther along the line, and just then, Davina, standing between St. Merryn and Charles, said loudly enough to be overheard, "It is really no concern of yours who gave it to me, Charles, so stop hissing at me. How do you do, Deverill? How daring of you to set foot in the lion's very den! Do not speak to Charles. He is being a beast." She fingered a pretty diamond brooch at her décolletage and fluttered her lashes at him.

Next to her, clearly goaded, Charles said, "Look at that thing, Deverill! If your wife suddenly turned up wearing such a dashed expensive spray of flowers, wouldn't you wish to know who the devil was so curst impudent as to give it to her?"

Sparing Gideon the need to reply, Susan, at Charles's other side, said, "Hush, Charles, you are drawing attention and holding up the line. Good evening, Deverill. Pray, pay him no heed."

Next to her, Seacourt said, "Susan, the orchestra is tuning up for the grand march. You will remain here with Charles to support your mother and father when Daintry and Penthorpe go in to lead it, and when you are released from your duties here, you will please be so good as to look after Catherine to be sure she is well entertained." Barely waiting for her stiffly murmured agreement, he added, "Come, Davina. Since Charles and Susan must remain to do their family duty, you will stand up with me for the first set of country dances, will you not?"

Davina laughed and fingered her brooch, casting a mischievous look at her husband. "To be sure, Geoffrey, I have been looking forward to dancing again with you this age. Come along, Deverill, we will find you an eligible partner."

Gideon had no objection, but he soon saw that although Seacourt apparently had no objection to indulging Davina's blatant flirtation, or to flirting with other pretty women, including Lady Catherine, the moment that the other members of the family appeared, his attention shifted to his wife. He did not dance with her, but he certainly watched her, and when Gideon claimed Daintry's hand for the first waltz, he saw that Seacourt was watching Penthorpe through ominously narrowed eyes.

"Geoffrey is making me nervous," Daintry confessed as she placed her hand in his and let him swing her into the pattern of the dance. "He keeps watching poor Susan like a hawk about to swoop down upon a rabbit."

"His own behavior leaves little room for him to complain, I should think," Gideon said, seeing Penthorpe lead Susan into the dance and hoping that he was right and Seacourt would not make a scene. A moment later, seeing that Seacourt was once more dancing with Davina, he began to relax and enjoy himself.

Daintry, too, had relaxed. "You have more color in your face tonight, sir. I trust you are completely well now."

"Oh, I think so," he said, smiling down at her.

She twinkled. "Do your servants still supply you with remedies, or do they too believe you have recovered?"

Chuckling, he said, "If you will glance down at my waistcoat pocket—the one with my watch in it—you will see that I am still well provided. The one thing that keeps me from knocking their fool heads together is that they both forgot them yesterday."

She laughed. "I think they must care for you, sir, and want to keep you healthy. Or perhaps you just pay them very well."

"I do." He guided her through an intricate pattern before he said, "You did not seem surprised to see me tonight."

"No, for Aunt Ophelia told me that she had sent you an invitation, and so did Penthorpe. He said I should look after you in case my father decided to cut up a little rough."

"Very pretty language," he said, grinning at her.

She looked surprised. "Good gracious, did it shock you? I merely repeated what he said, though I daresay I say such things on my own account frequently enough."

"No, it does not shock me in the least. You need not ever curb your tongue on my account." He gazed down into her eyes, and it seemed to him that something stirred there, a memory of other times, perhaps, and he wanted to take her in his arms right then and there and kiss her. The music stopped and he glanced hastily around, certain that his feelings must be apparent to everyone within a dozen feet of them. Taking her by the arm he escorted her back to where they had left her mother and aunt, to find Lady Ophelia sitting by herself.

"Letty's gone to bed," she said with a twinkle. "Felt a spasm coming on when she saw St. Merryn glaring at the pair of you. You needn't fret about him either," she added when Gideon looked quickly around. "He's gone to look after the guests in the card room, which means we shan't see him again tonight."

Gideon did not linger, certain now that he would be wiser to keep an eye on Penthorpe, and certainly the viscount was in a restless humor. He danced the cotillion with Daintry, but his attention was clearly divided, for he seemed to be keeping an eye on Seacourt and Lady Susan, who danced in the same set. Watching

them, Gideon decided Seacourt was spoiling for a confrontation, and decided to do something to prevent it. Hurrying to the
refreshment table, he demanded two cups of punch from a footman, and when the dance ended, he intercepted Penthorpe just as
he and Daintry returned to her great-aunt's side.

"Thirsty work," he said casually, handing one cup of punch to
Daintry and the second to Penthorpe. "Thought you'd like to wet
your whistles."

Smiling her thanks, Daintry sipped her punch.

Penthorpe's gaze swept distractedly over the crowd. "Much
obliged to you," he said. "Mighty thoughtful."

"Drink up, lad."

"Deverill," Lady Jerningham said, appearing as if by magic at
his side with a rather plain young woman in tow, "allow me to
present you to Miss Haversham."

Moments later, dancing a Scotch reel with Miss Haversham,
he looked around for Penthorpe but did not see him. His sense
of relief was short-lived, however, for when the dance ended, he
saw the viscount claim Susan's hand for a waltz. Cursing under his
breath, he looked swiftly for her husband. Seacourt seemed safely
occupied, since he was dancing again with Davina, until Gideon
saw Charles Tarrant moving purposefully toward them with a look
on his face that boded ill for the continued merriment of the gathering. Muttering more curses, Gideon moved to intervene.

"Not now, Tarrant," he said firmly when Charles tried to brush
past him. "This is not the time or the place, lad."

Charles looked at him in surprise but reacted just as Gideon's
military subordinates had reacted to that tone. "Yes, sir. Guess I
forgot where I was, but dash it all, she's got no business to be dancing a third time with that damned Seacourt. Bad enough he makes
my sister's life a hell. What can Davina—Here, what's o'clock?" he
demanded, staring past Gideon. "He's taking my wife into that private parlor yonder, damn his eyes!"

Gideon, following the direction of his gaze, saw at once that
Seacourt's eyes were blazing with fury as he strode toward the
parlor and that Davina was trying to hold him back rather than
to avoid going with him. He could not see Penthorpe or Susan

anywhere, but just as he was trying to decide whether he would be wiser to follow Sea-court and Davina or to attempt to keep Charles from doing so, he saw Daintry making her way quickly toward the parlor and the question was no longer at issue.

Leaving Charles several paces behind, he moved through the crowd as hastily as he could without drawing the eye of everyone in the room. As he reached the parlor, he heard Daintry cry out, "Don't you dare to touch her, Geoffrey! Don't touch either one of them! It was not what you're thinking at all, for I saw them. Susan was feeling faint, that's all. She has not been in spirits all evening, and it was plain as a pikestaff—No, don't!"

Gideon now saw that Penthorpe, who had apparently been seated beside Susan on a small sofa, had leapt to his feet to stop Seacourt, but Seacourt had shaken free of Davina's clutches and clearly intended either to knock Penthorpe down or thrust him aside to get to Susan. He was able to do neither, however, for Daintry dashed in front of him.

"Stop where you are, Geoffrey," she snapped. "You will bully no one in this house, do you hear me?" But her words ended in a sharp cry when Seacourt, clearly in a blind rage, backhanded her hard enough to send her spinning into a heap on the sofa.

Before Penthorpe could react, Gideon covered the space between in a few long strides, grabbed Seacourt by the shoulder, spun him around, and felled him with a right to the jaw.

Behind him, Charles exclaimed, "Well done, by God! Now pick the bastard up and give him to me, for I'm going to finish the job. First my wife, then my sister. By God, I'll murder him!"

"Charles, no," Davina cried. "You mustn't!"

"Won't do you a particle of good to stand up for the fellow, Davina. He hit my sister, and I've had my fill of him chasing after you, giving you presents—Oh, I could tell right enough, just by the way you were looking at him tonight, that he gave you that damned diamond brooch! I won't have it, I tell you."

Catching him by the arm, Davina said hastily, "That's not true, Charles. I bought the spray myself. It's a trifle, paste, I swear it! I did it to make you jealous. I thought you didn't care a button for me, but oh, Charles, you do, don't you?"

"Well, of course, I do," he said, looking searchingly at her. "Look here, Davina, what about all those other fellows?"

There were tears in her eyes. "I kept trying to get a rise out of you, Charles, but you'd just go off and play cards and drink, or flirt with some other woman. How was I to know you cared? You never said a word, except when you would get angry about me spending too much money on a gown or some such thing. And when I borrowed the rouleaux from Alvanley, I didn't know if you shouted at me out of jealousy or just because it was money."

Charles suddenly became aware of his interested audience, and said, "Look here, Davina, this ain't the place to chatter about this. We'll go somewhere and have a good talk."

"Oh, yes," she said. "Oh, how I wish I had told you all this before. It would have been so much simpler if we had both just said what we really felt straight out, instead of each of us expecting the other to know what was in his mind."

Susan, who had watched Gideon knock her husband to the floor without much change of expression, stepped from behind Penthorpe when Seacourt groaned and began to sit up, and said clearly, "Davina is right. One cannot expect things to change if one does not say one wants them to change. Geoffrey, if you please, since we will return to Cornwall when Mama and the others do, I want you to ask Catherine to make other arrangements. I am perfectly capable of running my household without her assistance, and I am certain that we shall get along a great deal better without her. Moreover, since Daintry will need help preparing for her wedding, Melissa and I will want to make frequent visits to Tuscombe Park to help her. Surely, you will not object to that, sir."

Seacourt, still shaken, did not speak until he regained his feet, but then, casting a look around at his audience, including Charles and Davina, who had been halted in their steps by Susan's Words, he turned a malevolent eye on his wife and said, "You seem to have forgotten your place, my dear, but you will soon be painfully reminded of it. As to visiting Tuscombe Park, you can forget about doing any such thing until you learn better manners. Moreover, you will go nowhere in Melissa's company. I thought I had made that quite plain to you before now." He looked around again, this time with a clear challenge in his eyes. "Does anyone here dare deny my right to command my own wife?"

No one did, and with a fulminating look at Gideon and a second at Penthorpe, he took his weeping wife out of the room.

Twenty

With tears in her eyes, Daintry watched Seacourt take Susan away, and knew the tears had nothing to do with the sting in her cheek. Daintry had bounced up at once after Seacourt had struck her and she had seen Deverill knock him down, and this time her emotions were unmixed. She felt only elation at seeing the bully brought to his knees, but what occurred afterward left her mind reeling, and when she saw Charles and Davina slip out behind Susan and Geoffrey, she got up at once to follow.

Deverill barred her way. "Don't move so quickly," he said. "That was quite a blow you took."

"But Aunt Ophelia can stop Geoffrey!"

"You would never get to her in time," he said patiently, "and you cannot go out there just now. Andy, go and fetch her a cup of punch, and get one for yourself." He smiled wryly. "Something tells me you did not drink the one I gave you earlier. What the devil became of it?"

Penthorpe was still staring at the door through which the others had gone, and Daintry saw that his hands were clenched into fists. When Deverill spoke his name a second time, he turned toward him, visibly collecting himself. Relaxing his hands, he said impatiently, "The punch? Oh, I gave it to Lady Ophelia. She was feeling the heat and said if I did not want it, she would be glad of it. I didn't, you know. Just took it because you were so dashed insistent."

"Good God," Deverill said, grimacing ruefully.

"What is it?" Daintry asked.

He did not answer at once, and Penthorpe said, "I'll get that punch straightaway. Dreadful thing to have done to you, my dear. The man deserves to be flogged."

Deverill said suddenly, "Take your time, Andy."

"What's that?" Penthorpe paused, and she saw them exchange a look before he shrugged and said, "I'll see what's o'clock."

Staring after him in bewilderment, she said, "Well, of all the odd things! Do you know, Deverill, I think he has already forgotten he was to fetch me some punch."

"Sit down," he said. "I have something to tell you."

"Why did you look so startled when he said he had given his punch to Aunt Ophelia?" she demanded.

The rueful look appeared again. "I had hoped to prevent just such a scene as the one that erupted here. He and Seacourt were clearly bound to collide, but I thought perhaps, if Andy got too sleepy . . ." He patted his waistcoat suggestively.

Understanding dawned quickly. "The powders? Deverill, don't tell me you mixed your powders into the punch and Penthorpe gave it to Aunt Ophelia! Merciful heavens, we must go and find her at once." She turned toward the door, but once more, before she had taken two steps, he caught her and pulled her back; and, once again she found herself much too close to him for comfort.

"You cannot go out there yet," he said gently. "The mark on your cheek is too pronounced not to draw comment." He touched it, and his hand felt cool but his eyes gleamed with sudden hot anger, and he said, "I did not hit him nearly hard enough."

She said mildly, "I'm glad you knocked him down, sir. He deserved it. Indeed I should have liked to do it myself."

"The last time I did it, you were angry."

"Only because you did not give me time to deal with him on my own terms. This was different."

He stroked her sore cheek again, and she looked up at him, aware of his nearness and remembering the last time he had kissed her. She could tell by the look in his eyes that he remembered it, too. He seemed to hesitate, but she waited, breathless, as nerve ends throughout her body came alive and her willpower evaporated. He bent nearer, and his lips touched hers, lightly, then again, harder, and then she was in his arms, and his kisses became more possessive. His hands moved over her back, caressing her. One moved to her waist, pulling her hard against him, and then slid up her side and around to her breast just as his tongue began to tease her lips, to part them, begging entry.

A sudden, quite unexpected wave of memory and fear swept over her, and involuntarily, she started and pulled away.

He let her go at once, looking both surprised and apologetic. "Did I hurt you? I forgot that you might have been bruised when you fell onto that sofa."

"No, I am not hurt. It's nothing, really." She could not meet his gaze, certain he would see the lie in her eyes.

His hands were on her shoulders now, and she trembled, unable to stop the horrid reaction, which she knew perfectly well had nothing to do with anything that had just happened and everything to do with what had happened to her at Seacourt Head.

Deverill's hands tightened, and he said, "You're shaking. What is it? Did I frighten you?"

She couldn't bear to tell him the truth. Even if she could somehow bring herself to put into words what Geoffrey had done, she had seen how angry Deverill could get, and if he were furious with Geoffrey, it would only make matters worse for everyone than they were already. So, instead, she said quietly, "I am pledged to Viscount Penthorpe, sir. This is very wrong. We must not."

He was silent, and she forced herself to meet his gaze. He did not look convinced, but after a moment, still holding her, he said gently, "I think your sister-in-law was right. The time has come for us to speak what is in our minds. Penthorpe, in case you have not yet noticed the fact, my pet, is more interested in your sister, Susan, than he is in you."

She smiled a little sadly. "I am not a fool, Deverill. Did you expect me to be shocked or distressed? In point of fact, however, it changes nothing. I only wish it were possible for Penthorpe to steal

Susan from Geoffrey and run away with her, so that she would be safe. Perhaps if he were cut from the same bolt of cloth as Lord Anglesey, he would try, but it would do no good, for Susan would not go with him if he did."

"I was not suggesting any such thing, you know. Your sister would be far wiser simply to sort things out with her husband."

"Don't be nonsensical," she retorted, annoyed. "The man is brutal, hard-hearted, and malicious. Why, I fear for her very life after what happened here tonight."

"You need not, I think," he said, his tone still gentle. "Just remember that to get out of the house he had to pass through that crowd out there, which is no mean feat, and then wait for his carriage. If my experience is any guide, people will stop them and chatter at them, and it will take time just to say their good-byes, especially since they will be forced to maintain an appearance of normalcy. Even without Lady Ophelia to intercede in person, the smallest respite ought to give him time to recall her will and the ease with which she can alter it."

"Well, I hope you are right, but I still think Susan would be safer to run away with Penthorpe. She would never leave Melissa, though." She brightened as another thought struck her. "Perhaps Penthorpe would take Melissa as well."

"He could not," Deverill said. "Even if your sister were to follow the lead of the Duchess of Argyll and secure a divorce in Scotland, no court in either country would award her custody of Seacourt's daughter. She would be forced to give her back."

"Then she would never go," Daintry said.

"You know," he said quietly, his hands still warm on her shoulders, "none of this has much to do with the point at hand."

"Certainly it does. Penthorpe is going to marry me, caring more about my sister than he does for me. I should say that has a great deal to do with the point at hand."

"Not when the point at hand, my pet, is us."

"I am betrothed to Penthorpe, Deverill. He is certainly too much of a gentleman to cry off, and my father is determined to hold me to my word of honor. Would you have me disobey him?"

"No, of course not, but I think if you and Penthorpe talk to him, a way might be found for one of you at least to be happy."

She stiffened. "Let me see if I understand you, Deverill. You want me and Penthorpe to tell my father that we agree mutually that we shall not suit. You do not mention which of us is to bring up the subject first, or how, but to do so would be pretty much the same as crying off in fact. But once I am free of Penthorpe, I am to cast myself into your arms. Is that it?"

His lips twitched. "I do not know that I would put it in such blatant terms as that, certainly, but if you were free of Penthorpe and could see your way clear—"

"You forget that my father would not under any circumstances permit me to marry a Deverill, sir."

He grimaced. "I confess, I did forget about that; however, since he did not precisely throw me out of here tonight, per—"

"Perhaps it will just chance to fall out the way you want it to, is that it? Well, since we are being frank with each other, sir, let me tell you that I do not think I would marry you even in such a case as that. You need not look at me as if you mean to show me otherwise, either," she added, stepping hastily away from him. "You seem to think that all you need do is sit back calmly and wait for fortune to smile upon you. I suppose, in school you were taught simply to do as you were told, or perhaps it comes of being a second son for all those years and knowing you need never take responsibility for anything, but—"

"Just a minute," he interjected. "I have never shirked a responsibility in my life. I was, if you will recall, a brigade major serving under Wellington at Waterloo, with a good number of men dependent upon me to lead them. If that is not responsibility, I should like to know what is."

"Pooh," she replied recklessly, "what of it? As I understand the matter, it was Wellington who decided what to do and you simply followed his orders. And, at all events, that has nothing to do with the present, since you are no longer a brigade major. Right now, you seem to think being heir to a great title is sufficient, and that if every-one else will just do as you think he or she ought to do, you will not have to lift a finger to secure your own ends. There is a good deal more to putting things right than merely wishing people would do what you want them to, Deverill."

"You don't know what you are saying," he retorted, his temper clearly on the rise.

"Oh, yes, I do. You say Susan would do better to learn to get along with her husband, because it is nothing to do with you, and you want me to talk my father and Penthorpe around because you have got it in your head that you want me. Notice that I say want, not love. If you loved me, you would at least have found a way to end the stupid feud. I've read every word of my aunt's journals, although the most interesting things in them are her views on novels written by the women of the last century, but I did it without prating about being in love. You, on the other hand, dismiss the feud, calling it stupid and idiotic and generally hoping it will go away and not annoy you, but you stopped looking for answers after going through a few papers."

"Now, wait just a—"

"No, Deverill, I am going to marry Penthorpe. I gave my word, and unless he asks me to break it, I will not."

He clamped his lips together, visibly fighting his temper now, but the tense silence that fell between them was broken when the door opened suddenly and Penthorpe entered, saying, "Beg your pardon but I think you ought to know Lady Ophelia ain't feeling quite the thing. Fact is, we can't seem to wake her up."

Daintry, reminded of the headache powders and Penthorpe's own contribution to her great-aunt's condition, felt a sudden, quite inappropriate, urge to laugh; but, seeing that Deverill did not share her amusement in the least, she said, "We will come at once, sir. She has been so tired of late, you know, what with all the preparations for the ball and having so many other social obligations as well, and she has suffered from insomnia since our arrival in London. I daresay it all caught up with her tonight."

They reached Lady Ophelia to discover that she had dozed off in her chair with her head resting against a marble column, and had drawn quite a crowd of concerned persons around her, including St. Merryn, who had been summoned from the card room, and who was, as a result, in no pleasant temper.

"She's asleep," he told Daintry indignantly. "I've shaken her, but she only mutters at me to go away. Upon my word, what will the woman do next?" He paid no heed to Deverill's presence other than to say to them all that something must be done, but it was Deverill who assumed direction of the proceedings, picking Lady Ophelia up in his arms and moving behind the row of columns in order to draw as little attention as possible as he made his way to the stair hall. Penthorpe stayed behind to explain to interested onlookers that her ladyship was suffering from no more than simple exhaustion, and Daintry went with Deverill to show him the way to her great-aunt's bedchamber, and to ring for Alma to see her tucked into bed.

When they went back downstairs, Deverill stopped at the landing on the drawing-room level and said, "I'll take my leave of you now, but I hope to see you again before you leave London."

She gave him her hand. "G-good night, sir. I . . . I hope you are not too dreadfully vexed with me."

"I have no cause," he said grimly. With a bow, he turned and went quickly down the stairs to the hall.

The ball seemed sadly flat after that, although a light supper was served soon after she returned and Penthorpe seemed determined to see to her every comfort. He seemed equally determined to be cheerful, and finally Daintry could stand it no more. Leaning across the small round table they shared, she said quietly, "Sir, if you are not happy with this arrangement, pray believe you have only to say so. I can quite understand that—"

"No, no," he said, flushing to the roots of his hair and looking directly at her, "no such thing. Completely happy, I promise you. Happiest man on earth. Good God, how could I be otherwise? Pleasing your father, pleasing my uncle, and of course, pleasing myself most of all. Dashed sorry if I've put any other notions in your head, my dear. If I seem a trifle upset over what happened earlier, it's because I cannot stomach cruelty, and if you'll forgive a little plain-speaking, that's just what it is, the way Seacourt treats your poor sister."

"I agree, sir." She said no more. If he was determined to plunge ahead with the wedding, she would not try to dissuade him. The

Tarrant family had already provided grist enough for the rumor mills, since word of the brawl in the parlor would spread, if only because Susan had been unable to hide her tears when Seacourt took her away. And if by some miracle that whole tale did not come out, Lady Ophelia's falling asleep in front of the entire company would give the gossips a good laugh at least. Daintry would not give them more by crying off from yet another betrothal even if her father could be persuaded to let her do so.

By the time she fell exhausted into bed that night, her thoughts were in a turmoil. She had, she decided, been perfectly horrid to Deverill, and though he had said he wanted to see her before the family left London, if he never spoke to her again, it would be no more than she deserved. Just to remember the way she had ripped up at him about never doing anything—and not ten minutes after he had sent Geoffrey crashing to the floor, too, which was a memory she would harbor fondly forever—made her ready to sink. How could she have been so idiotic as to fling such an accusation at him? He must think her utterly daft.

She had been completely right, Gideon thought as he strode along the flagway toward Jervaulx House. He *had* been waiting and hoping things would change, that somehow everything would fall out the way he wanted it to. He had hoped Jervaulx would come to realize that he had a son who was entirely capable of assisting him with his many duties. He had hoped the feud would somehow die out for lack of interest or that the key to resolving it would just turn up. And he had hoped that when everything else fell into place the way he wanted it, Daintry would discover she could not resist him any more than he could resist her.

She had been right, too, in blaming his past for his present attitudes. He *had* been taught at school to follow orders and do as he was told, and military life had reinforced those lessons. He could certainly claim, as he had, that as a brigade major he had carried grave responsibilities, but the truth was that he had simply waited for orders and then seen them carried out. His responsibilities had been clearly defined, his duties likewise. He had rarely had to sort things out and decide what was best to be done. No wonder he had felt all at sea when he first returned to England, for in truth, he had been uprooted. He remembered telling Penthorpe that Jervaulx did not know how to let go of past duties to take better care of present ones. He ought to have taken some small heed of his own observation. It was time, he decided, to step out of his old life and into the new.

Despite the lateness of the hour, he was not surprised to find Jervaulx still at his desk in the book room, reading some sort of document. The glow from the lamp reached no farther than the edges of the desk, and what tapers had been lighted earlier in the wall sconces had guttered. The only other light in the huge room came from the fire, still burning brightly and setting shadows dancing on the carpet and in the nearby corners.

Gideon moved to pull the bell cord near the hearth, and Jervaulx looked up at last. "The servants have gone to bed."

"Not all of them, sir. Thornton was in the hall when I came in, and though I told my own men not to wait up for me, I am nearly certain that both of them will still be up and about. You ought to have rung for more light, Father. You will ruin your eyesight. Yes, Thornton, I rang," he added when the footman entered. "Replace some of these candles, will you? It ought to have been done sometime ago."

"Yes, sir," Thornton said placidly, but even in the dim light, Gideon did not miss the oblique glance the man shot toward the marquess. "I've brought some with me, sir, thinking they might be wanted."

Jervaulx was watching his son.

"I suppose," Gideon said, returning the look steadily, "that you told them all you did not wish to be disturbed."

"Nothing further was required of them, and they must rise very early. There was no need, Thornton, for you to stay up."

"No, my lord. I'll just light these candles now." He moved toward the wall sconce nearest Gideon, and as he passed him he said quietly, "Mr. Peters is still up as well, Master Gideon."

Gideon nodded and moved nearer the desk. "I must ask you to stop now, Father, because I want to talk to you. I'd have waited until morning, but since you are up, I'd like to do it now."

"There is nothing so important that it cannot wait."

"On the contrary," Gideon said calmly. "Thank you, Thornton, that will be all. Tell Peters that his lordship will be up in half an hour."

"Yes, sir," Thornton said, slipping quickly out the door.

"Now, see here," Jervaulx began, "you cannot give orders like that in this house."

"You can certainly countermand them," Gideon agreed, drawing up a chair to the desk, "but I hope you will hear me out first, sir. May I sit down?"

Jervaulx shot him a look. "You must do as you please, of course. No doubt you will anyway."

Taking his seat, Gideon smiled. "I have not come to that yet, I promise you, but I have done a great deal of thinking tonight. Indeed, I walked all the way from Berkeley Square to Jervaulx House, and was so lost in thought that the journey seemed to take but minutes."

"You ought not to have walked such a distance," Jervaulx said harshly. "Any sensible man, having once been attacked in the street, must surely know better than to offer his person for a second attack. You are not fully recovered yet, and indeed, what does one keep a carriage for if not to use it?"

"I am perfectly stout again, sir, and I wanted to think. I had a few accusations flung at my head tonight that I fear were perfectly justified, and though I should like to think I have merely been keeping my own counsel these past months, I fear I have been little less than a coward."

"Nonsense, you are no coward."

"I am glad to hear you say so, sir, but I tell you frankly that I am presently quaking in my shoes lest I infuriate you when I tell you that I want you to turn over certain of your duties—specifically all of those relating to the Cornwall estates—to me, and that I would like you to do so at once."

"You fancy yourself as a magistrate, sir?" The tone was sarcastic, and Gideon had all he could do not to wince.

"No, sir, I don't. Not yet, at all events. I do not know nearly enough about the county or the law. But I can learn. Indeed, I wish to learn, and in the meantime, I am perfectly capable of finding someone to accept the appointment in your stead. And *that* I will do before the summer Assizes at Bodmin."

"And just how, knowing as little as you do about the county, not to mention the law, do you propose to find that person?"

"I will let it be known that a new appointment must be made, and that you wish to know who is willing to undertake the duties. I am an excellent judge of men, sir, and once we discover who is willing, it will not take long to learn which man is best qualified. Yours, of course, must be the final decision, since it will be upon your recommendation that the appointment will finally be made. However, I give you fair warning that if I should discover the Earl of St. Merryn to be both willing and best qualified, I will not hesitate to submit his name to you."

His tone was admirably firm, but it occurred to him as he fell silent that he could not more clearly have challenged the marquess if he had flung down a glove on his desk. He waited for the earth to shake. Instead, Jervaulx said mildly, "May I ask who was so misguided as to call you a coward?"

Looking narrowly at him, Gideon told himself he was crazy to think he saw a glint of amusement in Jervaulx's eyes, and said cautiously, "I'm afraid it was Lady Daintry Tarrant, sir."

"So the wind still sits in that quarter, does it?"

Certain that he wanted only to change the subject, Gideon said, "You need not concern yourself about that, sir. She is still very much betrothed to Penthorpe and says she will not have me in any case. At present, I should rather discuss Deverill Court. I know it must be a great disappointment to you that it will come to me and not go to Jack, but since it must—"

"Nonsense."

"I beg your pardon?"

"Utter nonsense," Jervaulx repeated roughly. "No father could be disappointed in a son who was mentioned in dispatches after such a battle as Waterloo."

"I meant—"

"I don't care what you meant, Gideon," Jervaulx said, getting up.

The look in his eyes now was one that had terrified Gideon as a boy, and even now, he discovered, it had the power to bring him instantly to his feet. "Sir, I think—"

"Be silent," Jervaulx snapped. "You will listen to me now, by heaven. I will not allow you to think for one more minute that I am disappointed in you."

"But—"

"Your brother coveted the Jervaulx title, Gideon, but he had little interest in the duties that go with it. He was a fine lad, sporting mad and popular with his friends, and I grieve for his death almost as much as I grieved for your mother; but Jack would have made a poor master unless he had changed his ways considerably. I thought you were the same. You showed little interest in the estates, and although I began to think you might when I learned you had turned the muniments room upside down, searching for information about that old feud, it quickly became clear that your main interest lay in seeing how many house parties you could attend. That being exactly the way your brother liked to spend his time, I thought you were like him."

"I thought you didn't want me to meddle," Gideon said, forcing calm into his voice, "and I had reasons of my own—"

"I know your reasons now. Had I not already begun to suspect them, they would have become clear when I saw you nearly leap out of your skin when that young woman had the audacity to challenge me in my own court. Since you still seem bent on making a fool of yourself in that direction, it is gratifying to learn that my initial opinion of you was not entirely justified."

Gideon stared at him. "You don't object to my interest in St. Merryn's daughter?"

"Of course I object, but you endow me with powers well beyond those I possess if you think I can stop you from marrying where you choose when you are fully of age. Or would you have me believe that you would never marry to disoblige me? And before you protest that you would honor my wishes, let me point out that I do have a considerable regard for your integrity."

Gideon spread his hands with a rueful grin. "You leave me with nothing to say, sir, but the point is a moot one since she is still under age—not to mention betrothed—and even if she were neither, I could scarcely insist that she disobey her father. Until the discord between our families is laid to rest, there is nothing I can do to further my cause. And since one of the accusations she flung at my head tonight is that I have done nothing to discover its key, I do wish you would tell me how the animosity between the two families began."

"All I know is that Tarrant was at fault and that some sort of threat was made, after which he refused to accept a challenge from your grandfather. More than that I was never told."

"Lady Daintry said there were rumors of Jacobite dealings."

"That is possible, of course. There was a good deal of that sort of thing in Cornwall at the time, but there cannot have been much to it, since there was no public accusation. The complete answer may he in the family papers, of course."

"That's why I turned the muniments room inside out," Gideon said, "but not knowing what to search for does rather impede my progress. I looked for mention of the Tarrants, of course, but aside from some matters of business between the two families—perfectly straightforward, as far as I could tell—there was nothing. When I return—" He broke off. "You managed to divert me from my point, sir, but I hope you do not mean to forbid me to take control of things at the Court."

"I have no objection."

"Then why did you never ask for my help? Indeed, you ought to have insisted upon it."

"A reluctant landlord is a bad one," Jervaulx said. "Had I seen you display more than a slight interest in the estate when you returned from the Continent, I would gladly have arranged for you to move into a more influential position there. But since I did not, there seemed nothing to do but to look after things myself until you did express an interest."

"I thought you disliked me," Gideon said, surprised at how just saying the words affected him. "I might never have dared."

Jervaulx turned suddenly toward the fireplace, his body stiffening. His voice was rough when he said, "I have never disliked you. After your mother's death, I found it impossible to allow myself the luxury of revealing such depth of feeling for anyone else. For months after her death, I was so afraid of losing you or your brother that I could not bear the sight of you on a horse, or swimming, or doing any of the other active things boys love to do. Indeed, my fear was so great that I thought it was certain to smother you. Jack was already at Eton by then, of course, and sending him back after her funeral was especially hard. I knew that if I was ever to send you there at all, I had to distance myself emotionally. And after Jack's death, I was alone, Gideon, and you were still at war, likely to be killed at any time. Can you imagine what it was like for me then? If I do not show my feelings, it is because I have not believed it safe or wise to do so, not because I do not have any."

Gideon found it hard to speak. At last, he said, "I will not fail you, sir. Do you return soon to the Abbey?"

"I must remain in London for some weeks yet," Jervaulx said, turning at last with a weary smile, "but I confess, I will be relieved to relinquish the duties of magistrate. I had expected to have to go to Deverill Court from here, but now I shall be able to go straight to the Abbey instead." He moved to put out the lamp on the desk. "Do not make a stranger of yourself there, my son."

"I-I won't, sir," Gideon said.

He lay awake that night for a long time, thinking over what Jervaulx had said, and wondering what his life would have been like if they had not been strangers for so many years. It was, he knew, nearly as much his own fault as his father's, and he vowed that no child of his would ever wonder what he thought of him. Thinking of children soon brought his thoughts to Daintry, and he wondered what she would say when he told her that his father would not stand in the way if she agreed to marry him. No doubt it would be something rude; however, he thought that if the opportunity arose before they left London, he would tell her.

But the next morning his vigilant servants, agreeing for once, thought it better not to wake him, with the result that he slept till well after noon, and when he went to Berkeley Square shortly after three, he discovered that St. Merryn had meant it when he had said they would stay only until after the ball. The knocker was off the door, and the servants were packing up to close the house. The family had returned to Cornwall.

Twenty-one

Looking out the carriage window at the passing countryside, Daintry sighed, thinking her father had whisked them out of London so fast that she had scarcely had time to snatch up the things she would need along the way. They had not departed until nearly two o'clock, however, and she had kept an eye on the square in hopes that Deverill would come to call before they left, but he had not. Perhaps he had thought better of it. More likely, he simply had not realized they had meant to leave so soon. Penthorpe, too, would be surprised by their abrupt departure, although her father had promised to send word to him.

"No point in staying longer," St. Merryn had declared before retiring the night before, "for there's no saying what mischief you'll be getting up to if we do. We came to town to find you a husband, after all, and now Penthorpe's back, it will be better to be married from your own home, and so I have explained it to him. He may not want to go to Cornwall at once, I suppose, but I shall make it clear that he is not to linger here too long."

Lady St. Merryn had objected, albeit weakly, when the plan was made known to her, but Cousin Ethelinda had attended to the details, and since all but the upper servants and their personal ones would be following at their own pace with the baggage, she could give no good reason not to leave at once.

Charles and Davina, much to everyone's surprise, had also decided to go. Davina, peeping into Daintry's room soon after Nance had wakened her that morning, had said laughingly, "It is dreadful to be rousted out so early when one would much rather sleep all day—especially after *such* a night—but your father is complaining that if we delay, we shall not be able to leave until Monday, and he is quite right because dear Mama St. Merryn will make a grand fuss if he tries to make her travel on a Sunday."

"You really are going with us, then."

"Oh, yes, for now that matters are clearer between us, we don't mean to spoil them again, and our habits have become so set, you know, that there is no telling what will happen if we go on larking about as we have been. I shall miss the parties and balls much more than Charles will, but I daresay I shan't miss them quite so much if I can spend more time with him."

That she might actually get to spend more time with him was evident by the fact that he had agreed to occupy a carriage with her rather than riding as he usually did, so although Daintry was not convinced that things would turn out as Davina hoped they would, she could not blame her for believing they might.

For once, she shared a carriage only with Lady Ophelia, who was looking particularly chipper. As the carriage left the cobblestones for the Exeter road, she said, "A pity we must leave just when I've finally had the benefit of a good night's sleep, though I cannot think what possessed me to drift off like I did."

Feeling sudden warmth in her face, Daintry was grateful for the dim light in the carriage, and hoped her great-aunt would not notice her reddening cheeks.

Lady Ophelia went on, "You know it was the oddest thing, my dozing off like that. I believe I have never done such a thing before in my life, and to think I did not so much as stir when I was carried upstairs or when Alma undressed me and got me beneath the covers. I am no lightweight either, you know. I hope whoever carried me did not do himself an injury."

"It was Deverill, ma'am. He had no difficulty."

"I do not suppose he would, though I own, I am surprised your father allowed him to penetrate so far into the house."

"Papa had other things on his mind, I suppose," Daintry said, thinking of Geoffrey and Susan and wondering what her father had heard about that unfortunate incident. She wished that she might have seen her sister before they left, to learn if Deverill had been right to think she would be safe.

Lady Ophelia chuckled. "Poor St. Merryn. What he must have thought, finding me sound asleep like that, but I tell you, I am too grateful to have had a full night's repose to concern myself with what a figure I must have made. Why, I had begun to believe I should never adapt to London hours this year."

Daintry bit her lip.

"What is it?" the old lady demanded. "You look like a cat that's been at the cream. What mischief have you been brewing?"

"It was not my brewing, ma'am, and was mischief only because it went awry, but I confess, your sleep was not entirely natural. When you said you were thirsty, Penthorpe gave you a cup of punch that Deverill had intended for him to drink in hopes of keeping him from getting into an altercation with Geoffrey."

Lady Ophelia stared at her, then burst suddenly into a peal of laughter. "What was in it?" she demanded when she could speak. "I tell you, I've never slept so soundly."

"It was a mixture Dr. Kingston had given Deverill for his headaches," Daintry told her. "I do not know what was in it."

"Well, we must find out, for I shall not go to London next year without some such thing by me, I can tell you. Miraculous, that's what it was, absolutely miraculous."

Relieved that she was amused and not angry, Daintry went on to tell her about the other events of the previous night, and if the tale distressed the formidable lady, she nonetheless tended to agree with Deverill that Geoffrey would not really harm Susan. "For you may depend upon it, my dear, that he knows folks will forgive his flying into the boughs when he jumped to the notion that Penthorpe was trifling with her, for that's understandable, but once people begin to believe he mistreats her, it will be quite another matter. And if he does not understand that, you may be certain that his precious Lady Catherine does."

"But Geoffrey always thinks he will be forgiven whatever he does, ma'am. I have frequently observed that."

"Well, of course, he does, my dear. Gentlemen generally do have that belief, and quite naturally, considering the way this world is ordered to suit them. After all, as angry as you may become over the way he mistreats Susan, he knows perfectly well that you are obliged to be civil to him when you meet, for if you are not, it is you who will be blamed for your poor manners, not he for having provoked them. In this life, manners are the glue that holds everything together, particularly for females." She smiled wryly, adding, "When a man—even one like Geoffrey— flies into a passion with his wife, the world wonders what she did to annoy him. When a wife does the same thing, the world believes she needs to be controlled, even disciplined, if only to protect her against the consequences of such distempered freakishness."

Daintry thought about that and decided that if she had to marry, it was better that she was marrying a man like Penthorpe, who would not attempt to mold her into a submissive wife, and not one like Deverill, who would; and, if she did not find these thoughts particularly cheering, at least they occupied her idle moments until they halted for the evening in Bagshot.

The journey back to Cornwall was accomplished more quickly than the journey to London had been, but it was tiring, and she was glad when the carriage finally rolled through the gates of Tuscombe Park. As they drew to a halt before the front entrance, she looked out the window expectantly, but although they had sent word ahead to warn of their arrival, there was not the least sign of a child on the watch at window or door. They had no sooner passed into the entrance hall, however, than the reason was made known to them, for Miss Parish hurried down the stairs to meet them, looking perfectly distracted.

Waiting only until she had exchanged greetings with them all, she said uneasily, "I am so sorry Miss Charlotte is not here to greet you, but indeed, no one said she ought not to go, and I did not quite like to forbid her to do so when you had not."

"Not here," Lady St. Merryn exclaimed, clasping hands at her breast. "Why, whatever can you mean?"

At the same time, Charles said, "What the devil are you talking about, Parish? Where is my daughter?"

"Oh, sir, she has ridden to Seacourt Head to visit her cousin. Indeed, she has done so several times whilst you were in London. I could see no harm, sir. I do hope you are not vexed."

Charles turned instantly to Daintry. "Did you tell Charley she could ride that distance on her own?"

"I did not. In fact—" She broke off, not wanting to make matters worse than they were.

Charles glared at her. "In fact you told her she was not to do any such thing. Is that right?"

Reluctantly she nodded. "She asked me several times, but I told her it was too far for her to ride alone. She is perfectly capable though, Charles, and I am sure she took her groom."

Miss Parish said instantly, "Oh, yes, my lady, she did indeed, and has done every time, but perhaps I ought to confess that I did tell her this morning, she ought rather to attend to her lessons. I am afraid she was a trifle impertinent, saying that you would be home soon, and it might be her last chance."

"Well, if that don't beat all," Charles said. "What sort of a governess allows a child to be impudent to her? Not that it ain't probably your doing, Daintry, if we but knew it. You were a saucy piece yourself, as I recall the matter."

"Perhaps I was, Charles," she retorted, "but if Charley is getting out of hand, you have only yourself and Davina to blame. The pair of you have scarcely paid her any heed at all."

"Well, that is about to change," her brother said austerely. He turned to the butler, entering the house behind them, and snapped, "When my daughter returns, send her directly to me."

Although Daintry was surprised by this change in her brother's demeanor, she could not be displeased, for she firmly believed that Charley deserved more attention from both her parents. It was dinnertime before the child appeared, the meal being served at five now that it was no longer necessary to keep town hours, and she came running in just as the family was about to sit down. Still wearing her riding habit, she had cast off her hat, and her curls were windblown and tangled.

Lady St. Merryn said, "Good gracious, Charlotte, you look as if you've been dragged backward through a bush! Go and tidy yourself at once."

"I beg your pardon, Grandmama; I will," Charley said, adding happily, "When I heard that Aunt Susan and Uncle Geoffrey had got home, I hoped all of you might be coming soon, too, but no one told me you would come today! What did you bring me?"

Sternly, Charles said, "There will be no presents today, my girl. You go straight up to bed, and don't give me any backchat about missing your dinner or anything else, for you are nearer right now to getting a spanking than you have ever been in your life."

Cousin Ethelinda gasped, and Charley's mouth fell open as she stared at her father in shock. "But—"

"Go," Charles commanded, pointing toward the door.

Charley glanced at Daintry, but there was no help to be had from that quarter, since Daintry was not pleased with her either, and when Charles suddenly scraped his chair back and looked about to get up, the child fled without another word.

As Charles scooted his chair in again, he cast a glance at his father, but St. Merryn was serving himself from a dish the footman held and paid him no heed. Shifting his gaze past Daintry and the others to Lady Ophelia, Charles said grimly, "I hope none of you means to tell me I was too harsh with the brat."

Neither Lady St. Merryn nor Cousin Ethelinda said a word, but Lady Ophelia, after refusing a dish of green peas and onions, said, "On the contrary, dear boy, I was too much astonished to hear you scold the child to consider whether you were too harsh, but I cannot think it will do her anything but the greatest good, you know. I will have some of that ham, please, Jago."

Davina said suddenly and for no apparent reason, "Charles and I had quite a long talk on the way home, you know."

St. Merryn said, around a mouthful of food, "Should think you must have, cooped up as you were for more than a week's time. God knows, Letty and Ethelinda kept up a steady stream of chatter whenever I had to ride with them for a spell."

Davina was looking hard at Charles, who seemed oblivious, and she said, "Charles has made a decision, haven't you, dear?"

"What's that you say?" He encountered a minatory look from her and said hastily, "Oh, yes, of course. Daresay now's as good a time as any." He looked at his father again. "I . . . that is, Davina and I have decided to take a house in Plymouth this summer, sir. It will be just the thing for us, I daresay."

"Damned expensive is what it will be," St. Merryn growled.

"Well, if you do not like it, sir . . ."

Davina said quickly, "It will not be so dear as all that, Papa St. Merryn, for I mean to take good care that it is not, but it will do Charles and me—and Charlotte, too, of course—good to . . . spend some time . . . that is . . ."

Daintry cut in swiftly before Davina faltered altogether, saying, "How wonderful for them, Papa! Just think how much Charley will enjoy living right by the sea for a few months, and they will be much nearer home than if they were to go to Brighton again. It ought to be much less expensive than that, certainly."

"Upon my soul, you may be right," St. Merryn said after a brief moment's consideration.

Davina cast Daintry a look of gratitude, and although St. Merryn grumbled a little more, his heart clearly was not in it, and when Davina had the happy notion to ask for his advice about how they might be sure to find just the right house, he entered into the conversation with much more enthusiasm.

Daintry went upstairs as soon as the gentlemen had been left to enjoy their port, for she wanted to talk to Charley before the child went to sleep. She was not surprised to find her still wide awake and suspected, in fact, that she had leapt beneath the covers the moment she heard her aunt's hand on the door handle.

Turning up the wick of the lamp on a nearby table until a soft golden glow lit the room, Daintry moved to stand beside the low cot before saying quietly, "I'm a bit disappointed in you."

Charley sat up and shoved a pillow behind herself, saying without remorse, "I was afraid you would be, but I had to go, for Melissa was lonely, and so was I. Right after you left, I got Teddy to take her a letter, and she sent one back with his cousin Todd, who works at Seacourt Head, but letters were not enough, so one day I just rode over. And then I did it again and again. Teddy always went with me though, so there was no danger."

Daintry, remembering the day she and Lady Ophelia had been attacked in the coach, as well as the many other incidents caused by disgruntled miners, repressed a shudder at the idea of Charley riding the cliff path alone, but remembering, too, her own childhood and the freedom she had cherished, she could not scold too vehemently. Instead, she said only, "You must not do it again, darling. Was Melissa happy to see her parents come home?"

Charley grimaced. "I don't know, for I never got to see her. I waited and waited at our place, for you might as well know, we decided from the outset that it would be better if Uncle Geoffrey never discovered that I was riding over to meet her, so Melissa always gave some excuse or other to her governess when we were actually riding on the shingle or exploring the smugglers' caves." She smiled. "We still have never seen one—a smuggler, that is—and I daresay we never will."

"But Melissa did not come to meet you today."

"No, and I waited and waited, and so finally I rode over to Seacourt. Before I got near enough to be seen myself, I saw that someone had arrived, for there were carriages in the drive and servants bustling about. I made Teddy go ask Todd what was coming to pass, and he came back and said they were home." She glowered at Daintry from under her brows. "Even Lady Catherine was there. Melissa does not like her. Why did she come back?"

"I must suppose she was invited to do so, darling," Daintry said, but her heart sank to hear it, and she hoped Geoffrey would remember Lady Ophelia's warnings and behave himself. "Perhaps we can invite Melissa to come visit us for a week or two."

"Uncle Geoffrey said before that he will not let her."

Remembering that he had said much the same thing in London, Daintry could think of no better reply than, "Well, maybe he will change his mind. At all events, I've learned some good news that will surprise you. Your mama and papa have decided to take a house in Plymouth for the summer and not go to Brighton at all this year. That ought to give you something nice to think about. But mind now, no more rides to Seacourt Head."

"I won't," Charley said with a sigh as she slid down in the bed and let Daintry tuck her in. "Good night, Aunt Daintry."

"Good night, darling." Daintry kissed her and turned down the lamp, pausing at the door to add, "Pleasant dreams."

"You, too," Charley murmured.

But, alone in her own bedchamber, Daintry found that sleep eluded her. It was plain that Charles and Davina looked forward to having a house of their own, even just for the summer. She approved of the change the decision had already wrought in her brother, and she had seen that Davina meant to encourage him to become even more decisive. Since that could mean only that Charles would become more and more the master of his household, when Daintry realized that she envied them, she could only wonder why on earth she should.

More than once on the journey home, St. Merryn had declared that the arrangements for her wedding must be put in hand the moment they returned. He was clearly determined to get her married before anything could intervene, and when she had once casually suggested that there could be no great need for such haste, he had nearly exploded.

There seemed to be no point in waiting, anyway, she thought now, since nothing could come of delay. Penthorpe had insisted that he wanted to marry her, and he was kind and funny. He would not be a difficult husband either, which was more than one could say for most males, and if her feelings tended to indicate a tenderness for larger, more passionate men, that was simply an unfortunate inconvenience, not only because she no longer had the luxury of snapping her fingers at a betrothal, but because she was not by any means convinced that marriage to anyone else would prove more tolerable. Nonetheless, when she tried to imagine herself sitting across the breakfast table from Penthorpe, it was always Deverill's image she saw in his place.

Gideon had not been able to leave London at once, because there were matters of business to discuss with Jervaulx before he could do so; however, he did not dawdle on the way, for he was anxious to take up his new duties. Kibworth and Shalton rode with the baggage, but so anxious were they to prevent his being forced to look after himself for so much as an hour at a posting inn, that their coach rattled along at nearly the same pace as the phaeton that Gideon drove, accompanied by his groom.

Kibworth and Shalton seemed to have reached an understanding after his injury, through sharing the self-imposed hours of care, and although each was still jealous of the other, their attitudes were so extremely polite that after traveling for days with them, he was only too glad to see Deverill Court again.

None of the house servants at the Court had traveled to London, so everything was in readiness for him, for the simple reason that it was always kept so for Jervaulx. The marquess rarely bothered to send word when he might be expected, and consequently, Gideon was able to sit down to a delicious supper upon his arrival, and to get straight to work the following day.

First he sent for Barton to explain that he was assuming control of the estate at Jervaulx's request.

"And about time, sir, if I may take the liberty to say so," the steward declared. "I've the books right here. There seems to be a bit of a ruckus betwixt the Sanderson lot over to Mulberry Mines and that group of tenants on the eastern bit of the moor. I've got the details all written up, for I meant to send word to his lordship, but perhaps you'll just look over what I've written. What I'd recommend is this." He proceeded to explain a number of things, and Gideon's respect for his father's ability to manage at once a myriad of affairs grew by leaps and bounds. It was a good time later before he was able to bring up the subject of documents and other records in the muniments room.

"When I was here before, Barton, I sorted everything pertaining to the years between my great-grandfather's death and my grandfather's marriage, but since I did not know what I was looking for, I found nothing of value, and there is still much to be examined. One thing I did discover is that only my father seems to have organized his papers into any proper order. My grandfather and everyone who preceded him just threw things into boxes and onto shelves, all higgledy-piggledy."

"That's a fact, sir," Barton agreed, "but there was actually some order to their methods, though you mightn't think it."

"Well, I daresay any order there might have been was disarranged by our previous efforts," Gideon said with a sigh, "but since you are bound to know more about all of it than I do, I wish you will come and help us look through it."

So it was that he had the assistance of his steward, his batman, his valet, and a young footman when he began his second foray into the muniments room. This time, they began at the beginning and proceeded quickly, thanks mostly to their efforts in sorting everything generally the first time. They divided up the work, and since Gideon was still convinced that anything that could be of use to him would be found in the years prior to his grandfather's marriage, that was where he began, leaving the material before that time to Kibworth and Shalton, and the material for the following years to Barton and the footman.

By the second afternoon, they had developed a routine, and the room was silent except for occasional murmured questions and answers. Gideon read steadily at the writing table, determined to read every word of every document until he found something that would help. So deep was his concentration that when Barton, standing beside him, cleared his throat suddenly and said, "Excuse me, my lord," he nearly jumped off his chair.

Collecting himself and taking the opportunity to stretch the stiffness from his arms and back, he said, "What is it, Barton?"

"Thought you might like to look at this, sir." He was holding a thick sheaf of papers, and Gideon felt a wave of hope that someone had found something important at last.

Taking the bundle and setting it down before him, he saw what it was even before he untied the string. "Grandmother's novel." He smiled. "I hadn't realized this was in here."

Barton said, "Nor it wouldn't be if the old lord hadn't had that habit you was just complaining about, sir. It were just dumped with an odd assortment of his personal papers in this here box that you all seem to have sorted through before."

"Shalton did that lot, I think," Gideon said, glancing at the box. "I told him just to organize things by whatever means he thought right, but I don't think this ought to be kept with the documents and records in this room, you know. Set it aside somewhere, if you will—or no, wait." Another thought struck him. During his trip from London, he had tried to think of a way to make peace with Daintry, and it occurred to him now that she might be amused to read a novel written by a noblewoman of the previous century. He did not think the tale would impress her very much, but he hoped she would appreciate both the source and the author. "Wrap it up, Barton. I know someone who might like to have a look at it. Ned," he added, observing that Shalton was watching them, "leave that for now. I've an errand for you."

Daintry received the brown-paper wrapped parcel from Clemons that afternoon when she went down to the stables with Charley to visit Victor and Cloud.

"What on earth is this, Clemons?" she asked in astonishment.

Glancing quickly around, the groom said, "The same fellow as brung that letter before brung this today, Miss Daintry."

She looked for Charley and, seeing the child happily engaged in discussing Victor's points with Teddy and his cousin Todd, she quickly moved a short distance away, set the bundle down on a bench, and untied the string. Opening the brown paper just enough to read the top page of foolscap, she saw inscribed there, *"The Handsome Duke* by Harriet Slocum, Lady Thomas Deverill." The last three words had been written in a slightly altered version of the same copperplate as the rest. Observing that a folded piece of paper had been laid on top, she removed and opened it.

Deverill had written, *I did not have the slightest notion what else to do with the enclosed, and though I doubt it compares with the work of the admirable Miss Haywood, I send it in hopes that it will amuse you. Perhaps if it makes you laugh a little, you will find it in your heart to forgive one who has only your best interest at heart,* and had signed with the single letter *D.*

Daintry replaced the covering carefully, retied the string, and called to Charley that it was time to return to the house. The child came at once, and for a wonder showed not the least curiosity about the parcel her aunt carried. Indeed, she seemed preoccupied, but when Daintry asked if anything was amiss, she looked up with her usual sunny smile and said, "Oh, no, not in the least. It must be nearly suppertime, don't you think?"

Daintry had no time to look at the manuscript until that evening, for immediately after supper Lady St. Merryn insisted that she help draw up a list of persons to be invited to her wedding, and before this task was well in hand, had thought of a number of others that must be accomplished before the date could be set. "And to think your father wants me to arrange it for next month," she said. "It cannot be done, not without it would be the shabbiest thing, for it is much too much for my nerves."

"Just as if," Lady Ophelia said when Lady St. Merryn had gone up to bed at her usual early hour, "your mama thinks she will have to manage every detail by herself." Setting aside her knitting, she took her journal out of her reticule and moved to the writing table.

Seeing that she was thus occupied, Daintry excused herself and went to her bedchamber, unwrapping the manuscript and setting it on the little table near her window while she fetched a branch of working candles to light the pages. She intended to read only a chapter or so, remembering her great-aunt's comments about the skill of the writer and finding that it was just as Lady Ophelia had observed. The writing was not only inept but was peppered with meandering little observations that seemed to have nothing to do with the tale that slowly began to unfold. Had the author not been Deverill's grandmother, she would have stopped after no more than half an hour's reading; however, because it was Harriet Deverill's work, the parenthetical remarks of the narrator began to seem at first rather amusing, giving one rare insight into the writer's personality, and so she read on.

Harriet seemed to have had a high opinion of herself and of her ability to manipulate her world as she chose, and it soon became clear that Lady Fanny, the heroine of *The Handsome Duke*, represented the author's view of herself, although surely Harriet had never been so beset by villains as poor Lady Fanny was.

Daintry lit more candles when the first ones guttered, and read on. When a casual reference to one of the characters as something of a Jacobite caught her eye, she began to read more carefully. Fifteen minutes later, her attention became riveted to the page as excitement vied with dismay for preeminence in her emotions. The sky was gray with the first light of dawn before she turned the final page and sat back, staring with unseeing eyes at the untidy pile of papers and chewing her bottom lip, wondering if anyone else would believe she had found the key to the Tarrant-Deverill feud in such an unlikely source.

Twenty-two

Daintry slept late the following morning, but as soon as she had dressed and eaten, and without saying a word about Harriet Deverill's novel to anyone else, she went in search of St. Merryn. Learning that he was closeted with his steward, she was forced to contain her soul in patience for yet another hour and a half, but having given orders that she was to be informed the moment he was alone, she was able at last to beard him in his book room, where she got to the point straightaway.

"Papa, I have discovered what began the feud, and it is all a parcel of nonsense."

"What's that?" St. Merryn looked up at her from the papers he had been reading, peering over his spectacles. "I am very busy, girl. A number of things transpired while I was in London that must be attended to now. What are you nattering on about?"

"The feud, sir, with the Deverills. I know what caused it. It was the fault of only one person, and she is long since dead."

"She? What can you mean, Daintry? Upon my word, I wish you will talk sense. How can you know anything about it?"

"I'll tell you presently," she said, for she had decided that if she were to inform him at once that the answer lay in an unpublished novel written during the previous century, and by a woman at that, he would order her out of the room. Instead, she said, "It was Deverill's grandmother who conceived the whole thing, sir. She was blindly jealous of Aunt Ophelia, whom she saw as her chief rival and as the only obstacle preventing Tom Deverill from proposing marriage to her. She did not believe Aunt Ophelia had no wish to marry, you see, for in point of fact, such a notion was foreign to most people then, just as it is now," she added with a speaking look.

"I hope you won't be telling me at this late date that you don't wish to marry, for I don't want to hear it," he said testily, "and what did Harriet's notion of Ophelia have to say to anything? Harriet got to marry Deverill, did she not?"

"Yes, but not for several years after she had arranged a quarrel between two good friends. I am not sure just how she put the matter to Tom Deverill, but you told me yourself that he was suspected of having connections to the Jacobites, and somehow she led him to believe that Grandpapa had threatened to expose him if he did not leave the field open for him to pursue Aunt Ophelia. You see, Grandpapa wanted her fortune, but Tom Deverill really loved her and was willing to give her up rather than drag her into the scandal Harriet had convinced him Grandpapa would brew if he did not yield. There was even a duel, sir, though it was given out that the two men fought over a card game or some such thing, because of course, gentlemen never admitted fighting duels over ladies. What with all the rules of good manners and proper conduct, Tom Deverill never did confront Grandpapa directly about the supposed threat to expose him—just as Harriet had known he would not—but he did let it be known that he was furious with his longtime good friend for betraying their friendship."

"Utter nonsense," St. Merryn snorted. "My father would never have done such a thing, and Deverill must have known it. Damme, they were best friends!"

"Yes, sir, but think how disillusioned Tom Deverill must have been even to think his friend would make such a threat. And if, the few times they did talk afterward, they talked at cross purposes—which might very easily have happened, you know—he would never have found out that Grandpapa knew nothing whatsoever about any threat. All Tom Deverill knew for a fact was that Grandpapa wanted more than anything to marry Aunt Ophelia for her fortune. He knew Grandpapa did not love her, and so he thought it entirely possible that greed could lead Grandpapa to threaten a scandal that would reflect as badly upon her as it would on Tom Deverill. So Tom Deverill, being noble about it all—and to my way of thinking, rather stupid—gave her up and turned his fury on the whole Tarrant family, refusing to speak to anyone in it and passing the anger on to his son, who is now trying to pass it on to his. You must end it, Papa, for it's all wrong."

"You must have windmills in your head, girl. Where did you get such a nonsensical notion?"

"Deverill's grandmother wrote a novel, sir," she said, knowing there was nothing more to be gained by equivocating. "It was never published because it is very badly written, but if one accepts that the heroine of the tale represents Harriet Deverill, one sees just how she convinced Tom Deverill to believe Grandpapa would betray him unless he gave up any claim to Aunt Ophelia's hand and left the way clear for Grandpapa to win her. Harriet made Tom believe his best friend was really his worst enemy."

"What? Upon my word, girl, a novel? How can one fool woman have created the Deverill feud? That must be nonsense."

"You told me yourself that Tom Deverill was thought to be a Jacobite. He risked losing Deverill Court if such an accusation was laid before the authorities, did he not?"

"Oh, that might be true enough," St. Merryn admitted, "but as to any plot to throw Ophelia into your grandfather's hands, that must be nonsense, for no such thing ever happened."

"No, sir, but it might have if she had not been so set upon remaining unmarried. At all events, surely you see that we have got to end it now."

"Upon my word, girl, why should we do any such thing?"

"Why, it was founded on a lie, sir. It cannot be allowed to continue. You simply must speak to Jervaulx."

"Pooh, nonsense, it was none of our doing, even if this stuff you're prattling has any truth in it. A Deverill began it, so only a Deverill can end it, but if you think you can get that stiff-necked

Jervaulx to apologize for anything—particularly for something you've got out of some damned romantical book—you're fair and far off, my girl. He won't listen to you now any more than he did when you made a fool of yourself in his courtroom."

"But if you went to him and explained, surely—"

"Upon my word, what will you say next? I shan't go near the fellow. Didn't I just tell you it is not my business to do any such thing? They began it; let them try to end it."

"Then I shall talk to Deverill."

"You will not. I've never heard of anything so improper! You are to marry Penthorpe, my girl, and you'll be making no assignations with anyone else until you're safely riveted. What you do after that is Penthorpe's business, not mine."

She did not give up easily, but he soon lost his temper, and when he ordered her out of the room, she went to seek solace of her great-aunt. Lady Ophelia heard her explanation of what had occurred more than sixty years before and agreed that Daintry had interpreted the novel in the most likely way possible.

"But who would have thought Harriet had such spite in her?" the old lady said. "Still I suppose the size of my fortune did lend credence to any tale she might have whispered to Tom."

"Papa says he does not believe a word of it."

"I shouldn't be at all surprised if the money don't add into that as well," Lady Ophelia said with a glint of amusement in her eyes. "He won't mind if it goes to Penthorpe, but his enmity has become so familiar to him, I doubt he'll relinquish it easily."

Daintry was still trying to sort this out in her mind when Lady Ophelia added bluntly, "What are you going to do about it?"

She sighed. "I do not have the least notion. Perhaps if settling the feud could make a difference to my future, I might decide more easily, but it will not affect me in the least. Papa insists I am to marry Penthorpe, and I did give him my word."

"You do not want to remain single," Lady Ophelia said gently. "That has long been perfectly obvious to me."

"Has it, ma'am?" Ruefully, she added, "It has not been so obvious to me until recently. If I were more like you, perhaps the single state would do very well for me, but I have come to believe that

I am singularly unsuited to it. I know you must think me a sad disappointment—"

"Merciful heavens, child, why should I think anything of the kind?" Lady Ophelia demanded indignantly.

"I should be failing your teaching quite miserably."

"You would be doing nothing of the kind."

"But you've always wanted me to be an independent woman!"

"I still want that," Lady Ophelia said matter-of-factly, "but just what do you think the term means, my dear?"

"Why, one who lives on her own, of course, and who can look after herself and be quite contented doing so. What else could such a term possibly mean?"

"Do I live by myself?"

"No, but you could do so very well, ma'am. Of that I have not the least doubt."

"Nor do I, but although I choose to live under your father's roof, I am nonetheless independent."

"But I do not want to continue living under Papa's roof. I want an establishment of my own just as badly as Davina does. I want to be my own mistress, to make my own decisions, and to control my own life, but since practically none of those things is likely to occur unless I break my word to Papa and insist upon living alone or with a lady companion, I must accept what is available, which is marriage to Penthorpe. At least as his wife, I shall be mistress of my own establishment, and I do not think he will prove to be a difficult husband, do you?"

Lady Ophelia did not answer at once. Instead, she subjected Daintry to a long and searching look. Then she said, "Do you love Penthorpe, my dear?"

Daintry said quietly, "I have come to the conclusion that to care deeply for a man leads only to a constant pulling of caps, which is no good way to live and does not lead to independence of any sort whatsoever. Penthorpe is kind and he says he wishes to marry me. In good conscience, there is no more to be said, for I cannot cry off from this betrothal even if I wished to do so, which, I assure you, I do not."

"An independent woman, my dear, is one who makes her choices freely and has the luxury to choose what will make her happy. That does not mean that she fails to heed the requirements or wishes of those who are dear to her, or that she ignores either her sense of honor or her deepest feelings. She takes all such matters under consideration. You expressed the thought earlier that I might be disappointed in you. I tell you now to your head that the only way you can disappoint me is by settling for second best when true happiness lies right within your grasp."

Daintry swallowed hard. "I-I don't know what you mean."

"Don't you? Then perhaps you had better consider the matter a bit more carefully. I must go and change my gown. Lionel Werring is going to dine with us this evening, and he has invited me to drive into Bodmin with him and back beforehand so that I can select a book from the subscription library there."

Feeling a sudden, strong need to get away from the house, Daintry sent an order to the stable to have Cloud saddled, went to her bedchamber to change to her habit, and was halfway down the stairs when she thought of Charley. Realizing the little girl would think herself ill-used if she were to discover her aunt had gone out without her, Daintry went back upstairs.

When she entered the schoolroom, Miss Parish looked up from the atlas she was perusing and said cheerfully, "Good afternoon, Lady Daintry. Here is your aunt come to visit you, Charlotte."

Charley got up at once from the bench by the schoolroom table where she was working, and Daintry said, "I wanted a gallop, so I came to see if you would like to ride with me."

"Oh, yes!"

Miss Parish coughed behind her hand and said apologetically, "I'm afraid not today, my lady. She has got a little behind in her work, you see, and must make up the lessons she missed."

Grimacing, Charley plopped back down on the bench by the long table, saying crossly, "Papa came up here this morning! Can you credit it, Aunt Daintry? It must be the first time he has ever set foot in the schoolroom, and it had to be today. He is no longer here, of course, for he and Mama have gone to Plymouth to look for their house for the summer, but before he left, he came to see me, and why? Just to blight my life, that's why."

Daintry chuckled. "You have no one to blame but yourself, darling, but if I remember correctly, you have complained any number of times that he pays no heed to you. I should think you would be grateful for his attention."

"Not this kind of attention," Charley said. "I'd have liked it much better if he had taken me to Plymouth to help look for a house, but of course, there was no reason for him to think of any such thing, and when I told him I wanted to go, he just said such matters were no business of mine. So here I sit."

"Well, if you get caught up today, we can ride tomorrow," Daintry promised. She left at once, just as glad to have the time to herself, and was soon lost in her own thoughts.

When she returned, refreshed by the exercise but without having come to any acceptable decisions, she found Charley at the stable feeding carrots to Victor and talking with the stableboys. Learning that it was nearly dinnertime and remembering that Sir Lionel Werring was to dine with them, Daintry did not wait for her but hurried inside to change her dress for dinner. She had no more opportunity to be alone with her thoughts until she lay in bed that night, but though she had meant to sort things out then, she was much too tired to do so, and soon fell fast asleep.

The dream began in darkness with a sense of someone touching her cheek, a weight pressing into the bed beside her, and the terrifying, breath-stopping memory of Seacourt's attack. Panic-stricken, she could not see at first, nor could she scream, for no sound came out when she tried, but the terror ebbed almost as swiftly as it had come. There was no reek of brandy, and the fingers touching her cheek were gentle, unthreatening. The weight beside her shifted and she went perfectly still, but she knew now that there was no cause for alarm.

A finger moved toward her lips, and she remembered Seacourt again and the way he had clamped his hand against her mouth, but though she still could not see, she knew the presence in her bed had nothing to do with Seacourt. The finger touched her lower lip, and as though the touch had somehow been a signal, a golden glow began to fill the room, moving from the walls toward the bed in a way that no light she had ever seen before had done. She still could not see the face beside hers, but she knew its features as well as her own, and when the glow finally touched his hair, revealing reddish highlights, she was not the least bit surprised. He shifted his weight, moving over her to kiss her, and she felt herself respond, her whole body leaping to meet his.

His lips were gentle, soft, and tender, tasting her mouth, her cheeks, and even her eyelids, and then she felt his hand on her shoulder, moving toward her breast. Instead of fear, she felt longing, and moved her own hands to caress his body.

He was naked. His skin felt smooth to her touch, and warm, but even as she became aware of those sensations, his fingers touched the tip of her right breast, and she realized that she was naked too. Her nipples tingled, but the caressing hand moved lower, to the tangle of curls where her legs met, and then he was touching her where she had once thought no one but a villain would touch her, but instead of recoiling, her body moved to meet his fingers and the warmth that spread through her was as nothing she had ever experienced before.

She moaned. The sound was audible, and his lips moved back to capture her mouth. His tongue plunged inside, and the fingers of his roving hand moved inside her too. She lost all sense of what she had been doing to him, too enthralled by the sensations he stirred in her, for his hands were everywhere now, caressing, possessing, and arousing her tingling nerves to ecstasy.

When his hands stopped moving, her body stirred of its own accord, and his hands moved again. The next time they stopped, she encouraged him with caresses of her own, and suddenly, almost overwhelmingly curious, she began to use her hands to explore his body, savoring the hardness of his muscles, his broad chest, his flat stomach, the tightly curled hairs of his—

She awoke sitting straight up in bed with sweat streaming from her body. The room was darker than it had been in the dream, and she knew that she was completely and utterly awake. Just thinking of the dream made her tremble, for she could still feel his caresses and her body still felt naked and vulnerable, although her nightdress covered her from neck to toe. Her breath came in sobs, and she wondered what on earth had possessed her to dream such wanton things, but one thing was perfectly clear. Under no circumstances could she marry Penthorpe.

Her sleep after that was fitful, but when she awoke the next morning with the smell of hot chocolate filling her room, she could remember no other dreams but the one she was certain she would never forget. Stealing a look at Nance, who had moved from setting down the tray to open the curtains, she wondered if the woman would sense any difference in her. Daintry was certain that she ought to, since she felt as if everything that had been done to her and that she had done ought somehow to be imprinted upon her for all the world to read.

"So you're awake, are you?" Nance said. "Let me straighten them covers for you, my lady."

She stayed very still, watching Nance, but the woman appeared to see nothing amiss, merely asking if she had learned some new way to drink her chocolate that would allow her to do so lying down, or if she meant to sit up like a Christian.

She sat up hastily, causing the newly straightened blankets to slip, which stirred a tingling in her breasts that made her feel as if she had been caressed again. It was as if Deverill had suddenly appeared in her bedchamber. Her cheeks burned at the thought, and as she took her chocolate from Nance, the woman put a hand on her forehead.

"Look a mite feverish, you do, miss," she said. "Are you feeling quite the thing?"

"Oh, yes," Daintry said, surprised that her voice sounded normal. "The room is a trifle warm, don't you think?"

"Don't feel it myself," Nance said, "but then, I was just at that window, and there's a bit of a breeze blowing across the moor and black clouds gathering overhead. Don't feel much like spring this morning. Will you be getting up at once, miss?"

"Yes, please. I'll want some writing paper, ink, and wafers, too, Nance, if you will send for some."

"Lady St. Merryn ordered gilt-edged cards for your wedding invitations, Miss Davies told me. Ever so pretty they must be."

"Well, they are not here yet, and I want to write a letter in any case, not invitations. And it will do you no good to pry, Nance, because I do not mean to tell you any more than that."

But when the materials were brought to her, it occurred to her that her task would not be as easy as she had hoped. Though she had decided her best course lay with writing to Penthorpe and being as candid with him as she could be, she had no idea where to direct her letter and dared not ask her father. The most she could do was to write to Deverill and tell him she had discovered the key to the feud. But that course, too, carried with it certain difficulties.

Not only had St. Merryn forbidden her to approach Deverill on the subject of the feud but she could not imagine telling him flat out that the whole thing had been his grandmother's fault. And to try to write out the details of the novel in such a way that they would be clear to him without causing offense would require a good deal more time and skill than she presently had at her command. The best thing, then, would be to send the manuscript back to him with a recommendation that he read it carefully, hinting only that it contained information about the feud and letting him draw his own conclusion just as she had.

That still left Penthorpe to be dealt with, but until he appeared, there was nothing to be gained by fretting about him, although she would have to make her position clear to Lady St. Merryn and the others before they began to write the invitations.

Having reached these decisions, she came suddenly to an impasse. It was all well and good for Aunt Ophelia to prose on about happiness and free choices, but since her own sensibilities seemed determined to bond her to Deverill as strongly as ever a pair of swans might be bonded, and since she was determined not to submit in body or spirit to any man—let alone to one as astute and as accustomed to commanding others to obey his wishes as Deverill was—and since her dream had made it completely ineligible to pretend to form any connection with poor Penthorpe, there could be no resolution other than to remain single and set up housekeeping for herself, with Lady Ophelia's financial assistance, the minute she was deemed old enough to do so.

That the prospect did not delight her was not a matter to be contemplated since she could think of no other way to retain both her dignity and her sense of personal integrity. Her father would be furious, of course, and she felt guilty at the thought of both breaking her word and of defying him so outrageously, but if it had to be done, it had to be done. It did not, however, have to be done all at once, and she still had to think of a way to do it which would not utterly sink her beneath reproach. In any case, she must wait until she could speak to Penthorpe.

Getting up at last, she allowed Nance to help her into a simple morning frock of rose-striped muslin.

"'Tis a lovely gown, this," Nance said as she fluffed out the bow of the pink-satin sash and straightened the trailing ribbons. "When do we expect my Lord Penthorpe?"

"Perhaps today," Daintry said, hoping that for once his lordship would not procrastinate but would travel into Cornwall with all dispatch. The sooner he arrived, the better, for the longer the world was allowed to believe them betrothed, the more difficult the break would be.

When she went down to breakfast, she had the room all to herself, and when she went in search of Lady Ophelia, she learned that her ladyship had already left the house to pay a call in the neighborhood. Although it was late morning by the time Daintry finished her breakfast, her mother had not yet come downstairs, but since Daintry had no wish to reveal her decision only to be drowned in tears and recriminations, she was just as glad.

She would have liked to ride, but since Charley had not yet come in search of her, demanding that she make good her promise of the day before, she decided it would be wiser to remain close at hand in case Penthorpe arrived. She decided as well that she would not be disobeying St. Merryn's command if all she did was to return Deverill's property to him, and so she went back upstairs, intending to go to her bedchamber to fetch the parcel, and met Miss Parish on the point of descending.

"Good morning, my lady," the governess said in her cheerful way. "You have been away rather longer—" Breaking off with an arrested look, she eyed Daintry from top to toe before going on to say, "But you must have returned some time ago, mustn't you, since you have already changed your dress and are even now coming *up* the stairs, rather than going down, but I bade Miss Charlotte most straitly to come right to the schoolroom when you returned.

That naughty child! I do so dislike to scold her, but I fear I must this time. Where is she, if you please?"

"I do not perfectly understand you," Daintry said, but she was only too afraid that she did understand. "Do you mean to say Charley led you to believe she was with me?"

"There was no *leading* about it, I fear," Miss Parish said, shaking her head. "She reminded me that you had said you would take her riding today, and insisted that you wanted to go first thing this morning because the sky looked as if it were clouding up to rain. Which it did," she added with a sigh, "but I collect that you had said no such thing to her, so where can she be?"

"I thought she was still too busy with her lessons to tease me to take her riding," Daintry said. "If that is not the case, I'm afraid she may have ridden over to visit her cousin again, and if she has done so, she must be punished." She glanced out the window to see even more dark clouds than before. "It is going to rain soon, so I daresay I had better go after her. Order my horse, will you? I'll go change into my habit."

She turned away only to hear her name spoken from below and, turning back, beheld the housekeeper with one of the younger maids at her side. The girl's eyes were red from weeping.

"Yes, Mrs. Medrose, what is it?"

"Begging your pardon, my lady, but Millie here has something to give you. She was told not to do so before two o'clock, but her conscience began to prick her—as well it should have done—and so she came to me, and I gave her a right good scold, for she ought never to have agreed to such a naughty thing. But here, Millie, you go and give that note to Lady Daintry right now."

Sniffling, her eyes downcast, the little maid came on up the stairs and handed Daintry a tightly folded bit of paper.

"Who gave this to you, Millie?" But she knew the answer even as she unfolded it.

"Miss Charley, m'lady. Oh, but I didn't know I oughtn't to take it. She's always so merry and kind, m'lady. Oh, please, ma'am, don't be vexed with me!"

Mrs. Medrose said sternly, "That will do. You go on about your business now and thank your stars Lady Daintry don't tell his lordship to turn you off without a character. The idea!"

Daintry paid no heed, for she was reading Charley's note:

Dear Aunt Daintry,

I have gone to rescue Melissa. Todd brought me a letter from her, and there is no more time to lose. Her papa has been very angry ever since he got home, and she is afraid of him, and afraid of what he will do to Aunt Susan, even though Lady Catherine says she will not let him hurt her again, but Melissa does not believe her and hates her, and Aunt Susan can run away again if Melissa does not have to stay with Uncle Geoffrey, for she said she would, only except Uncle Geoffrey will not let her take Melissa with her, and so that is why we are going. Tell Mama and Papa that I was sorry they did not want me to live with them in Plymouth, but it is just as well now, I think, because if they had wanted me to go with them, I should not have been here to rescue Melissa. Do not trouble your head about us. I will take very good care of her.

    Your own loving, Charley
    PS. Please do not blame Miss Parish, for I told her a false-hood, which I know I ought not to have done, but I could think of no other way.

Daintry stared at the note for several seconds after she had put herself in possession of its contents, fighting tears and wanting at the same time to murder Seacourt. Struggling to contain her emotions, she said with admirable calm to the waiting housekeeper, "Thank you, Mrs. Medrose, you did exactly right. Pray, say nothing of any of this to anyone, if you please. You, too, Miss Parish," she added, turning back to the governess. "Miss Charlotte has gone to her cousin, just as I feared, but I will leave notes for Lady Ophelia and my brother, so if you will see to ordering my horse for me, that will be all you need do."

The thought of Charles's likely reaction to his daughter's latest start was a bit daunting, but since it was partly his fault and Davina's for not making it plain to Charley that she was to live with them in Plymouth, Daintry would have no compunction about taking up the cudgels on Charley's behalf if she did not strangle the child first when she caught up with her.

As she hurried to her bedchamber to change into her riding habit, she realized that although she was fairly certain she knew where the children would go, she was going to need help if she was to return Melissa to Seacourt Head without running into trouble herself. That thought brought another on its heels, that Geoffrey might manage to find the children before she did.

The writing paper and manuscript were where she had left them, and ringing for Nance to help her dress, she sat down at once and wrote to Deverill, praying that he would be at home to receive her note and not have gone out somewhere. Then, dashing off notes to Lady Ophelia and Charles, she tied up the manuscript and slipped her note to Deverill under the string so that he would see it at once. She had just finished when Nance came in.

Ten minutes later, taking the parcel with her, she hurried to the stables and asked Clemons to see personally to its safe delivery. "I can trust no one else," she said, "and it is urgent that you see this parcel into Deverill's hands without delay."

The wiry groom eyed her askance. "I had orders to saddle Cloud, my lady. Surely, you ain't meaning to ride without me."

"I go the other way, Clemons, toward the sea."

"I'll get one of the lads to saddle up and go with you."

"I don't want anyone." If she did encounter Geoffrey, a stable boy would be of no help to her, and the fewer servants to know about any of it, the better. Clemons looked as if he might argue the point, but then he turned abruptly away, and a moment later, with relief, she saw him ride out of the stable yard.

Wasting no time, she put Cloud to a distance-eating pace, hoping that she would be the first, if not the only, person to realize where the girls were most likely to have gone. An hour later, before she made her way down the steep path from the cliff top, she scanned the shingle below with care. When she saw no sign of life, she breathed a sigh of relief and urged Cloud on, dismounting near the first cave and tying Cloud to a bit of scrub before she approached the entrance.

It was empty, as was the second, but as she crept into the opening of the third and largest cave, she heard voices at last. Even as she realized that at least one of them was masculine, a voice right behind her said, "Step right in, missy, the more, the merrier. Look what I've got here, lads!"

A hand in the small of her back propelled her roughly forward toward the dim glow of a small fire. In its light, she saw the frightened faces of her two nieces surrounded by a number of rough men, and as her dismay turned to shock she realized that all her dependence now must lie with Deverill.

Twenty-three

Gideon had spent the previous day reading documents, and the morning going over estate business with Barton. They had intended to ride out before noon to visit tenants who had requested assistance of one sort or another, but that plan was changed when, just before eleven o'clock, a footman showed Viscount Penthorpe into the estate office.

"Daresay I'm expected at Tuscombe Park," Penthorpe said when he had shaken hands with Gideon and been introduced to Barton, "but I must have passed the turn St. Merryn told me would take me across the moor. Next thing I knew, I was looking at the River Fowey, and I said to myself, it would be a good thing to drop in and visit you for a few days before going on."

"Procrastinating again, Andy?" Gideon said with a weary smile. He had not slept well. His thoughts seemed wholly taken up with matters that had nothing to do with estate business, and his ability to concentrate on things his steward wished to tell him had suffered as a result. He was glad to see Penthorpe. "Come along with me, and we'll order up some food, for you won't want to wait until five o'clock to dine."

"I have grown rather accustomed to dining whenever I take a notion to do so," Penthorpe said, following him upstairs to

Jervaulx's book room and looking around with approval. "Good view of the river and a cheerful fire. Very pleasant."

"It is my father's favorite room and has become mine as well. Sit down, Andy. How long do you mean to stay?"

"Trying to get rid of me already, old son?"

"Not at all, but since St. Merryn made no bones about wanting you wedded to his daughter without further ado, I must suppose he will be looking for your arrival with no little impatience." Seeing without much surprise that his friend did not return his smile, he added gently, "Blue-deviled, Andy?"

"No, no, not in the least. What stuff you say, Gideon! Good God, why should I be blue-deviled? Going to marry an heiress, ain't I? Bound to bring me a pretty penny when the old lady pops off her hooks. Stands to reason, no sensible fellow could help but be delighted."

"You had better not count on controlling that money," Gideon said, pouring two glasses of wine from the decanter on a nearby side table and handing one to him before ringing for a footman. "I've learned a bit about Lady Ophelia, and I can tell you she has more than a nodding acquaintance with the Chancery Courts. I'd wager a pretty penny, she will see that money tied up so that no mere male can ever get his hands on it."

"Is that right?" But Penthorpe did not seem particularly concerned. He stared moodily out the window at the river, saying nothing at all for several minutes. Then finally, and with an air of extreme casualness, he said, "I suppose Seacourt and his family are at home now, too, are they not?"

"I suppose so. I have heard nothing one way or another, only the same declaration you heard, that he intended to take his wife home and keep her there." He watched Penthorpe's profile carefully, but there was little reaction other than a slight tightening of his jaw. The viscount had himself well in hand.

A moment later Penthorpe turned and raised his glass. "To your very good health. I saw your father the day before I left. He was looking well, I must say, and actually greeted me as if I were someone and not just a bit of muck beneath his feet."

Gideon replied suitably, but as he kept up his part in the desultory conversation that followed, he tried to think of a way to get Penthorpe to speak more plainly. He was nearly as sure as one person could be of another that Penthorpe had no real wish to marry Daintry and only insisted he did because of social constraints, but since Lady Susan was married and there was no acceptable way to oust Seacourt from the picture, he could scarcely appeal to Penthorpe to declare his true position on the score of thus being able to secure his own happiness.

At last, having thought of no better way, when Penthorpe paused to sip his wine, Gideon said bluntly, "Look here, Andy, you don't really want to marry Daintry Tarrant, do you?"

Penthorpe choked and sputtered. Snatching a handkerchief from his waistcoat pocket, he dabbed at his mouth and looked in dismay at the spots on his coat. "Look what you've made me do. Those spots will never come out, and my valet will yap at me like a damned lapdog. Of course I want to marry her. Haven't I said so time and again. And even if I didn't—Lord, Gideon, even if that were true, you certainly couldn't expect me to admit it, so don't go startling a fellow like that again, will you?"

Gideon sighed. "I had hoped we could be plain with each other, Andy, but if you think I cannot be trusted with your honest feelings in this matter, of course I will say no more."

The door opened to admit the footman, responding to Gideon's ring, and after Gideon had requested food to be served within the hour and the man had bowed his way out again, Penthorpe said sourly, "You see what comes of such nonsense. Suppose I'd been fool enough to say just then that I didn't want to marry the wench—not that I said any such thing, mind," he added, keeping a wary eye on the door. "But even if I were to own that I should be happy to hear that a certain Captain Hackum had been given notice to quit, what then? It ain't going to happen, Gideon, and since it ain't, my best chance at happiness lies along the path I've chosen. Well, don't it?"

"I cannot think how."

"But it's as plain as a pikestaff! I can do nothing for her as things are, but as a member of her family, I'll have a chance to see her occasionally, to offer her some slight protection."

Holding his temper in check, Gideon said severely, "That's a damned poor reason to marry Daintry, my friend."

"Is it? I can't think of a better one, and not only am I betrothed to the wench but St. Merryn means to see it through and I'd look like a dashed reprobate if I were the one to cry off." He met Gideon's stern gaze and said impatiently, "Oh, well, since we are being plain with each other, I'll own that I'd change things if I could. I've spent hours plotting how to be rid of Seacourt. It even occurred to me that I might contrive matters so it looked as if the fellow had murdered me, and then once he had been hanged for it, I could reappear, hale and hearty, to ride off with his wife across my saddle bow. But that is the stuff of daydreams, old son, nothing more," he added morosely.

Gideon chuckled. "With your luck, Andy, the dream would turn into a nightmare. Seacourt would get himself acquitted of the charge, and when you reappeared, he really would murder you. And he'd get off scot-free, too, because he could not be tried for the same murder twice, you know."

"The law," Penthorpe said with a sour look, "is chuck full of ridiculous notions, to my way of thinking."

"Now, there you agree with your betrothed," Gideon told him, remembering the scene in his father's court with a certain fondness. "She holds a very low opinion of English laws. Told my father they were unfair to women, and though he did his best to persuade her otherwise by pointing out that women retain all sorts of rights under law and are even given license to run up debts, commit crimes, and bear bastard children for which their husbands are then held accountable, I doubt if he succeeded in convincing her that the law is at all fair to the weaker sex."

"Stubborn wench," Penthorpe muttered.

"You'll have your hands full," Gideon said.

"Anyone would, but look here, man, I've given my word, and that is all there is about it. Moreover, as I said, I've reasons of my own for desiring the marriage, and it's not as if anyone else wants the wench. Good God, who would?"

Gideon held his peace. Time enough to confess that he wanted her himself when he knew that she would look kindly on his suit, and that her father could be convinced to accept a marriage between the two families. In the meantime, he changed the subject and did his best to cheer Penthorpe out of the dismals. They were finishing their meal when Clemons was shown in.

He followed the footman into the book room, prompting the man to say apologetically, "I beg your pardon, my lord, but he refused to remain in the hall. Said he had to put that parcel into your hands personally, and without delay."

"You may go, Robert," Gideon said, seeing that Clemons was fairly bursting to speak. "What is it, Clemons?" he demanded when the footman had gone. "Did your mistress send you? Surely, not just to return that package!"

"No, my lord," Clemons said, pulling the letter from under the string and setting the package down on the table. "She wanted you to have this at once, sir." He glanced at Penthorpe. "I don't know if I ought to say more, my lord."

"Don't bite your tongue on my account, man," Penthorpe said, getting to his feet. "I'll leave you."

Gideon waved him back. "Don't go, Andy. This man is Daintry's groom. Lord Penthorpe expects to marry your mistress, Clemons, so the sooner he knows what's amiss now, the better." As he spoke, Gideon broke the seal and unfolded Daintry's note, finding another one tucked inside. He read hers first, then hastily read the other, his expression hardening as he read.

"What is it?" Penthorpe demanded.

Gideon glanced at Clemons, made his decision, and said crisply, "I am going to trust you to keep a still tongue in your head, Clemons, because I think we may need your help, but if I ever hear that you've mentioned a word—"

"I won't, sir. I know how to keep mum."

"Good man. Here, Andy, read these."

Penthorpe read quickly, and for once he did not show the least inclination to procrastinate. Twenty minutes later both men had changed to riding clothes and armed themselves.

Gideon had ordered Clemons to see that their horses were saddled, and to saddle one for himself as well, since the one he had ridden from Tuscombe Park was, as he diffidently informed them, "blown pretty well to bits." Clemons and Ned Shalton were both waiting for them when they entered the stable yard.

Shalton spoke before Clemons could do so. "Saw them asaddling your horse, Major, and had my own turned out as well. Whatever the fracas be, sir, I'm your man."

"Right you are," Gideon said, noting the holster fastened to Shalton's saddle. "You might prove useful, Ned." He glanced at the darkening sky and hoped the threatening rain would hold off.

"Where the devil are these caves she writes of?" Penthorpe shouted as the four men rode out of the yard at a lope.

"St. Merryn Bay, more than fifteen miles from here as the crow flies." He was riding Shadow, who was fresh and easily good for a fifteen-mile point, and he was not concerned for Penthorpe or Shalton, whose mettle he had challenged many times over the years. Glancing at Clemons, he decided the groom would do well enough, too. By the look of him, he would get to his mistress if he had to run to her on his own two legs. Gideon realized he had reacted much as if he were riding into battle and wondered if he had good cause for the reaction. The sky overhead and the distant murmur of thunder reminded him of Waterloo.

"Can't blame the child for running off," Penthorpe said the first time they slowed the horses to a walk to rest them, "but Lady Susan must be well nigh dead from worry about her. Daintry must not delay a minute taking her home, if she does find her."

"It won't be that easy," Gideon said, casting a warning look at Clemons, and at the same time recognizing the concerns that had been pricking at the back of his mind. "You saw what she wrote, that she fears to make matters worse if she simply takes the child home when she finds her. Seacourt is bound to be angry, no matter what excuse they can contrive for Melissa's having left, and if worse comes to worst, and they encounter him before then, heaven knows what the man might do."

Penthorpe grunted. "He's bound to cut up stiff, all right, and it stands to reason she must be afraid of him. Just look what he did to her that night at the ball. I always thought he was cut from the same bolt as your brother was, but I'll say this for Jack. He would never have bullied a defenseless female."

"Much obliged to you," Gideon said. He increased their pace, and they rode in silence except for an occasional exchange regarding their route until they came to the top of the cliff, where Gideon called a halt in order to search the shingle below. There was no sign of life.

"I'd have expected her to be on the watch for us," he muttered. "And where are the horses?" Clemons said diffidently, "One o' them caves is big enough for any number of horses, sir, and what with the sky looking like it's going to spit any moment, chances are, they will have taken them inside. Miss Charley's riding Victor, and she wouldn't want to leave him outside when it looks like thunder and lightning."

Gideon had hoped that the rain, having held off so far, would continue to do so until they found Daintry and the girls and got Melissa safely home again, but the thunder sounded nearer and the sky had darkened considerably. Looking at Clemons, he frowned and said, "Is Victor afraid of thunder?"

"Aye, sir. He near goes crazy."

Briefly Gideon wondered if the only reason Daintry had sent for him was that she feared she would be unable to deal alone with two little girls and a terrified horse, but the thought was a fleeting one. Had that been her only reason, she would have taken men from her own stables with her.

Dismounting, he crouched down to examine the marks in the path leading down to the shingle, and when he straightened again, he was frowning thoughtfully. He turned back to the others.

In the cave, Daintry sat against one damp, chilly rock wall, holding hands with the little girls sitting on either side of her. The horses were bunched in an alcove nearby, and their captors—five in all— sat near the tiny fire, talking in low tones. She could tell there was dissension among them.

At first she had thought they must be smugglers, but when she had spoken that thought aloud, the leader of the men had laughed. Tucking the pistol he carried into his wide leather belt, he said, "Glory be, mum, that ain't our lay. Honest men, we be, sure as check, but when the mines shut down, there warn't nothing for it but for us to take our shillings where we finds 'em, and that's the truth of it. Which ain't to say that none among us ain't never run with the free traders. Dewy there be an excellent spotsman, even a tubman from time to time when the dibs be out of tune, but don't go pratin' of such stuff," he warned, encountering a fulminating look from his henchman. "He don't like it known hereabouts."

Daintry had followed his glance, and when the man by the fire realized she was looking at him, his expression changed to acute embarrassment and he looked quickly away, but not before she gasped with recognition. "Dewy Warleggan!" Her temper flared. "How dare you take us prisoner like this? Just you wait until Feok learns what you've done!"

Dewy muttered disgustedly, "I told you, Nicca. I—"

"No use pissin' nettles, man," the leader snapped, "and no more names! We was promised there'd be no scufflin' over this business, and there won't be."

Charley said indignantly, "There will be big trouble when my papa and grandpapa find out what you did. They'll cut out your liver and feed it to their dogs. Just you wait!"

"Won't know nothing about it," the man called Nicca growled.

"And just how do you mean to prevent that?" Daintry asked.

He put a finger to his lips. "No need tattlin' before the nippers now, mum. What they don't know won't worrit 'em."

"If you mean to say that we shan't be able to tell anyone, I wish you will say so," Daintry said, giving the little hands tucked in her own a hard squeeze. A muffled sob from Melissa was the only response, but Daintry saw Dewy Warleggan exchange a silent look with the leader before he turned away to the fire.

Nicca said, "Come darkmans, it'll all come clear, but there ain't no need for weepin', I give you my word."

"What's darkmans?" Charley demanded. She was peering into the alcove where the horses had been put, and Daintry realized they were stirring nervously. One of them gave a nervous whinny.

Dewy Warleggan muttered, "Nightfall, miss."

"No more argle-bargle," Nicca snapped, glancing at the alcove, where there were sounds of yet more fidgeting.

"Did you hear thunder?" Charley whispered.

Daintry shook her head. Nicca, evidently thinking she had been cowed by his rebuke, went to join the others by the fire, and for what seemed to be a very long time, they grumbled and muttered amongst one another. Hoping that Dewy Warleggan and perhaps one other, a vocal man whose cant vocabulary made it impossible for her to understand him, might be pleading their cause, Daintry kept silent, moving only to ease stiffening muscles. Neither she nor the girls had been tied, and she wondered if perhaps they would find a chance to escape before nightfall. She could hear distant thunder now, and the horses moved restlessly. Victor whinnied again, and she glanced at Charley, but instead of pleading instantly for someone to calm her horse, Charley just kept watch on the alcove.

"He will be all right," Daintry whispered, wishing she could make herself relax. It was a few moments before she realized that it was not just the present situation that was making her nervous but one from the past. The rolling thunder outside was having much the same effect on her that it had on Victor.

Finally, she could stand it no longer and said in a louder tone than she had meant to use, "Are you holding us for ransom?"

Her words startled more than one man by the fire, but no one spoke until Nicca said, "That's as may be and no con—"

A tremendous crack of thunder echoed through the cave, and the horses seemed to go wild. Melissa's scream was drowned by Victor's as the huge gelding reared in terror, frightening the others. Crowded as they were into the alcove, it was a moment before Victor broke free and plunged toward the fire.

The men had leapt instantly to their feet, and several rushed to calm the frightened horses. Nicca was closest to Victor and reached toward him to catch his bridle, but the huge gelding reared again and one hoof caught the man on the shoulder, spinning him and sending him crashing to the cave floor at Daintry's feet, where he lay winded and gasping.

Quick as a flash Daintry snatched the pistol from his belt and said, "Move away with me, girls. Keep clear of Victor and watch those men with the horses." Once she was far enough along the wall to be sure Nicca could not simply snatch the pistol back, she waited for his eyes to open before she said in a calm, clear voice, "Do not move or I will shoot you."

The others had control of the horses now, including Victor, and her words echoed oddly through the cavern, causing the men to turn toward her as one. Dewy Warleggan took a step toward her.

"Stop where you are. If you think I won't kill him, you are very much mistaken. In fact, you ought to put another log on that fire before it burns too low, for I would hate to shoot the wrong man merely because I cannot see the right one."

Nicca sat up, rubbing his shoulder. "Do as the lass says." Then, watching her narrowly while Dewy obeyed, he began to get to his feet. "You won't blow a hole in a cove just for seeing if his bones are broke, will you, mum?" Once upright, he looked at her more speculatively. "Doubt you be a murderous mort when all's said and done." He took a single step toward her.

Dewy said sharply, "Don't do it, Nicca She don't like men, so she's as like to kill you as look at you!"

"Nay, lad, not her. I knows gentry-morts, ye see, and this one ain't gonna loose off no popgun at an unarmed man."

Had he leapt at her, Daintry knew she could very well have shot him, but if he simply kept walking toward her, she was just as sure that she could never fire the pistol.

"Shoot him," Charley cried. "Oh, shoot him!"

Daintry could see amusement in Nicca's eyes when he held out his hand and said, "You'll not do it, lass."

"She might not," Deverill said from the cave opening, "but I certainly will, and you won't really care who pulled the trigger when all is said and done." He held a pistol in his hand, and behind him, Penthorpe held another. "Now, back away from the ladies, and the rest of you lads step away from the horses and over by that wall so we can have a look at you."

Daintry said quickly, "The thunder, sir. Someone must hold Victor, or he will panic again."

"Clemons," Deverill said sharply, but Charley was already on her feet and had run to the gelding's head.

"I can steady him if only the others don't spook him again."

Deverill looked at Daintry, who nodded in reply to the unspoken question. He said, "Clemons, Ned, see to the others."

"My lord," Dewy Warleggan said, standing his ground when the two passed him, "we would not have harmed them, I swear it."

"As we saw," Deverill said grimly.

"He's cutting no whids, your lordship," another man said, and Daintry saw he was the one who had been so vocal earlier. "Happen we seen there was a damber in the ruffmans, and since we'd no yen t' deck the chates, we'd ha' binged a wast but for the rhino we was promised. A cuffin can't buy peck nor poplars without rhino in his drawers, m'lord, and times is hard."

Penthorpe said indignantly, "What's the fellow talking about? Dashed if I can understand a word of it!"

Deverill looked at Dewy Warleggan, but it was Nicca who answered, "He says it warn't altogether pound dealing, m'lord, which is fact, since the cove what hired us would ha' seen us swing had we'd done all he wanted us to do, and we'd ha' given him the bag but for the gelt he flung about so generous."

Daintry, still bewildered, looked quizzically at Deverill, who smiled at her and said, "Their principal is something of a scoundrel and since they don't wish to be hanged, they would have abandoned him altogether if he had not paid them regularly."

There was another sharp crack of thunder, and Victor reared, catching Charley off her guard. Nicca leapt to help her hold the gelding, and Deverill lowered his pistol. He looked from one to another of the would-be villains, then said, "What was the plan for today? In plain English, if you please."

Dewy Warleggan said, "We was told the bit lass there"—he pointed at Melissa—"had run off, and we was to find her but not to bring her straight back, only to keep her safe hid. One of the stable lads had been made to say where she was likely to be, and if Miss Charley was with her, we was to keep her, too, and to keep an eye out for Lady Daintry to show." He licked his lips. "We'd never have harmed her ladyship, my lord, not for nothing, but like Nicca says, times is real hard and money right scarce."

"A cove prefers to be rhinocerical," the vocal man muttered.

Nicca nodded, stroking Victor. The gelding's eyes were wide, but it stood quietly despite recurrent rumbling outside.

Dewy said pensively, "Doubt you'll credit it, sir, when I tell you who it was, but—"

"Not now," Deverill said curtly. "Just tell me this. Are you lot responsible for firing upon Lady Daintry's coach, inciting the riots at Mulberry mine, and shooting at me?"

Dewy grimaced. "I'd as lief not discuss the mine, sir. That were a separate matter and had naught to do with . . . with the cove I spoke of. Nicca did fire at you, but never to do harm, and he told him you was too quick for him both times. As to the rest, he never said the old griffin would be in the coach that day, nor Lady Daintry neither, just that we'd find easy pickings if we robbed it and he wouldn't cry none if them inside was killed. Think he meant them to be," Dewy added, "but he never said as much, and we lobbed off soon as we seen who it was inside. The cove's summat of a basket scrambler, your lordship, if you take my meaning."

Deverill nodded and Daintry, who had followed the conversation without much difficulty said suddenly, "Are you the same men who attacked Lord Deverill in London, then?"

Dewy shook his head. "Ain't never been to London, nor Nicca neither, but Sir—" He broke off, caught Deverill's eye, and went on, "That is, the cove I was amentioning might ha' hired someone else to do it. He's no friend of yours, sir," he added, "but we've no grief with you, none at all. Fact is, you, my Lord Jervaulx, and Lord St. Merryn are the only gentry we know who be trying to get the mines opened again. We don't bite off our own feet, so to speak, but we do what we can to earn a bit here and there without we commit murder."

"So you are willing to do what the man tells you, but only when it does not offend your conscience, is that it?"

Nicca grinned at him. "That's it. We work for the sheep-biter when it's to our good, m'lord, but we ain't scoundrels nor we ain't madmen, and that be the truth of it."

Penthorpe said suddenly, "What are we going to do with them, Gideon? We've got to get young Melissa home to her mother."

"No!" Charley cried. "You can't take her back!"

Melissa stood pressed against the wall beside Daintry, her eyes wide, her lips parted as she took in the scene before her.

Deverill looked at Daintry and said quietly, "We would do better to discuss this matter without so great an audience, I think, but I leave it to you to decide what must be done with these fellows, my dear. You were their victim, after all."

Penthorpe said angrily, "I'm for hanging the lot of them. Surely, you don't mean to let them go, Gideon!"

Deverill said, "Well, Daintry?"

Daintry, seeing that all the men were watching her, some of them most anxiously, said, "They did not hurt us, sir, and I do not believe they can be very villainous at heart, but to be sure, if they are the ones who fired upon our coach—"

"But missed, mum, by a mile," Nicca pointed out quickly, "and Cub there, he couldn't move his dexter wing for a sennight after. Old griffin plugged him neat as wax."

"That is perfectly true," she said. She looked at Deverill, expecting him to decide, but when he waited, the picture of patience, she knew he truly meant to abide by her decision. "Let them go, sir. I am sure they will mend their ways."

"We will," Dewy said, adding more hesitantly, "I say, mum, will you . . . that is, you won't say nothing to Feok, will you? What I meant is . . . well, Feok is . . . " He spread his hands.

"I will engage to say nothing if you will promise to help your brother on his farm—cheerfully, mind you—until the mine opens again or until you find some quite legal occupation that you like better. Is that a bargain, Dewy?"

"Aye, mum, it is." He glanced sheepishly at Nicca, who only grinned at him. A few minutes later the men and their horses had gone, and Daintry realized she had not heard thunder for some time. The light outside the cave opening was brighter, too.

Penthorpe snorted in disgust. "Well, they're gone," he said, "but I still say we ought to have hanged the lot for scaring poor Susan clean out of her mind, as I have no doubt they have done. Since they are gone, however, at least we can be getting Miss Melissa back to her straightaway."

"No," Charley said, "you don't understand!"

"Not another word," Deverill said sternly. "Ned, Clemons, take the other horses outside, and be sure those villains have departed. We'll be with you in a moment. And now, Charley," he added when they had gone, "you have ventured very near the edge of what I will tolerate, so I advise you to tread with care, but if there is something you believe you must say, say it now."

Charley looked at him, her mouth open, men closed it and looked down at the ground, nibbling her lower lip.

Daintry kept silent.

No one else spoke.

Finally, Charley said quietly, "We left a note for Aunt Susan, sir, so she won't be scared. W-we thought it would help her if Melissa ran away, because then she could run away too. If Melissa goes back now . . ." She could not finish, and Daintry saw that there were tears in her eyes.

Penthorpe started to speak, but Deverill silenced him with a gesture and said, "We are going to ride to Seacourt Head with you, Charley, and we will see to it that matters are properly explained so no one gets hurt. Will you trust us to do that?"

She nodded, but Daintry could see her reluctance and hoped Deverill could keep his word. Knowing he would find it easier to do so if he understood exactly what sorts of things Seacourt was capable of doing, she knew she had to make a clean breast of it at last, but when he commanded the others to ride ahead and drew Shadow alongside Cloud, she found she had no idea how to begin. Even if she did, she was by no means certain she could tell him the things that would matter the most. The storm had passed, and although there were still dark clouds drifting overhead, the sky behind them was blue again, and the thunder had stopped.

"Are you all right?" Gideon asked quietly.

"Yes, of course, though I suppose you mean to scold me for riding after them without getting someone else to come with me."

"I have no right to chide you, but I'd advise you to take care what you say to Penthorpe. He does have that right."

She swallowed, looking ahead to where the others were riding. "I didn't know he was in Cornwall," she said.

Gideon chuckled. "He hadn't quite got around to riding to Tuscombe Park, you see. It seems he put off turning across the moor until he suddenly found himself at Deverill Court."

She nodded, turned to him impulsively, then turned back and stared straight ahead.

Gideon watched her for a few minutes. Then, gently, he said, "What is it, my dear? I've seen that look on too many young soldiers' faces, when they have something they are burning to say but are afraid of the consequences. I have already said you have nothing to fear from me."

She looked at him, saw the warmth in his eyes, and said suddenly, "I'm not afraid of you, only of what you will think of me, but that's foolishness, for there are other, much more important matters at stake."

"Then suppose you tell me. I promise you, nothing you can say will alter what I think of you."

The warm note in his voice brought heat to her cheeks, but suddenly she found that she could talk to him as to herself, and the words flowed from her. She told him everything that Geoffrey had done to Susan. Then she told him about the night of the storm, and when she finished, and saw his lips pressed tightly together, she feared for a single, brief moment that he would blame her. Then he looked at her, and the fear melted away.

"Is that why you pulled away from me that one night?"

She nodded. "I-I couldn't help it. The memory came before I knew such terrors were lying in wait for me."

"We have some talking to do, some things to straighten out," he said, "but first I want a chat with Sir Geoffrey Seacourt."

They had reached the drive, and it was only minutes before they let themselves into the house. Daintry was surprised that there were no servants to greet them, but glad, too, knowing it would be best if the day's events did not become food for gossip.

She led the way to the drawing room, certain that at that hour they must find Susan there, but the others were close behind her.

As she drew near the doors, she saw that they were slightly ajar, and she heard angry voices. Motioning for the others to be silent, she crept nearer in time to hear her sister say, "I don't believe you, Geoffrey, and if you do not instantly tell me where you have hidden Melissa, I will kill Catherine."

Twenty-four

S eacourt said angrily, "Damn it, Susan, put that pistol down at once. You don't know what you're doing, and it could very well go off by accident! I tell you, Melissa ran away. I found a note from her and didn't tell you, because I had hoped to have her back before you realized she had gone."

"I don't believe you," Susan snapped. "You would not be sitting quietly here if you did not know where she was, Geoffrey. I know you have taken her to torture me because I asked you to send Catherine away, and if you do not instantly bring her back, I promise you, I will shoot Catherine."

"But damn it, I tell you, I cannot . . ."

Daintry, peeking through the narrow opening, was able to see Susan. She stood behind the chair in which Catherine sat, holding a pistol to Catherine's head. Susan's hand shook, and Catherine sat very still. Daintry could not see Geoffrey.

She felt Gideon beside her and reached out a hand to keep him from pushing the door open before she realized he had no such intention. Glancing up, she saw that over her head he, too, was peering through the opening, while behind him, Penthorpe danced with impatience. Charley and Melissa stood beside him, their eyes wide with fright, and Daintry knew that all three must have heard Susan's words as clearly as she had. For once she was grateful for Melissa's habit of silence, and she nodded approval when Charley put an arm around the younger girl. Now there was only Penthorpe to worry her, but though he was clearly itching to intervene, he seemed no more likely than Gideon to make a hasty movement. Having help from men accustomed to looking before they leapt was clearly an excellent thing.

Geoffrey said, "I command you to put down that gun, Susan. If you do anything to harm Catherine, I will have you clapped into Bedlam. As your husband, I have that power, you know, and in fact, if you actually should be so demented as to shoot her, you will certainly be hanged for it."

"No, she won't, Geoffrey," Daintry said, opening the doors just wide enough so that he could see her, and Gideon behind her.

"What the devil are you doing here!" Seacourt demanded.

"I came to visit my sister. Why else should I come? Oh, don't lower that pistol, Susan," she said in the same calm tone she had used before. "Indeed, I can think of no good reason not to shoot her, for you would then be rid of all your troubles at once, you know." She heard movement behind her and sent up a silent prayer that Penthorpe would not show himself just yet, or allow either of the girls to do so.

Seacourt said, "Good God, don't encourage her, Daintry! Are you as crazed as she is?"

"Oh, Susan is not insane at all, Geoffrey," Daintry said, forcing a smile. "Don't you remember what Lord Jervaulx said at the Assizes? My dear sir, if your wife shoots your mistress in your presence, the courts will assume—as indeed they must, by law—that she acted under your command and control. Therefore, it is not Susan but you who will hang, which is exactly as it should be." His look of dismayed fury was nearly enough to stir her to tell him exactly what she thought of him, but Gideon's hand on her arm recalled her to the moment, and she said quietly, hoping to calm her sister, "What brought this about, Susan?"

"He has hidden Melissa to punish me for demanding that he send Catherine away. Oh, Daintry, he has begun to behave as if she were his wife and I one of their servants. Indeed, he gave the house servants leave last night and ordered me to serve her last night in their place, and in front of Melissa, too! I told him I had had enough." She gestured toward a vivid bruise on her cheek. "This was my reward then, but now . . ." She hefted the pistol again. "Where is Melissa, Geoffrey?"

Catherine spoke for the first time, her tone a near whisper. "Please, Susan, this is not my fault. Why do you threaten me?"

"Be silent," Susan said through her teeth. "You came sneaking into my home to seduce Geoffrey with your cozening ways. Mincing around, pretending to be helpful, but in fact taking over my husband, my house, and my child. You made a mockery of my marriage and taunted me in front of Melissa and my servants. It was by your suggestion that Geoffrey made me a prisoner here and has forbidden me to go anywhere with my own child. Indeed, if the truth were known, you are no doubt the reason Melissa is gone now, so do not dare to tell me it is none of your doing."

"You are demented," Seacourt said. Then, glaring at Daintry, he said, "And you are, too, if you think any court in the land will believe this to be my doing. There are witnesses, you idiotic girl. You are one yourself, and Catherine and Deverill would have to speak against Susan as well."

"Catherine will be dead," Daintry said, "so what she might do does not signify, and if you think I will be a witness on your behalf, you have windmills in your head." Seeing her sister's hand falter and knowing Susan could not maintain what must be pure bravado much longer, she racked her brain for a clincher.

It came from an unexpected source. "You have no witnesses to support you, Seacourt," Gideon said calmly. "I certainly could not swear that you were not responsible for this."

"Would you lie in your father's court, Deverill?" Seacourt said with a sneer. "Somehow I doubt that. You, sir, are burdened with too much integrity to lie in any court of law."

"It would not be a lie," Gideon said. "You *are* responsible for everything that is happening here."

"That you are," Penthorpe said, pushing past Gideon and Daintry to confront Seacourt. "To stand up in a courtroom and say that Susan acted under your mastery would be as simple as breathing, Seacourt, for that is precisely what she is doing. Dash it all, she ain't a murderess! She's as gentle and kind as they make 'em, but you've dashed well pushed her to this, and so I'll tell anyone who will listen. But it won't come to that. Put down the gun, Susan. I'm taking you away from here."

She looked at him blankly but lowered the pistol. When Seacourt reached to take it, Penthorpe said sharply, "Leave it, you cretin, or by God, you'll answer to me!"

Seacourt stiffened. "You forget, Penthorpe, that my wife is no concern of yours. You will not take her anywhere unless you want to be landed with a suit for criminal conversation. And don't think I would not sue, for I'd take great delight in it. Susan, for the last time, give me that gun."

She looked uncertainly at him, then at Penthorpe.

Daintry said, "Don't do it. Geoffrey, leave her alone. She is going with us, and this time you will not get her back."

"She is my wife," Seacourt said, "and once this nonsense is ended, she will quickly be reminded of that fact. Moreover, your threats are meaningless, since I cannot believe you will, any of you, really encourage her to shoot Catherine."

"But, Geoffrey," Daintry said sweetly, "we do not have to encourage or allow it. As I recall, attempted murder is also a hanging offense, so all we need do is say that you had commanded her to kill Catherine but that we intervened in the nick of time to save them both. And there are three of us, you know, so even if Catherine should happen to tell another tale, she will not be believed, not once she is known to be your mistress."

"That's utter drivel," Seacourt exclaimed. He looked at Gideon. "Surely, you will not pretend to support such an absurd accusation, Deverill!"

"No," Gideon said, smiling at Daintry when she whirled to glare at him, "but Daintry forgets that it is not the least bit necessary to invent accusations against you, Seacourt. There are plenty of real ones that are more dangerous to you at the moment, or have you forgotten the attack on Lady Ophelia's coach, not to mention the villainous attack on me in London, both of which can be set at your door? I am certain it occurred to you that by eliminating Lady Ophelia you could keep her from altering her will, but what possible reason did you have to eliminate me?"

Seacourt flushed. "You have no proof of that!"

"Do not be so sure," Gideon said. "Melissa, come here."

Penthorpe said quickly, "If you truly want the children in this, they are in that little parlor across the way, for I took the liberty of putting them there when it looked like things might get ugly. Do you really want her, Gideon?"

"Melissa?" Susan's eyes lighted. "You found her?"

"All right and tight," he said, moving to take the pistol from her slackened grasp, then glancing at Gideon. "Well?"

Gideon said, "No, leave them. The point remains the same, Seacourt, in that they were not alone when we found them, and the rogues who held them prisoner were quite willing, after some encouragement, to chat about activities both recent and past."

"They did not admit to any attack in London," Seacourt said confidently, extracting a snuffbox from his waistcoat pocket and helping himself to a pinch as if he had not a care in the world. "Good God, man, as I understand the matter, you had only just arrived in town when that happened. I doubt they will admit to anything at all in the end, for to do so would be to implicate themselves. Moreover, I have done nothing whatsoever myself."

"Good God, I can't bear this any longer," Catherine said suddenly. Avoiding Seacourt's outraged eye and looking directly at Deverill, she said, "I don't know about the attack on Lady Ophelia and Daintry though I do believe he may have arranged it, but I do know that just then he wanted not only Lady Ophelia but Daintry out of the way, because he had got it into his head that if both were gone, Susan would inherit all the old lady's money. And he does torture poor Susan, and God help me, I behaved despicably to her, at first because I thought she was a fool not to try to be exactly the sort of woman he wanted, but later out of a rather odd but increasing sense of power that became nearly overwhelming to me at times. I cannot explain that part of it, but gradually I came to see that she did try to please him, that she tried too hard, and he took advantage of it. He is a cruel man, you know, but he seemed to care for me and I let myself be blinded to reality until today."

At last, she looked at Seacourt. "Today, when you let Susan believe you knew nothing of Melissa's whereabouts, even after she threatened to kill me, you proved how truly malicious you can be, and I would rather live in poverty than be thought an intimate of yours." She looked around at the others. "I know an apology can never make up for all I have done to increase Susan's misery, but if telling what I know in a court of law will help—"

"Are you mad?" Seacourt demanded.

"Not anymore, Geoffrey. What must I do, Deverill?"

Gideon let the silence lengthen until Daintry thought some-one—most likely, Geoffrey—would explode, then said quietly, "It need not come to that. What Lady Susan wants is her freedom and custody of her child. If Seacourt will grant those to her, there can be an end of this business today. No one was hurt, and none of us wants scandal. Do not mistake me," he added, looking sternly at Seacourt. "The men who held your daughter and Charley will be made to speak if it becomes necessary, and the crimes they com-mitted at your behest—even if only the abduction of the children and the attack on Lady Ophelia's coach can be proved—are serious enough to hang you. The case is compelling enough without Lady Catherine's testimony. Do you understand that?"

Seacourt glared at him, then at Catherine, but when she returned his look steadily, his gaze was the first to falter. He turned back to Gideon. "What do you want?"

"Your wife will require your written statement that you agree to divorce her and that you will put forward no claim to your daughter. Any settlement that was made on Lady Susan's behalf by you is to be considered her money, as is any dowry provided her by St. Merryn. If you will write out such a statement now and make no effort to prevent their immediate departure with us, no more will be said about charges being laid against you. That will hold true so long as you keep your part in the bargain, but any further harassment of her ladyship will free us to pursue whatever course we choose. Do you agree?"

"You leave me no choice, damn you."

While Seacourt wrote the required document, Penthorpe went to collect Charley and Melissa, and send orders to the stables.

Then, while he and Gideon remained to watch Seacourt and to sign the document as witnesses, Daintry took Susan and the children upstairs to collect Rosemary and help pack portmanteaus for Susan and Melissa, while Rosemary did the same for herself. When they returned, they learned that Catherine was also going to leave, and Daintry feared briefly that the woman and her maid expected to go with them, but when they reached the stables, she saw that two carriages had been prepared, the chaise Susan used to pay calls and the traveling carriage used for longer journeys.

Gideon had arranged for outriders to escort Catherine to St. Ives, where she had decided to take shelter with her relatives before deciding what next she would do; and Daintry, watching her being handed into the chaise, went to her and said, "We are much obliged to you for what you did today."

Settling herself against the squabs, Catherine smiled ruefully. "I am surprised the words don't stick in your throat, for you must wish me in Hades. I misjudged him, you know, and myself as well, but when it came to the sticking point, I knew I could not side with him. It was all greed, you know. A dreadful thing to admit about oneself, but after a dismally long year in Yorkshire, Seacourt Head and its charming master seemed too good to be true. They were not true, of course, and I know you will think I ought to have intervened when Geoffrey became violent, but the influence I exerted over him was remarkably small."

"You did send your maid to me that night, didn't you? I was not certain if you had, or if she acted on her own."

"Oh, yes, I sent Hilda. Geoffrey had made no secret of the fact that he hated you after that business at the Assize Court, and I had seen him watching you that night like a hawk watching a rabbit. When he did not come to me as he nearly always did, I was afraid he had gone to your room, so I sent Hilda to see. But I own, I never admitted to him that I had so much as suspected a thing, for there was never anything to be gained by taxing him with the dreadful things he did. He only became angry, and today I saw that he could be as cruel to me as he has been to Susan. I knew then that with her gone I'd end up either taking her place as his most convenient victim or being cast off altogether." She paused, then added thoughtfully, "Don't let her trust him too far in this divorce business, will you? He will not keep his word."

Daintry was still thinking of the warning when Hilda came out of the house, escorted by servants with Catherine's baggage, and Susan, Rosemary, and the two little girls were helped into the traveling carriage. Charley objected at first to being told she was not to ride Victor home, but when Gideon told her not to be childish, she subsided at once and announced that she would help keep Melissa entertained since they would be going by the road, which would take much longer.

"It will, too," Gideon admitted as he, Penthorpe, and Daintry mounted, "but your sister is in no condition to ride and neither is Melissa. We'll ride a little ahead of the carriages, I think, so we won't be suffocated by the road dust."

Shalton and Clemons rode behind them, the latter leading Victor, and the cavalcade proceeded down the drive to the main road. Caught up in her own thoughts, Daintry did not realize for some time that neither of her companions had spoken.

Gideon watched the road ahead, but Penthorpe was clearly in a brown study. She thought she knew what he was thinking about and considered for a moment whether she ought to speak her own mind or wait to see if he would speak his. Realizing that even now his strong sense of propriety would make it difficult, if not impossible, for him to do so, and remembering how quickly he had silenced her suggestion earlier that he might not be happy married to her, she had very nearly decided to take the bull by the horns when Gideon said abruptly, "I forgot to tell Shalton something. You two ride on ahead. I must speak to him."

Glancing at him, she saw that he was giving Penthorpe a commanding look. When he had dropped back, the viscount said quietly, "Ride a little ahead with me, will you, please?"

She saw that he was struggling with himself, for he kept glancing at her, then looking away, seeming not to know how to begin. Knowing exactly how he felt and taking pity on him, she said, "It is perfectly all right, sir. You need not say a word."

He shot her an apologetic look. "As plain as that, is it? Dash it all, I'm as great a knave as those louts who were holding you prisoner. Can't think what got into me, my dear, but I am prepared to . . . to . . . that is—Oh, dash it!"

"I am happy to release you from our betrothal, sir. That is to say, although I am very sensible of the honor—"

"Oh, dash it, Daintry, cut line! You're making me feel worse, and if that's your notion of the way one ought to end a betrothal—Look here, are you absolutely certain? I don't know what I'll do if you aren't, for I've every intention of seeing Susan and Melissa safe before I do anything else, but—"

"That is exactly what you must do," she agreed "Lady Catherine said we would be fools to trust Geoffrey to honor his agreement, and I think she was perfectly right. Indeed, I shouldn't be at all surprised if he came roaring over to Tuscombe Park in the morning to demand that Papa send Susan and Melissa right back to him. And I've got the most lowering conviction that Papa *would* order Susan back, too."

"That will not happen," Penthorpe said firmly. He was smiling now, and he glanced back at the carriage. "No sense in telling her yet all that I mean to do, but I'll tell you this much. Seacourt won't ever hurt her again. Gideon," he called. "Come up here and wish me—No, dash it, that's not the thing a fellow ought to say." He looked at Daintry, his eyes dancing. "Got carried away. Hope you won't be offended, but I daresay this will be the best thing for everyone concerned, you know. Ah, here you are, Gideon. You must excuse me, old boy. I've remembered a few things I want to say to Lady Susan. I'll just drop back now and ride beside her carriage for a time."

Gideon looked hard at him, and Penthorpe added insouciantly, "Oh, yes, and by the by, I'm afraid I've been given my *congé*, old boy. Lady Daintry informs me that we shan't suit." With another grin at Daintry, he turned his horse away to wait for the lead carriage.

"Is that right?" Gideon said a moment later.

She did not want to look at him, so she just nodded, saying carefully, "I daresay Papa will have a conniption fit and I shall be utterly sunk beneath contempt for breaking my word of honor to him, but under the circumstances I could see nothing else to be done. Penthorpe loves Susan, not me. I've known that for some time, of course, but since my father was determined that I should wed him, and since Susan is married to Geoffrey—What if he does not get a divorce, sir? Even with that paper he signed, I cannot be sure in my own mind that he will do as he promised."

"No, I am very sure he will not," Gideon admitted, "but that signed declaration will be enough to make certain she can get a divorce in Scotland, where just the fact of having been forced to accept Lady Catherine's presence in her house will be grounds enough for her suit. Anglesey's seduction of Lady Charlotte Wellesley was enough to gain one for his wife, after all."

"Will the divorce be dreadfully expensive?"

"Not nearly as expensive as an English one would be."

"Aunt Ophelia will frank her, I'm sure."

"That is not necessary, you know."

She smiled at him. "You mean that Penthorpe will bear the expense. I do know he would be happy to do so, but I think Susan would prefer to manage that herself and not hang on his sleeve."

"*You* would feel better under similar circumstances, my sweet, but I am not at all convinced that your sister's sentiments resemble yours at all, let alone to that degree. She is a much more dependent sort of woman, you know."

She sighed. "That's true, sir, but indeed, I cannot think she would want Penthorpe to frank her divorce from Seacourt."

"You may be right." He fell silent, and she could think of nothing to say to him. She was free of Penthorpe, but she still feared she did not know her own mind, and she certainly did not know his, for she had expected him to declare himself the moment he knew she was free, and it seemed he had no intention of doing so. After nearly a quarter hour of silence, she remembered that he still did not know she had discovered the origin of the feud. She said, "I found your grandmama's novel most interesting, sir.

"Yes, you recommended that I read it, as I recall. In the letter you sent when you returned it to me," he added when she looked bewildered. "Had you forgotten?"

"Good gracious, I suppose I did say that in that letter, but since I also wrote about going to find Charley and Melissa, I had completely forgotten. But you truly ought to read it, sir."

"Why? As I recall the matter, Lady Ophelia said it was dreadful—kittenish and cute. Not my style of thing at all."

"But you ought to read it," she insisted.

He turned suddenly and smiled at her. "Why? You can tell me about it. I am sure that would be much more entertaining."

"It might be entertaining, but I would find it difficult, sir, for in point of fact, in that novel lies the answer we have been searching for, the key to the Tarrant-Deverill feud."

"The feud doesn't matter anymore," he said, squinting his eyes against the setting sun. "I hope Lady Catherine is able to reach St. Ives before darkness falls."

Daintry did not care if Lady Catherine ever got to St. Ives. "Why doesn't it matter?" she demanded. "We have been searching for the answer for months and since it was all your grandmother's fault, my father won't do a thing to end it, which means your father must do so, but I daresay he will not—" She broke off, realizing he was smiling at her again. "What is the matter with you, Deverill? Did you even hear a word I said?"

"Every single one," he said, "and there is nothing the matter with me. Nothing at all." He began to whistle softly.

She stared, wondering what ailed the man, but he continued to squint into the sunset, and to whistle. She remembered his reputation, that he was a recognized flirt, and wondered if all the time she had thought he was falling in love, he had merely been toying with her, believing there was no danger of her taking him at his word since she was betrothed to another man. But that could not be, for when he had thought Penthorpe dead, he had said quite clearly that he intended to marry her, and his affections had seemed well engaged before they had gone to London. Until Penthorpe reappeared, only the feud had stood in his way, but then he had backed off. Had he lost interest since then?

She had not precisely encouraged him, ever, to believe his suit would prosper, and she had certainly never told him that she loved him. In fact, she had insisted that she was not really interested in marrying anyone and that, were it not for her father's demands, she would prefer to remain single. Maybe he thought that was why she had cried off today. She wished he would stop whistling and talk to her. As the thought flitted through her mind, she had a sudden mental image of Davina, and said tartly, "Do stop that awful whistling, and talk to me!"

"Certainly," he said. "What does your father think about the troubles at the Mulberry mine? Has he suggestions to make about what we should do with the miners who are out of work?"

It was not at all what she wanted to talk about, but since she could scarcely demand to know if he still wanted to marry her, she was obliged to accept a subject of his choosing. That one occupied them until the cavalcade came to the toll road leading to St. Ives, where they parted from Lady Catherine. Not until they rode on again did it occur to Daintry that Gideon had asked for her opinion as well as for her father's on a number of issues, and that he had listened respectfully to what she said. She remembered, too, that he had not scolded her for going alone to find Charley and Melissa but had seemed to assume that she had reason for doing so. Surely no other man would have done that.

They went on talking, but her thoughts continued to divert her attention until finally, after she had twice asked him to repeat himself, he said, "My sweet life, this is the outside of enough. I seem to recall being informed that *men* do not listen, that they constantly ask women to repeat themselves, but in fact I find that is not the case at all. Pay attention."

"I beg your pardon," she said contritely. "My mind seems to insist upon woolgathering, which is dreadfully rude, I know, but indeed, I cannot seem to help it."

"What thoughts can be so fascinating that they overcome your ability to pay heed to my words of infinite wisdom?"

"Do you still want to marry me?" The words were out before she knew she was going to say them, and hearing their echo in her mind, she forced herself to face straight ahead, though she could feel fiery heat in her cheeks and it was difficult not to turn away from him. Then she heard him chuckle.

"That is certainly a matter for conjecture," he said, "but we are not going to discuss the matter just yet."

She glared at him furiously, not certain if she ought to be humiliated, enraged, or simply relieved. At all events, she said not one more word to him even when he began to whistle again, and when the gates of Tuscombe Park loomed ahead in the dusk, she greeted the sight with relief, forgetting that more obstacles lay ahead. She was reminded of them the moment they entered the hall, for St. Merryn was there, talking with Charles and Davina, and he greeted their arrival with relief but no visible delight.

"Upon my word, what the devil is going on? Did you find Charley? Oh, there you are, child! Well, here is your papa and your mama at their wits' end from fretting about you."

Davina held out her arms, and Charley ran into them.

St. Merryn turned back to the others. "Good God, it's Deverill," he exclaimed when Gideon entered behind Susan, Penthorpe, and Melissa. "I suppose, because my wife's fool aunt invited you into my house in London—which she'd no business to do—you expect now to have the run of the place here."

"No, sir, I do not, but we have urgent matters to discuss, and this is not the place to discuss them. I suggest that we retire at once to your library."

St. Merryn glared at him, but the sight of one of the footmen descending the stairs to lend assistance with Susan's and Melissa's bags was enough to make him nod in agreement.

"I have to go with Melissa," Charley informed her parents as she attempted to free herself from Davina's embrace.

"Oh, no, you do not," Charles informed her sternly. "You, my girl, are coming straightaway upstairs with me to explain just what you meant by leaving the house today. And your explanation had better be very good, because you have worried your mama, and that I will not tolerate, as you will very soon discover."

Susan said anxiously, "Don't scold her, Charles, for indeed, I stand very much in her debt, but Charley dear, you need not come with us. Instead, I should like you to take Melissa up with you. We must talk with Grandpapa and you children have already seen and heard a great deal too much today. I will explain everything later, Charles, if you will do this for me now."

Charles exchanged a look with his wife, then said, "Of course, we will take them up. Charley, what can you have said to your aunt to make her think you would not be living in Plymouth with us? That much I will have explained to me if nothing else."

"Oh, Papa, I did think that, only Aunt Daintry told me I was mistaken, and indeed, I am very sorry if you both were worried." She was still earnestly explaining when Gideon shut the book-room door, cutting off all sound from the hall.

St. Merryn, moving to his desk, said curtly, "Now, perhaps someone will explain this farrago to me. Susan, if you have run away from your husband again, let me tell you—"

"Excuse me for interrupting you, sir," Gideon said calmly, "but before you say something you might regret, perhaps I ought to explain that Seacourt has agreed to a divorce."

"A divorce! We have never had a divorce in this family, and by God, we are not going to have one now. Susan, go and get your daughter at once. I'll take you back myself."

Penthorpe stepped forward then and said, "No, sir, you will not. It has been made plain to us today that Geoffrey Seacourt is responsible for an attack on Lady Ophelia's carriage that was intended to end in her death. It is our opinion that he wanted her dead so that he could claim his wife's inheritance before Lady Ophelia had opportunity to alter her will. We have it on good authority, too, that he also wanted Lady Daintry dead. If those events had come to pass, Susan's own life would not have been worth a sou, for he coveted her money and nothing more. And I'll tell you something else, too," he added grimly. "We are not going to wait for him to seek that divorce. Susan is going to petition in her own behalf at the Commissary Court in Edinburgh, and since she would be wise to leave first thing in the morning, she had better have something to eat now and get some sleep."

St. Merryn stared at him. "What is this? You, sir, are betrothed to my younger daughter, but that does not give—"

"No, he isn't, Papa," Daintry said. "We have agreed that we would not suit each other."

"By heaven, I told you I won't stomach that sort of thing again!" He glared at her. "I put my foot down!"

She said quietly, "You must, sir, for I will not marry him."

"Well, if you think that I'll bear the expense of another London Season for a witless chit who don't show the least gratitude for anything that's done for her, you had better think again. Whistling Penthorpe down the wind, when it was as good as settled! Upon my word, I don't know what to say to you."

Gideon chuckled. "You might wish her happy, sir, for she is going to be a marchioness one day."

"What's that? Nonsense, I won't have that either! Daintry, tell the man. By God, I'd rather see you remain single! An excellent notion, after all. By God, it is!"

"Yes, it is," Daintry said indignantly, furious that Gideon could declare himself so carelessly after refusing to discuss the matter with her before. He must, she thought, have windmills in his head if he still believed he could order things as he chose.

Twenty-five

While Daintry fumed, Gideon said to the bewildered earl, "A number of things have happened that must be explained to you, sir, but in a nutshell, Penthorpe is much more interested in setting your elder daughter free of her marriage than he is in marrying your younger one, while I am just as determined to marry Daintry as I was the first day I laid eyes on her."

St. Merryn growled, "I told you then—or rather when your gross deceit became known to us—that I would not hear of that, and nothing has come about to alter that decision, young man."

"Now, sir," Gideon said gently, "you know perfectly well, for I know Daintry must have told you, that the feud was begun by a woman who probably wanted shaking; however, that does not signify in the least because, in any event, it's as good as dead. My father has done nothing to end it before now, because he is cursed with a strong sense of duty, which includes a belief that he ought to support any stand taken by his father and, I suspect, because there was nothing to be gained by trying to end it. Things have changed, however. I call the tune at Deverill Court now, and I have believed for a long time that the feud must have been the result of damned foolishness. I certainly will not let it interfere with my future happiness, or that of your daughter."

"You heard her," St. Merryn said with a snort. "She won't marry you. And if you take my advice, you'll listen to the chit, for any man who did marry her would very soon learn his mistake."

"Papa!" Susan exclaimed. "How can you say such a thing?"

"Easily," the earl retorted, turning to peer at her through narrowed eyes. "Thought you were going to bed. You really mean to seek a divorce, do you?"

She looked at Penthorpe, then nodded. "Yes, Papa, I do. Will that put me quite beyond the pale, or may I still come to visit you and Mama and Aunt Ophelia from time to time?"

"Daresay you'll do as you please," he said gruffly. Then, shooting a glare at Penthorpe, and another at Gideon, he let his gaze come to rest upon Daintry before adding, "Daresay you'll all do as you damned well please."

"As to that, sir," Penthorpe said gravely, "I should like to discuss certain matters with you, but first I hope you will send Susan to bed before she drops down from exhaustion. And, Gideon," he added in that same decisive tone, "I will need to be getting back to Deverill Court to collect my traps if we are to leave Cornwall first thing in the morning."

Gideon had been watching Daintry, and without looking away from her, he said, "I will be at your disposal just as soon as I have attended to my own business here, Andy." Then, looking over his shoulder at St. Merryn, he said, "May I have some time alone with Daintry, sir? We have matters to discuss."

Daintry, ignoring her pounding heart, said provocatively, "There is nothing further to be discussed."

"We'll just see about that, my pet. Well, St. Merryn?"

The earl looked from one to the other, and suddenly his lips began to twitch. "Upon my word," he said, "if you can change her mind, lad, damme if I won't let you have her. Never thought I'd live to see it, damme if I did, but I remember the first day you came here. It was a pleasure to see you go to work with her. Susan, get along to bed, and you, Penthorpe, come with me. I daresay there's another room where we can have our talk."

A moment later, Daintry was alone with Gideon, and torn between wanting to slap him for his outrageous behavior and wanting to fling herself into his arms, she sought compromise in a rigid posture and refused even to look at him.

"Come here, sweetheart."

"No."

"Very well, then I shall come to you."

"No!" Abandoning hauteur, she stepped hastily away from him, knowing only too well the effect his touch would produce.

Still moving toward her, he grinned when she continued to retreat. "You are going to marry me, you know."

"I do not know it. I am still not by any means convinced, sir, that I can be happy with a husband who by his very nature will expect his every whim and decree to be obeyed."

Rather than promising instantly that he would never expect such a thing of her, as any sensible man in his position would have done, he said nothing at all. He just kept pace with her until she backed up against her father's desk and could go no farther. She tried to slip to one side, away from him, but when he put a hand on her shoulder to stop her, she froze.

Taking base advantage of the physical effect his slightest touch had on her—as, indeed, she had been certain he would—he drew her nearer, holding her wide-eyed gaze with the warmth of his as he bent his head and kissed her. The kiss was gentle, but it seemed to unleash something in him that was not gentle at all, for he suddenly grasped her by both shoulders and drew her close against him, and his kisses became more eager, more demanding, until she responded with a passion as ungoverned as his own. Then, when her body melted against his, and her arms went around him tightly, as though she would be one with him, his hands moved from her shoulders to her back and waist, and one slid up her side and around to cup her breast.

Daintry moaned with pleasure, and the horrors of the stormy night at Seacourt Head faded into oblivion as her body responded of its own accord to sensations that set her every nerve atingle.

Some moments later, he drew her to a sofa near the desk, and when they were seated, her head leaning comfortably against the hollow of his shoulder, he said, "I hope you do not mean to keep me dangling after such an enticing display, my love."

"You make me seem a wanton," she murmured. "I daresay you believe you will always be able to make me do as you want merely by touching me or kissing me."

He chuckled. "I doubt it will be so easy. Do you think any man could tame you to such a point, sweetheart?"

"You could, I think," she replied seriously, wrinkling her brow. Then, sitting up and turning so that she could watch his expression, she said, "I have just had the most awful thought. What assurance do I have that you will not turn out to be just like Geoffrey? Don't be vexed," she added hastily when his expression hardened ominously. "After all, Susan—all of us, for that matter—thought Geoffrey was charming and delightful, just as you are, but look what he did to her. She was once so merry. One would not know it to look at her now, but she was. It was Geoffrey who reduced her to the pale shadow that she is today. How do I know—Why are you laughing? No, Deverill, don't touch me. This is serious!"

The harsh look had vanished, and if he was not really laughing, he was certainly looking amused. He had reached for her, but at her command, he stayed his hand and said soberly, "I know you are serious, sweetheart, but I also know you are going to marry me, and I am perfectly certain that you do not for one minute believe I am cut from the same bolt as that scoundrel Seacourt. Even if I were, I can promise you, I would never let you discover it. Don't look so outraged. Only consider, my love, what would have been Sir Geoffrey's fate had he been so misguided as to marry you instead of your sister."

She considered that. "Susan said it would not matter, that no one could have stopped him, and indeed, he is certainly stronger than I am, as I had cause to discover."

His jaw tightened again, but his voice was even. "I can see that you have not carefully considered this matter. Seacourt certainly caught you at a disadvantage that night, but though you may try to convince me that had you been married to him you would have done nothing to protect yourself, I will not believe you."

"No?"

"Not for a minute. You and your sister are two very different people. You had the benefit of your Aunt Ophelia's teachings while Susan clearly was more strongly influenced by your mama and ladies of her ilk. Had you been in Susan's shoes, my sweet love, you would have murdered Seacourt before you had been married to him for a year, and you would have accomplished the deed in such a manner that no one would have entertained the slightest suspicion that he did not die of natural causes."

She grinned mischievously at him. "You are quite right, sir, and I am very glad you understand me so well. Are you certain you wish to marry such a dangerous creature?"

"I am, and I am pleased to see that you no longer spurn my caresses," he added, drawing her back into his arms.

"There was a reason for that, you know."

"I do. Seacourt still has much to answer for."

"I just hope he does not come storming over here tonight, but he did not do so last time, so maybe he will not."

"From what I saw of him, he was much more likely to drown his sorrows in brandy. But enough of him. Am I to understand from your present complaisance that you are willing—"

"Merciful heavens, here you are," Lady Ophelia exclaimed as she pushed the doors open and strode into the library. "I have been hearing the most outlandish tales from Charley about smugglers and from Susan about divorce that I cannot tell you whether I am on my head or on my heels, but when I learned that you were here, Deverill, I came at once to inquire—" Breaking off and peering at them in astonishment, she said, "Good gracious, what are you two doing? Not that I can say I am at all surprised, mind you, but I must say, I never—"

Daintry, sitting up quickly and pushing Gideon's hands away, said, "I beg your pardon, Aunt Ophelia, but I'm very much afraid I have actually fallen in love."

"Nonsense, my dear, it is plain to the meanest intelligence that you walked into the stuff with both eyes wide open. Now, Deverill, what I want you to tell me—"

"You aren't vexed with me?" Daintry was a little surprised. "I know you said you wouldn't be, but I thought you might at least be a bit disappointed."

"Good heavens, child, did I not tell you that being independent means making choices without having to knuckle under to anyone else's wishes? If your decision is that you wish to be a married lady, I must suppose you have discovered a man who treats you not only with affection but with respect." She glared at Gideon. "At least, I hope that is the case."

He said meekly, "It is, ma'am."

"Good. Now tell me, just what was in that stuff you put in my drink at the ball?"

They both stared at her in astonishment, and Gideon said, "I haven't the slightest notion what it was, ma'am. Kingston gave me those powders after the attack on my life, to help me sleep."

"Amazing stuff," she said. "I must have some. That is the reason I came to speak to you, but if this Kingston person is the source, I will write and tell him I shall want some made up for me next Season. I have no doubt I shall be dragged off to London again by someone, if not then, then certainly in a few years when Charlotte and Melissa make their come-outs, and a body likes to be prepared. But I'll not stand here bibble-babbling at you. I can see that you have other matters on your mind."

"Yes, ma'am." He reached for Daintry, but there was another interruption.

"Good God, Gideon," Penthorpe exclaimed, peering in through the open doors, "are you still dillydallying here? We must be on our way, old son. My affairs are finally in a way to being settled, and there's not a moment to waste!"

Gideon laughed. "Such sentiments sound very odd coming from the great procrastinator. Andy, you may wish me happy."

"Why?" He looked from Gideon to Daintry. "Oh, that. Good God, I knew that. Plain as a pikestaff. Know you'll be much happier with Gideon, my dear. Now, dash it, let's go! Beg pardon, ma'am," he added to Lady Ophelia, "but I'm in the devil of a hurry."

"I can see that," she said. Then, turning back to the others, she said sternly, "Take good care of her, Deverill."

"Oh, I will," Gideon said, giving Daintry one last hug and grinning wickedly down at her as he added, "If I cannot teach her to mind me, at least I can promise to teach her the hazards of trying to make a man live under the cat's paw."

And Daintry replied sweetly, "Your illusions are dangerous ones, sir, but all men may dream, certainly."

Letter from the Author

Dear Reader:

Since I am often asked where I get my ideas, I thought perhaps you might like to know a small part of the history of *Dangerous Illusions*. I frequently get ideas while I'm doing research, and the central theme of this book presented itself when I discovered that Englishmen, in attempting to legalize their domination and restriction of Englishwomen, had actually gone so far at one point as to make it possible for a wife to commit murder, openly and without penalty, and for her husband to suffer the consequences—including hanging. It was entirely too good an opportunity to pass up (as a writer, that is).

When I decided to add an elderly feminist to the mixture, I wanted her beliefs to have depth, which meant she could not just parrot the words of well-known late-18th-century feminist Mary Wollstonecraft (whose actions so rarely matched her ideas), so I began to search for other books Lady Ophelia might have read that could form a foundation for her opinions. Imagine how astonished I was to learn that novelists like Eliza Haywood had advocated women's rights as early as 1750, using many arguments we still hear today (including those favoring a woman's right to choose).

Of course, as many writers point out when asked the source

of their ideas, getting them is the easy part. Expressing them on paper is much more difficult, and there was still a great deal of work to do after I came up with that first kernel of an idea and that first character—minor details like creating a hero, a heroine, and a plot! Everything did fall into place in the end, and my earnest hope is that *Dangerous Illusions* has provided you with a few hours of entertainment, including some laughter and a chance or two to boo the villain and cheer the hero and heroine. That, after all, was the true purpose of the book.

Sincerely,

Amanda Scott

P.S. If you enjoyed *Dangerous Illusions,* I hope you will look for *Highland Fling* in your bookstore.

About the Author

A fourth-generation Californian of Scottish descent, Amanda Scott is the author of more than fifty romantic novels, many of which appeared on the *USA Today* bestseller list. Her Scottish heritage and love of history (she received undergraduate and graduate degrees in history at Mills College and California State University, San Jose, respectively) inspired her to write historical fiction. Credited by *Library Journal* with starting the Scottish romance subgenre, Scott has also won acclaim for her sparkling Regency romances. She is the recipient of the Romance Writers of America's RITA Award (for *Lord Abberley's Nemesis*, 1986) and the RT Book Reviews Career Achievement Award. She lives in central California with her husband.

THE DANGEROUS SERIES

FROM OPEN ROAD MEDIA

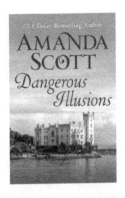

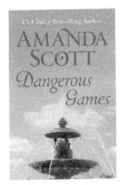

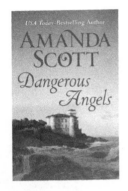

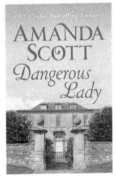

OPEN ROAD

INTEGRATED MEDIA

INTEGRATED MEDIA

Find a full list of our authors and
titles at www.openroadmedia.com

FOLLOW US
@OpenRoadMedia

CPSIA information can be obtained
at www.ICGtesting.com
Printed in the USA
LVHW09s1939051018
592410LV00006B/108/P